PAYBACK

PAYBACK

ROBERT WANGARD

AMP&RSAND, INC.

Chicago • New Orleans

Copyright © 2014 Robert Wangard

ISBN 978-1467545310

Design
David Robson, Robson Design

Published by
AMPERSAND, INC.
1050 North State Street
Chicago, Illinois 60610

203 Finland Place
New Orleans, Louisiana 70131

www.ampersandworks.com

———————

www.rwangard.com

Printed in U.S.A.

For my friends and loyal readers at the CSA

ONE

Even though he knew it was coming, Pete Thorsen couldn't help but flinch when the first shot was fired. The blast shattered the soggy stillness that hung over the field and ignited a frenzy of activity. Men in blue sack coats and forage caps stormed out of the trees screaming "Chickamauga! Chickamauga! Chickamauga!" and unleashed a hail of gunfire. Puffs of black smoke drifted skyward.

On the crest of the hill, Pete could see men hunkered down behind the earthwork and timber fortifications, their long-barreled weapons trained on the blue horde running madly across the field toward them. They held their fire, anxiously waiting for the foe to get closer, and watched as some of the attackers stumbled over the rough terrain and others stopped to perform the cumbersome task of reloading their muzzleloaders.

"Jeez, this is something, huh?" Harry McTigue said as he squinted through his binoculars. "It almost makes you want to become a reenactor."

"Very dramatic," Pete agreed. "I thought this was going to be like a Memorial Day ceremony with a bunch of septuagenarians in old

1

uniforms firing their guns in the air." He knew his comment would get Harry going.

Harry lowered his binoculars and stared disbelievingly at Pete from beneath his tattered brown slouch hat. "I know you're a smart guy," he said, "but sometimes I think you spend half your time under a rock. Thousands of people around the country are into Civil War reenactments in a big way. They keep our history alive."

"I guess it's as good a thing as any to do on a Sunday afternoon," Pete said.

"And you call yourself a patriotic American," Harry said disgustedly. I'll bet you wouldn't be so cavalier about it if some group were staging a mock Viking invasion of the Frankfort port. A bunch of savages in wolf skins and horned helmets in their strange boats, foaming at the mouth until they could reach shore and begin to rape and pillage."

"Sounds like a myth about the Norsemen started by some weak-kneed Scots," Pete said.

"Ha, you know it's true. But what you're watching now is part of a titanic struggle between two factions of a superior culture that was destined to rule the world for centuries."

"I'm always amazed by the way you combine eloquence with superior knowledge of so many subjects."

Harry got a faraway look in his eyes. "A newspaperman needs to be attuned to what's happening around him," he said earnestly. "You spend time under a rock in my business, you won't last long."

He resumed watching the mock battle and after a while turned to Pete again and said, "You probably don't know why the Union soldiers screamed 'Chickamauga! Chickamauga!' when they started their attack, do you?"

"Could it have something to do with the Union army's defeat at the Battle of Chickamauga?" Pete asked, feigning innocence. "Maybe a cry for revenge?"

Harry looked crest-fallen. "I'm surprised you knew that," he said.

"It's in the pamphlet." He tapped the pocket of his windbreaker. "Plus I once toured the Chickamauga battlefield."

Harry scowled at him as though not knowing what to say and then went back to watching the reenactment through his binoculars. The Confederates had begun to return fire from their dug-in position on the ridge, and the black powder smoke created by gunfire on both sides hung low over the field like bad smog on a windless day in Los Angeles. Northern Michigan didn't have a mountain range to hold in the smoke, but the heavy weather served the same purpose.

Pete inhaled the pungent odor of decaying leaves and tried to ignore the light drizzle that had been falling since they arrived. The moisture collected on his cap and in the tufts of sandy brown hair that protruded from the back and a trickle ran down his neck. He shuddered and brushed at his hair and zipped his L. L. Bean Weather Challenger jacket tighter around his neck.

The reenactment they were watching was one skirmish of the Battle of Missionary Ridge that took place near Chattanooga, Tennessee, in November, 1863, and was the centerpiece of the Thaddeus Clayton Festival. Pete wondered what the weather was like during that battle and contrasted the soggy conditions of the reenactment with the glorious spectacle of the day before when the vivid hues of sumac and Indian paintbrush and goldenrod and the flaming leaves of the hardwoods lit up the landscape in a celebration of splendid autumn weather. He consoled himself with the thought that it might be raining, but at least the icy talons of winter hadn't seized the area yet.

He was jolted out of his reverie by a new surge of action. The Union forces had split and some of them were mounting an all-out assault on the Confederates' right flank. Pete could see rebel soldiers on the ridge shift to that side in a panicky effort to shore up their defenses. Union troops who weren't involved in the flanking action dropped to their knees and commenced a withering barrage of fire to provide cover for their attacking comrades.

As Pete watched, he noticed the occasional puffs of white that mingled with the black smoke hanging over the field. Harry noticed it, too, and lowered his binoculars again and grinned. "You know what that white smoke is?" he said. "That's Cream of Wheat. A few of the guys pack the stuff into their muzzleloaders to add authenticity and realism to the battlefield."

Confident he'd regained the upper hand in the knowledge battle, Harry gave Pete a smug look and resumed peering through his binoculars. A few minutes later he said, "Oops, there goes Colonel Clayton's horse." The Colonel slid from the saddle and stumbled to the ground when his horse reared up on its hind legs. Clayton brushed some of the mud from his uniform and clamped his hat back on his head. Over the din of the gunfire and bugles, Pete could hear him resume shouting encouragement to his troops.

"The Colonel takes a hit in this battle, you know," Harry added.

"I assume that means he gets shot."

"Yeah, although reenactors use the term for someone who gets killed with a sabre or bayonet, too."

"What we just saw wasn't where the Colonel caught it I gather."

Harry, always eager to share his knowledge, said, "In the real battle of Missionary Ridge, Colonel Clayton's horse was shot out from under him before he caught a bullet himself. The reenactors are sticklers for detail, but I'm sure they feel they can't go around killing horses just for the sake of authenticity."

"Makes sense to me."

"Here's something else for you," Harry said. "Colonel Thaddeus Clayton served under the great General William T. Sherman who split the Confederacy by his march through Georgia to the sea. Did you know that?" he asked pointedly.

"I did know that."

"You must have read my newspaper this week. I laid out the whole story in my feature article."

"Yup," Pete said. "I read it there and again in the festival pamphlet which told the same story in more concise language."

"Concise language," Harry sputtered. "Did you notice that typo on the second page of the pamphlet? There couldn't be more than four or five hundred words in that scrap of paper and whoever proofed it still couldn't catch the typos."

"I didn't notice."

"Of course not," Harry said, snorting. "You lawyers are trained to spew out your lines and accuracy be damned as long as you can get someone to buy your half-truths. The first thing they taught us in J-school was to be careful with our spelling and editing. One typo can destroy the entire credibility of the story and its author."

Pete suppressed a grin. They'd had the same discussion several times before, and Pete had to admit that for a small town newspaper, *The Northern Sentinel* was as free of errors and typos as you were likely to find. Pete had a similar mania for accuracy and it was one of many factors that created his bond with Harry.

He resumed watching the simulated battle. The field was now strewn with the bodies of Union soldiers, and on the crest of the ridge, he could see numerous Confederates slumped over the fortifications as well. Plenty of troops on both sides had taken a hit, to use Harry's term.

Colonel Clayton, on foot since the incident with his horse, had his sabre drawn and was holding it aloft, exhorting his forces to continue attacking. Clayton alternated between facing the Confederate defenders defiantly and turning to shout encouragement to his troops. Suddenly he shuddered and clutched his chest. He continued to stand upright for a few seconds and then crumpled to the ground.

"I think he just took his hit," Pete said.

"That was it. That was the end for one of the most valiant heroes Michigan has ever produced. You have to admit that looked pretty damn realistic."

"It did," Pete said admiringly

On the battlefield, the Union troops still standing saw their leader fall. They bellowed with rage and intensified their attack on the Confederate defenses. The blue-coated men with Henry repeating rifles unleashed another hail of gunfire. The Confederates sensed that the tide of battle had turned against them and abandoned their positions and began to scramble down the back side of the ridge. The Union forces broke through what remained of the defensive line and fired at the fleeing enemy. Then they held their rifles triumphantly above their heads and let loose with screams that were even more primal than the ones with which they'd launched the battle.

The reenactors who'd taken hits began to rise from the wet ground and enthusiastically high-five each other in a display of exuberance over their performance. The three-piece brass band started to play the Union anthem, "The Battle Hymn of the Republic." The blue-clad soldiers, suddenly solemn, sang along in an off-key but spirited chorus.

Colonel Clayton remained on the ground. One of the reenactors went over to where he lay and said something to him. When the Colonel didn't move, the reenactor rolled him over, and after examining him for a moment, frantically called to the EMTs standing by an ambulance parked just outside the rope that separated the spectators from the reenactment area. The EMTs pushed the gawking reenactors aside and knelt by the Colonel's body. Pete had been watching everything through his binoculars, but his view was blocked when the mob crowded around the Colonel again.

"I think something's wrong," Pete said.

"You don't suppose he had a heart attack, do you?" Harry asked, plainly concerned. "That's Thomas Edinger playing the Colonel, you know. Edinger's the one who wrote all of the books about Clayton."

Pete continued to watch through his binoculars but couldn't see anything because the reenactors blocked his view. Then the sea of blue parted briefly and he saw what looked like a red stain on the front of Edinger's uniform.

TWO

Pete was stunned. He turned to Harry and said, "I think the Colonel really has been shot."

Harry lowered his binoculars and stared at Pete with widened eyes. "That's impossible. Reenactors don't use live ammunition."

"I'm sure I saw blood on the front of his uniform."

"Maybe it was dirt. The Colonel fell face down when he took the hit, remember."

"Possible," Pete said, "but it looked like blood to me."

Harry persisted. "The organizers of these reenactments have safety officers who check the weapons ahead of time to make sure no one has live ammunition. The Colonel couldn't have been shot."

"Harry, I'm just telling you what I saw."

"And you saw blood?"

"I saw blood. The crowd was milling around, and for just a second, I had a clear view of the Colonel. I'm sure there was blood on his uniform. Unless it was a gob of ketchup to add some more realism."

"If it were ketchup, the Colonel, or I guess we should say Thomas Edinger, would be up and celebrating with the others, wouldn't he?"

"You'd think so," Pete said.

Harry stared at him again and then said, "I have my press credentials with me. I'm going to see if I can find out what's going on."

With that, Harry was off at as fast a waddle as his elliptical body would permit. When he ducked under the rope, he was stopped by the sheriff's deputy who'd been on site for security purposes throughout the performance. Pete could see Harry talking to the deputy and waving his arms and pointing to what Pete assumed were his press credentials. After a minute, the deputy stepped back and Harry was off again at his awkward gait toward where the crowd was huddled around Edinger's body.

While Pete waited for Harry to return, he heard the sing-song wail of sirens in the distance. The sirens grew louder and soon two cruisers with sheriff's department markings and blue and red lights flashing pulled in and started across the field to where the crowd was watching in shocked silence. A voice over the loudspeaker in one of the cruisers instructed the crowd to move back so they could get through. An EMT came over to help clear a lane.

The cruisers stopped just outside the rope. Their light bars continued to flash and gave an eerie cast to the black smoke that still hung over the field. The newly-arrived deputies conferred with their colleague already on site, and after a couple of minutes, one of them pulled out a cell phone and punched in a number and carried on an urgent conversation with someone. The officer then slid back in his vehicle and over his loudspeaker instructed everyone to remain in the area pending further instructions.

Fifteen minutes later, a third sheriff's department cruiser with its siren wailing pulled in behind the other two and a bareheaded man in camouflage pants and a bulky brown turtleneck sweater got out. Pete recognized him immediately based on his distinctive body shape. It was the county sheriff, Franklin Richter.

Pete watched Harry hurry across the field to where Richter was conferring with his men. He tried to get Richter's attention and engage him in conversation. The sheriff finally held up a hand, said something to

Harry, then turned his back on him and continued to talk to his deputies. Harry stood there looking chastened, then made his way back to where Pete was standing.

"I'm going to have to wait to talk to the sheriff," Harry said with an air of resignation. "They're just deciding what to do."

"Why don't they get Edinger to the hospital?" Pete asked.

"That's something I did find out. Edinger's dead. He was shot in the chest just as you said."

Back on the field, Richter grabbed a bullhorn from one of his deputies and walked toward where Edinger was down. His deputies fanned out inside the rope.

"Ladies and gentlemen," he announced, "there's been a tragic incident. It appears that one of the reenactors has been shot. Until we sort everything out, we're going to have to impound all weapons and related gear. That includes all long guns and pistols, and all explosive charges, blanks, live ammunition, and smoke devices. My deputies are also going to search each reenactor's person and any equipment he has with him such as knapsacks, haversacks and similar items. Now I ask that the reenactors take their weapons and other possessions with them and form three equal lines in front of the deputies standing over there." Richter pointed to where the three deputies were stationed.

A deputy moved closer to Richter and whispered in his ear.

Richter raised the bullhorn again and said, "One more thing. Anyone who objects to having his person or possessions searched, or wishes to consult his attorney first before deciding whether to consent to a search, should line up in front of the fourth deputy over there," Richter said, pointing to where another deputy was standing.

"As for the spectators and other folks outside the rope, we ask that you remain on site and cooperate with us as members of our department circulate through the crowd and ask questions of some of you. Also, if anyone saw anything suspicious either before, during or after the reenactment, please report it immediately to Deputy Capwell over there." He pointed to Capwell. "This is going to take a while. I'm sorry for any inconvenience, but like I said at the beginning, we have a very serious incident here and I ask for everyone's patience and understanding."

The reenactors began queuing up in front of the three deputies who had been designated to inspect their weapons and other possessions. So far, no one lined up in front of the fourth deputy who was charged with dealing with those reenactors who objected to being searched. Two more sheriff's department vehicles arrived at the scene.

Pete continued to watch through his binoculars. It appeared the deputies were recording the name and contact information of each reenactor, affixing a tag to his weapon, and giving him a receipt for it. The deputies also checked the bags that each of the reenactors had with him and searched their pockets.

"Do you think these searches are legal?" Harry asked Pete in a whispered voice.

"No idea," Pete said.

"I was assigned to the crime beat when I was a cub reporter with the Chicago paper and seem to remember that the police had to get a warrant based on probable cause before they could conduct a search."

"Normally that's true," Pete said, "but this might be different. It looks like a crime has been committed here and everyone present presumably is a suspect, particularly if he has a weapon. The police don't have to enter a person's house or car to conduct their searches, either. The weapons are right out in the open. Plus, everyone seems to be voluntarily submitting to a search."

"So you think the searches might be okay."

"Look, I'm not a criminal lawyer. I'm just saying the searches look reasonable to me in the circumstances."

"If they find anything, it could be thrown out if the sheriff's wrong, you know."

"I know that. But what would you rather do in a case like this—take a risk that something you find might be deemed inadmissible in a court of law or let a killer walk out of here with the weapon that was used to kill Edinger?"

Harry was pondering that when a voice behind them said, "I'm not even surprised anymore when the two of you show up at a crime scene."

Pete recognized the voice and immediately knew he could expect some verbal hassling. He turned and said, "Hello, Sheriff."

"Harry I can understand," Richter continued. "He's a newspaperman and this is a news story. But why Pete Thorsen keeps showing up . . ." He shook his head as if he were puzzled.

"Nothing mysterious, Sheriff. I was just here watching the reenactment along with the rest of these folks."

Richter stared at him through narrowed eyelids. "Have you figured it out yet, counselor? Who did the shooting? Whether he had accomplices?"

"I have my suspect list," Pete replied, returning his stare with unwavering blue eyes that showed his amusement but no warmth. "It's probably the same as yours. Three hundred reenactors, give or take, are on it."

Richter fixed him with a sardonic smile. The sheriff's carefully moussed hair was beginning to droop in the drizzle and his sweater seemed to soak up moisture like a sponge and clung to his muscular upper body. He'd probably been pumping iron for an hour that morning, Pete thought, before heading out to do whatever he'd planned to do on his day off.

Harry wedged his way in between them. "When will you have a statement for the press, Sheriff?"

Richter abandoned his stare-down with Pete and said, "Not for a while, Harry. We have a ton of people here to process."

"Well, could you tell me this—and we can go off the record if you like—do you think there's any problem with these searches?"

Richter bristled. "Why do you ask that?" he snapped. "Has your pal Thorsen here been feeding you some of his nutty crap?"

"No, no," Harry said hastily. "Pete actually thinks the searches could be alright. But I was a crime reporter when I started my newspaper career in Chicago, and I remember—"

"Well, well," Richter said, fixing Pete with his cocky stare again, "don't tell me you've actually found something our office does that you agree with."

Pete didn't reply and Harry said, "I'm not trying to start a controversy. I was just wondering—"

"Legal business must be slow in Frankfort," Richter said, continuing to ignore Harry. "Are you trying to drum up business with the county by currying favor with us, Thorsen?"

Before Pete could answer, the department's lone plainclothes detective, the reed-thin Joe Tessler, came up and put a hand on Richter's arm and said, "Can I talk to you for a minute, Frank?" Unlike his boss, Tessler had a Chicago White Sox cap clamped on his head that kept his longish black hair dry.

Tessler avoided eye contact with Pete and led Richter away from the crowd. Pete had worked closely with the detective the previous spring when they were investigating Lynn Hawke's death and had gotten along with him fine. In fact, they'd developed a downright cordial relationship. Around Richter, though, Tessler had to be careful not to appear friendly with Pete.

Richter and Tessler carried on a quiet conversation twenty feet away. Pete saw Tessler point to one of the lines and whisper something that Pete couldn't hear. Then they ducked under the rope and headed for the line where a burly man in a Confederate uniform and a full gray beard was making a fuss over something.

Pete nudged Harry and said, "I think we have our first disagreement."

Harry listened briefly and then asked, "Can you hear what they're saying?"

Pete shook his head and said, "C'mon." He led the way through the crowd to an area that was close to the head of the line where the Confederate reenactor was standing with arms folded above his ample stomach.

When they got close, Pete heard the man say to the deputy, "That ain't good enough, son. I'll let you inspect my piece as long as you want, but when I leave, this here musket goes with me." He patted the musket's stock. "This is a genuine smoothbore and I ain't leaving it with nobody."

"What's going on here?" Richter asked the deputy.

"This gentleman is refusing to check his rifle with us," the deputy said. "He's not objecting to us inspecting the rifle, but he refuses to leave it with us for further examination."

"Correction, son," the reenactor said, "this here's not a rifle. As I told you, it's an antique smoothbore that's been handed down in my family for two hundred years."

Richter nodded and said to the man, "Sir, I appreciate your attachment to that weapon. But a man's been shot. We don't know who did the shooting, but it almost certainly was one of the reenactors on this field. Until we can determine the identity of the shooter, we're impounding all weapons. That's just the way it is."

The man studied Richter for a moment and his chin jutted out. "And who may I ask are you?"

"I'm in charge here," Richter said. "I'm the sheriff of this county." He'd pinned his shield to his sweater and tapped it with a finger.

He gave Richter a belligerent look and then said, "Well, I've made my position clear. I guess we've got ourselves a good old fashioned standoff."

"I guess so," Richter said. "This county is free of serious crime at the moment and all of the cells in our jail are empty. If you'd like, we'll gladly give you your choice of them so you can stay close to your firearm until we complete whatever inspection we desire to make."

"You can't do that!" the man bellowed. "I got a farm back in Tennessee that needs tending. Our bus home leaves first thing in the morning."

Another man, also in a Confederate uniform, came up and said, "Ezra, calm down, will you?" Then he said to Richter, "I'm Lieutenant Adams of the Seventh Tennessee Militia, this man's commanding officer. Could I talk to him for a minute?"

Richter nodded and said, "But please impress upon Ezra — either his weapon stays here with us or he stays along with it."

Harry elbowed Pete in the side and grinned. "You have to admit that the sheriff can be a cool sonofabitch."

"What's the operative word? 'Cool' or 'sonofabitch'?"

Harry gave him a disgusted look.

Lieutenant Adams and Ezra came back. Adams said, "If Ezra leaves his weapon, he wants to know what you're going to do to care for it and how you're going to get it back to him."

Richter conferred with Tessler again for a few moments and then turned to Adams and said, "We haven't worked out all of the details yet, but we'll probably lock up the weapons in our evidence room, and after we're finished with them, we'll ship them back to the owners at the county's expense."

Ezra said in a voice that could be heard all over the field, "You better insure those weapons! That's a goddamned valuable piece!"

Adams stepped between Ezra and Richter again and said, "That sounds reasonable, Sheriff. All we ask is that you take reasonable care of the weapons."

Ezra stared at the receipt for his musket, gave Richter another dirty look, and shuffled off to join some of his comrades who'd already checked their weapons with a deputy. Pete couldn't hear his words, but it was evident from the way he was carrying on that he wasn't mollified.

Across the field, the EMTs had loaded Thomas Edinger's body in the ambulance and, lights flashing, the vehicle was easing through the crowd toward the unpaved road that provided access to the field on which the reenactment had been staged.

"I bet they're going to take the body to the morgue in Traverse City for an autopsy," Harry said. "If the bullet stayed in Edinger's chest, they'll start trying to match it up with one of the weapons they've impounded."

Pete didn't reply, but knew Harry was right. He'd spent time at the morgue and knew the drill. He also cringed when he thought of the cold, antiseptic place with stark overhead lights that was filled with chemical odors and the smell of death everywhere.

THREE

Harry was hunched over his computer pecking away at the keyboard when Pete walked into to *The Northern Sentinel's* offices.

"Ready for dinner?" he asked.

"In a minute," Harry replied, not looking up. "I'm in the middle of some important background research for my story about the Edinger shooting. Here," he said, pushing a small stack of paper across his desk, "read these stories while I finish up."

Pete flipped through the newspaper articles. All of them involved past shooting incidents that had occurred at various Civil War reenactment events. One article was marked in the margin with a crude star in red ink and chronicled an incident that had occurred in 1998 at a reenactment of the Battle of Gettysburg. A young Charlottesville, Virginia man participating in that reenactment staged by thousands of Union and Confederate reenactors was shot in the neck by a Civil War-era weapon or a replica of such a weapon. The man survived, but the incident shook the reenactment community.

The other articles dealt with similar incidents. One told of an older man who was shot in the shoulder while portraying a member of the

Seventh New York Cavalry during the filming of a documentary at the Cedar Creek Battlefield in northern Virginia. Another dealt with an Alabama infantry reenactor who was shot in the groin during a Vicksburg II Campaign reenactment.

The stories raised a number of issues including whether the shootings were intentional or accidental, whether the shooter was a reenactor or a spectator, and whether the reenactment organizers had any legal liability. The stories didn't specifically identify the shooters in individual incidents, although one did describe the Gettysburg shooter as a "reenactor from France" without further elaboration or identification.

"This is all very interesting," Pete said, "but wouldn't it be better to get into what happened at our reenactment and what's going on with the investigation?"

Harry cocked an eyebrow at Pete over his half-glasses and said, "Are you telling me how to write a news story?"

"No, just making an observation."

"Well, how about this for an approach? Lead off with a couple of punchy sentences describing Edinger's death, get into what we know about the investigation so far—law enforcement confiscated all of the weapons on site, searched all of the reenactors, took the victim's body to the morgue for an autopsy—then provide some background about the Thaddeus Clayton Festival and the reenactment units that participated in it without mentioning any names. And to put matters in context, add a few paragraphs about other shooting incidents at reenactments that have occurred around the country."

"Sounds like a story that would keep me reading."

"Nice of you to say that after you know how a true pro intends to craft his story. A lawyer like you would probably start off with something like, 'Whereas a certain man believed to be Thomas Edinger, which cannot yet be confirmed, was shot on October such-and-such of such-and-such year at a reenactment commonly known as the Thaddeus Clayton Festival, and Whereas this writer has no idea whether any such incidents have ever occurred at other Civil War reenactments, either in the North or in the South, and Whereas while the shootee's body was taken to the morgue, this writer cannot confirm that he's actually dead because this writer did not personally check the allegedly deceased man's pulse, and Whereas . . ."

Harry paused and peered at Pete with a crooked grin as though he were expecting some comeback.

Pete only chuckled and said, "Actually, that's not bad, although I'd drop the 'allegedly' in your the last line."

They sat quietly for a few moments until Pete asked, "What do you know about Thomas Edinger?"

"A fair amount since I've been researching him in anticipation of the festival. He used to be a professor at a small college in Tennessee that's known for its Civil War studies and he wrote the definitive biography about Colonel Thaddeus Clayton. Clayton was from Michigan, as you know, and when people from this area talk about the Civil War era, Clayton is the first name they mention. That explains the strong interest in our reenactment. You want a Coke?"

Pete shook his head and Harry shuffled across the room to his small refrigerator, surveyed the contents, and plucked out a can. Back at his desk, he laboriously elevated his feet to his desk top, popped the tab, and took a healthy swallow of his soft drink.

"A few years after the biography came out," Harry continued, "which had the catchy title, *Colonel Thaddeus Clayton: A Definitive Biography*, in case you're not aware of it," prompting Harry to grin and take another long gurgling swallow of Coke, "Edinger wrote a follow-up book about Clayton except this time he wrote in a more readable, less academic style. Kind of like Stephen Ambrose, you know? He used a catchier title, too, *Heartland Hero*. That book made the *New York Times* bestseller list and stayed there for twenty-nine weeks. It established Edinger's reputation with the masses and he was off and running.

"After that, Edinger wrote a series of popular novels based loosely on Clayton's life. He had to go back in time because, as you know, Clayton was killed in 1863 at the Battle of Missionary Ridge. To hear Edinger tell of Clayton's career before that, he virtually led Michigan into statehood even though he was only eleven years old when Michigan was admitted to the Union in 1837, single-handedly calmed tensions between the Indian tribes and the white settlers, and performed all kinds of other heroic acts in the years leading up to the Civil War. Edinger claims Clayton was on President Lincoln's short list to command the Union forces after the South seceded.

"Edinger quit his teaching job at the Tennessee college about ten years ago, and a few years after that, he bought the old Bader property and renovated it into the showplace it now is. The reenactment was held on part of that property. I think Edinger moved up here to burnish his reputation as the foremost Thaddeus Clayton authority in the country." Harry grinned. "He's smarter than you and me because he also bought a place in Naples, Florida, where he spent the winter months."

"Did he start the Thaddeus Clayton Festival?" Pete asked.

"Not exactly. Clay Modrall started it. Clay's a distant relative of Colonel Clayton—I don't know the exact relationship—and got the idea years ago. At first, it was just a local celebration that involved readings commemorating the Colonel's life and stuff like that. Then Clay decided to stage a major celebration with a reenactment of the Battle of Missionary Ridge this year, which is the sesquicentennial of that battle, and named a board of directors and everything. Edinger got wind of the planned event, and with his big name, gradually took over."

"With Modrall's blessing?"

"Hardly," Harry said. "What's the barnyard expression for being elbowed aside?"

"Screwed over?"

"That pretty much sums up what happened."

"Was Modrall one of the reenactors?"

"He was. To throw him a bone, the directors of the event made him Colonel Clayton's adjutant."

Pete thought about that for a moment, then said, "I bet he winds up on Richter's short list of suspects."

"Clay?"

"Yes."

"That's bull."

Pete shrugged. "I know how Richter thinks."

"Clay might have been hurt over what happened with the festival, but he wouldn't harm a fly. Besides, we don't even know whether Edinger's shooting was an accident or intentional."

"True."

"But you still think Clay will be a suspect?"

"If they conclude the shooting was intentional, you can count on it. And remember, no one came forward this afternoon and confessed to accidently loading his weapon with a live round that just happened to kill Edinger."

Harry thought about that for a minute. "Sometimes it takes a while for a person to own up to what he did."

"That's also true, but I have a feeling that isn't what we're dealing with in Edinger's case."

Harry studied him for a long moment and finally said, "Are you sure you're not hoping that Edinger's shooting is classified as a murder so you have a new case to stick your nose into?"

"I don't think that comment even deserves a reply."

"No? We both know about the scrapes you've gotten yourself into the past few years. You seem to enjoy it."

"None of the scrapes, as you say, were of my making," Pete said. "And I don't know if anyone wants a repeat of seeing a man blown away before his very eyes." After a moment he added, "Did Edinger have other enemies you know of?"

"Other than Clay? Jesus, I don't know. I suppose." Harry thought for a while. "Maybe Dennis Bader."

"Bader's the one who used to own the property Edinger now owns, right?

"Yes. Dennis tells anyone who'll listen that Thomas Edinger stole the property from him. The property was in Bader's family forever."

"I know a little about that situation because it was all over the papers a few years ago. Edinger didn't *steal* the property from Bader; he bought it at a foreclosure sale."

"That's the legal aspect, but any way you cut it, Bader lost property that had been in his family for five generations. Things got pretty nasty."

"That's the reason I'll bet Bader finds himself on Richter's suspect list, too."

Harry peered over his reading glasses and said, "Why don't we just round up both Modrall and Bader and hang them by their necks on that deer rack in front of Jake's Outdoors? Justice for the community. Damn, what happened to the presumption of innocence guys like you are always preaching about?"

Pete looked at him and said, "It's alive and well. I'm just telling you the way Richter thinks."

Harry fidgeted with a pencil on his desk and finally said, "Do you really think that one of those people could have killed Edinger?"

"No idea."

"When do you think we'll have a better picture of the way this matter is headed?"

"You said it yourself. After they do an autopsy, we'll know whether the bullet lodged in Edinger's body or passed through," Pete said. "If they find the bullet, they should be able to trace it to one of the weapons the sheriff has locked up in his evidence room."

Harry shook his head.

"Hey, you're always complaining about the lack of hard news in a small town," Pete said. "I would have thought you'd be all over a story like this."

"I am all over it," Harry said defensively. "I just don't want to see good people in the community hurt by speculation is all."

"If we don't get something to eat soon, the morgue is going to have another body to deal with."

Harry looked at the clock on the wall and said, "Aw jeez, Rona is going to kill me. She wanted to close early tonight, it being Sunday and all."

"Look on the bright side. If she kills you, and I can get her off on justifiable homicide, we can lead a sweet life together so at least you'll be able to rest easy knowing that your darling is being cared for."

"I've warned you before, Thorsen, stay away from my woman."

"If we leave this minute, I promise to look only at my plate and not even steal a glance at her."

When they walked into Rona's Bay Grille, the restaurant was empty except for two tables where the diners were just finishing up. Harry started to explain, but Rona made a show of looking at her watch and gave him a look that would insulate the polar icecap from global warming for the next century.

FOUR

"I'm told that Richter insisted the Medical Examiner work on the autopsy all night," Harry said when he called the next morning to tell Pete of the latest developments in the case. "They recovered the bullet that killed Edinger. It was lodged just behind his heart."

"And?" Pete said.

"The forensics people believe the bullet came from a smoothbore musket. That means the weapon that fired the round didn't have spiral grooves cut into the inner surface of the barrel the way modern rifles do. The grooves are what causes the bullet to spin and greatly increases the accuracy, you know."

"That makes sense given the ancient weapons the reenactors used."

"Right, but here's the hitch," Harry said. "Ballistics may not be able to identify exactly *which* smoothbore fired the bullet. The grooves from a rifled barrel create the ballistic fingerprint that enables the forensic people to trace which weapon a bullet came from. No marks from the grooves, no trace."

"Even smoothbores must leave *some* marks."

"Not the kind they can trace I'm told."

"How many of the reenactors carried smoothbore muskets?"

"They're trying to sort that out now. According to Cap, the weapons they impounded are a combination of smoothbore muskets, Henry repeating rifles and carbines with rifled barrels. I guess at the time of the Battle of Missionary Ridge, both the Union and the Confederacy were converting to rifled weapons, but neither side had enough of them to go around. Reenactors are fanatics about authenticity—they make their own hardtack rations and everything—and I guess that's why some of them had one kind of weapon and others had another."

"Where do Richter and his minions intend to go from here?"

"Oh," Harry said, "one other thing came out of the autopsy I forgot to mention. The bullet that killed Edinger appears to have entered his chest area on a downward trajectory. In other words, it hit higher on his chest and then trended lower as it burrowed in."

"I know what downward means, Harry," Pete said dryly. "So the trajectory suggests that the shot that killed Edinger came from the Confederate side. They occupied the ridge above the attacking Union troops."

"That's what it looks like. But even then, there's some question. Edinger might have been bending over when the shot hit him. That would be another explanation for the trajectory. There's no way they can tell for sure."

"Okay, back to my question. Where does Richter intend to go from here?"

"Cap says the state crime lab is sending people up here to help with examination of the guns they impounded. There are three hundred plus total."

"That number should be cut down substantially if they release the weapons with rifled barrels," Pete said.

"It should. I'm going to try to find out how they intend to analyze the smoothbores in view of what I just said about the ballistic fingerprint problem."

"You're on this like a real Sherlock," Pete said. He could almost see Harry's chest puff out a bit when he made the comment.

"A good newsman has a healthy dose of sleuth in him. Before I end this call and get back to something more productive, I have a question. Did you take any pictures while you were at the reenactment yesterday?"

"Nope," Pete said, "I was just observing."

"I thought you might have used your cell phone to capture some of the action."

"I'm old-fashioned, Harry. I still use phones for talking and cameras for taking pictures."

"Well, Richter has put out a call for photographs taken before, during or after the reenactment. I guess they hope to spot something in one of them."

"Did you turn in your pictures?" Pete asked.

"Not yet."

"You did take some, didn't you?"

"Not really," Harry said after a long pause.

"Harry . . ."

"I was attending to my duties as a reporter. I didn't have time to take pictures. Say, I've got another call coming in that I need to take."

After Pete hung up with Harry, he got on the Internet to see what he could find about ballistic fingerprinting. The information he came up with from that source, while not always completely reliable, was consistent with what Harry had told him. Old smoothbore weapons left no distinguishing marks on the lead. He had no evidence to support his hunch, but did have a feeling the person who shot Edinger knew that.

He went to the window and stared out at the bay and thought about how he was going to spend the day. He'd felt restless since he got to the office and it was one of those times when he missed the hustle and bustle and nonstop action of Chicago. When he was practicing law there, he didn't have enough hours in the day to get everything done that needed to get done. There were deals to work on, disputes between partners to mediate, a law firm to manage. For the most part, he enjoyed the slower pace of northern Michigan, but on occasion he also felt relegated to the sidelines before his time. That's how he felt today.

He grimaced and resumed looking through the box of old family documents that he'd stored in his closet, searching for the letters home from his distant relative, Ottar Jacobsen, who had served with the Union forces during the Civil War. The reenactment had stimulated his interest in Ottar's exploits during that war.

Ottar Jacobsen was a relative on his mother's side of the family. Most of her family had immigrated to America during the early to mid-1850s. Ottar was a young lad when he came over with his parents, and shortly thereafter, at age fifteen, he'd joined the First Minnesota Norwegian Volunteers, one of two all-Scandinavian units in the Union army. The other was the Fifteenth Wisconsin Volunteer Regiment formed by Colonel Hans Christian Heg at Camp Randall in Madison. The Fifteenth Wisconsin was the more famous unit, but the First Minnesota prided itself on being the only unit composed exclusively of Norwegian-American immigrants.

Pete found the stack of correspondence he was looking for. Years earlier, he'd put the letters in individual plastic sheaths to protect the brittle paper. He held up a letter home from Ottar so he could see it better. The handwriting was meticulous, but he'd forgotten that it was written in Norwegian. He knew a smattering of the language, but not enough to interpret Ottar's letters.

Also in the box was a pile of yellowed photographs taken by the famed Civil War photographer, Mathew Brady. Most were staged photographs of the entire First Minnesota unit, but there was one shot just of Ottar posing bareheaded in his dark blue flannel sack coat. A yellowed newspaper article accompanied one of the group photographs and chronicled the unit's exploits at the Second Battle of Bull Run.

Pete's great-aunt had prepared a "family history" years earlier. Most of the material was little more than cryptic notes about Uncle Ole and Aunt Siv having lived in an old Victorian on Elm Street in Spring Valley, Wisconsin, from such-and-such date until such-and-such date. However, she'd also devoted several paragraphs to Ottar Jacobsen and his exploits with the First Minnesota. According to her account, the unit participated in some fifty Civil War battles and Ottar's only injury was when he had the lobe of one ear shot off by a musket round during some unnamed battle.

He wondered what Thomas Edinger would have been able to do with the material about Ottar Jacobsen. Edinger probably would have portrayed him as a larger-than-life new Norwegian-American who was next-in-line for the royal crown back home, but came to America to single-handedly save the Union cause. He smiled and put the family documents back in the box.

A look back at history hadn't taken away his restlessness. He checked the time and decided he had to get out of Frankfort for the rest of the day. He drove around Crystal Lake, and when he got to Beulah, he continued on to Traverse City with no purpose in mind other than to browse around the only music store he knew of that he'd willingly enter. Normally, he avoided those places like the plague and particularly disliked the speakers inside and outside the stores that blared the screeching voice of some adolescent pop star of the moment at decibel levels beyond what the normal human ear could tolerate. That's why he bought almost all of his CDs from infomercials on late-night television. They played snippets of songs by his favorite artists, and best of all, the CDs were cheap.

McGee's Music was different. He hadn't even been aware that McGee's existed until an old army buddy turned disc jockey came to visit for a weekend a couple of years earlier. He was into rock and roll oldies in a big way, and in fact was responsible for turning Pete on to the genre, and insisted that one of the things they had to do that weekend was visit McGee's. The store contained row after row of CDs by blues singers and jazz performers and country artists, and best of all, famous rock and roll musicians going back to the days when the music was in its infancy. And nothing blared over the sound system. If you wanted to hear a particular number, you went into a glassed-in room where you wouldn't disturb other music lovers who might prefer something different.

Cody McGee was tending the store as usual along with his wife, Anabelle. Cody was a Willie Nelson look-alike with a scraggly beard, weathered skin that looked like it had been glued to his face and neck in patches, and hair pulled back in a ponytail. Cody had just celebrated his sixtieth birthday, but looked ten years older. Pete often suspected that he consumed half a bottle of cheap whiskey instead of orange juice for breakfast.

"Pete," Cody said, "what brings a cheapskate like you to my store? Won't those places that let you avoid thirty cents in sales tax by buying over the telephone accept your credit card anymore?"

Pete chuckled and traded banter with Cody for ten minutes. He said, "Do you have anything new I might like?"

"You mean anything new that's really old?" Cody's laugh was a "heh, heh, heh" that seemed to chug on for minutes.

"Something like that."

"I just got in some music originally cut on 45s by Richard Wayne Penniman that now are out on a CD I think you'd like. Dynamite disc."

Pete furled his brow. "Penniman. Who's that?"

"Who's what?"

"Richard Wayne Penniman."

Cody McGee looked at him incredulously and said, "You don't know?"

"If I knew, I wouldn't have asked."

"Little Richard, for crissakes, Little Richard." Cody rolled his eyes.

"I know Little Richard. Why didn't you call him that?"

"Because I thought I was dealing with someone who knew his music."

"What else do you have from the sixties or seventies? Little Richard is old even for me."

Cody squinted at him and said, "Did you ever hear Penniman on a 45?"

"I never heard *anyone on a 45.*"

"Well, you got a treat coming. Hey Anabelle!" he bellowed, "take this cat into the listening room and play the new Penniman CD for him."

Anabelle McGee was a petite woman who dressed in western garb and claimed she'd been a rising star in Nashville until she chucked it all for Cody and turned to selling music rather than making it. Pete followed her into the glass-walled listening room and waited while she inserted the disc into the player. He watched her snap her fingers and close her eyes and groove to the strains of a Little Richard song.

She came alive when the Little Richard classic "Good Golly Miss Molly" started to play. She cranked up the sound to the max and began to gyrate wildly. Pete smiled in amusement; he knew Anabelle could be wild and unpredictable, but he'd never seen this side of her before. She wriggled past him and bumped him with a hip and grabbed his hand and forced him into a frenzied jitterbug that had him panting for air after one minute. Then she released his hand and went into a dance routine that was borderline obscene. Pete took advantage of the opportunity and slipped out the door. The handful of customers who'd come over to the glass wall to watch the spectacle clapped as he came out. Pete grinned sheepishly and walked toward the counter.

Cody McGee stood by the cash register with a smug look on his face and two CD cases in his hand. Pete paid without examining the CDs and left before his dance partner realized he was gone.

FIVE

wo days later, Pete was surfing a genealogy site to see if he could come up with additional information on Ottar Jacobsen when his telephone rang. "Pete, this is Matthew Stroud. You might recall that we met when I stopped to meet you when you hung out your shingle in Frankfort."

"Sure, Matt, I do remember. That was nice of you to come by."

The line was silent for a long moment, then Stroud said, "Umm, Pete, I go by Matthew, if you'll remember."

"Of course," Pete said apologetically. "I forgot. What can I do for you?" Matthew Stroud was the other lawyer in Frankfort, and while Pete had no intention of carrying on an active legal practice in the community of fewer than fifteen hundred people, Stroud seemed worried enough about the prospect to stop and gauge his intentions.

"I have a long-standing client who's consulted me on an important matter involving the Thomas Edinger shooting. He lives here in town. Walter Helwig, do you know him?"

"Not well," Pete said, "but I've talked to Wally a few times." Stroud didn't correct him and instruct Pete to call Helwig by his formal first name.

"This is a little awkward, but I have a question. Do you have any relationships that would prevent you from serving as co-counsel with me on that matter?"

"Before I answer that, maybe you should tell me what the matter is about."

Stroud was silent again, then he said, "I'm not comfortable discussing a matter this serious over the telephone. The government eavesdrops on all of our telephone conversations these days you know."

Pete rolled his eyes and said, "I'm in my office and not doing anything I can't put aside for a while. We can discuss it here if you like."

Stroud's relief was apparent even over the phone. "Could I come over in, say, fifteen minutes?"

"I'll be here," Pete said.

Pete knew from a conversation with Harry that Wally Helwig had been the safety officer at the Thaddeus Clayton Festival and assumed the sheriff wanted to talk to Helwig about the precautions he'd taken the day Thomas Edinger was shot. Like he'd read some of the same stories Harry had printed out from the Internet and knew that negligence was an issue that commonly came up in those investigations.

About twelve minutes after he called, Stroud walked in wearing a faded poplin suit that once had been dark blue and was more than a month past its summer season. A tear in one sleeve had been mended by a crosshatch of light blue thread. Stroud clasped Pete's hand with a weak grip and thanked him for seeing him on such short notice. He eyed Pete's dress which consisted of worn jeans and a semi-new flannel shirt and took off his suit coat and hung it on a hanger on the clothes tree in the outer office. Pete watched Stroud carefully adjust the garment on the hanger. He tried to keep the amused look off his face and strained to think of when he'd seen someone wear a suit in the county except at a funeral or the hospital fund-raising ball.

Stroud adjusted his narrow dark tie, as though it suddenly had become too tight, and accepted Pete's offer of coffee. "Is it okay if I sit here?" he asked, gesturing to the only side chair that was free of files and stacks of papers.

"Please," Pete said.

"I'm glad we could meet in your office. These stories about what the National Security Agency is doing with telephone records has everyone concerned."

Pete nodded solemnly. "You can't be too careful."

"In former days," Stroud said, "a person always felt he could trust his government. But with all of this electronic eavesdropping . . ."

Pete nodded again. "So what's this all about, Matthew?"

Stroud glanced over his shoulder at the outer office to make sure no one had come in who might hear, then said to Pete in a hushed voice, "Sheriff Richter wants to talk to Mr. Helwig about the shooting."

"That's what you said over the telephone. What's he suspected of?"

"It's about the security precautions he took as the chief safety officer for the Thaddeus Clayton Festival. I stayed at the office late last night and did some legal research. I think what the sheriff is raising is whether Mr. Helwig was negligent and therefore has some responsibility for what happened. I found several cases involving the theory of negligent homicide. The sheriff didn't use that term, but I believe that's what he's thinking."

"I see. Have you thought about your defense?"

Stroud's hands opened and closed around his coffee mug, telegraphing the tension that was coursing through his body. "I was hoping you could give me some ideas as my co-counsel."

Pete felt sorry for Stroud, who looked like he was stressed out over the prospect of meeting with Richter, but he didn't have the appetite for doing battle with the sheriff over an issue he didn't expect to go anywhere.

"Let's leave the co-counsel issue for later," Pete said, "but as a general matter, Wally should be careful to tell the truth. He'll be creating problems for himself if he doesn't."

"I've heard that Sheriff Richter is a bully."

"He is. But getting caught in a lie is the worst thing you can do with him."

Stroud fidgeted with his hands and said, "Walter tells me they took more precautions than they take at most reenactments."

"Does he have proof of that?"

"His experience, mainly. He's been to a lot of reenactments. He knows what was done in other situations."

"Okay," Pete said. "And the security precautions they had in place at the Thaddeus Clayton Festival were the same as those other reenactments?"

"Better, even, Walter tells me."

"Why don't you tell me what they were."

Stroud went to the clothes tree and extracted a folded sheet of paper from his suit coat pocket. He sat down again and unfolded the paper and studied it for a long time. "There are three points, really," he said. "Seventeen reenactment groups from around the country participated in the Thaddeus Clayton Festival. The commanding officer of each unit signed a form stating that he'd advised all of his men that live ammunition was strictly forbidden. Each of the commanding officers also inspected the weapons of his men and the items they were carrying to make sure no one had live ammunition."

"That's good," Pete said. "Does Wally have copies of those forms?"

Stroud's voice became a whisper again. "He has sixteen of them. He swears all of the commanders signed, but he can't find the seventeenth form."

Pete thought about that and imagined how Richter would react if he found out that Helwig didn't have all of the forms. He said, "So what are the other things Wally did?"

"He had a festival security committee consisting of himself and three other individuals. The committee split up the units and did a spot check of the reenactors and their weapons and the possessions they had with them."

"That's in addition to the inspections the commanding officers made?"

"Yes. The last thing Walter did was to announce what he called the 'rules of engagement' to all of the reenactors. He emphasized at the beginning and then again at the end that live ammunition was strictly forbidden."

Pete thought about it. "It seems like you've got a solid case except for the missing form."

"That's what worries me. I've heard about Sheriff Richter's reputation."

"You'll be okay. Just stick to the facts you just told me."

Stroud looked at him with a whimpering expression. "Now that you know the facts, are you willing to go with us to the sheriff's office as my co-counsel?"

"I think you'll be better off without me, Matthew, and I'll tell you why. Frank Richter and I have a history you might not be familiar with. Let's just say we don't get along. If I'm there, it might actually be tougher for your client because Richter will want to show me up. Just stick to your guns as I said and you should be okay. Besides, Richter's bluster about Wally having possible liability is just a side show. What he's really after is to establish either that Thomas Edinger's shooting was accidental or to identify and arrest his killer."

"Mr. Helwig couldn't have been the shooter because he didn't have a weapon of any sort and didn't participate in the reenactment."

"There you go. The notion that he was negligent doesn't seem valid either in view of what you told me."

"Are you sure?"

"I am."

Stroud seemed unsure whether he should wrap up the conversation or ask a follow-up question. Finally he came out with, "Could you give me some idea what I should expect from Sheriff Richter?"

"A couple of things. When you go to his office, he'll probably keep you and Wally waiting in an interview room to make you nervous and soften you up. That's called 'sweating' in police circles. Then he'll try to catch you in some inconsistency. If you stick to what you told me about all of things Wally did to assure safety, I can't imagine this will go any further than one round of questioning."

"Walter's the one who suggested I ask you to go along with us," Stroud said hopefully. "He knows about those other matters you've been involved in."

"Matthew, I explained why it wouldn't be wise for me to come."

"I know, but . . ."

"I'll tell you what, I'll give you my cell phone number. If you sense things aren't going well, ask for a brief recess and call me." He circled his cell phone number on one of his business cards and handed it to Stroud.

Stroud studied the card and then said, "And I'll be able to reach you right away at this number?"

"You will. This is kind of a halfway measure in case you really need me."

"And you'd come down to the sheriff's office then?"

"We can talk about it if you have to call, but I don't think you will." Pete got up and guided Stroud out of his office to where his suit jacket was hanging in the outer room. As Stroud put it on, Pete noticed the wetness under his arms.

Stroud's parting words as he left Pete's office were, "We're going to beat this thing, Pete."

Pete nodded and gave him a thumbs up sign.

SIX

After Stroud was gone, Pete tried to get back to his research on Ottar Jacobsen, but the meeting had fixated him on the Edinger shooting again and he remembered what Harry had said about the autopsy results. He sketched out the topography of the reenactment site as he remembered it and plotted possible areas the shot might have come from. Even though he'd spent several hours at the site on Sunday, his memory was fuzzy on some of the geographical features of the ridge and he kept making new versions of his sketch.

He leaned back in his chair and stared out at the bay. It was only mid-afternoon and he had plenty of time to get to the site and look around while it was still daylight. For a nanosecond, he thought about asking Harry to join him, but quickly rejected that idea. It would only provide his friend an opportunity to needle him about sticking his nose into another murder case. Or at least what *might* be another murder case.

The Edinger property on which the reenactment was held was just south of Elberta. He exited left off M-22 onto a narrow paved road that led to Edinger's house which, based on everything he'd heard, was quite grand. After going a short distance, he turned onto the gravel access road leading to the reenactment site.

Up ahead, he saw the field with the steep ridge at one end where the mock battle had been staged. Everything seemed to be the same as it was the day Edinger was shot. The rope that cordoned off the reenactment area from where the spectators watched was still up, and inside the rope, crime-scene tape was strung around four stakes that formed a fifty-foot square on the slope where Edinger had fallen. The yellow tape fluttered in the gentle breeze.

The barricades at the top of the ridge where the Confederate reenactors mounted their defense were also still there. The area had dried out and the fiery reds and oranges of the wooded areas that bordered much of the field glinted in the late autumn sun. Quite a contrast to Sunday when everything was cloaked in dreary gray.

Pete admired the scene for a while and then reminded himself that he wasn't on a color peeping tour. He ducked under the rope, walked past the taped-off area, and wandered into the trees at the base of the field where the Union reenactors had launched their attack with blood-curdling battle cries. Seeing the site from this angle reinforced his belief it was unlikely the shot that killed Edinger had come from this direction. He sketched the layout in his small notebook and made notes so he'd remember everything correctly.

He stared at the crest of the ridge. The shot had to have come from somewhere up there, either from one of the reenactors or someone else hiding nearby. But if the shooter were someone other than a reenactor, how did he escape the attention of all of the men around him? And the watchful eyes of hundreds of spectators?

Pete walked across the field to the picturesque split-rail fence on the far side to get a different perspective. Then he began to trudge up the hill. When he reached the crest, he noticed that the wood barricades and earthwork didn't extend all the way to the fence. He wasn't sure if that fact had any significance, but he'd learned from his army days working for Major Baumann of the CID to examine a crime scene from every possible angle.

As he walked through the trees and underbrush, he flushed a pair of ruffed grouse from their cover and the sudden explosion of wings startled him. He smiled. It took him back to his youth when he'd stroll through the autumn woods with his twenty gauge shotgun thinking of things that were more important to him than hunting. When the big birds exploded in front of him, they were usually well out of gunshot range by the time he'd pulled himself back to the present and taken aim.

Pete made his way along the ridge and looked for places a gunman could hide if he were targeting Thomas Edinger and wanted to avoid detection. He saw several places where the grass was packed down beside boulders or behind fallen trees, but concluded they likely were deer beds. He stepped into the dug-out earthwork just behind the timber fortifications and looked down the slope and tried to visualize the advancing enemy. As he stared at the scene, he heard a faint rustle behind him and a voice said, "It's nice this property ain't posted no more, ain't it? Just like it used to be. Except those yahoos could have restored this ridge, too."

The voice momentarily startled him because he hadn't seen anyone else in the area. The man standing barely fifteen feet from him had a shock of frizzy red hair stuffed partly under a dirty yellow cap with a "Gro-More" fertilizer logo on it and an unkempt beard that matched his hair except for the gray tinges. He cradled what appeared to be an old-fashioned rifle in the crook of one arm. Pete decided the man must be color blind because he had on a blue and purple checked shirt and wide brown suspenders with ducks taking flight from a marsh.

"We ain't been properly introduced," the man said. "I'm Calvin Seitz."

Pete climbed out of the earthwork bunker and said, "Pete Thorsen."

"Well, Pete Thorsen, you can't do no hunting without some kind of weapon. Funny, you don't look like no leaf peeper, neither."

"I'm not hunting and I'm not a leaf peeper, either, as you say."

"I been watching you for fifteen minutes," Seitz said. "Looking around at that police tape, casing the area, making notes in that little book of yours. You with law enforcement, Pete Thorsen?"

Pete chuckled and shook his head. "No, I'm not with the law. I was at the reenactment on Sunday and happened to be in the area again. I thought I'd have a closer look at the place where Thomas Edinger was shot."

"It was just a matter of time until that guy got what he deserved," Seitz said. "There were people lined up to get a shot at him."

"Really," Pete said. "I hadn't heard that."

"I been hunting this area for thirty years and all of a sudden this guy comes along with his money and buys half the property in the county and puts up all of these signs." Seitz pulled a wadded-up piece of paper from his pocket and smoothed it out and handed it to Pete. It was a standard "No Trespassing" sign that a person could buy in the hardware store.

Pete said, "Of course, if he owned the property, he could post it if he wished."

Seitz stared at him with narrowed eyes. "That's what a guy like Edinger would like you to believe."

"What do you mean?"

"You ever hear of hunter's easements?" he asked. "After a man's been hunting on a piece of property for so long, the new owner can't stop him from continuing to hunt on it."

"Who told you that?"

"It was right there in this hunting and fishing magazine I get. You can send in your question and a lawyer who knows all the rules and regulations gives you the answer. This lawyer says there's not even any question when it comes to a hunter's easement."

"Did Edinger ever tell you to stay off his property?"

"Oh, he told me a bunch of times." Seitz grinned slyly.

"But you didn't listen. Asserted a hunter's easement, huh?"

"I did that and had the equalizer here with me, too," Seitz said, patting the stock of his ancient weapon.

"I see," Pete said. "Were you at the reenactment Sunday?"

"Nope, couldn't come. The salmon are running on the Betsie River and I was busy catching a mess of them. A man's got to put away food for the winter at this time of the year. But I've kicked myself ever since. It would have been a real pleasure to see that idiot Edinger go down."

"Mmm," Pete murmured. "What kind of rifle is that?"

"Are you a hunter, son?"

"Not much anymore."

"If you were a hunter, you'd know not to call this piece a rifle. Doesn't have a single rifling in the barrel. This here's a smoothbore musket. It's the weapon our ancestors used to build this country. Ain't no finer piece ever made."

"Not too accurate though, right? I've heard that's why they started adding grooves inside the barrels."

Seitz looked at Pete like he was a total ignoramus. "You want to see accuracy, Pete Thorsen?"

Pete shrugged.

Seitz looked around the area. Pete started to say something and Seitz silenced him with a hand. Finally, Seitz whispered, "You see that squirrel?" He pointed to a tree that was thirty-five or forty yards away and it took Pete a moment to spot the animal hunched on a branch. Seitz swung the barrel of the smoothbore up, held it rock-steady while he aimed, and squeezed off a shot. The musket round tore into the branch and the squirrel tumbled to earth along with pieces of tree bark. Seitz looked at Pete with a crafty smile.

Pete knew enough about squirrel hunting to know that the most skilled hunters "barked" their quarry rather than shooting it straight on. "Impressive," Pete said. "What kind of range does this musket have?"

"I can put a round within four inches of center at a hundred yards nine times out of ten."

Pete nodded.

"Well, it's been good talking to you, Pete Thorsen. I got to get me a few more squirrels before dark. Make the best damn stew you ever tasted."

Joe Tessler wasn't available when Pete called so he asked for his voice-mail and left a message. Tessler returned his call an hour later.

"Where are you?" Pete asked.

"In my car, on my cell phone. I didn't want to be overheard talking to Public Enemy Number One on my office line."

Pete chuckled. "I'm glad to hear that I've maintained my standing."

"You have in the eyes of Top Dog. So what's up?"

"Before I get to that, I have a question. Has your department reached a conclusion on whether Edinger's shooting was accidental or intentional?"

"Nothing official, but my nose tells me it was intentional. The sheriff is thinking the same way."

"That's my uninformed guess, too, and makes the reason for my call even more relevant. I was just out at the Edinger place and—"

"Excuse me for interrupting, but what were you doing out there?"

Pete knew Tessler would raise that question and he was prepared. "Nothing special, just leaf peeping. Don't worry, I didn't tamper with your police-line tape or do anything to disturb the crime scene."

"Leaf peeping. What's that?"

"Admiring the autumn foliage," Pete answered casually. "The color is extraordinary at this time of the year on a sunny day."

Tessler was silent for a long moment. "Leaf peeping, my behind. You just can't resist nosing around in these things, can you?"

"You have an overly suspicious mind, Joe."

"Okay," Tessler said, sighing. "What did you just happen to discover when you were leaf peeping, as you say, at the Edinger's?"

"I was standing there admiring the color when this wild-looking guy with a bushy beard and a shock of red hair that looked like a fright wig popped out of nowhere and scared the bejesus out of me. Calvin Seitz. Ever hear of him?"

"Doesn't ring a bell."

"Anyway, Seitz claims he's been hunting on this property for thirty years and then spent the next fifteen minutes bad-mouthing Edinger for posting the property with 'No Trespassing' signs after he bought it."

"What's so unusual about that? A lot of people post their property."

"I agree, but Seitz doesn't recognize a landowner's right to do that. He claims he has a hunter's easement to continue hunting where he's hunted in the past."

"Hunter's easement. That's a new one to me."

"New to me, too, and I'm a lawyer. Here's the interesting part, though. Do you know what kind of weapon he was carrying?"

Tessler seemed to think about it and then said, "Probably a shotgun. It's bird season."

"A smoothbore musket."

"A smoothbore."

"Yes."

When Tessler didn't say anything, Pete added, "Edinger was shot with a smoothbore, wasn't he?"

"That's the way it looks like to us."

"Now do you see why I called? I think you should check this guy out. It may be nothing, but when I put together the smoothbore and the way he was bad-mouthing Edinger . . ."

"Several people we've talked to bad-mouthed Thomas Edinger. From what I can tell, he wasn't going to win many popularity contests."

Seitz had said the same thing and before Pete could add anything, Tessler asked, "Was Seitz one of the reenactors?"

"Not according to him. He claims he was over on the Betsie River catching salmon."

"Was anyone with him?"

"Don't know. You can only ask so many questions of a man with a smoothbore musket pointed in your general direction."

Tessler seemed to mull that over and then said, "I'll think about whether we should talk to Seitz, but if he wasn't one of the reenactors, it pretty much leaves him out regardless of how he felt about Edinger."

"Why do you say that?"

"Because of the accuracy issue. People tell me you can't hit squat with a smoothbore. Seitz couldn't have been lurking somewhere a couple of hundred yards out and picked off Edinger. It just wouldn't work."

"Smoothbores may be more accurate than people think," Pete said. He told Tessler about how Seitz had barked the squirrel and his boast that he could put rounds within four inches of center from a hundred yards.

"You saw him do that?"

"I saw him take out the squirrel. I didn't make him prove he could hit a four-inch target from a hundred yards."

"Frank will think I'm off my rocker if I tell him I want to question Seitz. He's bought into the accuracy issue and concluded that the shooter likely was a Confederate reenactor who was fairly close to Edinger. Once Frank gets something in his head, it's nearly impossible to get him off it."

"Okay," Pete said, "it's your call. I'm just reporting what I heard and saw. You didn't get any of this from me, okay? I don't want to become known as the town snitch."

He heard Tessler grunt over the phone. "I won't mention you for a lot of reasons, Frank being at the top of that list."

"I suppose it might gain me some points with the sheriff if he knew I was giving you information that might be relevant to his investigation."

"Fat chance! If Frank learns I'm talking to you for *any* reason, I'd have to try to get my old job in Chicago back."

Pete laughed. "Well, I'll pass on anything else I hear or see."

"It would make my life easier if you left any messages for me on my cell phone."

"Understood. Let me ask you one final question before I let you go. I understand that you have the bullet the medical examiner took out of Thomas Edinger. If you find a musket that you think fired it, I assume you can test it to determine if you're right."

"Not from what the ballistics experts tell us. They say they can determine if the musket and the bullet are the same caliber, but probably not if a particular musket fired a particular round. I don't know whether you know this, but ballistics fingerprinting depends on comparing the rifling inside a barrel and the marks that rifling leaves on the bullet. It's almost impossible to trace markings with a smoothbore I'm told."

That was the same as what Harry had told him and what he'd learned from his own research.

SEVEN

October's weather could be quirky, and with the temperature dropping from seventy degrees into the high forties and the sky looking like a hunk of tarnished pewter suspended low overhead, the last thing Pete wanted to do was go fishing for salmon on Lake Michigan. He was a fly fishing guy and trolling for fish a hundred feet down with tackle strong enough to beach a small whale somehow didn't appeal to him even in balmier weather. But Harry had been the high bidder at a charity auction on two tickets for the fishing outing and Pete agreed to go along out of loyalty to his friend.

The tickets had been contributed jointly by Jake's Outdoors, the hunting and fishing shop in town, and The Fusion, the popular Pan-Asian restaurant. Jake Rossum himself was on board the thirty-two foot Wellcraft Coastal for the outing. Pete had been in Jake's Outdoors a couple of times to stock up on dry flies, but he really didn't know Rossum.

Harry approached the fishing outing with the same gusto he brought to everything else in life, and as usual, his dress was something to behold. He wore insulated camouflage duck-hunting pants, a canary-colored slicker over a thick turtleneck sweater, and a pair of heavy gloves. He topped it off with his trademark beat-up slouch hat that was pulled low over his eyes and a red scarf knotted around his neck like the one Snoopy wore when he was on the tail of the Red Baron. Driving to the marina, Pete felt like he was sitting next to a nattily-dressed brown bear.

Pete and Harry were the first of the six ticket holders to arrive and Jake Rossum greeted them when they came aboard. Harry knew Rossum and introduced Pete. Rossum was a couple of inches shorter than Pete, maybe six feet even, and wore a Detroit Tigers baseball cap and had a neatly-trimmed moustache and beard.

Harry was soon was telling Rossum about all of the trophy salmon he'd landed when he was the outdoors editor of the Chicago newspaper he once worked for. Pete had known Harry for twenty years, but until that moment, wasn't aware that he had been the outdoors editor at *any* newspaper. Pete listened to their conversation a while and then wandered off to the other side of the boat and gazed out at the gray waters of the bay and wondered whether he should have worn another layer of clothing.

He heard loud voices and turned to see a group of three men walking out the pier toward their boat. One was carrying a beverage jug and a small plastic bag. The ebullient Harry assumed the role of greeter-in-chief for the boat and welcomed them aboard. After introducing the threesome to Rossum, he called to Pete, "Come meet Sal and his friends." Pete shook hands all around and then let Harry reassume his self-appointed role.

Pete went back to where he had been standing, and five minutes later, Harry tugged at his sleeve and said in a low voice, "Boy, this is going to be a great group." He took off a glove and looked at his watch and added, "We're still missing one. I wonder if he's going to be a no-show."

That question was answered two minutes later when a man in a hip-length brown coat and a stocking cap hurried down the pier. Harry watched him come and whispered to Pete, "Oh, jeez, this is going to be awkward. Do you know who that is?"

"No idea."

"Dennis Bader."

"Really?"

"Yes, really. I know Bader and that's him."

"So you're giving me the heads-up not to ask everyone on the boat if they know who Sheriff Richter is questioning about the Thomas Edinger shooting?"

"It's not a laughing matter, Pete. As I told you in my office, Dennis is a decent guy and I can't believe he had anything to do with it. C'mon, let's go over and say hello and make him feel welcome."

Pete followed Harry, and as soon as Bader stepped on the boat, Harry pumped his hand enthusiastically, introduced Pete, and made the other introductions. Harry talked to Bader for a few minutes and rejoined Pete while Jake Rossum showed Bader his fishing station.

As the boat pulled out of the harbor, Harry said, "This will be a good change of pace for us. I've never been out with Jake before, but he knows salmon fishing on Lake Michigan as well as anyone around. He's really respected in this part of the state."

"I'm especially anxious to get out on the open water on a balmy day like this."

"Are you cold?" Harry asked.

"I've been warmer."

"I could have given you a few tips on how to dress if you'd asked me."

Pete resisted the temptation to comment on Harry's attire and said in a low voice, "A better option would have been for you to bid on a paid fly fishing trip for two to the Au Sable River in early September."

"That wasn't one of the auction items. I guess I'd forgotten how venturesome you are, though," Harry said sarcastically as he shot Pete a look. "Me, I like to try new things even if I wind up reverting to what I'm familiar with. Besides, with Fusion providing the food, this outing should be something special."

"Kind of like that boat in the Chicago to Mackinac race that was written up in your old paper a few years ago, huh?"

Harry seemed puzzled for a moment, then his face brightened and he said, "Oh, I know the one you mean. The boat that serves gourmet food to its crew up and back. The chef is from the International Club in the Drake Hotel. Boy, I'd love to do that some time."

"Sail in the Mac or eat?"

"Both, wise guy. Sailors have to eat, too, you know."

Bader was standing alone gazing out at the water. Harry reverted to his low voice and said, "I really feel sorry for the guy."

"Do you think Richter has questioned him yet?"

Harry shook his head and whispered, "Don't know. Maybe he's scheduled to go in for questioning and is scared to death."

Sal and friends were enjoying Screwdrivers from their jug and arguing loudly among themselves as the helmsman guided the boat through the outlet onto Lake Michigan. Sal was barely five feet eight or nine inches tall and was dressed in a dark blue parka and matching rain pants and wore reflective sunglasses under a cap with "Navy" emblazoned across the front. "I wasn't there," Sal said in his outsized voice, "but from what everyone tells me, that writer guy was shot intentionally."

"Oh, boy," Harry said, "they're arguing about the shooting." He looked Bader's way to see if he'd over-heard Sal's comment. Bader continued to stare at the water.

The man Sal was arguing with said, "That's always the knee-jerk conclusion when there's an accident at one of these reenactments. Remember the Gettysburg reenactment a few years ago? The rumor was that the man was shot by someone with a grudge against him. It turned out that it was just an accident involving some flaky Frenchman."

"That's bull!" Sal said. "Frenchy was made a scapegoat by the incompetent local police. I have it on good authority that the whole affair was a cleverly staged attempted murder."

"What authority? The same conspiracy theory nuts who claim that Jack Kennedy was shot by a squad of Cuban commandos with backing from the Miami mob?"

After more arguing, Sal called, "Hey Harry! Come over here! We need a referee for a disagreement about the shooting at that reenactment." Pete saw Harry's face lose color in spite of the brisk wind that had flecks of red standing out on his cheeks. Harry shuffled over to where Sal and his comrades were standing, stealing a glance at Bader.

Sal put his arm around Harry's shoulder and said, "You're a newspaperman, right?"

Harry nodded.

"I assume you're up on the latest concerning that shooting then."

Harry said in a voice Pete could barely hear, "Pretty much. But understand, there might be information I've gotten from a confidential source that I can't disclose."

"Understood," Sal said. "Here's the disagreement. Eddie claims that the shooting up here was accidental and the person who did the shooting just hasn't been willing to come forward because he's afraid he'll be prosecuted. I say that's a crock and the writer . . . What was his name?"

"Thomas Edinger."

"Yeah, Thomas Edinger. I heard that this Edinger fellow had more enemies than a fish has scales and one of them used the reenactment for cover and plugged him. So, who's right?"

Harry glanced Bader's way again and said, "The sheriff is still investigating, I know that. I also don't think that they've determined yet whether the shooting was accidental or intentional."

"But you're not denying that Edinger had a lot of enemies, are you?"

"No, a lot of people have said that." Harry looked at the beverage jug and said, "You wouldn't have any extra Screwdrivers in that jug, would you?"

"Somebody get Harry a glass. He needs some lubrication to think. We need to resolve this argument before we get out to fishing water."

With his glass in hand, Harry then proceeded to catalog six or eight shootings at Civil War reenactments over the years and how some involved long guns and others pistols. Sal and his buddies seemed mesmerized by Harry's knowledge of the subject and crowded around him and listened carefully while Harry detailed each of the incidents.

"See?" Eddie said. "How many incidents was that, Harry? Six, seven? And all of the shootings were accidental."

Sal said, "That doesn't prove anything. Some of those cases are still open. Other shootings were only *assumed* to be accidental. People who know tell me there were at least two situations where the authorities suspected foul play, but they couldn't prove anything so they classified the deaths as accidental. Politics play a role in law enforcement, too, and the last thing an elected sheriff wants is to have an unsolved murder hanging around his neck."

"That's speculation and doesn't make any sense," Eddie scoffed. "If you were going to knock a guy off, wouldn't you plant a bomb in his car or something rather than do it in a crowd of hundreds of people?"

"Did you ever hear of cover?" Sal asked sarcastically.

"Cover bunk," Eddie replied. "I say that until we have proof to the contrary, the man who played Colonel Clayton was shot by accident like what happened at Gettysburg."

Pete listened to Sal and Eddie argue for a while longer and then his mind wandered off to his encounter with Calvin Seitz and his marksmanship with the smoothbore. He saw Rossum leave the helm and walk over to where Bader was staring out at the lake. He rested his elbows on the side of the boat and they carried on a conversation that Pete couldn't hear.

The chef came up from below deck with a steaming platter of Chicken Satay, Crab Rangoon, Spring Rolls, and Teriyaki Meatballs and walked toward where Harry was holding court with Sal and his group at the back of the boat. Harry could be surprisingly agile for a man of his girth when the occasion called for it and he managed to beat the others to the tray. He chewed approvingly while continuing to jaw with his new friends. For the moment, at least, questions of whether Edinger's shooting was an accident or something more nefarious took a back seat to sampling Chef Yoo's offerings.

When the feeding frenzy had subsided, Pete surveyed the leftovers and helped himself to two of the Spring Rolls that remained. Harry came over to him and said in an aside, "I wonder what Chef Yoo is serving for an entree?"

"I'm sure it's going to be good. Did you resolve the dispute over the shooting?"

"I think I made them see that there were two sides to it. I felt like I was a lawyer, saying 'On the one hand this,' but 'On the other hand that.'"

"It was those two days you spent in law school that did it."

Harry looked at him as though he were addled. "I never spent two days in law school. I was J-school all the way. I guess listening to you equivocate on everything all these years must have rubbed off on me and tainted my normal laser-like judgment."

"I'm sure you meant your association with me gave you a more open mind. Where are those guys from?"

"The Detroit area. Sal—he's the one in blue—was up here for another fishing weekend and attended the hospital benefit. He had the high bid on three tickets for this outing. Nice guy."

The other guests gradually took their fishing stations and peered intently at the water as the boat moved slowly through the area. Harry did the same for ten minutes and then nudged Pete and whispered, "I'm going below to ask the chef when he's serving the entree."

EIGHT

P ete pulled into his driveway in mid-afternoon after five hours on the lake. He was chilled to the marrow and had no fish to show for his suffering. He gazed east down the long stretch of Crystal Lake towards the small town of Beulah at the far end. On a clear day, he could see the outlines of buildings eight miles away. Today he saw nothing but gray.

After building a fire in the fireplace, Pete walked out to the road to check his mailbox. Most of the mail was fodder for his fire, but a registered letter notice caught his eye. It was in handwriting that would make encryption unnecessary if it were a CIA document and about all Pete could make out was "Michigan Supreme Court." He was tempted to leave it for the morning, but then curiosity won out and he piled back into his Range Rover and headed for town again.

The post office, normally a beehive of activity in the morning hours, was deserted when he walked in. He rapped on the counter a couple of times to attract the lone postal worker's attention and signed for the registered letter. Below "Michigan Supreme Court" at the upper left corner of the manila envelope was, "Attorney Grievance Commission."

When he was in his car, he sliced open the envelope with a finger and extracted a stack of documents. The one on top was headed "Notice of Complaint." He scanned the complaint quickly. It alleged that Pete was guilty of misconduct under Rule 9.106 of the Supreme Court's Rules in that, in essence, he had misrepresented himself as being the attorney for Lynn Hawke's estate, had misrepresented that he had the power to continue or set aside an executory contract between Hawke and Barbara Rodes, and that Ms. Rodes had been grievously harmed as a result of his actions. The actual allegations ran for five double-spaced pages and gave dates and examples of instances when he'd supposedly made misrepresentations.

Other documents in the package included a printed pamphlet with the Michigan Supreme Court Rules and a photocopy of a sheet that summarized possible disciplinary action that could be taken against an attorney who engaged in misconduct within the scope and meaning of the Rules. Finally, there was a request that Pete file a written response to the allegations "fully and fairly disclosing all facts and circumstances concerning the alleged misconduct" within twenty-one days of receipt of the letter.

Pete thought back to his conversations with Barbara Rodes when he was investigating Lynn Hawke's death earlier that year and anger boiled up inside him. He didn't remember exactly what he'd said to Barbara, but all he was doing was trying to get information that she should have freely disclosed anyway. She just had some screwy notion that her conversations with Lynn were somehow privileged and that she would go straight to purgatory if not hell if she disclosed even a fragment of those conversations. More to the point, the conversations had absolutely nothing to do with Barbara's death. That was the work of a counterfeiting ring that was interested in her for different reasons.

Pete stuffed the documents back in the envelope and flung the package against the passenger side door. On the drive back to the lake, he alternately seethed over the way the complaint mischaracterized his actions and tried to reconstruct his conversations with Barbara Rodes.

He reread the documents when he got back to his cottage. It was obvious that the complaint had been drafted by someone who had an intimate knowledge of the conversations he'd had with Barbara in her office, and on another occasion, during a telephone conversation with her. The complainant had the same last name as Barbara, but he couldn't make out the first name.

He reached for the telephone and dialed Angie DeMarco's number. Angie was his former law partner who had some background in the Lynn Hawke case. Her secretary answered. Gabrielle Summers told him that Angie was on trial and wasn't expected back until well after the close of business that day. He asked her to have Angie call him, and to make sure she knew he'd called, he also left a message on her voicemail.

He thought some more about the complaint. It was a bunch of bull, but he knew better than to take it lightly since the penalties that could be imposed by the Attorney Grievance Commission ran all the way up to loss of his law license in Michigan. Some years before, one of his former law partners, who also was admitted to practice in Michigan, was hit with what he viewed as a baseless complaint, too, and didn't take it seriously. Only when the Commission tentatively decided on suspension of his law license for a year did he scramble and succeed in getting the decision reversed.

Pete didn't practice law fulltime any more, but still coveted his standing as a practicing lawyer. Plus the stain on his reputation of having disciplinary action against him was something he couldn't stomach.

He fussed around the cottage for a while, hoping that Angie would get back to her office early and return his call. Finally he took his replica Viking longbow out back where he'd set up three army surplus silhouette targets. He placed his cell phone on a nearby tree stump so he wouldn't miss Angie's call. The longbow was made of polished yew wood that the best bow-makers had used for centuries and had been hand-carved for him by an elderly craftsman in Norway during a recent trip there. Pete coveted the bow and enjoyed practicing with it, particularly when he needed to let off steam.

The sky was darkening and a light wind tickled the lake's surface and kicked up frothy whitecaps. He drew the bow string back to his right ear a couple of times to regain the feel, then nocked an arrow and pulled the string back again and let the arrow fly. *Thunk!* The arrow tore into the target closest to him. He nocked another arrow, drew the string back, and let it go again. *Thunk!* Another hit. He felt pumped and reached for a third arrow.

In the past, he sometimes visualized the image of a hated adversary on the targets and gleefully plunked him with arrows. Harry knew of the practice and often chided him that it was bloodlust of his Viking ancestors coming out. At present, Pete had no adversary worthy of that treatment, but he was tempted to create one out of what's-his-name Rodes who'd signed the complaint. Pete kept launching arrows at his targets until it was too dark to see any longer.

Back inside, Pete threw another log on the fire and reread the definition of attorney misconduct in the materials from the Attorney Grievance Commission. It involved "conduct involving dishonesty . . . deceit, or misrepresentation" where "such conduct reflects adversely on the attorney's honesty, trustworthiness or fitness as a lawyer." He'd always prided himself on his high standards and the allegations in the complaint, regardless of how the facts were twisted, bothered him.

He mixed a vodka and tonic, using his signature Thor's Hammer vodka, and promised himself that it was the last of the season even though he'd made the same vow a week earlier. Then he checked his Caller ID to make sure he hadn't missed Angie's call and began to rummage through his music collection for something to listen to. He selected the second CD that Cody McGee had sold him the day he was in his store. It was a Johnny Cash collection, "With His Hot and Blue Guitar."

It opened with Johnny's trademark introduction, "Hello, I'm Johnny Cash," and followed with "I Walk the Line," the song that had put him on the music map. Pete hummed along with the familiar tune and when it came to " . . . because you're mine . . ." he hummed a little louder. He enjoyed the familiar boom-chicka-boom sound and walked over and made himself a fresh drink. He glanced at his watch; Angie must have stopped at Muldoon's with some of her litigation buddies after the day's court proceedings ended.

Johnny then launched into "Folsom Prison Blues" to the hoots and hollers and cheers of the prison inmates. "I hear that train a comin' . . ." Pete snapped his fingers to keep time and mouthed the words to the tune. It was one of his favorite numbers, why he didn't understand because he'd always viewed himself as a straight arrow and not one likely to wind up in the Big House. But the song struck a chord within him.

Pete was on his third Thor's Hammer and tonic and listening to the Little Richard CD at a considerably lower decibel level than Anabelle had played it when Angie DeMarco finally called back.

"So what's the urgency, Stud of the North?" she asked. She'd coined the name for him during a conversation they'd had the previous year, and now it was part of her standard line whenever they talked.

He ignored her greeting and said, "I want to read you a letter I just got. But first, how was Muldoon's?"

Silence, then, "How did you know I was at Muldoon's?"

"I have my sources. A lot of your trial buddies there?"

"A few. Speaking of watering holes, when are you coming to Chicago so you can take me to dinner at Gibson's for some good wine? That stuff they serve at Muldoon's is terrible."

"I'm not sure," he said. "I'll be down before the snow flies most likely."

"Let's be specific. The snow flies up your way sooner than it does down here."

"Let's split the difference and say before the snow flies in Benton Harbor," Pete replied, picking a town along the highway between Chicago and Frankfort.

"Oh Christ, you haven't changed a bit. Okay, what's the letter? I've got to prepare for court tomorrow. We have closing arguments in my trial."

"The letter is from the Attorney Grievance Commission."

Silence again. "You have a complaint against you."

"Right."

"I've told you before that you've been running too close to the line with some of the things you've been doing since you moved north. What is it, something you did in connection with the death of that woman who drowned?"

"No, it involves my investigation into Lynn Hawke's death. She died in a car accident early this year, remember? You helped me on the case."

"Sure," she said, "I remember now. What does the complaint allege you did?"

"Do you want the short version or the long version?"

"Short," Angie said. "I'm pressed for time."

"In a nutshell, the complaint alleges that I wrongfully represented I was the attorney for Lynn's estate and that I had the power to set aside or continue an executory contract between the decedent and another person."

"Did you?"

"Yes."

Angie groaned. "Oh, great. Who did you make the alleged misstatements to?"

"Barbara Rodes." He told her of the business relationship between Barbara and Lynn Hawke and how fudging the facts was the only way he could get the information he needed from Barbara, information that provided one of the links necessary for him to get to the bottom of Lynn's death.

"So you think the fact the misrepresentations got you some useful information justifies what you did?"

"You're damn right," Pete answered, feeling his anger beginning to rise. "Barbara Rodes had some horsecrap notion that conversations she had with Lynn were privileged. I had to make her see things in light of her own self-interest."

"I'm not convinced."

"You don't have to be convinced. All I want from you is some advice on the best way to deal with the complaint."

"Who did you say the complaining party is?"

"Some family member. Brother or maybe even the father. I can't make out the first name."

"Does the complaint say how they got the information?"

"No, and that's what puzzles me. No one besides Barbara was present when we had those conversations."

"Maybe she recorded them."

He thought about Barbara Rodes' office and said, "Possible. I only know the complainant has a lot of information, and except for nuances here and there and some twisting, it's pretty much as I remember the conversations."

"Okay. Have you looked into the procedure? What you have to do next and so forth?"

"I have to file a response within twenty-one days."

"So we have time."

"Yes, but I want to nip this in the bud. I don't want to have this thing hanging over my head."

"You should have thought of that before you lied to Barbara Rodes."

"Angie . . ."

"Sorry. Send me a copy of the documents and we'll talk again as soon as my trial is over."

"Don't spend all of your firepower on your closing argument tomorrow. Save some of it for me."

NINE

Rona Martin had been in Pete's office exactly once in three years, on the day he opened it, so he was surprised when she walked in.

"Hello, Doll," he said in his best gangster dialect. "Alone at last." When she didn't smile, he realized she hadn't stopped in just to banter with him.

"Am I catching you at a bad time, Pete? I need to talk to you."

"No," he said as he hurried to clear off the side chair that had been building up again with files after his meeting with Matthew Stroud. He hoped Rona's relationship with Harry hadn't hit a snag. He wasn't very good at counseling friends on matters of the heart.

"Water, coffee?" he asked.

"Water would be nice."

He got two bottles of spring water from his mini-refrigerator and handed her one. When he was seated again, he made a show of straightening some papers on his desk and added the documents from the Attorney Grievance Commission to the pile face down. He hoped Rona hadn't noticed them.

"I know you've been following the Edinger shooting case," Rona said. "Are you up to date on the latest developments?"

"More or less, I think. I understand the sheriff has some forensics people in from the state to help examine the firearms they've impounded and that they've been questioning several people."

"That's right." She gazed out the window at the bay. "One of the people the sheriff wants to question is my brother."

Pete stared at her and wasn't sure what to say.

"I know," Rona said, obviously picking up on his surprise, "you didn't know I had a brother."

He shook his head slowly.

"Let me explain. My mother died when I was nine and my father raised Carla and me. Dad was a military-lifer and his best friend in the army was a man named Nathan Dahl. They'd been in Vietnam together and everything. My father and Nathan made a mutual pact—if something happened to one of them, the other would raise his children. Shortly after that, Nathan was killed in a Jeep accident. Some people thought it was suicide. Post-traumatic stress disorder or some problem like that. Nathan's ex-wife was a junkie who'd long before moved to Nevada and was rumored to be working as a prostitute at a BunnyRanch type of place. My father knew that and made no effort to contact her after Nathan's death. He just took Nathan's son in and raised him as one of our family."

Rona paused and looked out the window again. "Carla and I had known the boy—his name is Spencer—from the time he was a baby so it seemed like the natural thing to do. It was like we instantly had a new member of the family and we even started calling him brother. But there was always something a little different about Spencer, and as Carla and I got older, we noticed it more and more.

"Spencer was between Carla and me age-wise, and it came to a head one night when I was home from college. I heard this commotion in Carla's bedroom, and when I went to see what the problem was, I found Spencer on top of Carla trying to rape her. I pulled him off and told my father. I think Dad was conflicted between what Carla and I told him and his pledge to Nathan Dahl to take care of his son. Anyway, my father tried to rationalize it, saying Spencer had been drinking, but he sent Spencer off to boarding school and after that to college. Carla hasn't spoken to him since that night."

"Okay," Pete said, "I get the picture. An ugly family situation. But how does this tie in to the Edinger shooting?"

"I'm coming to that. About six months ago, around the time you were investigating Lynn Hawke's death, Spencer showed up at my restaurant. I hadn't seen or heard from him in over twenty years. He said he'd decided to move up to this area to be 'close to his family.' I cringed. You know how you sometimes think you've put an unpleasant chapter of your life behind you, but suddenly find you haven't? Anyway, Spencer has rented an A-frame in the woods south of Elberta and makes his living teaching classes in mysticism and, when he can, selling his paintings."

"Does Carla know that he's back?"

Rona nodded. "I told her. She went crazy, as if I could do anything about it. Spencer also called her a couple of times, but she refused to talk to him."

Pete waited for Rona to continue.

"Then Spencer told me he's been carrying on an affair with Lorraine Edinger," Rona continued. "He put it more crudely, but that's the essence of it."

"Let me guess," Pete said. "Lorraine Edinger is the widow of the man who was shot, right?"

"Yes. The affair has been going on for months from what Spencer tells me. Sheriff Richter knows about the affair, too. How I don't know, but now he's eyeing Spencer as a suspect in the Edinger shooting."

"How did you learn that?" Pete asked.

"From Harry. He found out from his source in the sheriff's office."

Pete processed that and said, "Lots of people have affairs with other people who are married, but that doesn't usually provide a motive to kill their spouse."

"I know, but I think they have more than the affair on Spencer. I just don't know what."

"From what you know about Spencer, do you think he could have had something to do with the shooting?"

Rona scoffed and shook her head. "He's a low-life in many ways and exploits women, but he's not a killer. I don't think he's capable of planning and executing a murder. If something goes wrong in a relationship, he's likely to just move on to his next victim."

"Does Spencer know he's a suspect?"

"Yes. I felt I had to tell him even though Harry's contact in the sheriff's office swore him to secrecy."

"Harry obviously knows about Spencer."

"I told him when Spencer turned up last spring, but I asked him not to tell anyone."

Pete thought about that. Harry hadn't breathed a word about Spencer to him, which must have been hard knowing his personality.

"What did Spencer say when you told him that the sheriff intends to question him?"

"He blew it off. He said he didn't have time to worry about some country bumpkin sheriff. He said he was conducting a seminar on transcendental meditation this weekend and that he also had to finish a painting for a client. I urged him to take the matter seriously and bring a lawyer with him if the sheriff insisted on talking to him."

Pete nodded and said, "Good advice."

"Do you know how he responded? He asked what 'we' were doing for Thanksgiving and if it would be alright if he brought Lorraine with him. He's not playing with a full deck, Pete."

Pete stared at her for a long moment, then said, "I have a feeling you want me to give him legal advice, but I can't figure out why after what he did to your sister."

Tears welled up in Rona's eyes and she brushed them away. "I know I should hate Spencer, but I can't."

Pete waited for her to continue.

She bit her lip, then said softly, "He saved my life."

Pete didn't know what to say. He'd known Rona for nearly ten years, but had no idea of any of this before.

She brushed away the tears and continued. "When Mom died, I wanted to die, too, and be with her again. One day Spencer and I were playing near the river in back of our house and I saw my chance. I jumped into the water and began to float downstream with the current. Spencer knew I couldn't swim, and even though he was younger than me, he came in after me and managed to get me to shore. I would have drowned but for him."

Pete felt a lump in his throat.

"So for all the bad things he's done," Rona said, swiping at her eyes again, "and the bad human being he's become, I can't turn my back on him."

"What do you want me to do, Rona?" Pete asked gently.

"Call him and try to convince him that he needs to take this seriously."

Pete's jaw muscles tightened. The last thing he wanted was to become tangled up with someone like Spencer Dahl who sounded like a wacko, but he had a short list of people he truly cared about and valued as friends. Rona Martin was one of them.

He had to force out his response. "I'll do my best."

"Thank you, Pete. You're the only one I feel I can count on for something like this. I mean, I love Harry, but . . ."

TEN

After she left, Pete telephoned Harry at the newspaper. "Rona just left my office," he said when Harry picked up. "She told me about Spencer Dahl."

"That's an incredible story, isn't it? Did she tell you Sheriff Richter has Spencer on his suspect list for the Edinger shooting?"

"Yes. She wants me to talk to him and give him legal advice."

There was an audible sound as Harry expelled air. "I've met Spencer a couple of times. You're not going to like him."

"I suspect you're right based on what Rona told me. But I called to ask you a couple of questions. The first one we've discussed before. I gather there's no question that Richter is treating Edinger's shooting as a homicide, right?"

"That's what Cap tells me. They've given up hope that someone will step up and confess that he shot Edinger accidently."

"That's the impression I got from Joe Tessler, too. Next question. I assume Clay Modrall and Dennis Bader are on Richter's suspect list, and now Spencer Dahl. Anyone else you know of?"

"I heard that some crazy guy named Calvin Seitz just popped up."

"I know about Seitz."

Harry sounded surprised. "You do?"

"I suggested to Joe Tessler that they might want to take a look at him. Seitz had a grudge against Edinger and hunts with a smoothbore."

"You never told me any of that."

"It just came up," he fibbed. "Anyone else?"

"Wally Helwig, but I don't think they're seriously considering charges against the festival's safety officer. If they did, it wouldn't be a murder charge."

"Who's been questioned so far?"

"Both Modrall and Bader from what I understand. I think that's why Dennis looked so shaken on the boat that day. Clay is down on Richter's list because he was on the Union side and only had a pistol. The pistol uses a different caliber bullet than the slug taken out of Edinger. They don't see how he could have been the shooter."

"Do you know what they have on Spencer Dahl?"

"Richter knows that Spencer was sleeping with Edinger's wife, as I'm sure Rona told you, and that Spencer had a clash with Edinger before he was shot."

"Rona didn't mention anything about a clash," Pete said. "A clash over what?"

"I don't know the details. Cap just told me there was some kind of clash between the two of them."

"How is Richter getting all of this information?"

"Beats me, but he seems to know a lot about Spencer."

"How about the weapons Richter impounded after the shooting?" Pete asked. "Anything new there?"

"The state forensics people are helping with that as I told you. The only thing I've heard is that Richter is releasing the weapons with rifled barrels in view of what they've concluded about a smoothbore being the murder weapon."

"That's what we thought they'd do. How many weapons does that leave?"

"Seventy-five or eighty from what Cap tells me."

"That's still a lot."

"It is. But getting back to Seitz, how do you know about him?"

"I ran into him when I was at the Edinger place the other day."

There was a silence at the other end of the line. "You were at the Edinger place? You didn't tell me that either."

"I must have forgotten."

"Sure you forgot. Pete Thorsen the sleuth on the prowl again, huh?"

"I'm not a sleuth and not on the prowl again. I was just curious."

"Curious my fanny. You were investigating."

Pete ignored Harry's comment and said, "Seitz is a pretty good shot with that old smoothbore. I saw him knock off a squirrel with it at thirty-five or forty yards. He bragged about what he could do at longer range, too."

"Do you believe him?"

"I do, based on what he did to that squirrel."

"Was he one of the Confederate reenactors?"

"No, he claims he wasn't at the reenactment."

"Well, if he wasn't a reenactor, it couldn't have been him because I understand Richter has narrowed it down to a shot from the Confederate side based upon the trajectory and everything."

"The shooter still could have been someone other than a reenactor."

"You mentioned that before. What's your theory?"

"A marksman hiding in the trees is one possibility."

"Richter is hung up on the accuracy issue, and from what Cap tells me, he's discounting possibilities like that."

"Maybe he's right, but recall what I told you about Seitz."

"Mmm," Harry murmured.

"Anything else before I talk to your future brother-in-law?"

Harry grunted. "Spencer's not blood. I don't think there's much chance of him being invited to the wedding ceremony even if Rona and I were to get married."

"I don't know, he might just show up," Pete said. "He considers himself family from what Rona told me."

"Oh, ha! ha! And remember, everything I told you in this conversation needs to stay between us. I've already violated about ten confidentiality pledges. I can't even use any of the information in my stories."

After Pete hung up, he tapped his pencil on his desk and tried to get himself up for talking to Spencer Dahl. Finally he reached for the phone and dialed Dahl's number. No answer. He tried again a half-hour later and still got no answer. He checked with Rona to confirm he'd taken down Dahl's number correctly. He had. Rona said that she knew Spencer was around because she'd talked to him an hour earlier and told him Pete would be calling.

He tried calling Dahl a third time, again with no luck. He paced around his office and stared out his window at the deserted bay for a long time and thought about it. He decided that a visit to Dahl's A-frame would both get him out of the office for an hour or two and, with luck, give him a chance to size up Dahl personally.

Pete drove south on M-22 out of Elberta and watched for the unmarked gravel road exit Rona had described. It was just beyond the turnoff for the Edinger place which was marked by the kind of sign you'd expect to see in the Kentucky horse country.

After a quarter mile of navigating the pothole-dotted road and hearing the gravel ping against the underbelly of his Range Rover, he spotted the A-frame. It looked reasonably new, certainly no more than ten years old, and had a v-shaped glass window that ran from ground level up to the peak of the roof. The exterior of the house consisted of gray wood shingles.

A collection of pole-beam structures of varying heights and configurations were nestled in the woods at one side of the house. They reminded Pete of the kind of structure built by the hermit who lived across the road from his family's farm when he was growing up. Old Joe—the only name Pete had heard people call him—used the home-made apparatus to exercise, doing skin-the-cat and other maneuvers. A shirtless man Pete assumed was Spencer Dahl was doing the same on one of the structures.

Pete walked up to where the man was hanging from a cross-beam and said, "Spencer Dahl?" He hung there like a giant bat, eyes closed, muscles rippling, his body covered by a veneer of sweat. His straight blond hair was slicked back in a ponytail, like that professional football player in the television commercials. He had a broad forehead and wide-set eyes, although Pete couldn't actually see his eyes because his lids were closed. Pete was sure it was Dahl, and when he didn't answer, added, "Could I speak to you for a few minutes?"

Dahl's eyelids suddenly snapped open and he stared at Pete with intense green eyes that bored right through him. Pete stifled an impulse to jump back. He just hung there and stared at Pete and still hadn't uttered a word. "Spencer Dahl?" Pete asked again. The man released his grip and dropped three feet to the earth and stood facing Pete.

"You look like you could use some exercise, Pete," Dahl said. "You can join me in the rest of my work out if you like. We can meditate together. Cultivate our inner states of tranquility and equanimity so to speak."

"I think I'll pass on your offer today," Pete said. "Rona Martin asked me to talk to you about your legal situation."

"That was sweet of her," Dahl said. He began to do acrobatic exercises on a lower structure.

"I understand the sheriff wants to question you about Thomas Edinger's shooting," Pete said.

Dahl slid his legs over the cross-beam and without looking at Pete said, "So my sister tells me."

"Do you have a lawyer if you're called in?"

Dahl did another maneuver with his legs. "What do I need a lawyer for?" he said, beginning to breathe harder.

"You probably don't unless you care about protecting your rights. Just by growing to adulthood in our society, you must have heard that anything you say to law enforcement authorities can and will be used against you."

"That sounds like talk from a detective show I used to watch before I discovered the true path," Dahl said as he strained to execute another maneuver.

"Detective shows are fiction; this is real life. Do you have an alibi for the time Thomas Edinger was shot?"

Dahl swung his legs up again and curled around the beam. Then he dismounted the way a gymnast would do. He walked over to a chinning bar which consisted of a pair of upright posts with a steel bar across the top. He pulled on a pair of gloves that had been hanging on a nail on one of the posts and jumped up and grabbed the bar and began chinning himself. Pete was impressed by the ease with which he did it.

"I was in church that day," Dahl finally answered.

"All day?"

Dahl chinned himself another half dozen times, and then said, "Most of it."

Pete's patience for the conversation, or lack of conversation, was wearing thin. He said, "May I ask which church?"

Dahl eased himself up and down a few more times—Pete estimated that he must have done fifty chin-ups already—and said the "Church of the Universal Believers."

Pete could tell Dahl was toying with him, but played along and asked, "Do you know any parishioners who'll support your claim that you were there?"

Dahl continued his up and down motion. "One. Lorraine Edinger. We transcendentalized together for a long time that day."

"Transcendentalized?"

"Yes."

"I don't think I know what that means."

Dahl's breathing became more pronounced as he continued to do chin-ups. "You know," he wheezed, "we were having sex."

"Oh," Pete said, thinking that at least Dahl didn't make a secret of his relationship with Lorraine Edinger. "Well, if Sheriff Richter calls you in, be careful about what you say to him and the way you say it. That's my advice." He turned to leave, anxious to get back to the world of the sane again, and heard Dahl drop to the ground behind him. He grabbed a towel from a nearby sawhorse and began to wipe away the sweat.

"You can't come all the way out here and not see my paintings," Dahl said. "Maybe you can even convince my sister to buy one to hang behind the bar in her restaurant."

Pete made a show of looking at his watch. "If we can do it fast," he said. "I have someone else I have to meet."

"A parishioner at your church?" Dahl asked, showing his smirk again.

Pete ignored Dahl's comment and followed him into the A-frame. Most of the living room with its soaring ceiling and dramatic window looking out at the surrounding wooded area had been converted into a studio. Pete could see how the house would appeal to an artist or a person who fancied himself an artist. A series of unframed paintings filled the room. They had two things in common — the paintings were in various shades of black, with an occasional sop to the gray family, and all featured nudes in various poses.

"I'm still in my Rubensian period," Dahl said, apparently noticing Pete's expression as he stood staring at the paintings. "With my own touch, of course."

Pete resisted the impulse to roll his eyes and shake his head. Only the ample thighs and small breasts of Dahl's nudes remotely resembled anything the famous Flemish Baroque artist produced and then it was a stretch of titanic proportions to compare the paintings.

When Pete didn't say anything, Dahl said, "Which do you prefer, Pete?"

To be polite, Pete made a show of studying the pieces. "I'm not sure," he said, "I'd have to study them longer."

"If you like, you could take one with you on consignment. You look like the kind of legal eagle I can trust."

"Not today," Pete replied. "But I have a question. Do you work with live models or photographs?"

"Only live, Pete. You can't capture the essence of the female form by just looking at a snapshot."

Pete knew he should keep his mouth shut, but couldn't resist asking. "Do any of the models come from your church?"

Dahl actually grinned this time. "Are you asking whether Lorraine is the model for any of the paintings?"

Pete just looked at him.

Dahl shook his head. "Too big on top and too skimpy on the bottom," he said, continuing to grin.

ELEVEN

After scanning the newspaper the next morning, Pete called Rona and reported on his meeting with Spencer Dahl. She seemed embarrassed by Dahl's antics and disappointed by his continuing failure to recognize the importance of legal counsel if Sheriff Richter did call him in for questioning. Pete resisted calling Dahl a jerk, which is what he really thought, and ended the conversation feeling satisfied that he'd fulfilled his commitment to a good friend.

Pete reread the materials from the Attorney Grievance Commission. This time he looked at the complaint clinically, trying to divorce his personal emotions from the charges against him, and decided to try to find out more about the complainant just as he used to research opposing counsel in one of his deals. He felt that knowing who he was up against gave him an edge. Sometimes it did and other times it made no difference, but at least he satisfied himself that he'd covered all of the bases.

The documents didn't give an address or other contact information for the complainant. The last name, Rodes, was clear enough, and he again tried to decipher the first name. It started with the letter "J" and after that was just a wavy line. Probably "John" or "Joseph" or something like that. Pete knew Barbara Rodes had been living in Muskegon, Michigan, before her move north to Beulah, and during one of their conversations, she'd mentioned still having family in the small city on Lake Michigan. That would be a good starting point.

He did a Google search for "John Rodes" and "Joseph Rodes" and didn't come up with anything. Then he searched for lawyers in Muskegon and came up with several names including a Jeffery Rodes who practiced with the firm of Stojac & Rodes. That had to be the complainant. Stojac & Rodes didn't have a website, and he knew he couldn't very well call the firm directly and ask what Rodes did.

After thinking about it for a moment, he called Angie DeMarco's secretary, Gabrielle. He kibitzed with her for a few minutes, then asked her to call Stojac & Rodes and find out what she could about Jeffery Rodes. He suggested she use the ruse that Sears & Whitney was looking for legal counsel in the Muskegon area to help on a matter. Gabrielle knew of Pete's activities since he left the firm and immediately became suspicious about why he was trying to get information about Rodes. Pete took her into his confidence without telling her of the ethics complaint against him and soon Gabrielle had a mission he knew she'd attack with messianic zeal.

Pete was straightening up his office and waiting for Gabrielle's return call when Detective Joe Tessler walked in. "Have you had lunch yet, counselor?" he asked.

"Not yet. Are you buying?"

"Do you think I'd get a chit for your lunch past Frank?"

"If you can explain to him what you were doing in my office, I'm sure you'd be able to handle the receipt issue just fine."

Tessler laughed. "Seriously, let's get a couple of sandwiches and go to our favorite thinking spot. I'd like to pick your brains about something on the Edinger shooting. Off the record, of course."

"Okay, I might have to interrupt our conversation to take a call," Pete warned, thinking of Gabrielle, "but otherwise I have nothing pressing."

He handed Tessler a twenty dollar bill. "I'll even buy so you don't have to explain the receipt. One condition, though. You pick up the sandwiches. If we walk into Ebba's Bakery together, Ebba will have it spread all over the county within five minutes, and if I go in alone, we'll be talking about dinner before I get out again."

"Deal."

On the way to the Elberta overlook, Tessler said, "I see what you mean about Ebba. I think I've only been in there once or twice for a doughnut, but she knew who I was and started to grill me about the Edinger case and every other investigation we have pending. Finally I got desperate and told her I have a serious prostate condition and had to leave."

Pete laughed. "That's a good one. I'll have to remember that excuse."

Tessler slowed when they came to the Port City Marina. The marina was still open, but most of the boats were out of the water and either in storage or shrink-wrapped for the winter. "Remember when we found Arne Breit's body here last spring?" Tessler asked.

Pete nodded, but didn't say anything. He'd tried to put memories of that case in the past and wasn't interested in reviving them.

"Who would have guessed at the time that Breit was mixed up in something as big as it turned out to be," Tessler continued.

Pete nodded again.

"It was money, right?" Tessler asked.

"It usually is."

"A falling out among thieves," Tessler said pensively. "I see a lot of that in my line of business."

Pete didn't comment.

"I'm just sorry we didn't get there in time to nab that guy Gil Bartholome."

Tessler's comment struck a nerve with Pete. He wanted to see Bartholome in jail for a lot of reasons, not the least of which was the personal animosity he felt toward him for screwing up his relationship with

Lynn Hawke. "I still don't understand," he said. "I delivered him to you guys on a platter. Gave you the motel he was staying in and everything."

Tessler shrugged. "He was gone by the time we got there."

"No updates? That happened six months ago."

"Nothing I've heard. We're out of the loop these days since the feds are handling it and they don't tell us squat."

The Elberta overlook was deserted when they pulled in. Tessler parked five feet short of the protective cable that ran along the edge of the parking area. The beach below was deserted as well and the grass on the dunes away from the water was the color of autumn wheat. Lake Michigan hadn't yet taken on the angry look of winter and was smooth and gray with a thin dark band that defined where the water and cloudy sky met on the distant horizon. A long iron ore ship, a common sight on this part of the lake, powered slowly north.

Pete took in the scene and lowered his window a few inches to let in some fresh air. "The smell in your car isn't as bad as it was last spring," he said, intending his remark as a compliment. "You must have cut back on your smoking."

"It's been seven weeks since I had a cigarette," Tessler said proudly. "Nice of you to notice."

"What have you been doing to control your urges? I see drugs like Chantix extolled on television all the time by former hardcore smokers."

Tessler shook his head. "I went cold turkey. We Lithuanians are a tough bunch."

"Tessler doesn't sound like a Lithuanian name."

"Americanized courtesy of the folks at Ellis Island," Tessler said.

Pete took another bite of his sandwich. Ebba's breakfast sandwich wasn't the healthiest thing he could eat, but it was flat-out good. Two fried eggs on a lightly toasted oversized croissant with slices of baked ham piled high and a generous dribbling of melted cheddar cheese. He rationalized his dietary transgression by limiting himself to one of the sandwiches a week. That was difficult with Ebba's Bakery just a half-block from his office.

Tessler gazed out at the lake and worked on his own sandwich. Finally he said between bites, "I wanted to talk to you some more about your comment that the shooter might have been someone other than a reenactor."

"That's a possibility you have to consider, don't you think?"

"Let's say hypothetically that you're right. How would the shooter blend in so he wouldn't be conspicuous? There were several hundred reenactors at the mock battle area plus all of the spectators outside the rope. So far, no one has reported seeing anything suspicious."

"When I was out to the reenactment site the other day," Pete said, "it appeared to me that the shooter, if it wasn't a reenactor, would have had to be on one of the flanks. Probably on the Confederates' right flank, away from the spectators. Common sense says he wouldn't have positioned himself right next to the crowd."

"Edinger was approximately in the center of the field when he was shot."

"He was. And as I remember, he wasn't facing the Confederate lines the entire time. He was turning around and encouraging the Union troops behind him and doing all sorts of things."

"So someone hiding on the far side of the field could have shot him when he turned in that direction and maybe the bullet struck him when he bent over. That would explain the trajectory. It would still be a long shot, though. It would be a slam dunk for someone with a modern hunting rifle equipped with a scope. But with a smoothbore, I don't know. Even for as good a shot as you say Calvin Seitz is . . ."

"I didn't mean to shine a spotlight on Seitz, Joe. I just suggested you check him out because he hated Edinger and prides himself on being a marksman with that smoothbore."

"Maybe I put that wrong," Tessler said. "I should have said, if the shooter were someone *like* Seitz and not a reenactor. When you were out there, did you see anyplace a marksman could hide?"

"No really good place. I saw a couple of places with the grass packed down, but concluded they probably were deer beds. You might want to go out there yourself and have a closer look."

Tessler crumpled up his empty sandwich wrapper and said, "Maybe I'll do that."

"Have you looked at the Confederate reenactors who carried smooth-bores and tried to identify someone who knew and might have had a motive to kill Edinger?"

"We've started. But that gives us a universe of over fifty suspects. You don't look at that many people overnight."

Pete's cell phone burred. "I've got to take this," Pete said.

"Do you need some privacy?"

"No, that's fine. Pete Thorsen," he said.

"Pete," the female voice said, "I don't know if you remember me, but this is Carla Neville. We met at the ski resort last spring."

"Of course I remember you. Your daughter was part of the 'pink brigade' as I recall."

"Yes," Carla said, laughing. "Weren't they darling?"

"All budding young Lindsey Vonns."

Carla laughed again. "We'll see. I know this is *very* short notice, but I have two tickets to a concert at Interlochen tonight." She sounded awkward, but finally squeezed out, "Would you like to go?"

"I love Interlochen. What am I going to hear?"

"A bluegrass group called 'Detour.' My girlfriend was supposed to go with me, but her son got sick and now I'm looking for a stand-in. Interlochen is midway between us and I thought we could meet there if you're available."

"I accept on one condition. You let me buy dinner first."

"That would be wonderful. That's what Carolyn—that's my girl-friend—and I were going to do anyway."

Pete ended the call and glanced at his watch.

"Hot date?" Tessler asked.

Pete grinned. "An unexpected date. Now getting back to your case, if I were you, I'd look at reenactors on the Union side, too. Remember what we talked about a few minutes ago. Someone who was after Edinger would have a point-blank shot at him when he turned around and the trajectory would be explained if he were bending over at the time."

"That puts me right back where I was when we began this conversation, seventy-five suspects, give or take, plus an unknown number of non-reenactors."

"Who's on your list of suspects so far? Clay Modrall and Dennis Bader from what I hear."

Tessler looked at Pete with a half-smile. "Not many secrets in this town, are there?"

"Not many," Pete agreed. "How about Edinger's widow? I thought family members were the first place the police looked in a case like this."

Tessler stared straight ahead at the lake. "Frank talked to Mrs. Edinger. I don't know the details."

For the first time, Pete got the feeling that Tessler was being evasive. Pete threw out another feeler. "The only other name I heard mentioned is Spencer Dahl. Have you questioned him yet?"

Tessler looked at him with narrowed eyes and said, "I'm beginning to feel like you're interrogating me. Where did you hear Dahl's name?"

Pete shrugged and said, "Again, small town."

"You can do better than that, Pete. Who told you about Dahl?"

Pete feigned trying to remember for a few moments, then said, "I was in Dinghy's a couple of nights ago and some guys at the bar were talking about the case. Maybe that's where I heard his name mentioned."

"Do you know Dahl?"

Pete shook his head and said, "I've met the guy. That's why I picked up on the name when I heard it."

Tessler stared at him with narrowed eyelids. "If Cap is slipping information to Harry McTigue and he's disclosing it to others, there's going to be hell to pay if Frank finds out."

"I know nothing about any conversations Harry might have had with Cap, but I'm positive I didn't hear about Spencer Dahl from him."

Tessler didn't looked convinced and Pete decided to drop his efforts to get further information from the detective lest he put his foot in it again. He tried to end the conversation on a light note by saying, "And I suppose Calvin Seitz may or may not make your list depending on whether he can pass your smoothbore marksman test."

"Yeah," Tessler said dryly, "I'll let you know if he can pick off a canary at three hundred paces."

Pete grinned.

"Okay, I guess I better get you back so you can pretty up for your big date."

"If you have any tips for me, let me know before four this afternoon."

"How you can pretty up?"

"Yeah."

"Well for starters, I'd suggest changing your pants. Those jeans look like they could walk across Lake Michigan by themselves."

"I was planning to do that, Joe," Pete said sarcastically. "I thought you might have some constructive suggestions since you seem like a guy who understands women."

"I thought I understood them," Tessler said wistfully.

"That sounds like the past tense."

"It is."

"Wife or girlfriend?"

"Wife."

"What happened? Didn't she like your smoking?"

"I got married when I was with the Chicago PD. Two years later, I came home to our apartment one night and Tatyana was gone. Cleaned out everything we had of value and left me with a ratty old couch that we'd salvaged from the curb. Even took my extra socks."

"Tatyana. That's an unusual name."

"I kind of liked it. The guys down at the station called her 'TT.' They'd draw it out because what they were really saying was 'titty.' She was, you know, generous on top. I think they were jealous."

Pete stifled an impulse to laugh. "Did you ever find out where Tatyana went?"

"She moved in with a pimp who was one of my snitches. In one afternoon, with Mayflower's complicity, I lost my snitch and my wife."

"That's an incredible story. Did you divorce her?"

"We're not divorced. I'm thinking of taking a vacation to Mexico in November, and while I'm down there, getting one of those quickie divorces."

"Have you seen her since she left?"

"Once. At a neighborhood bar. She was dressed in a pair of low-slung gold lame pants and matching platform shoes that would make stepstools obsolete. I tried to talk to her. She just walked away and flashed me with her leopard-print thong."

TWELVE

Pete pulled into the parking lot of the tavern north of the Interlochen Center for the Arts ten minutes early dressed in freshly-pressed khakis and a soft green canvas shirt. Carla was not there yet so he leaned against the wall in the small reception area and waited. He figured he must look presentable because one of the women in a group of three being led to their table gave him an obvious once-over as she passed.

Five minutes later, a woman with short dark hair, a leather jacket and snug jeans pushed through the door and scanned the reception room. She looked different than he remembered, but there was no question it was Carla Neville. She spotted him and came rushing over. "I hope I'm not late," she said breathlessly.

"Actually," Pete said, grinning at her, "you're one minute early."

When they were seated, they ordered two glasses of wine. Carla fluffed her hair with one hand and said, "Thank you so much for coming on short notice. I had these tickets and was so looking forward to this concert . . ."

"No, thank *you* for inviting me. Let me ask you something. Did you cut your hair since I met you last spring? I seem to remember it being longer."

She fluffed her hair again and said, "I had six inches cut off. Do you like it?"

"Love it," he said. The soft curls framing her face reminded him of the way Angie DeMarco wore her hair.

"I got tired of wearing my hair long like everyone else these days."

"Oh, a contrarian."

"Only when it comes to my hair." She sipped her wine and looked at him.

"Tell me about this concert we're going to," he said.

"I bid on the tickets at a benefit and won. Let me tell you what the flyer says about the group." She pulled a sheet of paper from her purse and unfolded it.

"Sorry to interrupt," Pete said, "but is that the same benefit Harry and Rona went to?"

"Yes. In September. Were you there?"

"No, but Harry just dragged me along on a five-hour Lake Michigan fishing outing he won at that benefit. We didn't catch any fish, but I froze my buns off."

Carla laughed. "Harry played the high end of the silent auction. I stuck with what I could afford. Anyway, here's what the flyer says: 'Detour is a bluegrass powerhouse that features heartfelt originals, tightly focused harmonies, and high-stepping instrumentals from a superbly talented sextet of veterans of Michigan's bluegrass scene.'"

"Michigan. When I think of bluegrass, I think of Appalachia and places like that."

"Most people do, but the music is popular in many parts of the country. Anyway, I thought you might like them even though Harry says you prefer pre-twentieth century music." She had an impish look in her emerald green eyes.

"That's an exaggeration."

She shrugged. "That's what he tells me."

"I can empirically demonstrate that I have no music that was composed before 1952."

Carla laughed. "I'll tell Harry that after I check out your tunes. Of course, then he'll want to know what I was doing in your house. Seriously, though, you're not the only one who's into oldies rock and roll. I like that music myself."

Pete told her the story of how he got hooked on oldies when one of his army squad-room buddies played the music constantly to prepare for the day when he'd become a disc jockey specializing in the genre.

"If you like Johnny Cash and Waylon Jennings and Tammy Wynette, I think you'll like Detour. Bluegrass is a subset of country."

After they got their dinner orders in, Pete said, "You seem to know a lot about me, even if Harry has fed you a bunch of hogwash, but I know almost nothing about you other than that you have a beautiful young daughter named Jennifer. That's hardly fair, is it?"

"I like it that way."

"But you're not going to get away with it. So let's hear your story, lady."

"Okay," she said, sighing, "I'll start from the present and work back. I was divorced three years ago and still have a cordial relationship with my ex. I live and work in the metropolis of Cadillac which I understand you view as geographically undesirable—"

He shook his head disgustedly. "That sounds like Harry again. I told him once that Route 115 is a speed-trap and he immediately launches into some wild story about a girl he dated from the far southern suburbs of Chicago when he was just out of college who turned out to be geographically undesirable, and suddenly he ascribes the same tag to you because you live a few miles from me. In fact, I know Cadillac reasonably well and have been there lots of times."

"You date women from Cadillac all the time, right?"

He ignored the barb and looked at Carla's empty wine glass, then at his own. "Do you think we'll doze off at the concert if we have a second glass of wine?"

"I'm sure we won't."

With their glasses refilled, Pete said, "Okay, I have thirteen different women I date from Cadillac and rotate them according to my mood. Now that you've pried that out of me, I'd like to hear a little more about your life."

"Thirteen—"

"Your life, please."

"Gads, you're a tough guy to get off a subject. Okay, I work at a computer firm in Cadillac as a troubleshooter for people and businesses having problems with their equipment. Prior to that, allowing for some downtime, I worked in Washington for ten years."

"Doing what?"

"Research for a defense think tank."

"Sounds like you were an unofficial spook."

"Except I never carried, concealed or otherwise, didn't have surreptitious meetings in Prague or other world capitals, and never once met James Bond."

"What did you do, then?"

"Mostly clipped articles from newspapers and magazines. I have a reading knowledge of Russian. It was still pretty heady stuff. I got to rub elbows with former generals and admirals and CIA operatives on a daily basis."

"That sounds exciting. Cadillac must be pretty dull after that."

"You know," Carla said, sighing deeply, "it is. But life goes on. How about you? Aside from the thirteen women you date in Cadillac and your prehistoric music tastes, I don't know that much about you, either."

He told her about how he grew up on a farm in northern Wisconsin, spent two years in the army in Germany where he drove a Jeep for a major in the CID, worked his way through the university in Madison and then law school, and practiced law with Sears & Whitney in Chicago for twenty years.

"Is there some reason you didn't include solving crimes after you moved north?"

"I only tell things that are true."

"I know the real story."

"If your source is Harry, your information is hardly true."

"Umm, hmm. I suppose you're involved in the shooting death of that guy during the Civil War reenactment, too."

Pete chose his words carefully because of what Rona had told him about the relations between Carla and Spencer Dahl. "When you say involved," he said, "what exactly do you mean?"

"Tracking down the killer like you did in those other cases."

"No, I'm not tracking down the killer. As I understand it, Sheriff Richter hasn't even determined that the shooting was intentional."

"It must kill you to stay on the sidelines when something like that happens. Ordinary life can be so boring."

He grinned and said, "Are you talking about me or yourself?"

"You, of course."

"I'm satisfied with my life. Changing subjects, do you ever get out of Cadillac?"

"You mean on vacation?"

"Yes."

"It's hard with a six-year-old. Her interests are Disney World or maybe going to see One Direction."

"What's One Direction?"

"The pre-pub rock group."

"Oh. I once went with my stepdaughter and late-wife to see the Wiggles. Is One Direction like them?"

"Not exactly. See how things change in just a few years?" She looked at her watch. "Yikes! We've got to get going. The concert starts in a half-hour."

Pete tried not to show his disappointment. He wanted to have another glass of wine and continue their conversation.

THIRTEEN

The following morning, Pete was outlining his response to the ethics complaint and intermittently thinking about Carla Neville when Rona walked into his office. Spencer Dahl trailed behind her like a chastened schoolboy.

"Can we talk to you, Pete?" Rona asked.

Pete could tell from her expression that she wasn't happy. "Of course," he said. He cleared off his second side chair.

"Spencer got a call from Sheriff Richter asking him to come in for questioning this afternoon. He tells me he's not going."

Pete looked at Dahl whose face was void of the usual smirk. "Well, that's Spencer's choice," he said. "From what you said, it sounds like a request. There's nothing to compel him to go if he doesn't want to."

"See, Rona? I don't know anything about that idiot Edinger's death. I don't have time for this bull."

Rona ignored him and asked Pete, "What will happen if he doesn't go?"

Pete considered her question. "Knowing Richter, he'll either come out to Spencer's house and try to talk to him there or he'll subpoena him. The sheriff has a short fuse, and if that happens, he'll probably be even more aggressive than he usually is in his questioning."

"That'll be worse, right?"

"In the short run, probably. Long run, it'll depend on the facts."

Rona appeared to process what he'd said. "What would you do, Pete?"

"If it were me, I'd go. But then I'm a masochist. I kind of enjoy doing battle with Richter."

Dahl rolled his eyes.

Rona turned to Dahl and said, "You should go, Spencer. You'll just make things worse for yourself if you don't. Pete will go with you."

Pete was about to protest, but caught himself. He didn't want to embarrass Rona.

"I told you, I don't need a lawyer. I know nothing about that guy's death."

Rona ignored him a second time. "Will you go with him, Pete? I'll pay your fee."

Pete tried to ease the tension. "I have to warn you," he said, grinning, "it'll be pretty steep. Maybe a free dinner at your restaurant with a piece of key lime pie. Harry can pay his own way if he comes along."

Dahl rolled his eyes again and said, "Oh, God." He glanced at Pete and added, "It looks like it wouldn't kill you to miss a meal."

Rona seemed visibly relieved. "Does that mean you'll go?"

"If Spencer wants me."

Rona looked at Dahl. He had a disgusted expression on his face and just shrugged.

"What time did Richter ask you to come in?" Pete asked him.

"I don't know," he mumbled. "1:00 p.m. or something."

"Which is it, 1:00 p.m. or 'something'?"

"1:00 p.m., okay?" He turned to Rona and said, "See? That's why I never deal with lawyers. This guy's as big an ass as that sheriff."

No one spoke until Pete said to Rona, "I'd like to ask Spencer a few questions before we go to see Richter. I think it's best that you not hear our conversation."

She rose to leave. "Okay, I'll be —"

"She's family for crissakes!" Dahl exploded.

"I'd still like to talk to you in private."

When Rona was gone, Pete looked at Dahl for a long time before saying, "Let's get some things straight, Spencer. I'm doing this for Rona, not you."

"Whatever you say, Petey."

"The other thing is I don't like to be surprised. That means I need to know about everything that might come up before we go in, including your relationship with Lorraine Edinger."

"I told you when you barged in on my workout and interfered with my meditation. We were transcendentalizing when old hubby caught the bullet. Or if you prefer, we were having sex. What more do you need to know?"

"Let me be the judge of what I need to know or don't need to know. How did you first meet Lorraine?"

"At one of my classes."

"You teach mysticism, right?"

Dahl shook his head disgustedly. "Only an ignoramus would call it mysticism."

"How would you put it then?"

"I run classes in transcendental meditation, Unitarian universalism, and Eastern religiosity."

"And that's where you first met Lorraine Edinger? At one of your classes?"

"I think that's what I said," Dahl answered sarcastically.

"When did you start sleeping with her?"

"When did the first trillium appear in the woods last spring? Who can remember things like that?"

"Well why don't you give it a try? I assume it was sometime within the last six months since I understand you weren't up here before that."

"I suppose."

Pete stared at Dahl. "Did you ever meet Lorraine Edinger's husband?"

"The guy who writes those comic books he passes off as history?"

"You know who I mean."

"Once."

"Only once?"

"You have trouble with the English language, don't you Pete? I met the guy exactly once. He came to my home and complained about my teachings. He didn't like some of the thoughts I was putting in Lorraine's head. Or something I was putting someplace else." He grinned lewdly.

"He knew you were sleeping with his wife?"

Dahl shrugged.

"Or suspected you were sleeping with his wife?"

Dahl shrugged again.

"I'll take that to mean yes. Thomas Edinger was a rich man, wasn't he?"

"I suppose."

"Did Lorraine ever make a contribution to your 'church'?"

"Once or twice."

"For how much?"

Dahl shrugged a third time. "I don't remember."

"Edinger didn't have children from his marriage to Lorraine I understand, but did have two children from a prior marriage. Do you know if Lorraine would inherit part or all of his wealth if he died?"

"I don't concern myself with mundane details of life like that."

"But you concerned yourself with those mundane details enough to accept contributions to your church."

"What are you saying, Pete?"

Now it was Pete's turn to shrug. "Nothing, just trying to get a clear picture of what was going on, that's all."

"Are we done?" Dahl asked. "Rona promised to make me an organic salad before my charming lawyer goes with me to meet this Barney Fife sheriff."

"Anything else you can think of that might come up?"

"Not a thing, Petey."

Pete wanted to punch the smug jerk in the face, but held his temper and said, "I'll pick you up at the restaurant at 12:30 p.m. We can ride over together. On the way out, Dahl grabbed his leather bag from a table and slung the strap over his shoulder.

As soon as he was gone, Pete dialed the number for the sheriff's office and left a message for Richter that he would be accompanying Dahl that afternoon. He couldn't bring himself to call Dahl his client, but he hoped that alerting Richter in advance would ease some of the tension when he showed up with him.

Then he called Harry, but before he could get into the reason for his call, Harry said, "How was your date last night?" He shook his head. News certainly gets around.

"We had a good time."

"I bet you did. Are you planning to see her again?"

"Jeez, Harry, I hadn't thought about it," he said, knowing Harry would realize what he said was a lie. "It was only twelve hours ago."

"She's a nice woman, isn't she?"

"Very nice."

"I told you I saw a spark between you two last spring."

"That's not why I called. I have something to ask you."

"She's a little out of the way," Harry said, forging right on, "but quality women are worth it. She even likes old music the same as you."

"Bluegrass isn't old."

"Didn't she tell you she liked Tammy Wynette and June Carter—that was Johnny Cash's wife—and people like that?"

"I know who June Carter is," Pete said dryly, "but the reason I called was to—"

"Maybe we could double-date some time. You know, two sisters and two guys who are kinda like brothers."

"That would be swell, but I have to leave in a few minutes and wanted to ask you if you heard anything new about the investigation."

Harry switched gears and said, "You're going with Spencer to see the sheriff, right?"

"Right."

"Be on your guard. Cap tells me that the sheriff has some new information and Spencer has risen to the top of his suspect list."

"That's what I've been trying to get to for the past ten minutes. Did Cap give you any insight into this new information?"

"None. He just wanted to give me a heads up."

Pete thought about it, then said, "I just spent a half-hour grilling Dahl and only two things came out—the guy's a jerk, which I already knew, and he's been sleeping with Edinger's wife, which I also knew."

"He was sleeping with the wife at the time Edinger was shot, right?"

"That's what he claims."

"It seems like an open-and-shut case then."

"Nothing is open and shut with Frank Richter."

"That's why you shouldn't let them surprise you."

"It would be easier not to be surprised if I knew what they had."

"Sorry I can't help you, brother. You know the situation in the sheriff's office. Richter has frozen Cap out of everything meaningful, but he can't get rid of him because he has twenty-two years of service and hasn't done anything specific to warrant dismissal."

"Well, I expect I'll soon know. If that bastard Spencer lied to me . . ."

"On another matter," Harry said, "there's a new restaurant in Traverse City and—"

"Harry, I'll talk to you about it later. I have to go."

FOURTEEN

Richter didn't keep Pete and Spencer Dahl waiting this time. The woman at the front desk led them down to the same cozy interview room Pete had been in twice before and the sheriff showed up three minutes later. Joe Tessler followed him in, and after giving Pete an embarrassed glance, avoided eye contact with him.

"You can put your briefcase over there," Richter said to Dahl, pointing to a small table in the corner of the room.

"It's not a briefcase. It's my man bag."

Richter gave him a blank look. "Your what?"

"My man bag. For my toothbrush, car keys, a granola snack, other things."

"Oh," Richter said, looking mildly amused after hearing Dahl's explanation. "You can still put it over there."

"If it bothers you, I'll put it on the floor." Dahl set the bag next to his feet.

Richter fussed around for a minute and then said to Pete, "I'll record our conversation again, if you don't mind." He placed a small device on the table and clicked the "on" switch.

"I do mind," Pete said.

Richter looked up at Pete. "You didn't object before."

"As I recall, I objected for the record, but I finally agreed."

"Why is this any different?"

"It just is." Out of the corner of his eye, Pete saw Dahl smirking.

"Recording our conversation is just for convenience."

Pete shrugged.

"We really don't need your permission to record you know."

"You have two choices—you don't record or Mr. Dahl and I walk out of here."

"It won't do you any good. We'll just subpoena him."

"Feel free."

"Okay, counselor, have it your way. I have a court reporter standing by just in case." He walked out of the room and returned a few minutes later with the court reporter dragging her machine. No one spoke while she was setting up.

"Okay, shall we begin?" Richter said when the court reporter was ready. "Mr. Dahl, would you state your full name and current address for the record?"

"You've got to be kidding," Dahl said. "You know my name."

"It's for the record. State you name, please."

Dahl rolled his eyes, but said "Spencer L. Dahl."

"And your current address."

"General delivery, Elberta."

"Is that in Michigan?"

Dahl laughed. "What kind of bull is this? I can almost see Elberta from here. If this crappy little room had a window."

Richter told the court reporter to record Dahl's address as general delivery, Elberta, Michigan.

"Now, Mr. Dahl, where did you live before your current address?"

"Around," Dahl said.

"Around where?"

"Around the country."

Richter said to Pete, "It's going to be a long day if we have to go through this with every question."

Pete turned to Dahl and said, "Tell the sheriff your former address."

Dahl gave an address in Roanoke, Virginia.

"And your address before that?"

"Gosh, I forgot to bring my life history along. Somewhere out West. I've moved around quite a bit."

"You didn't move around for three years before you moved to Roanoke, did you? You lived just outside Roswell, New Mexico, from what I understand."

Dahl suddenly looked fidgety. "That sounds right," he muttered.

"In the state correctional facility there?"

Pete looked at Dahl. Rona hadn't said anything about her brother being in prison and Dahl certainly hadn't mentioned it when he'd questioned him before coming to the sheriff's office.

"A lot of people are wrongfully incarcerated in this country. The United States has the largest prison population *per capita* of any country in the world. I was just another unfortunate statistic."

"And what were you *wrongfully* incarcerated for?" Richter asked, clearly feeling he had the upper hand.

"Some baloney charge," Dahl said sullenly. "I don't remember the details."

"Let me refresh your memory, Mr. Dahl. Didn't—"

Pete interrupted him. "What does all of this have to do with Thomas Edinger's shooting, Sheriff? I suggest we get back to questions that are relevant to that matter."

Now it was Richter's turn to smirk. "Let me explain a few things that I wouldn't expect a corporate lawyer like you to know. First, we're not bound by evidentiary rules as to relevancy in our questioning. We're trying to clarify Mr. Dahl's background here. And second, when you hear what Mr. Dahl was incarcerated for, I think even you might see a curious connection between what happened in that case and what we think could have happened with Mr. Edinger."

Pete didn't say anything.

Richter continued, "Now as I was saying, Mr. Dahl, weren't you in the Roswell facility because you were convicted of fraudulently trying to bilk a woman out of a large sum of money, and in connection with that, you were suspected of having something to do with the unexplained death of the woman's husband?"

"I didn't try to bilk money out of anybody," Dahl said, "and the court found I had nothing to do with the husband's death."

"Correction, Mr. Dahl. Your attorney struck a plea bargain with the state and you were never *tried* for that offense. The court didn't find you had nothing to do with it." Richter turned to Pete again and grinned sardonically. "Even a corporate attorney should be able to appreciate the difference."

News of Dahl's prison record had Pete off-balance and he was angry at Dahl for not telling him. He said to Richter, "Can we recess for ten minutes? I'd like to talk to my client in private."

"Sure, Mr. Thorsen, take all of the time you need. I'm sure you want to lecture Mr. Dahl about not being upfront with you about his past."

Pete started for the door with Dahl, then turned and said to Richter, "Maybe we should put off all of the questioning until later."

"We can do that, Mr. Thorsen, but then you're going to force us into making a decision you probably don't want us to make."

Pete gave Richter a look and then said, "We'll be back."

They walked down the hall and out of the building. When they were in the parking lot, Pete resisted the urge to grab Dahl and bang his head into his Range Rover, and said in as calm a voice as he could muster, "Why didn't you tell me you had a prison record?"

Dahl shrugged nonchalantly and said, "Didn't think it mattered."

"It might not matter in the long run, but you made me look like an idiot in there. Don't you see what Richter is doing? He thinks that other offense you pleaded guilty to is part of your *modus operandi* of taking advantage of women. Plus the husband died in that case, too. See the connection?"

"I really don't."

"Well, Richter seems to," Pete said, exasperated. "I told you before, if I'm going to represent you effectively, I need to know everything. Can you think of anything else Richter might spring on us?"

"No," Dahl said, shaking his head.

Pete sighed deeply. "Alright, let's go back in and get this over with."

When they were seated at the table again, Richter looked at them and then said to Dahl, "I don't see any blood on your shirt. You must have convinced Mr. Thorsen that it was just an oversight you didn't tell him you're an ex-con."

"Can we finish with your questions?" Pete said tersely. "We all have other things to do."

Richter gazed at Joe Tessler with a self-satisfied look. Tessler, who'd looked uncomfortable throughout the questioning, continued to avoid eye contact with Pete.

"To finish up with your background, Mr. Dahl, were you ever in the military service?"

Dahl frowned and said, "A long time ago."

"The army, right?"

Dahl nodded.

"What did you do while you were in the army?"

Dahl smirked and said, "Marched and ate chow like everyone else."

"And shot rifles?"

"Everyone shot rifles."

"What were the rifle qualification categories when you were in the army?"

"I don't remember."

"Let me refresh your memory. The lowest level was 'marksman,' right?"

"Sounds right."

"The next level up was 'sharpshooter,' am I right about that, too?"

"If you know all of this crap," Dahl said, "why are you asking me?"

Richter ignored his comment and said, "And the highest qualification level—the pinnacle of a man of arms so to speak—was 'expert,' isn't that true?"

"Whatever you say," Dahl said sarcastically.

"Where did you fit in this hierarchy, Mr. Dahl?"

Dahl didn't say anything.

"My, my, Mr. Dahl, aren't we having a convenient lapse of memory today? You were in the expert category, weren't you? As a matter of fact, according to your service record, you were the best of the best and captain of your battalion's rifle team and regularly represented your unit in competitions against other units, isn't that true?"

"Sheriff," Pete said, "where is all of this going?" He glanced at Dahl and said, "It must have been more than twenty years ago that Mr. Dahl was in the army."

"The point I'm making, counselor, is that Mr. Dahl here is a crack shot. Thomas Edinger was shot from a distance by someone who clearly knew what he was doing."

"With a smoothbore? I'm told you can't hit something twenty feet away with a smoothbore."

"Unless you're an expert marksman."

"Whatever. I don't think they had troops practice with smoothbores when Mr. Dahl was in the army."

Richter was visibly irritated. "You don't see any connection between the Edinger shooting and a man who's an expert shot?"

"I really don't," Pete said. "I was a pretty good shot in the army, too, and I probably couldn't hit the side of a barn now."

Dahl seemed to be enjoying the zingers that were flying back and forth between Pete and the sheriff.

Richter looked disgusted. He studied his notes and looked at Dahl again and said, "Moving on to the next subject, do you know Mrs. Thomas Edinger?"

"You mean Lorraine?" Dahl said.

"I think that's Mrs. Edinger's first name."

"She was in one of my classes." Under questioning from Richter, Dahl explained that he ran classes in transcendentalism meditation and related subjects.

"What's your relationship with her?"

"Teacher and student."

"Anything else?"

"What else would there be?"

"You had a sexual relationship with Mrs. Edinger, didn't you?"

Pete was about to object again, but realized it would be futile. Richter obviously knew all about Dahl's relationship with Lorraine Edinger.

"Maybe," Dahl said.

"Maybe?"

"I have an active sex life," Dahl said. "I don't remember every woman I've had relations with."

"Come on, Mr. Dahl," Richter said, "we know you've had a sexual relationship with Mrs. Edinger for the past three or four months."

Dahl said nothing.

Richter shook his head, studied his notes and then said, "Did you ever have discussions with Mrs. Edinger about money?"

Dahl was slow to answer. Finally he said, "Lorraine supported some of my causes."

"How much 'support,' as you say, did she provide?"

"I don't remember exactly."

"Let me refresh your memory, then. Mrs. Edinger gave you checks for $7,500 on one occasion and $15,000 on another, didn't she?"

"She could have. I'm not an accountant."

"And her husband objected, didn't he? That's why he came to see you two weeks ago, wasn't it? To warn you to stay away from his wife."

Dahl didn't reply.

"And following that encounter, Mr. Edinger put a monitoring system in place at the bank that would alert him if Mrs. Edinger attempted to transfer additional funds to you, didn't he?"

Dahl again remained silent.

"Mr. Dahl, did you have conversations with Mrs. Edinger about how you could get around those restrictions?"

Once more, Dahl didn't say anything.

"Last question," Richter said, looking at Dahl disgustedly. "For the moment anyway. Have you seen this before?" He handed Dahl a sheet of paper encased in a plastic sheath.

Dahl glanced at the sheet of paper and slid it back across the table to Richter. "Looks like a poem. I'm not into poetry."

"My question was whether you ever saw it before?"

"Not that I remember."

Richter's face lit up with a "gotcha" smile and he asked, "Then why are your fingerprints all over the paper?"

Pete interjected, "Could I see that?"

Richter slid the plastic-covered sheet across the table to him and waited while Pete read it. It consisted of eight lines of type laid out in poetic form.

"Where did you get this?" Pete asked Richter.

"We found it in the deceased's study."

Pete glanced Dahl's way and then said to Richter, "How do you know the poem was sent to Thomas Edinger? I don't see his name on it. Was it in an envelope addressed to him?"

"No envelope, but the poem was in Mr. Edinger's study. That proves it was sent to him."

"It doesn't prove anything of the sort. The poem could have been intended for someone else, or maybe someone planted it in Edinger's study. There are all kinds of explanations."

"That's bull," Richter said. "Your client sent the poem to Mr. Edinger and you know it!"

"That's the wonderful thing about our system, Sheriff. The state can't simply decree something to be true that they wished were true." He stared at Richter for a minute or two and then said, "Are we finished?"

Richter's face reddened and he signaled the court reporter to stop transcribing. He picked up his papers and stormed out of the room. Joe Tessler followed him without looking back.

In the car driving back to Frankfort, Dahl sat with the usual smirk on his face. He glanced at Pete and said, "I think that went pretty well. You kicked butt on that poem. You rose in my esteem with the way you handled that, Petey."

"Yeah, it went really well," Pete said sarcastically. "The sheriff knows you're an ex-con with a history of preying on women, knows that you're an expert marksman, knows that you've not only been having sex with Lorraine Edinger but also taking money from her, knows that Thomas Edinger came to see you to warn you to stay away from his wife, and knows that Edinger received a death poem with your prints all over it. I'd say that's a real positive outcome."

Pete was about to leave his office when his phone rang. He recognized the number as Joe Tessler's cell phone.

"Why didn't you tell me you were representing Dahl?" Tessler demanded angrily.

"It so happens that I didn't represent Spencer Dahl at the time we talked on the bluff, Joe. Rona Martin barged in my office this morning with Dahl in tow and said he'd been asked to come to your office for questioning. She badgered me into going with him."

"Rona Martin is that woman who owns the restaurant, right? What's her interest in this?"

Pete explained the relationship between Rona and Spencer Dahl.

"Are you going to represent Dahl if this case progresses?"

"I hadn't thought about it. But speaking of disclosure, why didn't you tell me about the things you claim to have on Spencer Dahl?"

"You know I can't get into the details of our investigations with civilians."

"I see," Pete said sarcastically.

"You really pissed Frank off today."

"About the poem you mean?"

"The poem, refusing to let us record the meeting, everything."

"Frank is pissed at me when he gets up in the morning. Why should this be any different?"

"Oh boy."

"I'd hate to see this affect our relationship, Joe."

"Me too. But you don't make things easy."

FIFTEEN

Pete had just walked into his office the next morning when his step-daughter, Julie, returned his call. He wanted to talk to her about her latest cell phone bill. She'd spent seven weeks taking art classes in Paris this past summer, and since she returned, her international cell phone charges had gone through the roof.

"I'm sorry I didn't call you back last night, Dad," Julie said, "but I was in the library until it closed cramming for a mid-term test. I know you go to bed early, so . . ."

"So you called this morning. That's perfectly alright. How are your classes going so far?"

"An A in everything, except I have an A- in art history. The teacher knows I studied in Paris last summer and I think she's holding that against me out of spite."

"Oh I doubt that's the case."

"You don't know her. She's a bitch."

"Watch your language."

"It's true."

"Can't you—"

"Suck up to her?"

"I wasn't going to put it quite so crassly."

"That's what you were going to say though, right?"

"I guess."

"I don't see why I should have to do that, Dad. I feel art's my strongest subject and I have a lot of real-life experience. I'll bet my teacher has never even been to the Louvre."

"You don't know that."

"How much do you want to bet? I can tell she's jealous of my experience."

"Speaking of things French, do you hear from your friends over there?" he asked, trying to ease into the cell phone bill issue.

"I talk to them once in a while."

"I'm looking at your latest cell bill, Sweetie, and it looks like you talk to them more than once in a while."

Silence, then, "That was probably my calls to Remy. I've been missing him a lot lately and maybe we talked a little long. How much is the bill?" He told her. "That's really not so bad when you consider how much a plane ticket would cost to go over and see him."

"I didn't realize that was an alternative."

Silence again, then, "Remember our conversation about long distance relationships, Dad? Last year when you were having all of the problems with Lynn?"

"Sweetie, I explained that. We weren't having problems. She'd just made her choice and was living with another man."

"The same principle applies, though. Two people have to make an extra special effort to make the relationship work when things are long distance."

"All I ask is that you ease off on the calls to Paris a bit. Try writing letters once in a while or using e-mail."

"That's so impersonal," Julie said disdainfully. "So twentieth-century. Besides, my cell phone bills will go down when Remy comes to visit."

Now it was Pete's turn to go silent, and after a few moments, he said, "I didn't know Remy was coming."

"We just decided. He's coming in mid-November and will stay for a month. That way he'll be with his family for Christmas."

"Does he have friends or relatives over here that he can stay with?"

"Dad, he's going to stay with me. We're in love."

Pete chose his words carefully. "I thought the school had rules against guests staying in student's rooms."

"They never enforce those things. I know lots of kids who've had guests stay with them."

"Julie, how old are you?"

"You know I'm seventeen, *Dad*."

"Don't you think that's a little young to have a boy stay with you?"

"Oh for God's sake! I might have known that would come up. Mom wouldn't bat an eye about this if she were alive."

"No, Sweetie, she wouldn't bat an eye. She'd just say you couldn't do it."

"You're trying to run my life again! I'm seventeen, not seven! When are you going to lighten up! I can't do this, I can't do that! I'm going to ask Wayne," she said, referring to her biological father who had legal custody over her. "If he says yes, I'm going to do it!" The phone went dead.

He pursed his lips and tapped on the desk with a pencil as he thought about the conversation. He still missed his late wife Doris, but never more than at times like this. Julie, whom he loved dearly, was becoming a handful to deal with and sometimes he felt that he wasn't up to the challenge. Julie regarded Pete as her father notwithstanding the legal technicalities involved and he'd lurched back and forth between giving her the space she wanted and trying to rein her in a bit. Teens were hard enough to understand, but he was finding a girl doubly so.

Pete called Rona. He'd called the previous night to give her a report on his visit to the sheriff's office with Spencer Dahl, but she was in Glen Arbor for a meeting and he left a message that he'd call again in the morning. He was so sick of Dahl at the time that it was a relief to put off their conversation.

Rona wasn't at the restaurant and the man who answered the phone told him that she was working around home that morning. He walked the two blocks to the Victorian house on Forest that Rona shared with Harry and found them cleaning out the garage. Rona was dressed in jeans and a ratty oversized sweatshirt and was energetically sweeping up a pile of refuse. Harry was examining some paddles for the yellow kayak that was stored along one wall.

As Pete walked up, Rona blew a few strands of hair out of her face and removed one of her work gloves to free her hand to reposition the green barrette that held her hair back. It was obvious from her demeanor that she was eager for news of the questioning so he jumped right in and summarized what had happened at the sheriff's office. When he told her about Dahl's stay at the New Mexico correctional facility, her face lost color and Pete was afraid she might faint. Tears welled up in her eyes. "He never told you about that, did he?"

She sniffled and shook her head. "He didn't tell me, either," Pete said. "And according to Richter, the offense Spencer was in for was similar to the situation with Lorraine Edinger. He took money from both women and their husbands turned up dead."

"You said Thomas Edinger went to Spencer's home and demanded that he leave his wife alone. Is that what happened in New Mexico, too?"

"I don't know all of the facts of that case," Pete said, "but Richter seems to see a pattern."

Pete went on to tell Rona about the poem Dahl had allegedly sent to Thomas Edinger. "When Richter hit him with the poem, I managed to deflect things by suggesting some possibilities that poured water on his theory that Spencer had sent the poem. That backed Richter off a little, but do you know what Spencer said to me on the way back to Frankfort? He was almost giddy over the way—his words—that I'd kicked Richter's butt on the poem question. Here's a guy who's under suspicion for murder and he was chortling over the fact I made Richter squirm."

Rona brushed the tears from her eyes and grabbed the push broom and began to sweep again with vigorous strokes. Dust swirled around the garage, causing Pete to back out of the door. Harry coughed and rubbed his eyes and watched Rona sympathetically. Then he went over and kissed her on her cheek and said, "Here Hon, I'll do this. Why don't you go inside and finish your conversation with Pete."

She let loose of the broom without saying anything and went over to the wall where cardboard boxes were stacked and began to move them around. The bottom fell out of one box that obviously had been damaged by water and the contents scattered across the floor. She stared at the mess and tears gushed from her eyes again.

Pete grimaced, then took Rona's arm, and said, "Let's go inside like Harry suggested."

Rona sagged against him. Her face was streaked from the tears and her eyes were red. They went inside and sat on facing loveseats in front of the living room fireplace.

She sniffled and asked, "Do you think he did it, Pete?"

"I honestly don't know."

"The more I hear, the more I wonder. I thought he'd get his life straightened out as an adult, but . . ."

"He hasn't been a model citizen, that's for sure."

"What should we do?"

"I'm not a criminal lawyer, Rona. You know that. But there are some chinks in Richter's case against Spencer. They have an obviously sleazy guy—and I say that not intending any offense—and a few things besides that. But nothing that really establishes guilt. No murder weapon, no witness placing him at the scene, Spencer claims he has an alibi in the person of Edinger's widow. That's a lot for the state to overcome, even if Spencer isn't likely to be a very sympathetic character in the eyes of a jury. I know the Prosecuting Attorney for the county. I'm not sure he'd take the case to trial based on what Richter presently has."

"Everything just *sounds* so bad," Rona said.

"It does. But remember—and even a corporate lawyer knows this—the state has to prove guilt beyond a reasonable doubt. That's a tough standard."

"Will you continue to represent him?"

"He needs a criminal lawyer, Rona."

"He told me he doesn't have any money. That's why I asked for your help in the first place."

"Hold on," Pete said. "Richter claims he has evidence that Lorraine Edinger gave Spencer over $20,000 to date."

Rona shrugged. "That's what Spencer told me. He says he's broke."

Pete thought about it for a minute. "Let's let it play out for a few days. See what Richter does. Then we can decide what to do."

"Thanks, Pete. There's no one I trust more than you. I know you don't like Spencer, but . . ."

"I wouldn't do this for anyone but you, Doll."

Rona laughed for the first time since Pete came over.

SIXTEEN

In their conference call that just ended, Pete and Angie DeMarco mapped out a strategy to defend against the ethics complaint. The strategy had three prongs: First, Pete would admit that he'd shaded the truth when he told Barbara Rodes that he was the attorney for Lynn Hawke's estate, but explain why he'd made that statement and argue that it had absolutely nothing to do with Barbara's death; second, they'd point out that Barbara Rodes wasn't Pete's client and that he owed no special duty to her; and third, Pete would line up testimonials from clients, former law partners, and other attorneys attesting to his good character and high ethical standards.

Pete was at his desk preparing a list of possible character witnesses when Matthew Stroud walked in his office looking far more ebullient than the first time he'd come to see him. "I thought you'd like to know how the meeting went between my client, Walter Helwig, and Sheriff Richter," Stroud said.

Pete motioned for him to sit and asked whether he wanted coffee.

"I don't need any caffeine in me," Stroud said. "I'm already pumped."

Pete gazed at the Walter Mitty figure sitting across from him and half expected him to begin to rip off his faded blue poplin suit coat and display his Superman garb underneath. "So what happened?" he asked.

"For starters, we got to the sheriff's office right at the appointed time," Stroud said, sitting bolt upright and doing his best to puff out his concave chest. "The sheriff was maybe a half-hour late, but I was expecting that. I tried to keep my client relaxed by talking about his family and the high school football team and duck hunting. You know, small talk."

Pete nodded and waited for more.

"Then the sheriff comes busting into the room without knocking. He had two gentlemen with him — a deputy and another man who must have thought it was his day off because he didn't have his uniform on."

"Joe Tessler?"

"I didn't catch his name. Real sinister looking guy. I guess the sheriff thought by coming in numbers, they'd put us on the defensive."

Pete controlled his smile. He couldn't wait to tell Joe that Stroud had described him as "sinister looking."

"Anyway, I was prepared and after the preliminaries, I laid out why my client couldn't have been guilty of negligence. The committee under Walter's direction had searched the reenactors' weapons, they got statements signed by the unit commanders, Walter announced twice that live ammunition was strictly prohibited. I showed the sheriff the written statements, all arranged alphabetically, and even had copies ready in case he wanted them. The sheriff read one statement and paged through the others, but didn't say a thing. He didn't even notice that one form was missing."

"That's good," Pete said.

"We were out of the meeting in twenty minutes. You know what the sheriff said to me when he was escorting us out? He put his hand on my shoulder and thanked us for coming in and said we'd done the right thing by being so forthright with him. He also told me confidentially that they were looking seriously at the possibility that the shooter wasn't even one of the reenactors."

"It sounds like the meeting went as well you could have hoped."

"I'll tell you, Pete, one thing they don't teach you in law school is the importance of preparation. I think that's what carried the day for us."

"Wally Helwig must have been happy."

"Happy? The man was flying! I've got a client for life after the way I pulled that case out of the fire for him."

After Stroud left, Pete smiled at the thought that he now had a more formidable competitor around town for future legal business. It wasn't good news for Spencer Dahl, though. The sheriff obviously had Dahl squarely in his cross-hairs and his statement to Stroud that the shooter might not have been one of the reenactors was just one more sign.

If there was any doubt about the way Richter was thinking, it was put to rest when Pete got a call from the sheriff's office later that day asking him to bring Dahl in for follow-up questioning. Dahl, predictably, didn't answer his telephone calls so Pete had to enlist Rona's assistance to track him down and convince him he should continue to cooperate.

Pete picked up Dahl at his house and listened to him bad-mouth Richter all the way to Beulah. He complained about the country turning into a police state and insisted on meditating for five minutes before entering the County Government building.

Richter and Tessler were waiting when they got to the familiar windowless interview room. Anticipating Pete's objection, they already had a court reporter in place to record the session.

"What's the issue, Sheriff?" Pete asked. "Didn't we just spend over two hours with you?"

"It'll be clear in a moment, counselor."

Richter went through the usual hoops of getting Dahl's name and address for the record again. Then he asked, "Mr. Dahl, where were you between 11:00 a.m. and 3:00 p.m. on the day Thomas Edinger was shot?" He gave Dahl the exact October date.

Dahl looked at Pete and asked, "Do I have to answer that question?"

Pete asked for and was granted a brief recess. In the hall, he said to Dahl, "You don't have to answer; it's up to you. But if you were with Mrs. Edinger as you said, you might want to answer even if it's embarrassing."

"What's he trying to do?"

"He's trying to establish that you don't have an alibi for the time Edinger was shot."

"I was screwing Lorraine. I told you that."

"Which I assume she'll corroborate, right?"

"Of course. She's crazy about me."

"Well, my advice from a minute ago stands, then. But to repeat, it's entirely up to you how you answer."

Back in the interview room, Richter reread the question for Dahl.

"I was with a woman."

"Where?"

"At her house."

"What's the name of the woman and where does she live?"

Dahl paused for a moment, then said, "Lorraine Edinger." He told Richter he didn't know her exact address, but said she lived north of his own house maybe a half-mile.

Richter raised his eyebrows and nodded several times. Then he retrieved a document from the pile in front of him. He paged through it, then paged through it again. "That's funny," he said, looking up at Dahl. "Mrs. Edinger swears she was in Beulah shopping at Crystal Crate & Cargo and some other places during that same time period."

Dahl's face lost color and his eyes widened. "She must be mistaken," he said. "She was with me."

"Maybe I misread her statement," Richter said. He studied the document again. "No, I had it right. It says right here on the second page of her statement that she was shopping."

"She's lying!" Dahl screamed.

Pete looked back and forth between Richter and Dahl and tried to figure out what was going on. From the beginning, Dahl had cockily claimed he was having sex with Lorraine at the time Thomas Edinger was shot. Now his claim apparently was contradicted by Lorraine's statement.

Richter held the document up so Dahl could see the last page and said, "That's Lorraine Edinger's signature, isn't it?"

Dahl glanced at the document and turned away with a pinched look on his face. "I'm not a handwriting expert," he muttered.

"Could I see that?" Pete asked.

Richter gave him the statement and Pete paged through it. The statement was clear about Lorraine Edinger's whereabouts at the time her husband was shot; she was shopping and not, according to her, with Dahl. On another page, he saw Lorraine's statement that she'd given money to Dahl under duress. Pete gave the document back to Richter.

"We can get an expert to review this document and corroborate that the signature is actually Mrs. Edinger's," Richter said to Dahl. "Is that what you'd like us to do?"

Dahl didn't say anything.

"Want to change your story, Mr. Dahl?" Richter asked.

Dahl just glared at him.

Pete started to say something, then caught himself. He'd been blind-sided again and there was nothing he could do in the short run to mitigate the damage. He thought about asking for another short recess to talk to Dahl, but decided that wouldn't be fruitful.

"Are we finished?" Pete asked Richter.

"Here, but we'd like to look around Mr. Dahl's place if you don't mind."

"You goddamned storm troopers!" Dahl screamed. He erupted from his chair and tipped the conference room table toward Richter and Tessler with a violent shove. Pencils and pads of paper clattered to the floor and they caught the table just as it landed in their laps. "You don't have my permission to go crawling around my home!" Dahl screamed again.

Richter and Tessler returned the table to its upright position. Richter, in particular, seemed to be enjoying Dahl's histrionics.

Pete said to Richter in as even a voice as he could muster, "You aren't going near Mr. Dahl's house without a warrant."

"Why am I not surprised to hear you say that, counselor?" Richter said with feigned weariness. He shoved another document across the table to Pete. "Does this satisfy you?"

Pete scanned the document. It was a warrant signed by a county judge that authorized the search of Dahl's house and surrounding grounds and his vehicle. Items mentioned in the warrant included smoothbore weapons, long guns as well as pistols, and ammunition for such weapons including powder, patches, wads, caps, balls and other paraphernalia. Pete handed the warrant to Dahl who swatted it away and sent it flying across the room. Pete retrieved the warrant and slid it back across the table to Richter.

"We're headed out to Mr. Dahl's place now," Richter said to Pete. "You and your client are welcome to come with us as long as you don't interfere with our search."

"We're coming, dick head!" Dahl screamed before Pete could say anything. "If you put one scratch on anything that belongs to me, the county is going to have a lawsuit on its hands faster than you can blink!"

Pete was aware of the problems of suing in a case like that, but didn't say anything. Dahl screamed about the Gestapo tactics of Richter and his men nonstop on the drive to his house and berated Pete for letting them run roughshod over him. Pete was tempted more than once to tell Dahl to stuff it, but remained silent.

They pulled into Dahl's yard just behind Richter and Tessler. Three police cruisers and an unmarked car were already parked there. Pete counted nine law enforcement officials lounging against the vehicles and obviously waiting for Richter to arrive. Pete assumed that the three plainclothes men were state forensics people helping out with the investigation.

The front door to Dahl's house was unlocked and the investigative team followed Richter and Tessler inside. For the next three hours, they poured over every inch of the house. Periodically, Pete looked through the open door and saw them prying up floor boards, checking the rafters, examining furniture and cushions, testing the bricks in the fireplace for ones that might be loose, checking Dahl's paintings and art supplies, and looking through every nook and cranny and appliance in the kitchen. He couldn't tell what if anything they'd found.

Dahl had calmed down. He sat on the ground and stretched and assumed the Lotus position and appeared to be in a trance much of the time. Pete assumed he was meditating and let him be.

Five members of the search team moved outdoors and began examining every man-made and natural object in sight. Sawhorses, the woodpile, window sills, eaves, the crawl space under the house, Dahl's vehicle. Dahl, still in his own world, seemed not to notice as they scoured his property.

The outdoor fireplace fifty feet from the house was constructed of fieldstones with a chimney that was maybe eight feet tall and a semicircular concrete bench in front of the fireplace opening. Pete watched one of the investigators poke around in the ashes with an iron poker. He called a colleague over and soon they were scooping up ashes from the fireplace with a red flat-bladed snow shovel and depositing them in heavy plastic garbage bags. They labelled each of the bags.

Other members of the team were examining the homemade workout structure. They tapped on posts and on horizontal beams. One man used a board to put upward pressure on a crossbeam he couldn't reach from the ground. The crossbeam came loose at the end. Another man went in search of a ladder and set it against the post and climbed up so he could examine the area where the post and crossbeam intersected.

Pete moved closer to Dahl and whispered, "Is something up there?"

Dahl seemed to be reengaged in the world and whispered back, "Just some weed." He sounded relaxed and mellow, like illegal drugs were nothing.

The post obviously was hollow at the top and the man on the ladder put on a pair of plastic gloves and reached into the cavity. He withdrew something, examined it and dropped it in a plastic bag. He continued to reach in and withdraw other objects.

"Must be a lot of weed," Pete whispered.

Dahl shrugged. "That'll get me what? A fine? Maybe probation?"

The men on the ground huddled together and examined the items they'd found in the hollowed-out post. Richter joined them. They whispered among themselves for what seemed like an inordinately long time. Then Richter and two of the deputies walked over to where Dahl was sitting next to Pete and asked him to stand.

"What's going on?" Pete asked.

"We're taking Mr. Dahl into custody."

"On what grounds?"

"Possession of a large amount of a controlled substance with an obvious intent to sell," Richter said. It was a close question whether the sheriff or Spencer Dahl would win in a smirk contest.

A deputy slipped handcuffs on Dahl and Richter read him his Miranda rights. Halfway through, Dahl interrupted him and said, "I've heard all of that crap before. What's the judge going to give me for selling some weed?"

"We'll see, won't we?" Richter glanced at Pete with a "gotcha" look and added, "Oh yeah, extortion and attempted extortion are other charges. There may be additional charges as well."

"Extortion? What do you have to support that?"

"You saw the poem that the suspect sent to the Mr. Edinger. Since we questioned the suspect, Mrs. Edinger confirmed that the reason she gave Mr. Dahl money was because he threatened to go public with whatever he had on the vic. It's all in Mrs. Edinger's statement."

"That's a lie!" Dahl screamed. "Lorraine gave me money to support my church and other causes! Nothing more."

Pete asked him to be quiet.

Richter smirked again and said to Pete, "Feel free to come along and watch as we book your client."

"Are you taking him to the county jail?"

"For the time being at least."

Pete watched as they led Spencer Dahl away.

SEVENTEEN

Rona leaned against Harry in her postage-stamp office at the rear of the restaurant and listened as Pete summarized what had happened during Spencer Dahl's second round of questioning and the subsequent search of his house. When Pete got to Dahl's arrest, she began to sob and buried her face in Harry's flannel shirt. The small office felt even more claustrophobic with her outburst of emotion.

Harry tightened his arm around Rona and after a few moments said, "The marijuana doesn't surprise me, but the other stuff, the extortion charges and everything. That's a shocker."

"Plus if you believe Lorraine Edinger's statement," Pete said, "Spencer has no alibi. She's denying he was with her at the time of the shooting."

"Do you think her statement is truthful?"

"I have no idea."

"You said Spencer seemed surprised when the sheriff showed him the statement," Harry said.

"It looked that way to me."

"Let's turn it around, then," Harry said. "How do you suppose Spencer thought he'd get away with claiming he was having sex with Lorraine if he wasn't?"

"Harry, you keep asking me questions I can't answer."

Harry studied Pete. "And you didn't see the other stuff they found in that hollow post, huh?"

"No, but my impression is that it was more than just weed."

"Did Spencer seem surprised at what they found?"

"Not at the marijuana. He seemed to expect that they'd find that, and didn't appear too worried. Like selling a little weed was nothing. As I said, we couldn't see what else they found."

Rona had been listening to the conversation between Pete and Harry and interjected to ask, "Did they take Spencer to the county jail?"

"That's what they told me," Pete said.

Harry jumped in again and said in his take-charge manner, "I'm going to verify that. Cap will know."

Rona wiped her eyes. "What happens next, Pete?"

"There'll be an arraignment at some point, I expect. That's when they'll formally charge Spencer." Pete looked at her for a long time. "Rona, I'm not bailing out on Spencer in his moment of need, but I'm really not qualified to handle a criminal case like this."

"But I've watched you in recent years," Rona said. "You have the ability to get to the bottom of things. You're the only one I really trust."

"I can follow a suspicious trail and see where it leads, but criminal defense isn't what I do. I'd get eaten alive by a prosecutor who knows what he's doing. As a favor to you, I'll help if I can. But my advice is for Spencer to get a good criminal lawyer to handle the procedural aspects of the case, and if necessary, to represent him at trial."

"How about that guy from Chicago you brought in to defend John Hicks?" Harry said. "Maybe we can get him again."

"Ira Manning? He's one of the most expensive criminal lawyers in the country. He only represented Hicks *pro bono* because I called in a favor and he thought he'd get a lot of publicity that would help him get new clients in the future. I know he wouldn't be interested in a run-of-the-mill drug case and probably not even in a case involving extortion. He's a murder guy. Besides, you said Spencer doesn't have any money."

They were all silent for a couple of minutes. Then Rona said, "I could take out a loan on the restaurant."

Before Harry could say anything, Pete said, "Let's sleep on it and decide tomorrow."

On the way out, Harry said to Pete, "What did you do when Spencer turned the table over on those guys?"

"To tell the truth, it happened so fast I didn't have time to do anything. One second Richter was saying he was going to search Spencer's house and the next Richter and Joe Tessler were hoisting the table off their laps."

"That sounds like something you'd do to Richter."

"Only in my dreams."

Pete opened a bottle of Pinot Noir, poured himself a glass, and put on an Eagles CD. He propped up his feet and settled back to listen. The easy lyrics filled the room.

Rona was right. He had become good at getting to the bottom of things. He'd also been pretty good at getting himself in nasty scrapes and wasn't eager to jump into another one just now. Besides, he had his own problems with the ethics complaint hanging over his head. He couldn't neglect that.

Then there was Spencer Dahl himself. He genuinely disliked the guy. He disliked his arrogant manner, disliked the way he preyed on lonely women, disliked the way he used and apparently sold drugs, disliked all of the mysticism crap, disliked his general lifestyle. As a matter of fact, he couldn't think of a single thing he liked about Dahl. He didn't have to worry about that with corporate clients. On occasion, he'd agreed to represent someone he didn't care for personally, but his feelings never rose to the visceral level they did with Dahl.

He poured a second glass of Pinot Noir and thought about the extortion charges and the line in the poem Dahl allegedly gave Edinger. He tried to remember how it read, but it was something like " . . . the Colonel's horse he'd ride and his past he was determined to hide . . ." It was unclear whose past the poem was referring to—Thaddeus Clayton's or Thomas Edinger's. Edinger's if he had to guess based on the language.

Pete's thoughts shifted to Carla Neville and the good time he'd had with her at dinner and the Detour concert. She reminded him a lot of Angie DeMarco, minus the flamboyance that could grate on him sometimes. Plus she was single and didn't carry the baggage that becoming involved with a married woman entailed. He stared at the telephone for a long time, poured another glass of wine, and finally dialed Carla's number.

"Hello?"

"Carla, it's Pete Thorsen."

"Oh, hi."

Have you put the budding Lindsey Vonn to bed?"

"Yes."

"I'm sitting here having a glass of wine and thinking about what a nice time I had at the Detour concert. Thanks again for inviting me."

"Okay."

"I wondered if you have any plans for Saturday night. There's a nice restaurant in Cadillac I used to go to with a client, and I thought we could have dinner there if you're available."

"Saturday might not work for me." The tone of her voice didn't invite an alternative proposal.

Pete had expected a more enthusiastic reception and scrambled for a graceful way out. "Why don't we do this, then? Call me when you know your schedule. I'd love to do dinner on Saturday if you can make it. If you can't, maybe we can do it some other night."

"Okay. Say, I've got to go."

Pete was deflated when he hung up the telephone and tried to figure out what was behind the chilly reception he'd just received. He wasn't blowing smoke when he told Carla he'd had a good time at dinner and the concert. He thought she did, too. He poured another glass of Pinot Noir and continued to brood about it.

EIGHTEEN

The next morning, Pete went for a run along the lake to quiet the annoying demons that were creating the pulsating beat inside his head. Killing an entire bottle of Pinot Noir had a way of bringing them out in force and they seemed reluctant to retreat.

Pete squinted into the low autumn sun as he loped east along South Shore Road and felt the crisp air on his face. Signs of the death of one season and the beginning of another were everywhere. The lake was steel-gray and dry birch leaves blew across the sandy beach and collected in the tangle of the surrounding brush. Across the road from the water, in the open areas between clusters of lilac bushes and beech saplings and patches of dune grass, boat piers and hoists were stored upside down for the winter and resembled the work of some urban sculptor as their pipe footings protruded skyward in random patterns.

He had the road mostly to himself. The only vehicular traffic was the occasional pickup that sped past with an aluminum ladder sticking out of its box and other tools of the tradesman's craft piled alongside. In one case, he heard the sounds of Waylon Jennings blaring from the driver's side window that had been cracked slightly, probably to let the cigarette smoke escape. An uncomplicated life, he thought with envy. His body heat was up and he unzipped his nylon athletic jacket a few inches.

Pete tried not to think about his conversation with Carla Neville the night before, but her cool response to his suggestion of dinner kept crowding out his other thoughts. Either he'd completely misread her on that first date, which was a possibility, or something else had come up. Maybe she was involved with someone and just hadn't told him. Or maybe—just maybe—she'd found out somehow that he was representing Spencer Dahl. He knew from Rona's comment that she still detested the guy for what he tried to do to her years ago.

He shook his head at the thought and retraced his route back to his cottage. After going through his morning routine, he drove to town and parked in front of Ebba's Bakery. It must have been a slow day because as he approached the door, he saw Ebba with her flaming tresses standing near the plate glass window watching him come. She clutched him in a bear-hug embrace the moment he walked in, and as she held him close, he could feel her stiff undergarments dig into his chest.

After he disentangled himself from her arms, the torrent of words started and all of them were about Spencer Dahl. Pete desperately wanted one of Ebba's breakfast sandwiches—comfort food that his body craved on this morning even though a week hadn't yet passed since his last—but first he had to endure her hail of questions. She wanted to know if it were true that Sheriff Richter was going to remodel the jail to build a more generous cell for Dahl out of concern for his contacts with the netherworld. And whether it was true that mystics of various stripes were already pouring into town and gathering outside Dahl's cell window and chanting and meditating and communing with unseen spirits. And on and on and on.

His headache was back by the time he finally got to his office. He ate his sandwich and sipped from a carton of orange juice and read the report that Angie DeMarco's secretary had compiled on Jeffery Rodes, the complainant in the ethics case.

Rodes was a graduate of Wayne State University Law School in Detroit and had been in practice for nineteen years. His practice was typical of a small town lawyer. A mix of trusts and estates, tax, small business representation, and some criminal work, primarily representation of clients accused of DUIs. He belonged to the American, state and county bar associations with the committee memberships you'd expect in light of his practice areas. He'd published several articles in bar association journals over the years including one on mediating disputes between heirs to a small business. Nothing particularly revealing.

Pete resumed work on his list of character references, adding some names to the tentative list he'd compiled and scratching off other names. He wound up with a final list of seventeen—four partners from his former law firm, Sears & Whitney, six other lawyers from around Chicago who'd worked with him and knew him well, and six clients. The seventeenth name, which he'd scratched off and then added again, was the retired dean of his law school. It was a long list, but the strategy was to inundate the Attorney Grievance Committee with testimonials in hopes of nipping the complaint in the bud.

He began to call the people on the list. All of his former partners were squarely on board as soon as he explained the circumstances of the complaint. He got the same reception from former clients. Several asked whether he'd ever considered moving back to Chicago and resuming his law practice. To a person, they said if he did come back they'd prefer having him handle their legal affairs again, while emphasizing that didn't imply that they were unhappy with the lawyers to whom Pete had transitioned their business. The Chicago lawyers were equally supportive, and one went so far as to say he was going to help Pete shove the complaint right up some unspeakable orifice in Jeffery Rodes' body.

On a morning when he was feeling down, the telephone conversations helped buoy his spirits. Now the challenge would be to chase in the testimonials so they could be filed with his response on a timely basis.

He began working on a draft of that response. He completed the first two pages, but then the words didn't flow anymore and his thoughts kept drifting off to the Thomas Edinger murder investigation. Something about it wasn't right and he began to wonder again, as he had in the past, whether it was another example of Sheriff Frank Richter jumping on the most obvious suspect in sight or just Pete's suspicious nature. And he couldn't shake the look of genuine shock he'd seen on Dahl's face when Richter told him Lorraine Edinger had denied his alibi.

His telephone rang and Harry was talking before he even got the receiver to his ear. "They've just added a murder charge to the other charges against Spencer!" he said breathlessly.

"Slow down. Who told you that?"

"Cap. He got it from another deputy."

"What's the new charge based on?"

"Evidence they discovered during the search of Spencer's house. Besides the drugs, I guess they found a lot of stuff for smoothbore muskets in that hollow post."

"Umm," Pete said. "Anything else?"

"Yeah, and this is the dagger. Remember you said they took the ashes from Spencer's outdoor fireplace?"

"Yes."

"Do you know what they found when they sifted through the ashes?"

"Tell me, Harry. I don't feel like playing guessing games today."

"Someone burned some clothes in that fireplace. They have scraps of unburned cloth they're examining, but I guess the thing they're most excited about is the buttons. They recovered several metal buttons from the ashes—I don't know how many—with 'Confederate States of America' on them."

"A uniform."

"Yes, a uniform. Richter and his people now think that the way the shooter blended into the reenactment scene was to wear a Confederate uniform and pretend to be a reenactor. Apparently they've checked with several reenactment apparel manufacturers and found some that produce uniforms with 'Confederate States of America' on the buttons."

Pete mulled over what Harry had said and shook his head. "That's so obvious," he mused as much to himself as to Harry.

"It is now."

"There were seventeen Civil War reenactment groups involved in the festival from what I'm told," Pete said. "I don't know what the breakdown was between Union and Confederate, but let's assume that it was fifty-fifty. We also know that the groups came from different states. Some of the reenactors might know each other, but I doubt that all of them did."

"Exactly," Harry said. "Richter thinks Spencer took advantage of the situation, shot Edinger, and then slipped away and burned his uniform."

"Spencer or someone else."

When Harry didn't say anything, Pete asked, "Does Rona know any of this?"

"No, I called you first. She's going to be devastated."

"If there was any doubt before, there isn't now. Dahl needs a criminal lawyer."

"So where does this leave us?"

"You mean where does this leave Dahl."

"Is that your answer?"

"It might be if I were dealing just with Spencer. But given the fact Rona is so emotionally vested in this case, I'm going to call in the rest of my chips and see if I can interest Ira Manning now that it's a murder case."

"Do you think you can get the big guy?"

"I don't know. I'll try. Sit on this with Rona until I get back to you."

"Thanks, Pete. I knew you wouldn't just walk away."

"I would if I had any sense," Pete said. "Before I let you go, have you talked to Carla in the past day or two?"

"We talked yesterday afternoon. She called about running some ads for her company in *The Northern Sentinel*. Why do you ask?"

"I called her last night to ask her out to dinner and it was like talking to a glacier."

Harry was quiet for a moment, then said, "Crap, I think I know what happened. After we talked about the ads, she asked almost as an after-thought if the rumors were true that you were representing Spencer Dahl. I couldn't very well lie to her since she'd find out the truth sooner or later. I said that as far as I knew, you were just covering things until Spencer could get a regular criminal lawyer."

"That explains it. Why didn't you warn me?"

"I intended to, but my conversation with her just happened and I got busy with this week's edition . . . Sorry. Maybe I could call her back and assure her you're trying to line up Ira Manning to represent Dahl."

"No," Pete said wearily, "let it be for the moment." He thought about how to repair the damage, then shook his head glumly and called Manning.

"Norske!" Manning boomed. "How the hell are you?"

"Fine, Ira. Keeping busy?"

"Listen to this. I've been in the office by eight each morning, six days a week, for the past three months. Does that tell you anything?"

"Murder must be big business these days."

"You know that fellow Thomas Malthus? That guy from the old days who worried about the population problem? My clients are doing their best to help him out and keep the population numbers down."

Pete laughed. "All of your clients are paying on schedule I assume."

"That's the good thing about my line of business. There's usually no problem getting paid. Especially when you get your money up front. The only time I ever have problems is when I break my own rule out of good heartedness. Did I ever tell you about that babe Stella Lord I represented on a charge of killing her husband, and after I got her off, she wiggled her fanny and did everything to avoid paying the rest of my fee? Well I had ol' Stella in my office and—"

"Ira, sorry to cut you off, but I've heard that story twelve times. The reason I called is that I have a problem. I have this client who I think is going to be arraigned for murder and—"

"Now it's my turn to interrupt, Norske. Didn't you call me last year about another client of yours who'd been charged with murder, too? Hicks or something like that?"

"Hicks wasn't my client. I was just doing a favor for a friend."

"Oh that's right. You called for Harry something or other. Short fat guy."

"I don't think he'd like to be described that way."

"Which, short or fat?"

"Neither. Anyway, the new guy's name is Spencer Dahl." Pete proceeded to lay it out for Manning, including the fact Dahl had already been arrested on other charges and was about to be indicted for murder as well.

When he was finished, Manning said, "That sounds like Hollywood blockbuster material."

"It does. I haven't talked to our Prosecuting Attorney yet, but I expect Dahl will be arraigned in the next few days."

"That's a piece of cake. Just tell that Dahl fellow to stand up when the judge tells him to and say 'Not guilty.'"

"I've been practicing law long enough to know that things don't always go according to script. Plus, there are bail issues, aren't there?"

Manning was silent for a moment. "There will be. So what you're leading up to in your meandering Scandinavian way is to ask if I would come up there and hold this guy's hand."

"Yes."

"I could probably do that. Let's see, at my standard rate plus travel time, my fee shouldn't exceed fifteen grand. That okay?"

"Umm, Ira, I don't think this guy has fifteen grand."

"How much does he have?"

"His sister tells me he's broke."

"Damn, Norske, don't you ever represent clients with money?"

"Not many these days I'm sorry to say. I thought you could drive up and Harry and I could take you to dinner at some really special place.

Sort of in celebration of the time I helped your impecunious uncle sell his scrap metal business before he died of alcohol poisoning."

Manning cut loose with one of his patented belly laughs. "You're about as subtle as a pile of horse turds, Norske. Okay, when do you need me there?"

"I'll call you."

When he was off the phone with Manning, he called Harry to tell him that he'd lined up Ira Manning to handle Spencer Dahl's arraignment and bail hearing. After that, they'd either have to convince Manning to continue or make other arrangements.

Pete could hear Harry breathe a sigh of relief, followed by a chortle. "It'll be good to see that big toad again," Harry said. "He was masterful the way he handled the John Hicks case."

"That's Ira."

Pete told him about his commitment to treat Manning to dinner. "We could take him to Rona's restaurant and have the chef whip up something really special," Harry suggested.

"I thought about that, but I'm not sure that would be a good idea with Rona and all."

"There's this new place in Traverse City that I've been dying to go to," Harry said. "I started to tell you about it the other day, but you cut me off. We could go there."

"That sounds fine."

"Ira eats a lot, doesn't he?"

"He eats a lot, then he has two desserts to top it off."

"Boy," Harry said, chortling, "this is going to be some kind of evening. I might even do a profile of him in *The Northern Sentinel.* I bet he has a ton of stories I could use."

"I'm sure he does."

"Did he ask about me?" Harry asked tentatively.

"Asked how you were," Pete said. He didn't mention Manning's short and fat descriptions.

"Do you think he'd sit for an interview with me while he's here?"

"Might, if you feed him well."

Pete and Harry agreed to meet at the Bayview Grille and deliver the news to Rona together. Even with Ira Manning's agreement to represent Dahl at the arraignment and the bail hearing, it didn't go well.

NINETEEN

arry McTigue wasn't known for being an early riser, but he called just as Pete was rolling out of bed and gave him the sparkling weather forecast for the day. To make it up to Pete for enduring five hours of frigid weather on Lake Michigan, he proposed they attack the trout in the Betsie River on what was likely to be the best remaining day of the season. Pete considered Harry's proposition for all of five seconds and then agreed. He needed a little diversion.

Harry was standing in his driveway waiting when Pete pulled up. As usual, he was already clad in his waders, fishing vest and other angling attire. He tossed the gear he wasn't wearing in back along with a large wicker picnic basket and wedged himself into the front seat beside Pete. Before he'd buckled himself in, he started waxing on about the weather and how the water-level of the Betsie was just right for optimal trout fishing, then launched into a tutorial about the kind of flies that were likely to attract the lunkers that day. He concluded his soliloquy by mentioning that he'd invited Jake Rossum to join them, but Rossum had to decline because the kid who worked for him part-time had classes that day at the community college and he had no one to tend the shop.

The mercury was edging over the sixty degree mark when they got to the stream and their favorite stretch of water was void of other fishermen. It had been a dry autumn except for the weekend of the Thaddeus Clayton Festival and most of the leaves were still on the trees. They blazed with reds and oranges and yellows and bronzes in the soft sunlight.

Harry, fully dressed for combat when they arrived, rolled out of the car first and was already in the river by the time Pete started to pull on his waders. Pete reveled in the autumn splendor and took his time assembling his equipment. He went downstream a couple hundred feet from where Harry was earnestly working an eddy and waded into the river. The current was slow-moving, but Pete could feel the pressure against his waders as he moved out in the stream. A small animal—probably a muskrat—made a "v" in the calm water as it swam toward a tree that was uprooted and partially submerged in the river.

Pete drew his rod back to the one o'clock position and flicked his line toward a patch of water that was shaded by overhanging branches and began to work his fly. Several more casts yielded a decent-sized brook trout. He carefully disengaged the hook and released the trout back into the stream and continued to cast. As he methodically worked the water for the next hour, he thought about everything that was happening in his life.

"Hey, Pete!" Harry called. "You ready for some lunch?"

Pete checked his watch and smiled. He could always count on Harry not to let fishing interfere with food. He waded upstream to the sandbar where Harry was withdrawing items from the wicker basket and laying them out on a red and white checked tablecloth he'd draped over a tree stump.

"Jeez," Harry said, "Rona's guy outdid himself with this lunch." There was cold salmon, smoked whitefish and crackers, red grapes, a salad for each of them in plastic containers, and a long loaf of fresh French bread. Topping it off were several half-bottles of Pinot Grigio.

They sat on a fallen log and wolfed down the food. Pete passed on the wine, but Harry finished his first half-bottle and was eyeing another.

"How did you do this morning?" Harry asked as he chewed on a hunk of French bread lathered with smoked whitefish.

"One brookie. Fifteen, sixteen inches."

"I got shut out, but it's great being outdoors on a day like this, isn't it? Too bad Jake couldn't join us."

"Yeah," Pete said, feigning disappointment. He was more interested in just being outdoors than socializing.

Harry popped grapes into his mouth and while he chewed, mumbled, "I haven't talked to Jake since they arrested Spencer. He's probably relieved that Dennis Bader is out from under the cloud of Edinger's murder."

Pete looked at Harry and said, "Is he close with Bader?"

"They looked pretty close on the boat that day, don't you think?"

Pete shrugged. "I thought he was just being polite because it was his boat."

"Maybe you're right," Harry said. "What do you think Ira's defense of Spencer is going to be?"

"Don't know. He has some things to work with, though."

"What do you know that you haven't shared with your friends?"

"Nothing concrete, but don't you think the case against Spencer seems a little too pat?"

Harry seemed to consider that. "In what way?" he asked.

"I don't know. Just a feeling."

"Oh, that's a big help. Is the feeling in your gut or in your head?"

Pete shot him a look and didn't say anything. He just watched the gentle flow of the river.

"You have a plan, don't you?" Harry persisted.

Pete furled his brows. "Plan. What are you talking about?"

"You have a plan. You're going to let Manning handle the technical details of the defense while you sniff around and try to find out what really happened."

"That's nonsense."

"Is it? I know you pretty well and I've seen you act like this before."

"You ought to stick to news reporting and leave psychiatry to the professionals."

Harry rambled on. "For Rona's sake, I hope you're successful. But there's a downside for you, too. If Carla finds out you're helping Spencer, particularly after you lined up Manning, you can kiss your chances of building a relationship with her goodbye."

Pete looked at him cynically. "I've already kissed them goodbye."

He helped Harry pack up what remained of the food and then took his rod and headed back to the river. Cloud cover was rolling in, turning the vibrant scene of the morning to gray, which matched his darkening mood.

When Pete got back to his office in late-afternoon, he found that his voicemail had been pressed into duty overtime. Seven calls were from his list of character references asking questions that ranged from how long the testimonial letters should be to how much detail they should provide. He returned the calls and patiently answered all questions. Then he called Angie back, and when he didn't reach her, left a message that he'd have a draft of a response to the ethics complaint to her by the following evening.

His telephone work done, he resumed work on the response. The words flowed better than the previous day and he was making good progress when Harry called.

"Didn't I just spend the day with you?" Pete asked.

"I beg your pardon," Harry replied, feigning hurt feelings. "I come up with a great idea to get you out of the office on a beautiful autumn day and feed you the best trail lunch you've ever had and you thank me by giving me grief. You Norwegians don't know how to show gratitude, do you?"

"We're a well-known bunch of ingrates," Pete said. "I thought you were going to some newspaper dinner tonight and had to leave early."

"That's why I'm calling. Jake Rossum just called me. He drove his old pickup today, but now it won't start and he asked if I'd take him home."

When Harry didn't say more, Pete said, "And you want me to give him a lift as a repayment for the day, right?"

"Could you? Rona and I are dressed and we have to leave right now to make the dinner. Jake lives somewhere south of Benzonia. It shouldn't take you long."

Pete said he would and wrapped up work on his draft. When he pulled up in front of Jake's Outdoors, Rossum was standing in front of his shop waiting for him. He got in Pete's Range Rover and looked around the interior and said, "Your car is almost as old as my pickup."

Pete grinned. "Old, but reliable. And comfortable. My stepdaughter says it fits my image of owning nothing that was made in this century."

"Kids."

"Do you have any children, Jake?"

"None I know of."

Jake guided Pete on the route to his home. Neither of them seemed much for talking and the drive was mostly silent. Then Pete remembered his conversation with Ira Manning about smoothbores and asked, "Do you sell smoothbore equipment in your shop?"

Rossum shook his head. "Not enough demand. Why do you ask?"

"The lawyer from Chicago I brought in to represent Spencer Dahl is a city boy and asked me to brief him on the weapons. It's kind of the blind leading the blind because I don't know anything about smoothbores either."

"I know a little," Rossum said helpfully.

"Enough to give me a tutorial?"

"I think so."

"Could I stop by sometime and have you give me a demonstration?"

"Sure. We could consider it payment for the lift home."

"If stores like yours don't sell smoothbores," Pete said, "where does a person who uses one of those weapons get the paraphernalia for them?"

Rossum smiled. "You mean the 'fixings'?"

"Is that the term they use?"

"A lot of them do."

"I suppose that's the lingo a guy like Calvin Seitz would use. I ran into Seitz when he was hunting squirrels with a smoothbore. Do you know him?"

Rossum thought for a moment. "Crazy looking guy with a mop of red hair and a beard?"

"Sounds like him."

"Seitz was questioned too, I understand."

"Right. He had a grudge against Edinger and is a crack shot with a smoothbore."

"Was he at the reenactment?"

"He claims he wasn't. He says he was fishing on the Betsie River."

"I wasn't there either," Rossum said. "I was in Grand Rapids for an outdoor trade show that day. But people who were there say it was something until Edinger's shooting put a damper on things."

"It was."

"Getting back to your question, a lot of smoothbore people, particularly if they're purists, make their own stuff. I think there are a couple of mail order houses that cater to that crowd as well."

"Okay."

The Rossum place had once been a farm and in addition to the two-story clapboard house, there was a barn with peeling red paint and a sagging roofline, a silo, and another small out-building. A newish Toyota Tundra was parked near the house.

"Have you lived here long?" Pete asked.

"A few years. I'm just renting the place."

Pete saw a woman in a plain blue dress come out from behind some clothes she was hanging on an outdoor line. She fixed her eyes on them and stared.

Rossum called, "It okay, Mother. I'm home."

The woman edged her way toward them and appeared to eye a pitch-fork that was leaning against a stone chimney. Rossum seemed embarrassed and said to Pete in a low voice, "Sorry, Pete, she's not well."

The woman was now within twenty feet and continued to stare at them. Rossum repeated, "I said it's okay, Mother."

"Who are you two?" she asked.

"It's your son, Jake. This is Pete Thorsen. He gave me a ride home."

"That isn't Jacob's car." She moved closer to Pete's Range Rover as if to inspect it.

Rossum said to Pete in a low voice, "You probably should go. Thanks for the ride. Let me know when you want to come to the shop for that smoothbore tutorial."

Pete headed around to the driver's side of his Range Rover and as he started to get in, he noticed Rossum's mother following him. Rossum quickly stepped forward to block her path.

TWENTY

Ira Manning was in fine form as they drove to the county jail. Spencer Dahl's arraignment was the following day and they had an appointment to see him that afternoon.

"What's this guy Dahl like?" Manning asked.

"Jerk would be too kind of a word to describe him."

"Is he guilty?"

"Hell, Ira, I don't know. He claims he's being set up."

Manning cut loose with one of his belly laughs. "They're all being set up. I haven't met a criminal defendant yet who wasn't as innocent as a baby lamb. I learned that when I first started practicing law and represented this street guy who was in the slammer for blowing away another dude with a sawed-off shotgun in front of about seventeen witnesses. Do you know what he wanted me to argue in court?"

"No idea."

"That it couldn't have been him for two reasons. First, he had arthritis in his hands as a result of sleeping on the streets when he was a kid and couldn't pull the trigger of a shotgun. And second, it was a case of mistaken identity because all black folks look alike to white people, never mind that sixteen of the seventeen eyewitnesses were black themselves." Ira launched another booming laugh that came straight from his belly.

"That doesn't sound like the kind of high-end client who can afford your fees."

Manning looked at him and said, "You lead too sheltered of a life, Norske. My fee came to three hundred grand in that case."

"Really?" Pete said, showing his surprise.

"Once a week his old lady—for you white-shoe types, that's his squeeze, not his mother—would show up in my office with a brown paper bag stuffed full of fifties and hundreds. By the time the case was over, I think I had my three hundred grand and then some."

"No kidding."

Manning looked thoughtful. "I'm not sure I'd agree to be paid that way again, though. My secretary refused to count the bills out of fear they might be contaminated with drugs or maybe even dried blood that carried the HIV virus." His booming laugh filled the car again.

County jails in small towns had the same kind of security as their big-city counterparts, with one saving grace. They were less bureaucratic when a lawyer came to visit his client. Pete and Ira Manning waited in a small room divided by what Pete assumed was bulletproof glass. Spencer Dahl was led into the room by a deputy no more than ten minutes after they arrived. He was dressed in a jail jumpsuit and had cuffs on his hands and shackles on his ankles. The deputy closed the door behind him, but Pete could see him watching them through a small window in the steel door.

They all picked up their phones. Dahl stared at Manning for a few moments and then said to Pete, "Who's your tiny friend?"

Pete was relieved that at least he didn't call Ira his "big, fat friend." "This is Ira Manning. He's a criminal lawyer from Chicago. He's going to represent you at your arraignment and bail hearing."

Dahl looked at Manning again and said, "You should get a new suit, Ike."

"Ira," he corrected him. He grinned at Dahl. "And I think my suit is a cut above yours."

For the first time since Pete met him, Dahl actually laughed rather than just smirked. "I like this guy," he said to Pete. "He's not a tight-ass like you."

Pete ignored the jibe and listened quietly as Manning and Dahl went over the facts of the case and what the sheriff had found when they searched his house and surrounding environs. The deputy who'd been periodically monitoring them through the window opened the door and said, "Time's up, gentlemen."

"Could we have ten more minutes, Deputy?" Pete asked.

"Time limits are time limits."

"What harm would there be in giving us an additional ten minutes?"

The deputy seemed to consider it and said, "Okay, ten minutes." He closed the door again.

"That would never happen in Chicago," Ira said, grinning. "Time's up means time's up there."

"Why don't you two wrap things up," Pete said, "and leave five minutes for me. I need to ask Spencer about something."

When they were finished, Dahl said, "What's your question, Petey?"

Pete ignored Dahl's smart-alecky tone and said, "The poem Richter claims they found in Edinger's study. I don't remember the exact wording, but one line seemed to make reference to Edinger's past. What did you mean by that line?"

Dahl smirked at him. "You're assuming I wrote the poem, aren't you Petey?"

Manning seemed to be about to say something, but Pete put a hand on his forearm and said to Dahl, "Listen wise guy, I can think of ten places I'd rather be instead of sitting here in the slammer playing stupid cat-and-mouse games with you. You know you wrote that ditty and also that you sent it. Your fingerprints are all over it. Now I'm going to ask you again—what did you mean by that line?"

"You told the sheriff he couldn't prove that I sent it, remember Petey? That was the only good thought you've had since I've known you."

Pete banged his free hand against the glass and Dahl lurched backward in surprise. The deputy wrenched open the door again and shouted, "What's going on in here?"

Manning said in a soothing voice, "Pete was just demonstrating something. I think he hit the glass a little harder than he intended to."

"Well, your time is up anyway. You two counsel have to leave now so I can take the prisoner back to his cell."

"Give us two minutes," Manning said. "That's all we need to wrap things up."

The deputy looked at them skeptically and peered at his wrist watch. "Alright, two minutes, then this party is over. And no more violence in here or Mr. Dahl is going to have two new cellmates." He closed the door again.

"I've been listening to your conversation with Mr. Thorsen," Manning said to Dahl. "You might want to answer his questions in a civil tone. If you don't, we're both going to walk out of here and never look back."

Dahl looked back and forth between Pete and Manning and apparently decided they were serious. He said, "I heard that Edinger had some incident in his past."

"Who told you?" Pete asked. "Lorraine Edinger?"

Dahl snorted derisively. "Where else would I hear it?"

"What precisely did Lorraine say?"

"I don't remember."

"Bull you don't remember. You referred to it in that poem you sent to her husband."

"It was just some stupid thing old hubby did while he was teaching at some Podunk college."

"Which college?"

Dahl shrugged and shook his head.

"Okay, then what did he supposedly do?"

"She didn't say."

"Based on the conversation you had with her, what do you *think* he did?"

"I don't know, Petey," Dahl said in a whiney tone. "Maybe he banged the dean's wife or something. Or maybe it was his daughter." Dahl leered at him lewdly.

The deputy opened the door again. "Okay, you two counsel have to leave right now. No more extensions of time."

Pete and Manning left and walked out of the building. On the way back to Frankfort, they were both quiet until Manning asked, "Your hand sore?"

Pete looked at him with raised eyebrows. "No. Should it be?"

"You slammed that glass pretty hard, Norske."

Pete didn't respond to his question, but directed one of his own Manning's way. "Was I right about him being a jerk?"

"Spot on. I guess I'm more used to dealing with people like that than you are. For a minute there I thought we might have the first jailhouse homicide in the history of your county."

Pete grinned. "Thanks for restraining me."

"Now I know what my uncle meant when he said you can be a real barracuda when you get your back up. What's bugging you about that poem?"

"I wish I could tell you. It's more intuition than anything else."

"But you think it could have something to do with Edinger's shooting."

"Could have," Pete said, shrugging, "but I can't draw a connection."

"Do you plan to check it out further?"

"If I can. It's clear that Thomas Edinger didn't inspire love in a lot of people and I'm wondering whether his death has something to do with his past rather than with some lowlife sleeping with his wife and leeching money off her."

Manning looked at him a long time. "When you form an opinion about someone, it's hard to get you to change, isn't it?"

Pete glanced Manning's way, but didn't reply.

"You know what Angie says about you?" Manning continued. "That you're a frustrated sleuth."

"Angie's a good friend, but she can be preachy."

"A pretty damn good looking preacher, though. You ever think of making a move on her?"

"Maybe when I've had too much Thor's Hammer vodka."

Ira's belly laugh erupted again. "I'll tell her that."

"You do and Thor himself will come to visit you and do surgery on both of your legs with his hammer."

Ira looked at him. "You're serious, aren't you?"

"Deadly serious. He won't come until you're finished representing Spencer Dahl, though."

"Now hold on, Norske. I signed on to represent this innocent man at his arraignment and bail hearing. That's one more day of my time. I didn't promise to do anything beyond that."

Pete shot him a sly smile. "Maybe you'll change your mind after you see how much publicity this case is going to generate."

Ira furled his brow and said, "I've been thinking about how this case might generate some pub. Guy gets killed with a nineteenth century weapon, some creepy guy who lives in the woods and is into witches and spirits has been banging the deceased's wife and taking her money. That's the kind of stuff the media eats up."

"See? You're weakening already."

"I'm weakening not because of your horsecrap logic, but because my gut hasn't had any sustenance since this morning. I hope Harry made an early reservation somewhere."

"You can count on it with Harry. But it's a forty-five minute drive to Traverse City. That's if the traffic isn't a problem."

"Forty-five minutes. Jesus, Norske, I might need a snack along the way."

"That's Harry's department. I'm sure he won't be hard to convince."

TWENTY-ONE

Pete skipped breakfast with Harry and Ira Manning and went directly to his office. He planned to hook up with Manning later at Spencer Dahl's arraignment and bail hearing.

He logged on his computer and began to search for information on Thomas Edinger. There was plenty, beginning with Edinger's official website which was a slick affair with trailers for each of his books and a ton of blurbs from big-name historians and authors. The Google search ran for nine pages and referenced everything from Edinger's books to interviews he'd given, including three that appeared in the *New York Times*, to stories about his Civil War knowledge. Pete scanned the material, looking for something of interest.

He skipped over what he already knew from Harry and noted that Thomas Edinger was born in Toledo, Ohio, and after attending high school there, had gone on to what was now Wittenberg University. He then pursued graduate studies in history and earned his Ph.D. from the University of Virginia. His first college teaching job was an assistant professor at the University of Tennessee. After five years at that school, during which he produced an impressive number of academic articles focusing on the Civil War, he joined the faculty of Ridge College in its history department. Ridge College was a four-year liberal arts institution located in Chattanooga, Tennessee, and noteworthy primarily for its Civil War studies. Edinger spent eleven years at Ridge College, leaving after his second book on Thaddeus Clayton was published. He then published the popular novels based on Clayton's life.

Pete leaned back in his chair and tried to remember exactly how Dahl had described the rumor concerning a blot on Edinger's past. The only thing specific was that the rumored incident occurred at a college where Edinger had taught. That was a small universe since Edinger had only taught at two. Maybe he'd get a chance to grill Dahl further at the court hearing that afternoon.

Pete never had the occasion to be in the county court before, and as he sat with Ira Manning at the counsel's table waiting for Dahl to be brought in, he was struck by what a nice facility it was.

He leaned over and whispered to Manning, "A lot tonier than 26th and California, huh?" referring to the large criminal court complex in Chicago.

"And a lot safer," Manning replied. "There's not even a chain link fence around the lot where we parked."

Pete turned and waved to Harry who was sitting in the front row of the spectator's section which was mostly filled. Word had obviously gotten around that Spencer Dahl was being arraigned that afternoon. Murder cases could be counted on to draw a crowd regardless of how large or small the venue.

Pete leaned over and whispered to Manning again. "If we get a chance, I want to ask Dahl some additional questions about that poem."

"After the way he jerked you around yesterday?" Manning whispered back.

Pete nodded.

"Okay. I'll try to steer the conversation in that direction if we have some down time."

Two deputies led Dahl into the courtroom. Even though he was an athletic man in top physical condition, Dahl shuffled along like an octogenarian with the constraints of the leg irons and handcuffs. He dropped into the empty chair between Pete and Manning. Manning motioned for them to huddle closer and whispered, "You all set, Spencer? Just say, 'Not guilty' when the judge asks you how you plead."

"This is bull!" Dahl said in a voice that sizzled with anger. "I want the judge to know I'm being set up!"

"Keep your voice down," Manning admonished him.

"No, I want to cut this off right now! The judge needs to know what's going on. Lorraine is lying and someone planted that stuff at my home. This Barney Fife," he said, using the old television series character to describe Sheriff Richter, "is railroading me just because he needs a scapegoat for that guy's murder."

Manning grabbed him by the forearm and his knuckles whitened with the pressure. "Listen to me, Spencer. The judge won't hear anything you have to say today other than how you plead to the state's charges. We'll have plenty of time to make our case later."

The judge walked in and took his black leather chair behind the bench as the bailiff announced him and called the court to order. Dahl's case was one of only two on the calendar that afternoon. The bailiff called their case first and Ira Manning stepped forward with Dahl shuffling along behind him. The bailiff read the charges against Dahl and the judge asked how he wished to plead.

Pete saw Manning shoot Dahl a stern look. "Not guilty," Dahl muttered compliantly.

The judge then questioned Dahl briefly about his plea and instructed the bailiff to enter a not guilty plea.

"Now I understand you have time constraints, Mr. Manning, and you've requested that the bond hearing be held this afternoon. The

Prosecuting Attorney says he has no objection and I'll hear that part of the case immediately after I deal with the next matter."

Manning and Dahl returned to the counsel table. Manning whispered to Dahl, "While we wait, Pete has some additional questions for you about that poem."

Dahl looked at Pete and then back at Manning and said, "Unbelievable. Who's my lawyer here? This guy's not even a criminal lawyer. He's just a paper pusher."

Pete jumped in and said in a low voice, "Listen, Dahl, I've had enough of your crap. Why don't you try being civil for a change."

Dahl glared at him but didn't say anything.

"Why are you so resistant to talking about things we need to know to defend you?" Pete persisted.

"Because your nutty questions about that poem have nothing to do with my defense," Dahl hissed. "You should be trying to find out who set me up. You should start with Lorraine Edinger."

"Let Ira and me decide what's relevant to your defense. How did Lorraine happen to bring up the incident you referred to in that poem?"

Before Dahl could answer, Pete's cell phone burred and he hastily turned it off. He saw that the caller was Angie DeMarco and he got up and walked out of the courtroom. He called Angie back and said nothing about where he was. She was in court herself, and during a brief recess, she wanted to pass on some additional thoughts for him to take into account in his draft response to the ethics complaint. He finished the call and returned to the courtroom.

Dahl saw him coming and rolled his eyes. "What did my sister want?" he said after Pete seated himself again.

"That wasn't your sister. In fact, I didn't know you had a sister."

A sardonic smile creased Dahl's face. "Now who's playing games?"

Pete ignored his comment and said, "To get back to my question, how did Lorraine Edinger happen to bring up her husband's past?"

"You really have a one-track mind, don't you? We were communing and it came up."

"C'mon, Spencer. You must know what she was referring to. People don't just say, 'My husband has a soiled past' out of the blue."

"Maybe in your world, Petey. But when people are really communicating with each other, things come out."

"I'm wasting my time here," Pete said to Manning. "Call or stop by my office before you head back to Chicago."

"I feel so exposed now that my paper-pusher lawyer is deserting me," Dahl said tauntingly. He feigned a sorrowful look.

Pete stuffed his papers in his briefcase and said nothing as he prepared to leave.

"Say hello to my sister, Petey."

"Which one—the one who's trying to save your butt or the one you tried to rape?"

Pete stalked out of the courtroom. Harry tried to beckon him over as he passed, but Pete kept walking.

He was in his office staring out at the bay when Manning and Harry walked in. "I suppose you're going to report that Spencer Dahl is free as a bird pending trial, walking around the streets of Frankfort and looking for someone else's wife to have sex with and give him money."

Manning shook his head solemnly. "The judge denied bail."

"Really?"

"Really. The Prosecuting Attorney strongly opposed it, and the judge found that Dahl has no real ties to the community and is a flight risk."

"There was no room to propose a compromise of any kind?"

"I tried. I proposed house arrest with ankle bracelets to monitor Spencer's movements, but the judge wouldn't buy it."

Pete stared at him. "So what now?"

"I've got to get back to Chicago. Let me think about it for a day or two, then we'll talk."

"Thanks for coming up on short notice, Ira."

"One more thing, Norske. I continue to believe you may be onto something with that poem. If I'm going to be involved going forward, and I'm not yet ready to commit, you have to have some skin in the game, too. You have to continue to dig around into Edinger's background."

When Manning was gone, Harry said, "Ira told me about the crap Spencer was giving you in the courtroom."

"And before that, in jail. The guy's a jerk, Harry."

"I warned you that you wouldn't like him."

Pete looked out at the bay again and didn't say anything.

Harry seemed to be uncomfortable with the silence and said, "What are you going to do?"

"I don't know."

"I mean about digging into the background of that poem."

"I know what you mean."

"Any ideas?"

"I need to think about it."

"Should we walk down to Rona's and have dinner? The three of us can talk. Maybe we can come up with some ideas,"

"Thanks, but not tonight," Pete said.

Harry hovered around the office, like he was hoping Pete would change his mind. He had a look on his face that Pete had seen before. The one that said he recognized there was a problem, but didn't know what to do.

"Tell Rona I'll talk to her tomorrow," Pete said.

Pete continued to sit in his office after Harry left, staring out the window as the shadows lengthened and darkness began to set in. Then he picked up a hard copy of the draft of the response to the ethics complaint and made some pencil changes. He couldn't concentrate on the words and his heart wasn't in it. Whenever he looked up, his reflected image stared back at him from the window.

He closed down for the night and headed home. He took the scenic route, the one where he was run off the road one night years earlier when he was investigating the drowning death of Cara Lane, and slipped a Johnny Cash CD into the player and lost himself in the music as he drove along the dark road.

TWENTY-TWO

A good night's sleep improved Pete's outlook on the world and he arrived at his office with a mental checklist of things to accomplish that day. The first was to call Rona, also an early riser, and tell her what he'd committed to do for Ira Manning: Try to get to the bottom of the veiled reference to Thomas Edinger's past in the poem Spencer Dahl had allegedly sent to him. Pete and Rona knew each other well enough that he didn't have to come right out and say that he was really doing it for her, but that seemed to be understood from the way she thanked him.

Before doing anything else, though, he had to revise the draft of his response to the ethics complaint and get it to Angie for her input. He spent the next three hours going through several versions of the response, incorporating Angie's suggestions from the previous day, and tweaking the language. He downplayed some points he'd made in earlier drafts and amplified others and played with the words. Finally he felt the draft was in good enough shape to e-mail it to Angie.

He walked down the street to the bakery, and after dodging Ebba's pointed questions and listening to her cluck about the criminal element

around town these days, he returned to his office with a healthier sandwich than the one he really wanted—roast turkey on wheat bread
without mayonnaise. He propped his feet up on his desk and ate his
sandwich and thought about Lorraine Edinger. The feeling that she'd
turned on Dahl for some reason kept nagging him. Dahl's violent reaction when the sheriff confronted him with Lorraine's statement contradicting his alibi and the rest of his story was too spontaneous, too
genuine not to be real. If he were right, the question was why?

He wondered if Lorraine Edinger would be willing to talk to him.
Even if she stuck to the story in the statement she gave the sheriff, which
he had to expect, it might provide an opportunity for him to probe into
what she knew about the alleged incident in Thomas Edinger's past. He
knew the odds were against it, but decided to give it a try.

The Edingers weren't listed in the local directory. Pete used a service he'd used before and came up with two unlisted telephone numbers for them. He called both numbers and each time got a voicemail
message. One message had a man's voice and the other a woman's.

After puttering around his office for an hour, he tried again. No
answer this time either. Pete thought back to when he was trying to
reach Spencer Dahl. Dahl was home, but either hadn't heard his phone
ring or didn't want to talk to Pete and was avoiding his calls. Lorraine
Edinger might be doing the same thing. With Dahl, he'd just showed
up at his house. Maybe he'd get lucky with Lorraine as well.

Pete wound up what he was doing, jumped in his Range Rover, and
headed for the Edinger place south of Elberta. He exited M-22 when he
came to their sign and followed the winding ribbon of asphalt through
the six hundred acres of property Thomas Edinger had amassed. Pete
continued on the road past the turnoff that would have taken him to the
field where the reenactment was held and suddenly the manor house, as
the locals all called it, loomed in front of him like something from the
pages of *Architectural Digest*.

The house had been built in the Greek Revival style that would
have fit perfectly with the plantation houses on an antebellum tour of

Georgia or Louisiana. Pete could almost imagine Scarlett O'Hara leaning languorously against one of the soaring white Doric columns at the front of the house watching him as he approached. The house reflected the author, but certainly not the protagonist of his books; Colonel Thaddeus Clayton was born and raised in a four-room log cabin in the wilds of Michigan.

As Pete got closer, he had to smile when he thought of Calvin Seitz with his bushy red beard and wild mop of hair and outlandish dress insisting on continuing to hunt on the property as he had in the years before Edinger acquired it. He could imagine Seitz stalking through the maples and oaks and other hardwood trees that blazed with color matching his hair, and Thomas Edinger in turn reacting with rage when he saw him picking off squirrels in his front yard with his old smoothbore musket.

A spotless black SUV stood in the circle drive that was paved with cobble stones. The SUV was a Mercedes GL550 4Matic that seemed to fit the house perfectly. Pete parked a prudent distance behind the Mercedes lest the small rust spot he'd recently discovered above the wheel housing of his twelve-year-old Range Rover might be contagious. Pete got out and admired the view of the surrounding countryside briefly and then headed for the entrance.

He banged on the front door with the iron knocker and half expected a butler in formal wear to answer. After a couple of minutes, he repeated the routine. Finally a woman with heavy eye makeup and a black Lycra top that showed enough cleavage to make Dolly Parton blush opened the door and squinted at him in the bright sunlight. A blend of burning incense and some brand of heavy floral perfume he didn't recognize wafted through the open door and assaulted his nostrils.

"Lorraine Edinger?" he asked casually.

She looked at him suspiciously and finally said, "Yes, and who may I ask are you?" The heavy makeup slathered on her face would have played better in softer light.

"Pete Thorsen, Mrs. Edinger. Could I talk to you for a few minutes?"

"Thorsen," she repeated. "How do you spell that?"

He told her.

"That sounds familiar. Are you from the sheriff's office?"

He said, "No, but I know some people in that office, including Detective Joe Tessler."

"The skinny man with hair the color of mine?"

"That's him. Could we go inside and talk for a few minutes? This shouldn't take long."

"Talk about what? You've interrupted my meditation."

"I'm sorry. I need to talk to you about your husband."

"My husband is dead."

"I'm aware of that."

"They've arrested his killer. I'm sure the sheriff can tell you all about it if you're interested." She started to close the door.

Pete put his foot in the opening to block the door and said, "His *accused* killer. The man they arrested is entitled to a trial. But I need to ask you some questions, Mrs. Edinger. It really would be better if we went inside rather than trying to carry on a conversation out here."

"Mr. Tessler was more courteous than you are," she said. "At least he waited to talk until I'd finished my meditation."

"I can wait, too, if that works better for you."

She looked at him like he was an uneducated ignoramus. "You don't know anything about meditation, do you?"

"Not much," he agreed.

"If you did, you'd know it's not easy to get back into a state of consciousness once you've been interrupted."

"Maybe we should have our conversation now, then, so you can get back to your meditation without further interruptions."

Lorraine Edinger blocked his path as he started to gently nudge the door open. "If you're not with the sheriff's office, why should I talk to you at all?"

"Because it's in your best interests. A man named Spencer Dahl was arrested because he's suspected of shooting your husband. I'm aware you know Mr. Dahl. He's being represented by a lawyer from Chicago named Ira Manning, one of the most famous criminal lawyers in the country. I'm working with him to investigate the background of the case."

"Spencer Dahl," she said, screwing up her face and shaking her head. "Awful man. I'm not the least bit interested in talking to you about him." She tried to close the door again, but Pete still had his foot in the way.

"You have two choices, Mrs. Edinger. You can talk to me informally, which is what I hope you'll do, or Mr. Manning and I can subpoena you and force you to talk to us that way."

"Subpoena. What does that mean?"

"Essentially, it's an order by the court instructing you to meet with us and answer our questions. If that happens, you'll be under oath and could go to jail if something you say is untruthful." He knew he was slanting the truth a little, but it was close enough.

She seemed to consider that and then said, "I think I should call Detective Tessler and see what he says."

Pete knew that getting Tessler involved would throw everything into a cocked hat and said casually, "You can call Mr. Tessler if you wish, but we have a right to subpoena you regardless of what he says. I'd like to make this easy for everyone."

She looked at him suspiciously and said, "How do I know I'll be safe if I'm in the house with you alone?"

"Do I look like an axe murderer?"

For the first time since she opened the door, Lorraine actually smiled. "You're kind of cute, actually."

She stepped back and let him in. They sat on facing love seats in the small seating area just inside the door and Pete asked some preliminary questions to get the ball rolling. It was a close call whether the incense or the strong perfume irritated his eyes more.

"You admit you know Spencer Dahl, do I have that right?"

"The killer?"

"The *alleged* killer," he reminded her again.

"I know Mr. Dahl." She wrinkled her nose and tugged at the top of her outfit.

"How did you meet him?"

"My girlfriend and I went to a meeting at that shack of his in the woods last summer." She rolled her eyes. "We sat around his fireplace and he tried to convince us to accept him as our spiritual leader and teacher."

"Did you?"

"Accept him? Absolutely not. I know more about transcendentalism than he does. I could have been *his* spiritual leader."

"Why did you hang around with him for several months then?"

"I didn't *hang* around with him. I went to a few meetings, that's all."

"Alone or with others?"

"Now you're getting personal, Mr. Thornburg or whatever your name is. I think I'll end this interview right now." She rose to her feet and stood glaring at him.

"Sorry."

"You're not a very considerate man," she admonished him.

"Look, Mrs. Edinger, we can end this interview if you like, but then we're just going to have to subpoena you as I said earlier."

"How much longer is this going to take? I hear my mother's voice talking to me. It isn't often that we're able to get in touch with each other."

"Fifteen minutes," Pete said.

"Okay, fifteen minutes and then you have to leave." She sat down again and closed her eyes.

"Mrs. Edinger?" Pete said after a few minutes.

Lorraine opened her eyes and said, "I was just communing with my mother."

Pete was beginning to feel like he was the one who should be concerned with being in the house alone with Lorraine Edinger, not the other way around. He decided to get to the most pressing questions.

"Mr. Dahl said you gave him money on two occasions to support his causes. Is that true?"

Lorraine Edinger studied her long fingernails coated with dark purple nail polish and after a few moments said, "I loaned that creep some money, but he never paid it back."

"There seems to be some misunderstanding concerning the money. Spencer said you gave him the money as a donation and the sheriff said that he extorted the money from you by threatening to expose an incident in your husband's past, something I understand you told him about."

Lorraine looked confused. "I'm not supposed to talk about that. It's confidential between me and Sheriff Richter."

"It's not confidential because I already know about it. I'm only looking for details."

Lorraine tugged at her top again and said without looking up, "I didn't tell that awful man Dahl anything about my husband's past. Thomas had a wonderful reputation. He was a world-famous scholar and author. If he had any secrets, I'm sure I'd know."

"If what you say is true, why did Spencer send your husband a poem referring to some incident based on what you told him?"

She looked fidgety. "I don't know anything about a poem."

"Then you may want to see Sheriff Richter again and clarify the statement you gave him."

Her eyes widened. "How do you know about my statement?"

"The sheriff showed it to me."

"Doesn't anyone have any integrity anymore? I gave that statement to him in confidence and now you say he showed it to you. You have to leave now, Mr. Thornburg. You've taken up enough of my time." She rose to her feet again and crossed her arms under her breasts.

Pete got up as well, but said, "You might want to take a look at another part of your statement as well if you go back to the sheriff's office. Spencer claims he was with you when your husband was shot, and in your statement you say you were shopping in Beulah. Both of you can't be telling the truth."

Lorraine Edinger looked aghast. "He said he was with me? Why would he be with me? We didn't have any classes scheduled that day."

"He claims the two of you were being, how shall I say, intimate at the time."

Her demeanor changed to indignation. "Intimate? You mean like having sex?"

"Yes."

She threw her head back and laughed wildly. "That's unbelievable," she said. "I was a happily married woman until that creep took my husband from me. I certainly didn't go around having sex with other men."

Pete shrugged. "That's what he claims."

"He claims he knows everything about meditation, too, but he doesn't know anything."

"One last question, Mrs. Edinger. What possible motive would Spencer Dahl have to kill your husband?"

"You don't get it do you? He was after my money. He must have thought that without my husband around to protect me, it would be easier for him."

"Okay."

As he was walking to the door, Lorraine said, "I've been sitting here thinking your name sounded familiar. Did you know Barbara Rodes?"

"The accountant? Yes, I knew her."

"I thought so. You have a reputation for misrepresenting yourself to get information from people, Mr. Thorsen. You told Barbara Rodes that you were the attorney for some woman's estate, but we all learned after Barbara was murdered that wasn't true."

"Who told you that?"

"Barbara was the Edinger family accountant, too. Barbara and I got to be friends."

"I see."

"Barbara's brother also told me there's a lawsuit against you for unethical behavior."

"That's not true. There's no lawsuit against me."

She jabbed a long, purple-coated fingernail at him. "He said there's a lawsuit in the Michigan Supreme Court to take away your law license."

"It's not a lawsuit. It's a bogus complaint filed by Barbara's brother."

She smirked in a way that would make Spencer Dahl proud. "You can't go around lying to people, Mr. Thorsen. When you came here, you wanted me to think you were from the sheriff's office so I'd talk to you, didn't you? Then you changed your story and said you're helping investigate my husband's murder. You threatened me with one of those subpoenas if I didn't talk to you. I'm going to call Jeffery Rodes and tell him about today and ask what I can do to help with his case. People like you shouldn't be allowed to go around deceiving other people to get what they want."

As Pete drove away from the Edinger house, he wondered if he'd put his foot in it again.

TWENTY-THREE

Pete was thinking about his meeting with Lorraine Edinger and considering other ways to check on whether the rumor about Thomas Edinger's past was true when his office telephone rang.

"Dad, I've been trying to call you all day. I left three messages for you."

"Sorry, Sweetie. I've been out of the office."

"Don't you carry your cell phone when you go out?"

"Not today, I'm afraid. I forgot it."

There was silence at the other end of the call that Pete could only interpret as speechlessness. "How could you forget, Dad?" Julie finally said. "How can you stay in touch with your friends and everything if you don't have your cell phone with you?"

Pete thought about giving her his usual response about being wired differently than she was, but decided to save his energy. He'd just have to give the same explanation the next time she tried to reach him and he didn't have his cell phone with him.

"Generational differences, Sweetie. Anything important in your messages?"

"Well, *yeah*. I think I've worked out a solution to our disagreement."

"What disagreement is that?" he asked.

"Earth to Dad. Earth to Dad. I mean our disagreement about Remy staying in my room when he comes to visit."

"Oh," Pete said, "what's the solution you've worked out?"

"Well—and you're going to be so proud of me—there's a room on the floor below me that isn't occupied and won't be occupied until January. I talked to a woman in the housing department and she said Remy can stay in that room as long as he goes through the application procedure and we vouch for him."

Pete wasn't born yesterday and knew all about co-ed dorms on college campuses, and while prep schools probably were stricter, he also understood the ingenuity of teenagers. But having Remy in a separate room on a different floor was at least better than what she was proposing when the subject first came up.

"What do we have to do? Verify that we know Remy?"

"It's a little more complicated than that, Dad. We have to put up a damage deposit and pay the room charge for a month. Oh, and pay a prorated portion of the meal plan charge. He'll have to eat, you know."

"Remy would pay those charges, right?"

Her tone changed from ebullience to sheepishness. "He might need some help."

"Help?"

Julie hesitated and then said, "He doesn't have any money."

"No money."

"Dad, everyone knows that artists don't make money until they're like fifty years old or something."

"Can't his parents pay the charges?"

"They're poor. Besides, they're already paying for his plane ticket."

"I see. So you want me to pay, is that what you're saying?"

"Not you personally. My trust."

In Julie's eyes, the trust established by her mother, his late wife Doris, had limitless resources. The reality was that it had very modest funds and he'd been quietly paying over half of Julie's school and personal expenses from his own pocket.

"The trust is short on liquid funds right now, Sweetie. I don't think it can handle any additional expenses without cashing in some investments."

"I knew it!" Julie exploded. "I just knew you'd find some excuse to keep Remy and me apart! He's coming and he's staying in my room!"

If cell phones had cradles, the crack could have been heard all the way on the West Coast. He sighed. After the mess with Spencer Dahl was resolved, he needed to have a good long chat with Rona about how to handle a teenage daughter who was exploding with hormones.

His thoughts shifted back to Thomas Edinger. He'd already tried the one person who was closest to him, his wife, and had come up blank as far as information about his past was concerned. He also knew that if there was something in Edinger's past, he wasn't going to find it on a website or from some other public source. It was going to come from someone who knew Edinger. The tricky part was finding that person and getting him or her to talk to him.

The plus side was he knew where Edinger had worked at various times in his career because it was on his website. Pete just didn't know who to call to ask about him. He also didn't know where the incident had occurred, assuming the rumor were true, or if the incident was job-related.

Edinger had spent the most time at Ridge College where he was a professor in the history department before he left and became a best-selling author. He searched the college website and found all of the information about the school he could. He wrote down the names of the current college president and the chair of its history department. Realistically, he didn't expect to get anything from them, but decided to call them in the morning anyway. If he struck out, as he anticipated, he could always do more checking at the school or go back further in Edinger's career.

He locked up for the night. Most of the businesses at this time of the year closed at 5:00 p.m., but the pizza place two blocks down the street was still open and he picked up a carryout cheese pizza. Driving home, the smell from the back seat tantalized him. He resisted pulling over and wolfing down a piece.

His telephone was ringing when he walked into his cottage. He was torn between answering the call and ignoring it and getting to the more serious business of eating. He checked Caller ID and saw that it was an unknown number. He picked up the receiver with the intention of immediately hitting the "End Call" button, thinking it was probably a telemarketing call.

Before he could do that, a female voice said, "Pete?"

"Yes?"

"Hi, it's Carla."

He was surprised. After their conversation the other night, he didn't expect to hear from her again.

"Well hi," he said.

There was a pause at the other end of the line, then, "I probably wasn't as friendly as I could have been the night you called. I was in a bad mood and didn't want to talk to anyone."

Pete scrambled to think of something to say. All he could come up with was, "No problem, as the kids like to say. We've all been there."

"No, no, I was wrong. I should have been more civil."

He wanted to explain his role in the Spencer Dahl situation, which is what he was convinced was on her mind the night he called, but thought better of it. Instead he said, "No need for apologies. I was hoping you were calling to say you'd be happy to have dinner with me."

"Girls aren't supposed to be so forward."

"Oh spare me! These days?"

Carla laughed. "I'll tell you what. How would you like to have dinner tomorrow night at my house with my daughter and me?"

"Depends on the menu. I'll only come if we have mac and cheese."

She laughed again. "It's in the same family. I cook this pasta dish that will knock your socks off. I've trained Jennifer to eat real food, not the garbage they have on the children's menu at restaurants."

"Sounds wonderful. Can I bring anything?"

"A drinkable Chianti would be nice. And bring along a couple of your favorite CDs. I want to hear what you listen to at 3:00 a.m. when you entertain the neighbors."

"Who told you about that?" he asked sheepishly, thinking back to the night a couple of years earlier when he'd played music loudly in the wee hours of the morning after he'd had too much to drink and his neighbor, Charlie Cox, came over to complain. Charlie had been cool to him ever since.

"I told you, I know a lot about you," she teased.

When Pete was off the telephone with Carla, his pizza was stone cold. He tore off a couple of slices and zapped them in the microwave. As he washed down the pizza with a bottle of spring water, he thought about some of the embarrassing things he'd done in his life. The incident involving Charlie Cox ranked right up near the top.

He shook his head and looked across the room at his wine rack, but opened up another bottle of spring water instead. He had to be at the top of his game for dinner the following night.

TWENTY-FOUR

Pete walked into *The Northern Sentinel's* offices and greeted Harry, then said, "You're in early."

"Busy."

"What's your slant going to be on the Edinger case in your next edition?"

"See for yourself." Harry pushed a yellow legal pad across his desk.

The pad showed "Edinger Killer Arrested" at the top and below it several variations of that headline.

"Richter could have written that," Pete said. "It sounds like Dahl has already been convicted. I assume your story is at least going to mention the chinks in Richter's case—no murder weapon, no eyewitness placing Dahl at the scene of the crime, his contention he has an alibi for the time of the shooting."

"You sound like a mouthpiece for the defense team."

"I am part of the defense team whether I like it or not, remember? But my point is, I believe you owe it to your readers to put out a fair and balanced story."

"That's what I intend to do," Harry said defensively.

"It doesn't sound that way from your headline. It sounds like the jury has already decided."

"What do you suggest, then, genius?"

"I don't know, something like, "Man Arrested for Edinger Slaying.""

Harry thought for a moment, then said, "That's actually not bad, but Richter probably wouldn't like it. I'm sure he'd prefer something more conclusive."

"You'll have to decide whether you want to be a journalist or a shill for the local sheriff."

"That's insulting," Harry said, bristling. "I'm not a shill for anyone, but I also don't want the sheriff upset with me. In a small town like this, if Richter thinks I'm against him, I won't get a thing out of his office in the future."

Pete shrugged. "You have a problem, then. Rona won't be too happy with you either if your story makes it sound like Spencer Dahl is dead meat."

Harry appeared to think about that and after a few moments said, "Good point. Maybe I'll go with your alternative headline."

"It's factually accurate—Spencer Dahl has been arrested—and it leaves open the question of his guilt or innocence."

"Let me think about it. I've got two days before we go to press."

"Shifting gears," Pete said, "now that Dahl has been arraigned, has Richter cleared the other suspects?"

"Not officially from what I've heard. The only person he's commented on publicly is Wally Helwig. He said at his news conference that he didn't see any charges being brought against Helwig because Wally and the other festival organizers took all the precautions they could reasonably be expected to take in the circumstances."

"He finally got something right," Pete said.

Harry looked at him and shook his head.

"The fact Richter hasn't cleared the other suspects suggests that he might not be sure of his case against Dahl, doesn't it?"

"Not according to Richter," Harry said.

"How did he handle the evidence they found at Dahl's place."

"He was doing everything he could to contain his glee when he told us about the smoothbore equipment they found in the post and the remnants of the burned Confederate uniform they retrieved from Spencer's outdoor fireplace."

"How about the marijuana?"

"That was almost an afterthought."

"Did the question of Spencer's alibi come up?"

"Richter said they have a credible witness who disputes the alibi."

"Credible? Lorraine Edinger?"

"That's what he said. He didn't mention Spencer's claim that he was having sex with Lorraine at the time Thomas Edinger was shot."

"That was big of him."

"There are reputations to think about. Lorraine Edinger is a sympathetic figure now, being the widow and all."

"One of them is lying, Harry, either Spencer or Lorraine Edinger."

Harry furled his brow and nodded a couple of times.

"You ought to consider doing what I suggested a minute ago and at least mention the holes in the prosecution's case. That's the role of the press in a free society."

"I know what our role is," Harry said, "but I don't want to get into that again. I said I'd consider your points and I will."

"Okay," Pete said, sighing.

Harry looked at Pete with narrowed eyes and said, "You're sounding more and more like you think Spencer didn't do it."

"As I told you that day on the river, the case against him is a little too pat."

"I remember you saying that," Harry said.

"Anyway, the reason I stopped in was to check on whether you still carry me as a contributing editor of your paper."

"Sure," Harry replied, "you haven't contributed anything for about seven years, but I still show your name and title. Don't you ever read my paper?"

"I do, but I usually don't pay attention to that box."

"Unless you have something to gain."

Pete grinned. "Unless I have something to gain."

He squinted at Pete over his glasses again and said, "Why do I have a feeling that you intend to masquerade as one of my reporters again?"

Pete explained that the line from Dahl's poem implying that Thomas Edinger had some baggage from the past stuck in his mind and that he'd promised Ira Manning to try to get to the bottom of it. He went on to say that he planned to approach the president and others at Ridge College to see what he could find out."

"Why don't you just ask Spencer?"

"I did. Twice."

"He must know what it's about if he referred to it in that poem."

"He says he doesn't. He says it was something he picked up from Lorraine and he was just trying to use it against Edinger. Getting a straight answer from that jerk will drive you nuts. Especially when he thinks he now has one of the top criminal lawyers in the country representing him and views me as excess baggage."

"Is that why you stormed out of the courtroom?"

"You're so perceptive it's almost criminal."

"No need for sarcasm. And just so you know, Rona really appreciates what you've been doing for Spencer. She knows you don't like him."

"Mmm," Pete murmured.

"Do you think the people at Ridge College will talk to you?"

"Probably not if I approach them as Pete Thorsen the lawyer. Maybe yes if I approach them as Pete Thorsen the freelance journalist who's going to publish stories that will extoll the virtues of their college."

Harry studied him again. "This case has your juices flowing, doesn't it?"

"I'm just trying to live up to a promise I made to your woman."

"Bull," Harry said. "Course if it helps Spencer . . ."

"Between you and me, I'd just as soon see Spencer rot in jail. But unlike some people I know, I happen to believe even scum is entitled to a fair trial and that requires ferreting out all of the facts. Plus, I've got Ira Manning to consider."

Harry snorted. "Some warrior for justice you are, referring to your client as scum."

"Only in the privacy of your office."

"Well, don't do anything that reflects badly on my paper. The last time you masqueraded as one of my reporters, you got a man killed."

"I didn't get anyone killed, Harry. I just happened to get caught in the middle of something and almost got myself killed."

A concerned expression crept over Harry's face. "You be careful, okay? I can't afford to lose my number one fly fishing buddy."

"By the way, have you talked to Carla again recently?"

"Yesterday as a matter of fact. She said she was calling about the ads again, but I think what she really wanted was to pump me about the rumor that some big gun from Chicago had taken over representation of Spencer Dahl. I confirmed the rumor and didn't say anything about your continued involvement. She sounded happy at the end of our conversation."

Pete left and headed for The Bookstore to pick up the copies of Thomas Edinger's books he'd had the store order for him. He shook his head as he thought about the way Carla seemed to be monitoring every move in the Edinger murder case. For the moment, at least, he apparently was back in her good graces, but he knew he had to be careful. He was on his way back to his office when he heard an angry voice.

"Hey Thorsen! I've been waiting for you to apologize!"

Pete looked up the street and saw Calvin Seitz standing on the sidewalk in front of the hardware store glaring at him. He held a three-pronged garden implement with the tag still affixed in one hand and a plastic bag in the other. His frizzy red hair and unkempt beard looked even wilder than it did the day Pete ran into him in the woods on Edinger's property.

"Hi, Calvin, nice to see you again."

"Don't give me none of your flowery talk. I know you sicced the sheriff on me."

"I don't know what you mean," Pete said, scrambling for a way to deflect the ire of the madman walking his way.

"I don't know what you mean," Seitz repeated sarcastically, spitting on the sidewalk. "I ought to bury this here implement in your chest."

Pete decided that his best course was to come semi-clean. "Look, Calvin, I ran into Joe Tessler, who's a detective with the sheriff's department, and told him that I'd met you at the reenactment site. I suggested that they might want to rethink their analysis of the Edinger case because you demonstrated that smoothbore weapons are more accurate than most people assume."

"You phony! This Tessler guy came out to my cabin and questioned me for two hours. He weren't looking for no demonstration of smoothbore accuracy. He was eyeballing me as a suspect in the shooting. I told him that Edinger deserved to die, but I wasn't the one who had the pleasure of doing him in."

"I'm sorry, Calvin. I had no idea—"

"They got the real killer in jail now and you owe me an apology, buster."

"I'm sorry if what I told Tessler caused you any problems."

Seitz snorted. "If I was you, Thorsen, I wouldn't go roaming around the woods no more. Some squirrel hunter's aim might be a little off and a lead ball might find its way into your sad carcass."

Seitz turned and stalked down to where his claptrap pickup was parked and got in. The truck sputtered to life and emitted a cloud of gray smoke from its tailpipe, then clattered off down the street. Pete shook his head and resumed walking to his office.

He flipped through Edinger's books. The novels looked like quick reads, but the first academic tome was going to be more of a challenge; it had seventy-two pages of end notes.

Then he began to work the phone. His first call to Ridge College was eventually passed along to its public affairs office. He explained who he was for the fifth time and said he was doing a feature on Dr. Thomas Edinger, a prominent former member of the college's faculty who'd been tragically shot at a reenactment of the Battle of Missionary Ridge. He said he expected the story to be picked up by the national media because Edinger had such a high profile.

The public affairs woman was giddy over the prospect of the publicity her college would receive from the article and offered to provide all of the information he needed. He thanked her and said he was coming to Ridge College in the next day or two to develop material for his feature. Before he was off the phone with her, he persuaded her to give him the direct phone numbers and e-mail addresses for the college's president and the chair of its history department.

He waited an hour and then dialed the number for Dr. Edmond Stephens, President of Ridge College, and got some administrative person. He explained that he was working through the public affairs office, but wanted to check and see if Dr. Stephens would be available to meet with him briefly and provide a few quotes he could use in his stories. He was put on hold for five minutes and finally patched through to Dr. Stephens who confirmed that he would be on campus all week and Pete should call when he arrived. He repeated the drill with Professor Dawn Austin, chair of the history department, and got a similar response.

Pete had one more stop to make before he went home, cleaned up, and headed for Cadillac for dinner with Carla Neville and her daughter, Jennifer. Jake's Outdoors was void of customers when he walked in, and Rossum was moving boxes of ammunition around and dusting a shelf. He looked toward the door when the chime sounded and said, "Hi, Pete."

"Housecleaning time?"

Rossum grunted. "Dust seems to settle in no matter how tight the building is. I had new windows installed two years ago but they don't seem to make much difference."

"You have a lot of stuff in here."

"I wish more of it would walk out the door with paying customers, but with the economy . . . Say, I'm sorry about my mother the other night."

"No apology necessary," he said, thinking of his father who was in a facility in southwestern Wisconsin with advanced Alzheimer's. "Is this a good time for that tutorial on smoothbores?"

"Good as any. As I explained, though, I'm not an expert on those weapons so you'll have to take what I say as generalizations."

"All I need to know is the basics so I can pass on the information to Ira Manning."

"Is this part of your defense?"

"I don't know how Ira plans to use the information. He's like me, though. Amass all of the information you can and decide later what to use or not use."

"Makes sense," Rossum said. He walked over to a display case, unlocked it, and took out a single-barrel twelve-gauge shotgun. "You'll see in a minute why I picked a twelve-gauge. Do you know the difference between a shotgun and, say, that thirty-thirty over there?" He pointed to a classic Winchester lever-action rifle in another glass case.

"The shotgun has a smooth inner barrel whereas the Winchester has grooves inside."

"Right. A gun with grooves is far more accurate which is why firearm technology moved that way in the nineteenth century. I don't have a smoothbore or any loads for them so I'm going to simulate how they work by making up some equipment."

"Fixings, right?" Pete asked, grinning.

Rossum nodded and pried out the slug from a twenty-gauge shotgun shell. "A smoothbore load might have a different shape than this," he said, "but this ball will illustrate the technology if I can use that term for these weapons." He then found a piece of cloth and cut two pieces from it.

"I don't have any black powder, but if I did, I'd put some in the barrel like this." He pretended to pour powder down the barrel of the twelve-gauge. "Most people who use these weapons put a hard card wad down next. The final step is to place a cushion patch around the lead ball and slide it down the barrel." He illustrated again by sliding the patch and lead slug down the barrel of the twelve-gauge. "My make-shift load is loose, but if it were a real load, it would fit snuggly down the barrel. Until percussion caps became common, the powder was ignited by the gun's flintlock and the explosion propelled the shot from the barrel."

"I'd be afraid to load one of these things," Pete said. "The whole thing would probably blow up in my face."

Rossum shrugged. "Hundreds of thousands — maybe millions — of musket balls were fired with these weapons."

"Why would someone use a smoothbore when modern rifles and shotguns are far more accurate?"

Rossum shrugged again. "Tradition, maybe, or possibly they want to feel like they're in touch with their ancestors. Your friend Seitz is an example."

Pete nodded.

"And of course with the reenactors, authenticity is everything. As I'm sure Harry told you, that's why a lot of them carried smoothbores."

Pete nodded. "And I understand that among the things the sheriff found at Dahl's place was the paraphernalia necessary for a smoothbore."

"That's what I heard, too."

Driving back to his cottage, Pete felt he was now better equipped to explain smoothbores to Ira Manning. It was one thing to read about the weapons on the Internet; it was another to see an actual demonstration. He grinned when he thought about how similar smoothbore aficionados were to someone like himself who preferred a classic longbow to the modern compound bows that now dominated the market. There was one critical difference, however: The choice of a smoothbore in the Thomas Edinger shooting was likely motivated by something more nefarious than tradition.

TWENTY-FIVE

When Pete got home, he searched his music collection for just the right numbers to take along to dinner. Carla obviously enjoyed bluegrass, but he knew little about her other musical tastes except for what Harry had told him. Most of his CDs were compilations of the greatest hits of prominent artists. In a few minutes, he had CDs spread out before him by Johnny Cash, Dusty Springfield, Moody Blues, Roy Orbison, Aretha Franklin, Tammy Wynette, Otis Redding, and Linda Ronstadt.

He stared at the discs and tried to make his selection. He resisted the temptation to select Johnny Cash, probably his personal favorite, and picked Roy Orbison instead. Balance might be nice for his second choice. A female artist. He examined the Linda Ronstadt label but thought about bluegrass again and put Ronstadt down and picked up a Tammy Wynette CD. If Harry knew what he was talking about, Carla was fond of the vocalist who helped define the role of women in country music during the 1970s. He decided he couldn't go wrong with Roy Orbison and Tammy Wynette.

He headed for the shower, and when he was out, he thought about what he'd worn to the first dinner with Carla and selected a sky blue shirt that gave him a different look. Then he checked his wine rack and didn't see a single bottle of Chianti. Plenty of Pinot Noirs and a range of whites, but no Chianti. The grocery store in town carried a lot of wine, but usually nothing memorable and he wanted to make a favorable impression. He looked at his watch; he had time to detour through Traverse City and visit his favorite wine shop there.

When he arrived in Cadillac, he drove through the streets for fifteen minutes to kill time and knocked on Carla's door exactly at the appointed hour of 6:00 p.m. with a bottle of Chianti Classico in one hand and the two CDs in the other, feeling like a teenage boy on his first date. Carla opened the door with Jennifer clinging shyly to one of her legs. It looked like Carla had fussed over her outfit, too. She wore stylish black pants topped by a green sweater that accented her eyes and had subtle silver threads running through it that picked up the light. Jennifer wore a pink tee, apparently her trademark color, with bears romping playfully across the front.

"Right on time," Carla said.

Pete grinned. "Hungry," he said. He inhaled the aroma coming from the kitchen. "Smells wonderful. What's this knockout dish you tantalized me with?"

"Surprise." She took the wine bottle from him and examined the label. "Mmm, perfect."

Pete laid the CDs on an end table. Carla looked at them. "My, my. One boy and one girl. Someone trained you well."

"Random choice," he replied casually.

Carla's house was small but immaculate. Pete could see the streaks across the carpet from the vacuum cleaner, and the pillows on the couches were arranged precisely. They sat in the living room on facing loveseats with Jennifer snuggled close to her mother.

"So who's the client that made you so familiar with Cadillac?"

"Former client," Pete said. "He's dead." Pete didn't want to put a damper on the evening by telling her how the Colonel passed on, but did tell her the name of his company.

"That was your client? I've driven past their plant lots of times. Real modern building?"

He nodded.

Jennifer had been listening to the conversation and watching Pete intently. Then she blurted out, "Do you like my Mom?"

Color rose in Carla's cheeks and Pete smiled at the comment and Carla's discomfort. "I sure do, Jennifer. Everyone likes your mom. I'll bet you like her, too."

"Yeah," she said, looking up at her mother fondly and snuggling even closer.

"Are you going to ski again this year?" Pete asked Jennifer.

"There's no snow."

"But when there is snow."

Jennifer looked up at her mother again and asked, "Mom, am I going to ski?"

"You sure are."

"Mom says yes," Jennifer said, just in case Pete hadn't heard. She looked at him quizzically. "Do you have any kids?"

"One, a daughter."

"Why didn't you bring her with you so I'd have someone to play with?"

"She's away at school."

She considered that for a moment, then said, "Why did you send her away?"

Pete was becoming uncomfortable with the probing questions of a six-year-old. "I didn't send her away," he said. "She's seventeen and attends boarding school. The school's a long way from here."

"I have to finish up a few things so we can eat," Carla said. "Jennifer, why don't you show Mr. Thorsen your room?"

Jennifer jumped off the couch and grabbed Pete's hand and led him toward her bedroom. On the way, she said, "Mom made me pick up my stuff before you came. She said she didn't want you to think that two pigs lived here."

Pete shot a grin at Carla over his shoulder and saw her roll her eyes and shake her head.

By the time they finished the bedroom tour, Carla had set the small table in the dining alcove and was bringing out the food. Pete went into the kitchen to open the wine, and when he came out, Jennifer was arranging place cards written in a first-grader's hand with herself in the middle and Pete and Carla on either side. Carla had put on the Roy Orbison CD with the sound turned down low.

Dinner was chicken parmigiana over linguini, French bread, and a tossed salad. Eat your heart out, Harry, Pete thought as he loaded up his plate. They exchanged small talk while they ate. Pete was eying another piece of chicken when Jennifer said, "When are we going to have dessert, Mom?"

"Wait until everyone finishes eating, Honey."

Jennifer waited impatiently until Carla brought out the Tiramisu. "I have to confess that I didn't make this," Carla said. "I picked it up in this shop I go to in Traverse City."

"An honest woman. And a terrific cook. That was great."

"Worth the drive to a geographically undesirable household?" she asked impishly.

"For the tenth time, that was Harry's term, not mine."

Carla just smiled.

Pete helped Carla clean up the kitchen before she bundled Jennifer off to bed. Jennifer insisted on giving him a kiss before she said goodnight.

"I think you've won her over," Carla said when she came back.

"Cute girl," Pete said. "Don't forget, I have the advantage of having gone through this once," thinking of Julie.

Carla started the Roy Orbison CD over and turned up the volume slightly. "You probably didn't think I knew who Roy Orbison was, right?"

"I thought you might know who he was, but I'll bet you don't know as much about him as I do."

"Oh yeah?" she said. "Let's have a contest to see who knows most. You go first — ask me something about Roy Orbison. Anything."

"Okay," Pete said, thinking for a moment. "What's the title of Roy's new CD that came out in June of this year?"

"That's almost insulting. Roy Orbison died in 1988. Okay, my turn. Where did he die?"

"Madison, Tennessee."

"Hmm, not bad. You must have studied up before you came."

"My turn?" he asked.

She nodded.

"What was Roy's nickname?"

"The Big O," she answered. "Okay, let's name some of the songs he made famous. And you can't use 'Blue Bayou,' 'Only the Lonely,' 'Bye Bye, Love,' or 'Crying.' Everyone knows those."

They continued to play the game until neither could name any more songs. Then they listened to the Tammy Wynette CD.

Carla got the wine bottle and moved to the loveseat next to Pete and tried to add some wine to his glass. He put his hand over the top and said, "I have to drive home on that speed trap, Route 115, and get up early tomorrow morning to catch a plane."

She raised her eyebrows. "Any place exciting?"

"No, just business," he replied, realizing he was at a delicate moment. He was determined to stay away from any reference to Spencer Dahl and said, "The separation agreement with my old law firm requires me to do things on occasion."

"Sounds like the agreement I signed when I left the think tank."

"What do they require you to do?"

Carla got a brooding look on her face and said, "I'd tell you, but then I'd have to kill you. I don't want to have a body lying around and traumatize my daughter."

They both laughed. "Fair enough," Pete said. "We'll each keep our dark secrets to ourselves."

Carla looked at him impishly and said, "Are you sure I can't give you a teeny, weenie final sip of wine?"

"Okay, but make it a small sip."

She leaned against him and poured a splash of wine in his glass. She looked at him with bedroom eyes and he kissed her on the lips. "Umm," he said, "too bad that bottle is empty."

"Do you need wine to kiss a woman?"

He didn't reply, but put his free arm around her shoulders and drew her close and kissed her again, longer this time, the hunger coming out and his passion growing.

"Why are you kissing my Mom?"

The small voice startled him and he looked up and saw Jennifer standing in the living room doorway watching them. He scrambled for words and said, "To thank her for dinner, Jennifer. Don't you kiss your mother after she cooks you a good dinner?"

"Sometimes."

Carla regained her composure and said, "You should be in bed, Angel."

"I'm waiting for you."

Pete and Carla looked at each other and tried to suppress their smiles. Pete said, "I've got to be on my way, anyhow. I have a long drive home."

They saw Pete out, and as Jennifer clung to her leg, Carla squeezed Pete's hand and gave him a peck on his cheek. "I'll call you when I get back," he promised.

TWENTY-SIX

By the time he got off the plane at Chattanooga Metropolitan Airport, Pete felt like the poster boy for airline transfers. He was the lone patron at the rental car counter, and after signing more paperwork than it took to close one of his corporate deals, he programmed the navigation system in his rental Ford Explorer and drove to his hotel.

He checked in, took a shower, and changed clothes. Then he hiked to a steak house named Hennen's for dinner. According to the desk clerk, Hennen's was "just around the corner." It turned out to be around the corner and six blocks down, but he didn't mind the walk after his day in airports and sitting in airplane seats designed for passengers with a maximum height of five feet six inches and weight of under a hundred and twenty pounds.

He'd come up with Hennen's by perusing his Chattanooga guidebook, and judging from the crowd, he'd stumbled on *the* place to dine in the city. He had bang shrimp to start, a meal in itself, and then the stuffed flounder for his main course.

His mind drifted back to the previous night and the marvelous time he'd had. It made him feel like he had a life again. He knew it all would have exploded, though, if he'd told Carla what he was really planning to do on his "business trip." He felt bad about deceiving her, but knew he had to walk a tightrope until the situation with Spencer Dahl was resolved.

As he ate, he planned his visit and made notes. He knew he had to go through the charade with the Ridge College public affairs person or he'd never have a chance to meet the college president or the chair of its history department. He resigned himself to sitting through a couple of hours of spin with the public affairs lady whose sole job was to put the college's best foot forward.

Walking back to his hotel, he felt a surge of excitement that he knew came from being off the sidelines and back in the arena. He'd never bared his feelings with anyone, not even close friends like Harry and Angie DeMarco, although they seemed to suspect what was driving him. The fact was he *needed* to put himself on the line occasionally.

Ridge College was nestled in a wooded area along the Tennessee River. The leaves were just beginning to turn, adding a touch of color to the pastoral scene. The college's old brick buildings, many with white Doric columns, gave it the appearance of the quintessential established liberal arts school. Cars were banned from campus, and as he walked across the quad toward the administration building, he saw students crisscrossing the area on the way to their next classes. Their attire was hardly formal, but it wasn't grunge either. It reminded him of the dress when he was in college.

Pete climbed the stairs to the second floor of North Hall for his meeting with Amy Colbert, the public affairs person. It was another case where he was going to have to use half-truths to get what he wanted. He'd been lectured by both Angie DeMarco and Harry McTigue for doing that—it was the core of his problem with the ethics investigation, after all—but he saw nothing wrong with it. It was just a trick-of-the-trade he'd picked up from his old boss in the CID, Major Baumann. The major often used a similar technique to get the information he needed. No one was hurt and it usually worked out for the best all around. Pete knew he couldn't be so blatant in framing his defense to the ethics complaint, but that was the truth no matter how Jeffrey Rodes tried to make it look sinister and unprofessional.

Amy Colbert's office was at the far end of the corridor in a complex of offices that housed many of the administrative personnel. The woman who served as the common receptionist informed Ms. Colbert that he had arrived, and less than a minute later, a scrubbed-looking young woman who didn't seem much different from the coeds he'd seen on the quad bolted from her office and rushed to greet him.

"Mr. Thorsen," she said, "I'm so pleased to meet you."

"Please, call me Pete. Good of you to make time for me."

She took him to her small office, which elevated neatness to new heights, and after the social preliminaries, they got down to the task at hand. Pete again explained what he was doing and that his interest in Thomas Edinger stemmed from the fact the late professor was the foremost authority on Colonel Thaddeus Clayton who was from Pete's part of Michigan. He also explained that he was with a small newspaper in that area, but that he expected his story or stories—he wasn't exactly sure of the format yet—to be picked up by the national media because Thomas Edinger was such a high profile person.

"When I heard the news, I couldn't believe what happened," Ms. Colbert said, looking horrified. "The whole campus is in mourning."

Pete nodded. "I was at the festival when it happened. They were reenacting part of the Battle of Missionary Ridge that took place right here in your city."

"It's part of our history," she said sorrowfully. She moved a bulging manila folder to the center of her desk and said, "I've compiled all of

the material on Professor Edinger I think you'll need for your stories."
She began to withdraw the papers.

For the next hour, Amy Colbert took him through the materials.
There were summaries of Edinger's early life and his years as a professor at Ridge College and reviews and other materials on each of his
books. Pete had seen most of that material when he browsed the Internet, but nevertheless listened attentively.

"You've been busy," he said when she finished.

"Professor Edinger was one of our most prominent alumni," she
said. "Not in the sense he graduated from here, but I think you know
what I mean."

Pete nodded. "Did you know him personally?"

"Oh no, I only graduated from the University of Tennessee at Chattanooga three years ago. The professor was gone by the time I got here."

"Mmm," he murmured. "How about Dr. Stephens and Professor
Austin? Did they know him personally?"

"I'm sure they did." Suddenly she got a worried look on her face. "You
don't have to talk to them, too, do you?"

"I'd like to."

"They're both very busy. That's why I took the time to put together
all of these materials. So you'd have everything you need."

"I checked with them before I came down," Pete said. "They both
told me they were going to be on campus this week and would be happy
to see me."

"They did?"

Pete nodded again. "I want to get quotes from senior people here at
the college to add depth and texture to my stories."

Amy seemed to process what he said. "I could have them write out
some quotes and e-mail them to you," she said hopefully.

"Not the same. The best quotes are those that flow from a conversation. It's like candid shots with a camera. Dr. Stephens is in this building, isn't he?"

"Yes, but without an appointment . . ."

"Why don't you check with him? He knows I was coming, as I said. All I need is ten or fifteen minutes of his time."

"Is this really necessary?" Amy pleaded. "Dr. Stephens depends on me to handle these things."

"Well, if I can't talk to Dr. Stephens, I'll just have to state in my stories that college officials declined to talk to me about Professor Edinger."

"Would you really do that?"

Pete acted nonchalant and shrugged and said, "I'd have no choice." He continued to look at her.

"I'll see if Dr. Stephens is available," she said with an air of resignation. She got up from her desk and disappeared down the hall. She returned ten minutes later.

"Dr. Stephens said he can see you for a short time. He has an important meeting with the people from *U.S. News & World Report* in an hour and has to finish preparing. The rankings that magazine puts out are so important to colleges you know."

Amy led Pete down the hall to a suite of offices with "President" in brass letters on an adjacent wall. A dour looking woman, obviously the gatekeeper for the college president, occupied a neat desk in the outer office. "Wait here," she commanded after she gave Pete the once-over. "I'll see if Dr. Stephens is ready for you."

She disappeared through a polished wood door into the inner sanctum and a minute later reappeared and beckoned to Pete. She held the door for him and then closed it quietly behind her.

A man maybe sixty years old who reminded Pete of pictures he'd seen of the famous poet T. S. Elliott—thinning hair combed straight back, wire-rim glasses, a dark three-piece suit, even a watch fob—came around to meet him. His formal appearance seemed to fit the décor of his dark paneled office.

"Mr. Thorsen," he said, grasping Pete's hand warmly. "Welcome to Ridge College. Did Amy take good care of you?"

"She did," Pete said. "A talented young lady."

Dr. Stephens smiled appreciatively. "She's the face of our college in so many ways. We were fortunate to attract her. I understand you'd like a couple of quotes for your story about Professor Edinger. Tragic situation, really, tragic. I'm afraid I don't have a lot of time, though."

"I'll get right to the point then. Did you know Professor Edinger well?"

"No, I'm sad to say. I took over my job here about the time he was leaving the college. Professor Edinger did launch a couple of his books here, though. I got to know him that way. A wonderful scholar. He contributed greatly to our understanding of the Civil War."

"I understand that's what Ridge College is noted for."

"Yes, history is our largest department and over half of the professors in that department specialize in the Civil War period. Our biggest challenge is keeping our faculty. The Ivy League schools are always trying to pick them off because of their reputations."

"That's a problem a lot of colleges and universities have these days."

"It is," Dr. Stephens said sadly.

"Getting back to Professor Edinger, to your knowledge, did he have any detractors? My stories are going to be positive, but I was just wondering for my own background."

Dr. Stephens smiled wisely. "Who among us doesn't have detractors? I understand you were a lawyer before you turned to journalism, Mr. Thorsen. Law firms and college faculties are a lot alike. Herding cats is an expression that's commonly used. When people are competitive, you can always find someone who's critical of someone else."

"What kind of criticism was levied against Professor Edinger?"

"I can only speak to my personal experience."

"That's what I'm asking for."

"Historians, including those who specialize in the Civil War period, are divided between scholars who view events primarily through the prism of military action and those whose focus is broader and centers on social and economic issues. The latter often look down their noses at the military-oriented people. Professor Edinger's focus was on the military side."

"I see. So any sniping at Professor Edinger was purely professional. Nothing personal or ethical."

"Heavens no, not that I've heard anyway."

As the conversation dragged on, it became clear that Dr. Stephens wasn't going to be much help providing Pete with what he wanted. He politely took down a couple of contrived quotes about Edinger. Dr. Stephens then looked at his watch, apologized for his tight schedule that morning, and ushered Pete out.

Pete walked back to Amy Colbert's office and found her sitting upright behind her desk with a worried expression on her face. When she saw him walk in, she asked nervously, "Did you get your quotes?"

"A couple of good ones, actually. Dr. Stephens is a very engaging man."

"Then you got along okay?"

"Very well. He's an impressive fellow and obviously a true intellect."

Amy appeared to relax a bit. "Yes he is," she said. "There are rumors he's being considered for one of the senior positions at Oxford University. I certainly hope we don't lose him."

"That would be a blow," Pete agreed.

"So you have what you need to write your stories?" Amy asked hopefully.

"Mostly," Pete said. "But I'd also like to speak to speak to Professor Austin. I understand she's the chair of your history department."

Amy Colbert exhibited her anxiety again. "If you got good quotes from Dr. Stephens, do you need to talk to her, too?"

"Just to close the loop, as they say."

"Professor Austin isn't in this building."

"Tell me what building she's in and I'll walk over."

"She's in South Hall. Should I try to set up an appointment for you?"

"Not necessary. She knows I'm on campus. If she's tied up, I'll wait. I'm in no hurry."

Amy looked at him apprehensively. Pete scooped up the materials she'd prepared for him, thanked her, and walked out to locate South Hall. The weather was ten degrees warmer than it was in northern Michigan and the sky had clouded over since he arrived.

South Hall was directly across the quad from North Hall and was its clone. The antique brass plaque in the lobby said Professor Austin's office was on the third floor, and after surveying the creaky elevator, Pete opted for the stairs. He asked a student for directions to Professor Austin's office and was directed to the end of the corridor again where it seemed that all important offices were located. A senior lady with her hair done up in a bun occupied a desk that was strategically located in an open area on the way to Professor Austin's office and two others.

Pete gave his name to the lady and reminded her that he'd contacted the college and been told that Professor Austin would be available to talk to him. The woman walked to the open door at the back of the complex and said something he couldn't hear and returned to her desk. Soon a second woman, Professor Austin he assumed, came out of the office and asked if she could help him. Pete again explained who he was and said he'd just come from President Stephens' office. He said that Stephens suggested he talk to her about the late Thomas Edinger. Pete banked on the fact that Stephens was probably in his meeting with *U.S. News & World Report* and wouldn't be available to verify his story if Professor Austin called to check.

"It sounds like you have everything you need," Austin said. "I'm not sure what I can add." Her pinched face was void of makeup and her ill-fitting tweed clothes hung on her frame like a sack draped over a post. She stood looking at him with humorless gray eyes.

"That may be true," Pete said, "but even that would be useful. Corroboration if you will. Should we go somewhere where we can talk?"

"I'm working on something and have papers spread out all over my office. I'm sure this won't take long, but if you insist on sitting, I assume this will suffice." She gestured toward two wing chairs in the common area. Pete sized up the situation and decided that was the best he was going to do. The likelihood of getting something useful out of this woman seemed remote at best, particularly when they were in a public area where everyone could hear them.

After they were seated, Professor Austin crossed her legs and steepled her hands and waited for him to begin. He summarized what he'd been told before and her only response was to say, "Sounds like I remember it."

Then Pete got to the crux of what he was interested in. "Just for background, I'm wondering if there's anything in Professor Edinger's past that might embarrass him in some way. My stories are going to be positive — and God knows there's enough positive in Professor Edinger's life to fill ten stories — but for my own background, can you think of anything in his past that might diminish his reputation? No person is perfect," he said with his most disarming smile.

Professor Austin stared at him for a long time. "You must think I'm a complete fool, Mr. Thorsen. That's what this is about, isn't it? You want to besmirch the reputation of one of the most prominent former members of this college's faculty. Well, you won't get your dirt from me, sir." She stood and added, "I have to go. Have a good day." The young man standing patiently with a bundle of documents under his arm followed her into her office and one of them closed the door.

Pete had been blown off by some pretty slick characters in his life, but Professor Austin set a new record for speed and curtness. He made a show of sorting out his papers and inserting them carefully in his briefcase to give himself time to think. Either Professor Austin knew something about Thomas Edinger that he wasn't going to get out of her short of using enhanced interrogation techniques or she had identified him in her mind as a charlatan who was intent on besmirching the memory of a former colleague. Which, he couldn't be sure.

As he walked past the elderly receptionist, she looked around and seeing no one, handed him a slip of paper with a name and telephone number on it. "Call Professor Tate," she whispered and then went back to tapping on her keyboard. Pete wanted to ask her some questions about Tate, but it was clear from the woman's demeanor that she didn't want to say anything more.

When Pete reached the parking lot, he got in his rental Explorer and looked at the slip of paper. The number had a Chattanooga area code. He punched in the number on his cell phone.

TWENTY-SEVEN

"Andrew Tate," a gruff voice finally answered.

"Professor Tate, my name is Pete Thorsen. I'm a former lawyer turned journalist and I'm writing a series of articles on one of your old colleagues, Thomas Edinger." He told Tate that he'd already been to Ridge College and met with, among others, President Edmond Stephens. He said he was touring the Missionary Ridge battle area just then and asked if he could stop by and talk to him about Thomas Edinger.

"You want to talk to me about Professor Edinger?"

"Yes. You might have heard that he was killed."

"I heard. Where did you get my name?"

"A secretary or an administrative assistant in the history department gave it to me as I was leaving."

"Sounds like Millie," Tate said after a moment. "She's about the only one over there who talks to me anymore."

Pete wondered about his comment, but didn't say anything.

"What would you like to know about Thomas Edinger?" Tate asked.

"I'm looking for some background for my stories. What he was like, that sort of thing. You were in the history department the same time as he was, right?"

"Yes."

"Do you have time to talk?"

Tate paused, then said, "I think I'm going to pass."

"I caught you at a busy time, huh?"

"No, I'm not busy."

"Why won't you talk to me then?"

"I have a separation agreement with the college that bars me from talking about college personnel."

"I see. Is there some way we can work around that agreement? Thomas Edinger is dead and left Ridge College ten years ago."

"I don't think that matters. The agreement covers people who are living or dead and whether they're currently with the college or used to be with the college."

"Pretty comprehensive, huh?"

"Very."

"Let me suggest something. How about if I stop by your house? Then if we can't work something out you're comfortable with, I'll leave."

"I guess I can't argue with that."

"I'm planning to have a quick look at some of the monuments on Missionary Ridge and could come over in about an hour. Would that work?"

"Yeah, fine."

"I checked your address on the map. It looks like you live close to Missionary Ridge."

"Pretty much right on it."

Pete laughed. "I guess that shows I can still read a map."

"Are you familiar with Chattanooga?" Tate asked.

"I've never been here before, but my rental car has a navigation system."

"It's good you're coming in the daylight hours. This area can be a little rough at night."

After he got off the phone with Tate, Pete programmed the navigation system to pass by a couple of Civil War monuments on the way to his house, including the Illinois Monument at the Bragg Reservation, marking the spot where Illinois troops broke through the Confederate lines, and the Colonel E. H. Phelps Monument.

Pete was poking along enjoying the scenery when he glanced in his mirror and saw another vehicle rapidly coming up behind him. He hugged the right side of the hilly road and the vehicle swerved left to pass. As the menacing-looking black muscle car with tinted windows drew even, the driver gunned his engine several times, causing ear-shattering roars to fill the air, then shot past him and swerved into the right-hand lane again where it braked suddenly. Pete slammed on his brakes in a panic to avoid rear-ending the car and his tires squealed. The passengers, a bunch of teens it looked like, leaned out the windows and screamed at him and made obscene gestures with their hands. Then the car shot forward again with more roars of its engine and disappeared from sight.

Pete collected himself and swore under his breath. He slowed down further to put some distance between the car and himself. He remembered what Tate had said about the area being dangerous at night. Apparently it wasn't just at night because it wasn't even twilight and the crazies were out already. He watched for the car as he drove slowly up the hill. If he saw it, he was prepared to make a fast U-turn and head straight for Tate's house.

It was a nice day and he had the windows cracked a few inches. In the distance he heard *Pop! Pop! Pop!* Like a series of gunshots. He stopped and scanned the road ahead. There were no signs of the other vehicle. He proceeded again and saw something in the middle of the road as he rounded a bend. An animal of some kind. As he drew even, he saw that it was a dog. He pulled over on the shoulder and looked around. He didn't see the black car.

He got out and walked over to the dog. Blood was pooling on the pavement under its body and the dog was whimpering fitfully. He swore again, this time out loud. The idiots in that car apparently had shot the dog as they drove past. The Golden Retriever looked at him with mournful eyes. Pete knew he couldn't leave the dog in the middle of the road; it would either die of the gunshot wound or another vehicle would come along and hit it. He reached down to grab the Golden's fur and drag it to the side of the road. The dog snapped at him. He drew his hands back and after a moment began to stroke its fur. The Golden continued to whimper. After a few moments, he again tried to move the dog. It snapped at him a second time, but finally let Pete drag him to the side of the road.

Pete debated what to do. The dog was safe from vehicular traffic, but the way it was bleeding, it was a matter of time until it died. Not knowing what else to do, he called the local 911 number and explained what had happened. The operator patched him through to the Chattanooga Humane Society. Tears and hand wringing and gnashing of teeth followed when the woman who answered the phone heard what happened. Eventually, the woman said she'd have someone pick up the dog and asked if Pete would stay on the scene until the person arrived. He was already late for his appointment with Professor Tate, and nervous about hanging around on the side of the road with crazies driving around the area, but agreed. The rescue team arrived a half-hour later. Pete stroked the Golden's fur one last time before he left and saw the agony in its eyes. He wondered if the dog would survive.

Pete headed directly for Professor Tate's house. Ten minutes later, he pulled up in front of the Federal-style brick house just off Crest Road. The doorbell didn't work so Pete rapped on the door several times before Tate appeared.

"Sorry I'm late," Pete said, "but as I told you on the phone, some hoods shot a dog and I had to wait until the rescue team showed up."

Tate brushed a hand through his thinning gray hair and said, "You're lucky it wasn't you they shot. I told you this can be a rough neighborhood.

Not like it used to be. These days, the boys in the hood prey on tourists who are driving around looking at the monuments. Night's the worst, but even during the day there are incidents."

Tate led Pete into the living room. It was about what one would expect of a college professor who lived alone and dressed in shapeless tweed jackets and knotted his ties into something only a veteran sailor would recognize. Tate clicked on a couple of lamps and the light illuminated the veneer of dust that covered just about everything. A glass with amber-colored liquid and a pair of reading glasses rested on a small table next to the threadbare wing chair where Tate had been sitting.

He motioned for Pete to take a companion chair and before sitting himself, said, "The cocktail hour caught up with this time zone while you were nursing that Golden. Can I pour you a little something?"

Pete looked at Tate's glass, and to be polite, said, "I'll have the same as you're having."

Tate shuffled off to the kitchen and came back with Pete's drink. "I hope neat's okay. I know you northern folks like your ice, but the stuff dilutes good whiskey."

"Neat is fine," Pete said. He took a sip and a fiery sensation snaked down his throat. He tried not to show his reaction.

Tate held his glass up so he could study the liquor against the light from one of the lamps. "You're drinking genuine Tennessee Whiskey made according to the statutes of this state."

Pete took another, smaller sip and said, "I didn't realize the state had an official liquor."

"I don't know if it's official, but to be called 'Tennessee Whiskey,' it has to meet all of the criteria specified in the statute."

"Which are?"

"Besides being produced here, the law says that 'Tennessee Whiskey' has to be made from at least fifty-one percent corn, be filtered through maple charcoal, and be aged in new, charred oak barrels."

"So a moonshiner can't just cook up a batch of whiskey and call it Tennessee Whiskey, huh?"

"Not legally anyway. The new barrel requirement of the statute is the most controversial."

"Mmm," Pete murmured, taking another, even smaller sip. "How long did you teach at Ridge College?" he asked.

"Exactly twenty seven years. Then they put me out to pasture."

"Mandatory retirement?"

"No, they said they wanted to make room for new blood in the history department. Some of those spoiled brat kids I was supposedly making room for by moving aside wouldn't know history if it bit them in the butt."

Pete laughed. "I've been thinking about your separation agreement," he said. "Would it satisfy you if we went off the record and I didn't attribute anything you told me as coming from you?"

"That would be a start. There may be some things that I won't be able to answer, period. I can't afford to lose my retirement benefits from the college. Royalties from college text books don't amount to a hill of beans."

"Fair enough," Pete said. "From what you told me on the phone, Thomas Edinger was at the college when you were there."

"Saw him come and saw him go," Tate said, sipping his Tennessee Whiskey.

"For my background, what kind of a guy was he?"

"You mean as a scholar?"

Pete shrugged. "That and other ways."

Professor Tate looked across the room and appeared to be choosing his words carefully. "Bright enough, I suppose, if you apply the current standard. Not a tremendously hard worker. Ambitious."

Tate looked at Pete's glass. "I'm going to get a refill. Join me?"

"Thanks, not yet," Pete said. He wasn't used to drinking straight whiskey and his throat already felt like it was anesthetized. He still had to find the airport that night, too.

When Tate came back, Pete said, "I know that writing a book involves a tremendous amount of work. Edinger wrote two—both biographies of Colonel Thaddeus Clayton—while he was here if my information is correct, plus a number of scholarly articles that were published in professional journals. That doesn't seem like the output of a lazy man."

Professor Tate grunted, a little derisively Pete thought. "Did you ever hear of graduate assistants? And co-authors?"

"Sure."

"There you go. Edinger was a master at using other people, although I didn't say that."

The conversation then shifted to the professors in the department when Tate was at the college, the politics of academia, and the Civil War battles fought around Chattanooga.

"As I understand the system," Pete said, trying to get things back on track, "a young professor on his or her way up aims for promotion to full professor and tenure. Publishing is the most important consideration, isn't it?"

Professor Tate sipped his whiskey and said, "At Ridge College, a person is evaluated on three things: teaching, scholarship, and service."

"Thomas Edinger was a full professor when he left so I assume he passed on all accounts."

"The advisory committee recommended him."

"You sound like you have reservations."

Tate gazed at him for a long time. "Before I answer that, tell me your real interest in Thomas Edinger," he finally said.

"I'm writing some feature stories on him."

"That's what you said, but I sense there's something more." He drained the rest of his glass and played with the bows of his reading glasses and continued to look at Pete. "Candor requires that information flow both ways, you know."

Pete decided that if he was going to get any more information out of Professor Tate, he'd have to come clean. He said, "You're right, there is more. The part about my feature stories is true, but my mission down here is doing double duty." He went on to tell Tate how a low-life named Spencer Dahl had been arrested for Edinger's shooting, but there was at least a serious question in his mind regarding whether he actually did it.

Tate rose again to get another drink and gestured toward Pete's glass. Pete accepted this time. He wasn't a Southerner, but he was aware of the bonding power of a few glasses of neat whiskey. Tate returned and handed Pete his refilled glass. He said, "Tell me why I should do anything to help Thomas Edinger?"

"You wouldn't be helping Edinger. You'd be helping a man who might be innocent."

Tate took a sip of his fresh drink. "Let's put it another way, then. Why do you want to help a man you just called a low-life?"

"I'm doing it for Dahl's sister who is decidedly not a low-life. Plus, I'm a lawyer, remember? We don't just take on popular causes."

"I know," Tate said, waving his hand, "every man accused of a crime deserves a fair shake and all of that stuff." He took another sip. "By the way, I think we should get on a Pete and Andy basis. You can't share Tennessee Whiskey with a man and stay formal."

Pete nodded and said, "Getting back to the advisory committee —"

"Before we go any further," Tate said, "I want your ironclad assurance again as an attorney and a journalist that anything I tell you won't be attributed to me."

"You have it, Andy. And I'll go one step further and deny that we ever talked."

Tate nodded and said, "I'm taking a risk you know, but I trust you."

Pete glanced at his watch while Tate was looking away. It would be tight getting to the airport if he left that very minute, and there was no way he was going to leave when he sensed he was on the cusp of getting some useful information.

Andy Tate continued to sip his whiskey and gaze around the room. "So you want me to give you the real dope on Thomas Edinger, huh?"

It was as much a statement as a question. Pete waited for him to continue.

"To back up a moment, Edinger was in the process of being evaluated for promotion to full professor which under our system would have given him tenure. For the scholarship aspect, he relied on a series of articles he'd published in journals, including one in the University of Chicago Press, and a partial manuscript for a book he was co-authoring with another candidate for tenure. The book had already been accepted for publication by Cornell University Press. Edinger's co-author was an associate professor named Marlin Hines."

"I assume that was the book Edinger eventually published as *Colonel Thaddeus Clayton: A Definitive Biography*."

"Yes, but that wasn't the initial plan as I said. Originally Edinger and Hines were collaborating on the book. I wasn't real close to Hines, but I always thought of him as superior intellect who'd breeze right through to full professor."

"Is Hines still at the College?"

"I'll get to that in a moment," Tate said. "Both Edinger and Hines were proceeding through the evaluation process, but then one day Hines sent a letter to the advisory committee withdrawing his name from consideration. At the same time, he informed us that Thomas Edinger was responsible for most of the original research that went into the manuscript for their book as well as for the writing of the draft chapters that had been accepted by Cornell."

"Did you see the letter?"

"I was on the advisory committee."

"What exactly did the letter say?"

"I don't remember the precise wording and I don't have a copy. But it was pretty much as I just described."

"Umm," Pete murmured.

"The advisory committee never had a case like that before and initially opinions were all over the place. Ultimately, the committee members decided to go forward with their recommendation that Thomas Edinger be promoted to full professor. That carried with it tenure, as I said, and a substantial increase in salary. I was the only dissenting vote on the committee."

"You opposed the recommendation?"

"I didn't necessarily oppose it. I just thought that Edinger's case should be given further scrutiny because it was so unusual."

"I see."

"Three months later, Hines resigned from the college and moved out of the area."

"Where did he go?"

"Ohio. I have the address somewhere." He looked at Pete's glass. "Can I freshen that up for you?"

Pete had given up on the possibility of catching a flight out of Chattanooga that night, but any more liquor and he'd have to sack out on Tate's living room floor for twelve hours. "Thanks, this is good stuff, but I think I better limit myself to two," he said.

"What was the mood on campus after word got around?" Pete asked when Tate returned.

"The whole thing was kept quiet. Of course, the students knew he was gone and they were sorry to lose one of their favorite professors. But life goes on."

"And Thomas Edinger went on to publish his book and we know what happened after that."

"Yes, we know." Tate sloshed the whiskey around in his glass. "I went to see the college president and tried to get him to place consideration of Thomas Edinger back on the table." He took another sip of his drink. "That was the beginning of the end for me."

Pete looked at Tate sympathetically. He'd seen enough of organizations to known how they could invoke collective denial and circle the wagons when something untoward happened in their midst.

"So what do you make of it?" Pete asked.

Tate swirled the whiskey around in his glass again and stared at the floor. "All I can think of is that Edinger had something on Hines that he was holding over his head."

Pete raised his eyebrows. "Like what?"

"I don't know."

"Not even a hunch?"

"No. I've thought about it a hundred times and haven't been able to come up with anything that makes sense."

"Did you stay in touch with Hines?"

"Tried to. But when a person never responds, you kind of get the message and leave things alone after a while."

"When did all of this happen?"

Tate appeared to think about Pete's question. "Ten years ago maybe? I can get the exact dates if you like."

"That's close enough for now." Pete was in no hurry to leave now that his travel schedule was irrelevant. Besides, he needed to allow time for the liquor to wear off.

"What are you doing these days?" he asked Tate.

Pleased to move on to happier subjects, Tate's face brightened and he said, "My new book came out three months ago." He walked over to some volumes piled on one end of his bookcase and came back with a copy. It was titled, *The Battles for Chattanooga: Personal Histories*.

He handed it to Pete who paged through it. The author page showed "Andrew H. Tate, Professor of History Emeritus, Ridge College." He looked up at Tate. "It seems you haven't severed *all* ties with the college."

Tate smiled ruefully. "That was my lawyer. He was looking out for my interests down the road. You have some smart people in your profession."

Pete handed the volume back to Tate. Tate put a hand up palm out. "That's yours, Pete. From me to you."

"I'll accept this book only if you autograph it for me." Pete watched as Tate inscribed the book and autographed it with a flourish of his hand and a pleased look on his face.

TWENTY-EIGHT

With two plane changes and the usual waits between flights, Pete got into Traverse City at mid-afternoon the following day. An hour later, he was in his office and set about returning his telephone messages, beginning with one from Angie DeMarco.

"Been out fly fishing?" she asked.

"Nope. I was out of town and just got back."

A pause, then, "You weren't in Chicago, were you?"

"No, dear."

"If I found out you were here and we didn't go to Gibson's, I'd really be burned."

"Rest assured, I wasn't in Chicago."

"Where did you go then?" she asked suspiciously.

"Just a trip for a client."

"Do you work for the CIA these days so you can't tell me where you were?"

"Keep your voice down," he whispered. "It's MI6, not the CIA. Last summer, I was behind this woman on my way to Beulah. Her license plates had '007 Girl.' I've been thinking about getting plates with '007 Man' on them."

"Did this '007 Girl' have big boobs?"

"Not on her back."

"Ha! ha! Aren't we the comedian today, Mr. Stud. Anyway, I read your draft response to the ethics complaint. I never realized how humble you could be."

"Not humble, just adaptable."

"I'll let that one pass," Angie said. "I have some suggested changes to the draft and I'll e-mail them to you the first thing in the morning. Anything else I should know about your case?"

"Funny you should ask. The other day, I went to see the widow of the man up here who was shot. She seems to know all about the ethics complaint against me."

"How?"

"Her family's accountant was the same woman referred to in the complaint. She knows the whole story, or at least Jeffery Rodes' version of the story. She threatened to help Rodes."

"I hope you didn't give her any ammunition."

Pete paused. "She claims I implied I was with the sheriff's department in order to get her to talk to me, which is pure bull, and then changed my story and said I was helping lead counsel for the defendant in her husband's murder case and threatened to subpoena her testimony if she wouldn't talk to me voluntarily."

Angie groaned.

"Now don't get your fanny in an uproar. I *am* helping Ira Manning who's now involved in the case, and as you know, we have a right to subpoena her if necessary so there wasn't any misrepresentation in what I said."

"How about the sheriff's office part?"

"I told you, that's pure bull. All I said was that I *knew* Joe Tessler who's the detective in the department. I never said I was with the department or worked for Tessler."

"You should get out of that case or at least keep a lower profile until the ethics complaint is resolved."

Pete thought about that for a moment and said, "I don't think I can."

"Why, may I ask?"

"Two reasons. I promised Rona Martin, who's kind of the defendant's brother but more importantly is a good personal friend, that I'd stay involved and try to get to the bottom of what happened in the case. Then I made the same promise to Ira, particularly with regard to the poem the defendant allegedly sent to the murder victim. I just uncovered some information that may be the key to that."

"And the third reason is that you really don't want to get out, do you?"

Pete didn't say anything.

Angie sighed and said, "I suppose I should have learned by now that it's fruitless to try to talk you into doing something you don't want to do."

Pete continued to remain silent.

"Do you think the widow will follow through on her threat to weigh in on the ethics complaint?" Angie asked.

"No idea."

"Well, first things first. Let's get your response filed with the Attorney Grievance Commission and deal with the widow if we have to. I'll e-mail my proposed revisions first thing in the morning as I said."

The other voicemail messages were of lesser importance. He returned two of the calls from people in Chicago who were providing character references to support his answer to the ethics complaint and then called Harry.

"I thought you were coming back a day ago."

"I got delayed."

"Well, at least you didn't get yourself shot or beaten up. Those southern boys don't cotton to northerners, you know."

"No problems. I didn't even need my passport to get into or out of Tennessee."

"Want to grab some dinner and tell me about it?"

"Dinner sounds good, but first I need to do something. I'll meet you at the restaurant in a half-hour."

Pete had been getting his money's worth for the fee he paid the service for finding the telephone numbers of people he was trying to track down. He logged on to the service's website and input the name "Marlin Hines" and the Toledo, Ohio address Andy Tate had given him. A response flashed on his screen ten minutes later informing him that no telephone listing for Marlin Hines had been found. He expanded the search to cover the Toledo metropolitan area and got the same result. Then he tapped the service's premium feature and ordered searches for an unlisted number for Hines or his cell phone number. Again, the search results were negative.

Harry was at their usual table when he walked in the restaurant. He was in deep conversation with Rona Martin and had one of his hands over hers. When they saw him, it was clear they were eager to hear what he'd learned on his trip to Chattanooga and whatever they'd been talking about could wait. He spent fifteen minutes briefing them on his visit.

"So the college people basically weren't talking," Harry said, "but this Professor Tate gave you some inside dope you think could be useful."

"That sums it up," Pete said. "And what Tate told me is based on his suspicions and suppositions, not facts. By the way, you can't tell anyone about the conversations I had with Tate or even that I talked to him. He has an agreement with the college not to talk about college personnel and I absolutely have to make sure that nothing comes back to bite him as a result of his conversations with me. He put his pension from the college at risk by talking to me."

"Understood," Harry said. "But what Tate told you is based on pretty good suspicions and suppositions, right?"

"That's my guess," Pete said. "It seems to confirm that there might be something in Thomas Edinger's past that he didn't want to come out."

Harry leaned forward in his chair and eagerly asked, "So what's the next step?"

"I'm going to follow the trail of what Tate told me and see what turns up."

They sat quietly until Rona said, "I feel guilty about this. My sister thinks you're out of the case."

"That was my impression when I saw her the night before I went to Chattanooga. Either that or she's decided just not to make it an issue between us."

"That would be nice," Rona said, "but I know my sister. She's reasonable about everything except when it comes to Spencer Dahl."

"With a little luck," Pete said hopefully, "I might be able to resolve the poem issue one way or the other before the issue comes up again with Carla."

"Maybe you can preempt the issue by telling her you're out of the case except for your commitment to Ira," Harry suggested.

Rona shook her head.

"Let me think about it," Pete said.

"If you want," Harry said, "I could talk to her."

Rona shook her head again. "I told you, it's impossible to talk to Carla about anything that has to do with Spencer Dahl."

Harry persisted. "Carla and I have always gotten along well. I bet I could bring her around."

Rona put her hand on Harry's and said, "Let Pete and Carla work it out, dear."

"I'm not trying to interfere or anything. I just want all of us to be friends."

"I understand Carla's feelings," Pete said. "Putting myself in her position, I'm not sure I'd react any differently. Attempted rape by someone who's almost a member of your family is a hard thing to forget."

No one said anything. Pete's eyes flicked toward Rona and for a moment he thought she might make things easier for him by offering to let him back out of the case altogether if he wanted to, but she didn't. He wasn't sure how he'd react even if she had.

TWENTY-NINE

While Pete waited for Angie's comments on his draft response to the ethics complaint to come through, he did some further research on Ottar Jacobsen's exploits during the Civil War. He reread his great aunt's family history and her cryptic reference to his service in the Second Battle of Bull Run. To refresh his memory about that battle, he went on the Internet and spent the next hour reading about the Union's defeat and the outcome of some other famous battles in the war.

He also made a note to query the editor of *Viking* magazine about whether she'd be interested in an article that dealt with the First Minnesota Norwegian Volunteers and drew on original source materials.

Angie's e-mail appeared on his screen and he printed out a hard copy of the answer with her suggested edits. He adopted most of them and spent the next three hours finalizing the response and assembling the character reference letters that had come in. He was still missing letters from two people who'd promised to write on his behalf, but decided to let the package go anyway. He made two photocopies of everything, including one for Angie, and walked to the post office to mail the package.

While he was waiting his turn in line, he saw a slight woman with unkempt gray hair and an old brown coat that looked like, if offered, Goodwill would reject, walk in and go over to the bank of mail boxes along one wall of the post office. He recognized her immediately as Jake Rossum's mother. She fumbled with her key trying to get her box open. He turned away slightly. She might not recognize him, but he didn't want to risk a repeat of the awkward moment at her house that night.

Pete walked out of the post office feeling good. He'd launched the opening salvo in his counteroffensive against the ethics complaint and was satisfied he'd made a persuasive case. Now it was wait and see time. He hated that, but knew he had to let the situation play out at the Attorney Grievance Commission.

His adrenaline sank back to its normal level and he had to decide what to do for the remainder of the day. He called Harry to invite him to a late lunch, but he wasn't around and the woman who answered the telephone at *The Northern Sentinel* didn't know where he was. He wandered down the street and looked for a place that was open to grab a sandwich. He decided against Ebba's Bakery because he didn't feel like being interrogated again by Ebba and settled for the sub shop. He emerged with a long hunk of French bread piled high with ham, turkey, cheese and lettuce and wrapped in baker's paper.

While Pete ate his sandwich, his thoughts returned to Thomas Edinger like iron drawn to a magnet. When he finished eating, he called Andy Tate, reached him on the third ring, and after the usual pleasantries, told him that he'd been unable to find a telephone number in Toledo for Marlin Hines.

Pete said, "You told me you wrote to Hines a couple of times at the Toledo address. I assume the letters never came back."

"I wrote to him twice and sent a newspaper clipping another time. Oh yeah, and sent a Christmas card the first year he was gone. Nothing came back and I assumed he just didn't want to hear from anyone at Ridge College."

"Do you think he could have moved and had his mail forwarded?"

"I can't help you there, Pete. I honestly have no idea."

"Might the college have a forwarding address for him?"

"Possible. I don't have the foggiest. If I were to make an inquiry now, the administration would wonder what I was trying to stir up and manufacture some cockamamie argument that I was violating my separation agreement."

"Would Millie know Marlin Hines' forwarding address if the college has one?"

"She might."

"Is she trustworthy? I mean in the sense that she wouldn't go blabbing to the administration if you asked her."

"Oh hell yes. Millie's a mound of integrity in that den of weasels over there."

"Would you be comfortable asking her?"

"Sure. We talk every now and again."

Pete waited anxiously for Tate to call him back. He did an hour later. "Millie says that the only address she has for Hines is the one I gave you. He never gave the college a forwarding address. Millie would know, too, since she's in effect the secretary for the history department."

"I appreciate your help, Andy. By the way, I read the first six chapters of your book on the way home and really enjoyed them. Where did you come up with all of those old letters you quoted from?"

Pete could tell from the way Tate reacted that he felt good about his comments. "I've been collecting letters from families here in the city for the past twenty-five years. In many ways, I'm closer to them than I am to my own family." He went on to tell Pete how he'd developed the relationships and how having access to the letters enabled him to piece together a picture of the Civil War in the Chattanooga area from an intensely personal and human standpoint. One of the fascinating things, Tate said, was that so many of the families had Union sympathizers even though their menfolk fought mostly on the Confederate side.

"Did you hear from anyone at the college when your book came out?"

"I received one comment. A four-by-six card from Dr. Stephens that said, 'Congratulations on your new book'."

"That was it?"

"That was it."

Pete had been on the phone with Tate for over an hour by the time he finally got off. During the last ten minutes, Tate tried to persuade Pete to make another trip to Chattanooga. He promised to personally take him on a tour of the Civil War battlefields in the area and to introduce him to some of the families that had provided material for his book. He also promised to have an ample supply of Tennessee Whiskey on hand for Pete's visit. Pete's head already balked at the thought.

Another visit to Chattanooga wasn't on Pete's travel schedule, but it took him less than fifteen minutes to decide to make a trip to Toledo to see if he could locate Marlin Hines. He got out his atlas and plotted a route. It looked simple enough; east to I-75 and then a straight shot south. He estimated it would take about the same amount of time as it took him to drive to Chicago. He'd grown to hate long drives, but it was preferable to putting up with the airports again.

Pete checked his watch. He still had enough daylight to do something else he'd been wanting to do since the killer's *modus operandi* became apparent; have another look at the crime scene. He grabbed the keys to his Range Rover and headed for the reenactment site. When he arrived, everything was the same as the last time he was there. The crime scene tape was still up, as were the Confederate fortifications on the crest of the ridge. Pete ducked under the rope and climbed to the top of the ridge and looked around.

The remnants of the burned Confederate uniform found in Spencer Dahl's outdoor fireplace, whether planted as Dahl claimed or not, was pretty strong evidence that the killer had dressed up in a Confederate uniform to blend in with the other reenactors on the ridge. Then he'd shot Colonel Clayton, or Thomas Edinger playing the Colonel, when he got close enough and presumably bided his time until he could slip away unnoticed in the pandemonium of the simulated battle. The perfect opportunity for that came either when the Confederate forces, sensing that they were about to be over-run, fled wildly down the backside of the ridge or maybe when they climbed to the top again after the battle was over and rejoined their fellow reenactors for a boisterous victory celebration.

Logically, the killer wouldn't have wanted to park his vehicle in the area where all of the other vehicles were parked since then he'd be too conspicuous when he left. That meant he'd probably parked it out of sight somewhere to the right of the reenactment field and stationed himself on the right side of the Confederate defenses. Assuming he drove that is. If he left the scene on foot, it was still likely that he'd been on the right side of the defenses for the same reason. That did not augur well for Spencer Dahl since his house was at most a half-mile away through the woods.

As Pete was studying the terrain, a gunshot split the silence and he heard something strike a branch no more than ten feet from where he was standing. A squirrel tumbled to the earth. Pete immediately froze and turned his head in the direction he thought the shot came from. Calvin Seitz came out from behind a tree and said, "Didn't I warn you, counselor? These woods ain't safe for a man to walk around in leaf peeping, especially if you don't wear hunter's orange."

Seitz began to reload his smoothbore and periodically looked up at Pete as he tamped powder and another load down the barrel. The shock of red hair and twisted expression on his face scared the hell out of Pete because he wasn't sure what the goof would do next.

"Didn't you see me standing here, Calvin?"

"I seen that squirrel," Seitz replied as he continued to tamp the long rod down the barrel of his ancient weapon and eye Pete. "That's what I was getting at on the street that day. Hunters can be an intense bunch and sometimes they don't see nothing but their quarry in front of them."

"I'm going to report your reckless conduct to the sheriff," Pete said.

"And maybe try to point a finger at me again for that Edinger shooting? You didn't do so good the first time, did you?"

Before Pete could answer, Seitz swung his smoothbore up so that it passed across Pete's body and came to rest at a target over his head. He pulled the trigger and the blast shattered the silence again. Pete's ears rang and smoke billowed from the barrel and he could smell the odor of burning powder. Another squirrel fell to the ground.

Now Pete was livid and he screamed, "You crazy sonofabitch!" He started for Seitz, knowing that his smoothbore was empty, but pulled up when he saw the weapon was pointed at him with the rod down the barrel.

"Seitz shook his head and said, "I don't think it's wise to go around attacking a peaceful hunter, Mr. Thorsen."

"You're nuts!" Pete screamed again.

"Why don't you go ahead and tell the sheriff that the hunters in this area are a little careless," Seitz said. "Maybe you'll fare better than the first time you accused me of something."

THIRTY

As Pete drove south on I-75, he was still seething over his latest encounter with Calvin Seitz and the telephone conversation he'd had with Joe Tessler when he called to report the incident. Tessler said he could go out and question Seitz, but emphasized that Pete had no evidence of Seitz's reckless behavior except for his word and that when members of his department had questioned him the first time, Sheriff Richter had wound up apologizing to Seitz for wrongfully considering him as a person of interest or a suspect. Pete got the impression that Richter had bad-mouthed him in the process.

The City of Toledo loomed just ahead of him. Pete had never physically been there before, but felt like he knew the city because growing up, he'd adopted the Toledo Mud Hens as his favorite minor league baseball team. He thought the Mud Hens, the AAA farm affiliate of the Detroit Tigers, had the coolest name ever and embraced the team as his own and vowed that someday he'd pitch for the Hens and they'd be his stepping stone to the majors. He wrote to Mud Hens management and got on their team mailing list and had a Mud Hens jersey mounted on his bedroom wall above a wooden bat and old fashioned glove signed by some Hens star from the past. His brother, with whom he shared their jail-cell sized bedroom, would get mad and tear down the display because he regarded the Mud Hens as little more than a sandlot team and certainly not worthy of idolatry. When his brother wasn't around, Pete would quietly restore his edifice to baseball immortality and gaze lovingly at the display.

Marlin Hines' address that he'd gotten from Andy Tate was 941 Grover Court in the city itself. After a lot of trial and error, including going down one-way streets that wouldn't let him turn for three blocks and having to backtrack because other streets didn't go all the way through, he found the 900 block of Grover Court. The neat bungalow at the 941 number was shaded in front by a solitary Maple tree that had just begun to shed its leaves. A green and yellow plastic tricycle lay on its side on the front walk.

A pleasant young woman in jeans with an infant snuggled on top of one hip came to the door when Pete knocked. Pete introduced himself and told her he was looking for Marlin Hines. The woman looked puzzled and explained that she'd only lived there five months. She suggested that he talk to Bill and Karen Emerson next door.

The Emersons weren't home so Pete moved on to the next house. A fit young man in a tight tee shirt and jeans and his perky wife came to the door at the same time. When Pete introduced himself, they stumbled over each other in their eagerness to be friendly and said they were new to the neighborhood as well and didn't know Marlin Hines. They suggested he talk to Armand Lukitsch across the street. The wife pointed to a modest brick ranch house with neatly-trimmed shrubs in front and lowered her voice as though afraid their across-the-street-neighbor might hear her. She said Lukitsch had lived on the block for forty years and knew everyone and their comings and goings. Her husband warned in the same hushed voice that Lukitsch would talk his leg off

Pete knew the sort of person they described and girded himself for the experience as he crossed the street. He thought he saw a curtain covering one of Lukitsch's windows fall back into place as he approached the house. He didn't have to knock because the front door swung open when he was coming up the walk and a man in a plaid shirt and baggy khaki pants stood poised to greet him. Two cats rubbed against his leg. The odor that wafted through the open door suggested those weren't the only two felines that made the house their home.

"Armand Lukitsch," the man said, extending a hand. "What are you selling? I saw you going house-to-house across the street."

Pete shook Lukitsch's hand and introduced himself and said, "I'm not selling anything. I'm trying to locate someone who used to live on your block."

"Well why don't you come in and let me see if I can help. I'm just brewing some tea. Would you like some?"

Pete's drink of choice was iced tea with a strong dose of lemon, but he really didn't care for hot tea. Nevertheless, he accepted Lukitsch's offer to be polite. As he sat on the couch in the living room waiting for Lukitsch to return from the kitchen, the full measure of the kitty odor closed in on him. Pete thought it incongruous that Lukitsch wouldn't do something to control it because he appeared to be fastidious in all other respects. The two cats that greeted him at the door had followed Lukitsch into the kitchen, but a third cat with bright orange fur materialized out of nowhere and hopped into Pete's lap.

"Freddy must like you," Lukitsch said when he returned with their tea. "Freddy is short for Frederick the Great. Normally he doesn't warm up to strangers right away."

Pete munched on one of the small cookies Lukitsch served with the tea. He didn't know whether Lukitsch always had his tea from a ceramic pot with matching cups and saucers exquisitely decorated with pink roses and green vines or whether he'd trotted out the good stuff for his guest. Either way, it was a nice touch.

"How many cats do you have?" Pete asked.

"Seven counting the two kittens I just adopted from the humane society. They're good company." Two more cats appeared and jumped into Lukitsch's lap. "Does the odor bother you?"

"No," Pete lied.

"It bothers some people," Lukitsch said. "I just bought a new brand of kitty litter that's supposed to soak up all the odor, but haven't gotten it out yet. Are you a cat person or a dog person, Pete?"

"I don't have either at the moment."

"Most people fall into one camp or the other. Rarely do you see a person that has both." Armand Lukitsch droned on about the merits of cats versus dogs and Pete half-listened politely. He wanted to get on with his questions about Marlin Hines, but at the same time, he knew you had to take things slowly with some people.

When there was a brief lull in the conversation, Pete handed one of his business cards to Lukitsch. Armand held the card with thumbs and forefingers on each side and studied it the way Japanese businessmen study a card that's been given to them.

Lukitsch looked up from the card and said, "A cousin of mine is a lawyer in Columbus." That led to an extended discussion of what his cousin did and whether he was happy practicing law and the traditions and state of the legal profession in modern society.

Pete saw an opening and said, "I'm told that Marlin Hines once lived on your street."

"Marlin and Carrie Hines," Lukitsch mused. He looked at the ceiling for a moment and added, "941 Grover Court." Then he gave the month and year they moved in and the month and year the house was sold to another couple that preceded the current owners in the chain of title.

Pete was impressed. "Can you do that with every home on the block?" he asked.

"Only for people who moved in or out of the neighborhood in the past thirty eight years. Thirty eight years and seven months to be more precise. Before that, I'm a little sketchy."

"Where did the Hines move to when they sold their house here?"

"I'm not sure where Carrie Hines moved. As far as I know, she didn't give anyone a forwarding address."

"When you say you don't know where Carrie Hines went, does that mean she and Marlin split up?"

Lukitsch stroked one of his cats and said, "I guess you could say that. Marlin Hines died."

"Natural causes?"

Lukitsch looked at him and said, "Promise you won't spread this around?"

"Promise," Pete said. "I'm just trying to locate the heirs to a small estate. Mr. Hines is one of them. I'll keep anything you say confidential."

"Marlin Hines killed himself," Lukitsch said in little more than a whisper. "Carrie went to the basement one day and found him hanging by the neck."

The news jolted Pete. "Suicide."

"That's what the police concluded. There wasn't much of an investigation, I understand. I guess they found no evidence of foul play."

As Pete was digesting that, Lukitsch said, "Do you see now why I asked you to keep it confidential? If news of a suicide or a murder in a house gets around, it can make that house nearly unsalable and affect the value of all the other houses in the neighborhood."

"Does the current owner of the house know what happened?"

"I don't think so," Lukitsch said. "The man who bought it from Carrie Hines knew, but it didn't seem to bother him."

"I see," Pete said. "What about the newspapers? Did they print anything?"

"I watch the obituary pages very closely. One paper carried a three-line obituary announcing that Hines had died, not giving any cause of death, and saying only that he was survived by his wife. Didn't even mention his son who was in the army at the time. Carrie was a basket case over the incident so I suppose the paper had to pretty much piece things together from what they had."

"Mmm," Pete murmured. "What else can you tell me about Marlin Hines?"

"Fairly young man. He was a professor or teacher of some kind. I believe he taught history at the community college. He didn't talk about himself much, but that's what I understand."

"Any children other than the son in the army?"

"Not that I know of. Of course, there might have been some. That happens sometimes. I can't keep up with all members of everyone's family," he said modestly.

There probably wasn't much about the affairs of people on the block that Lukitsch didn't know, Pete thought. "What was Marlin Hines like on a personal level?" he asked.

"Not very sociable. We have a block party every summer and he and Carrie never came in the short time they lived in the house. I don't like to speak ill of the dead, but he also wasn't a very good neighbor. Didn't take care of his property, that sort of thing. I remember once when Marlin and Carrie were on a trip somewhere and I had to go over and mow their grass. It was six inches high and becoming a real eyesore. People depend on each other to keep their property looking good. It creates an image of the entire neighborhood and affects the values of all of our homes."

The conversation drifted off to other topics and as his neighbors across the street had said, Lukitsch certainly never lacked for something to talk about. And talk about and talk about some more. It was nearly dark when Pete got on I-75 again and headed north while munching a cheeseburger and fries from a fast-food place and thinking about Marlin Hines' suicide and whether it had some connection to Thomas Edinger's death.

THIRTY-ONE

"I searched the morgues of the Toledo newspapers like you asked," Harry said. "Your chatty friend was right. The only obituary I could find for Marlin Hines was the short blurb in the Toledo daily."

"Is that usual?" Pete asked.

"With a suicide, yes. I was surprised to find *anything* in the papers, to be honest. An editor who's worth his salt wants to protect the privacy of family members in a case like that. I suspect that's what happened with Hines."

"Okay, thanks."

When he was off the telephone with Harry, Pete flipped through Thomas Edinger's first book on Colonel Thaddeus Clayton again and reread the three-page acknowledgements section. There was exactly one mention of Marlin Hines; he was listed along with four of Edinger's research assistants as having contributed to the book. That seemed unusual in view of the fact Edinger and Hines once represented to the tenure committee that the work was their joint product.

Pete tapped on his desk with the end of his pen and thought for a while, then called the Toledo Police Department to see if he could find out whether there'd been an investigation at the time of Hines' death. A frustrating two hours later, after talking to four different police officers, being disconnected twice and waiting close to an hour for a callback from one officer who promised to plug Marlin Hines' name into the department's computer to see what popped up, he didn't know any more than he did when he first called. The officer who said she'd run the search told him that Hines' name didn't appear in the computer so there wasn't any more she could do.

As he considered his options, he briefly thought about trying to enlist Joe Tessler's help since the Toledo police were likely to take a request more seriously if it came from a sister police department rather than some lawyer who called over the telephone. But he knew it was a pipe dream to expect Tessler to help. Tessler almost certainly would refuse to make a request of the Toledo Police Department without Sheriff Frank Richter's blessing and the chances of Richter giving that once he knew Pete was behind the request were practically nil, particularly since Pete was trying to prove that Richter had the wrong man in custody for Edinger's murder.

The only alternative he could think of was to try to track down Carrie Hines and see if she would talk to him. Pete knew that wasn't going to be easy since based on what he'd been told, she'd dropped off the face of the earth after her husband's suicide. He knew a little about the computer searches private investigators used to locate people, but he was going to need at least Carrie's full name including her middle initial to run a search. The information he'd uncovered in Toledo gave him a perfect excuse for a follow-up call to his new friend, Andy Tate.

Tate seemed pleased to hear from him again, and after a few minutes of social chit-chat, Pete told him about Marlin Hines' suicide. Tate took some time to digest the news and then said, "I guess that explains why I never heard back from him, doesn't it?"

"It does. I realize you didn't know Hines that well, but did you notice any change in him around the time he left Ridge College?"

"A lot of change. I stopped in his office to say goodbye when he was packing up to leave and it seemed pretty clear to me that he was depressed. He was a different man from the colleague I'd observed in the years before that."

Pete told Tate he wasn't successful in getting any information about Hines' suicide from the Toledo Police Department and that he was interested in reaching his wife, Carrie, to talk to her about her husband. He asked if Tate knew her full name and had any idea of where she was from just in case she'd returned home.

"I don't know where she's from, but I do know her real first name is Catherine. I bet Millie could tell us what her middle initial or name is."

Tate hung up to call Millie and five minutes later got back to Pete. "Her full name is Catherine R. Hines. Millie didn't know what the 'R' stood for."

"That's a big help, Andy."

"You never did say how Marlin committed suicide."

"He hung himself in the basement with a long piece of heavy electrical cord."

"God," Tate muttered. "And Carrie found him?"

"That's what his former neighbor told me."

"Something about this smells, doesn't it, Pete?"

"It does. I just can't get my arms around it yet."

"You and I are a lot alike," Tate said. "I smelled something, too, when Hines withdrew his candidacy for tenure and resigned from the college. That's why I made a pest of myself at the time."

"Something that didn't serve your own interests very well."

"No it didn't."

"I feel like I'm getting myself in the same box," Pete said.

"Sometimes a man has to stand up and do the right thing. I get the feeling that's the way you live your life, too. Well, let me know what your search turns up."

Armed with Carrie Hines's full name and nothing else — he didn't have her Social Security number, where she'd moved to after she left

Toledo, her place of birth or any other relevant information — he began to run some computer searches. The first thing he found was that information available to the general public varied from state to state. To get around that, he tried The Nationwide Locator service and paid to order a Social Security search, an address update, a national surname search which turned up several thousand people with the name Hines, and a NIS package that included things like a driver's license trace, a motor vehicle registration trace, an asset search, and a criminal record trace. None of the searches turned up anything useful, but a notice on his computer screen informed him that his credit card had been charged two hundred forty-seven dollars for the searches.

He called Andy Tate to tell him he had no luck locating Carrie Hines. Tate didn't say anything for a moment, then said, "It doesn't have anything to do with finding Carrie, but have you considered the possibility that Edinger was blackmailing Marlin Hines?"

Pete thought about that for a moment. "That might be relevant if I were investigating Marlin Hines' suicide, but what connection do you see to Thomas Edinger's shooting?"

"There may not be one," Tate said. "It's just a thought I've had over the years when I considered the situation."

When Pete got off the phone, he thought more about what Tate had said. There wasn't any obvious thread connecting Hines' suicide to the Thomas Edinger murder, but Pete decided to look into it further anyway.

He stretched and decided he'd had enough of the Thomas Edinger case for the day. The weather was still warm enough to cook outside. He'd go home, slap a steak on the grill, have a glass of wine, and read a few more chapters of Tate's book.

When he got back to his cottage, though, he found a notice of another registered letter from the Attorney Grievance Commission in his mailbox. He hadn't expected a response to his to his ethics complaint submission this soon. He drove back to town without even going inside his cottage and signed for the letter at the post office.

He opened the envelope when he was back in his Range Rover and read the cover letter. It acknowledged receipt of his response and supporting documents and asked that he respond to the supplemental ethics complaint against him, a copy of which was enclosed, within five days. The supplemental complaint had been filed by Lorraine Edinger based on Pete's actions when he'd gone to her home uninvited. It chronicled her version of what had occurred during that visit and accused Pete of abusive, inappropriate, and unprofessional conduct.

The original complaint worried him because it was factually correct even though he was convinced he'd done nothing wrong, but the supplement was, in his opinion, entirely different. It was nothing more than a bunch of baseless charges made by an emotional woman who he was convinced was playing her own double game. Anger boiled up inside him. For tactical reasons, he'd struck a contrite tone in the response he just filed. This was different. This time he intended to come out swinging.

THIRTY-TWO

e scanned the latest materials from the Attorney Grievance Commission into his printer/fax machine and e-mailed a copy to Angie DeMarco with a cover message that he'd call her in fifteen minutes. This time she was in her office and not on trial or at Muldoon's.

"I warned you not to—"

He cut her off and said, "No lectures, please, Angie. How long have you known me? A dozen years? Does what Lorraine Edinger put in her statement have the ring of truth?"

"No, but—"

"But nothing. That woman is playing some kind of a game in the murder case we've got going up here and is making ridiculous charges against me because I've been nosing around."

"I don't understand."

"Lorraine Edinger's been sleeping with this guy Spencer Dahl and Dahl claims that's what they were doing at the time her husband was shot. Suddenly she does a back flip and claims she was actually shopping at that time. That left Dahl hanging and now he's been arrested for Thomas Edinger's murder in part because she denied his alibi. She's trying to make life difficult for me because she's afraid I might stumble onto something."

"Isn't Dahl the guy you yourself called a slime-ball who couldn't be trusted?"

"I trust him on this. The more I see, the more I'm convinced that Lorraine Edinger is the one who's lying."

"How does she even know about the original ethics complaint filed against you?"

"Barbara Rodes was the accountant for the Edinger family as well as for some others involved in the Lynn Hawke murder case. From what I can figure, she's kept in touch with the Rodes family and knew that way."

"Okay, how do you propose to answer the latest charges?"

"Take the gloves off. We struck the right tone in my response to the primary complaint, but this is different. Lorraine's statement is a crock and we need to tell the Grievance Commission so."

Angie sighed. "You have five days to file a supplemental answer, right?"

"Five days, but I want to respond tomorrow. Are you going to be around tonight?"

"Until about ten. I have a brief due in two days."

"Can you find a half-hour to look at my proposed response if I e-mail it to you before you leave?"

"For you, dear, anything."

Pete abandoned his plan for a quiet steak dinner at home and picked up a small pizza from next door and ate a slice while he outlined his response. Then he set about keying it in. He was a two-finger man on the keyboard, but tonight his fingers flew faster than usual as the anger boiled in his mind. He ate a second slice of pizza, which was now cold, while he edited a hard copy of the response. Then he keyed in the changes he'd made, edited the text again, and e-mailed the draft to Angie.

His office telephone rang twenty minutes later. "From our conversation earlier," Angie said, "I thought I'd get something than would singe the page. This has an edge to it, but I think it'll fly. It has the right blend of outrage and reason. I only have a few suggestions." She spent the next ten minutes going over her suggested changes, refinements really, and Pete keyed in the ones he agreed with as they went. It was 9:00 p.m. when they finished.

"You really owe me when this is all over."

"Only if I'm still able to practice law in Michigan," Pete said.

"You will be."

"You know, when you're representing a client and someone else's interests are at stake, it's a lot easier to be sanguine. Understand I'm not talking about you personally. But when your own hide is on the line, it makes you nervous as hell."

"Are you concerned about how this will end up?"

"Yes I'm concerned. Just because I don't practice full-time anymore doesn't mean my law license isn't important to me. It's more than my ticket to an occupation, it's part of who I am. If I had that stripped from me just because I was trying to do the right thing ..."

Pete spent the next half-hour finalizing his supplemental answer and getting it ready to mail first thing in the morning. Then he took the scenic route home. During the summer months at this time of the night, he'd be greeted by a magnificent view when he came over the last hill and saw Crystal Lake spread out before him. It was autumn and too dark for that view, but the shimmering light on the water from the Harvest Moon provided a different kind of beauty.

He got a heavier jacket from his cottage and wandered down to the water's edge and admired the scene. Besides the moon, the Heavens were ablaze on a cloudless night. He identified Ursa Major and Ursa Minor and Orion and Capella. It was one of the positive things about being in the north where the stars and constellations weren't obscured by a ceiling of emissions that were the product of urban society. It also reminded him of his youth in northern Wisconsin when he would lie in the grass and look up at nature's handiwork and dream of what he'd do when he was finally able to move on with his life.

His mind drifted off to his last telephone conversation with Andy Tate and the question he'd raised regarding whether Thomas Edinger had been blackmailing Marlin Hines. Maybe Tate was onto something. Certainly it would explain a lot of things, such as why Hines bailed out of university life just when his career was ascending and why he committed suicide shortly after that. And, most importantly, it would explain the line in the poem Spencer Dahl had sent to Edinger obliquely referring to something in Edinger's past, even if Dahl didn't understand what he was writing about.

There was a missing piece, though. If Hines were still alive, that would be the obvious place to look since Hines and not Dahl could be the killer. But Hines was dead. Or at least he was reported dead due to suicide.

As Pete thought about the possibilities, he reminded himself again that maybe Spencer Dahl really did kill Edinger. Maybe it was as Lorraine Edinger said, that Dahl thought she'd be an easier mark with her husband out of the way and all of her millions in inherited wealth there for the taking by an unscrupulous man with a record of conning women. But there was too much that didn't fit with that scenario, either, beginning with the fact Dahl hadn't in the past exhibited violent tendencies and the way he'd reacted in Sheriff Richter's office when it appeared that Lorraine Edinger had turned on him.

The only logical course forward seemed to be to probe further into Marlin Hines' background in the hope that something would come to light to make sense of the whole situation. That meant making yet another call to Andy Tate in the morning to get additional information. He suspected that Andy wouldn't mind hearing from him again since they seemed to have developed a common interest in unraveling the mystery.

Julie called just as he was getting ready to turn in. "Hi, Dad. I was just thinking about you and decided to call before the clock struck the magic hour of 10:30 p.m. and you went to bed."

"You know that there's no deadline if you want to call me. Or if you *need* to call me."

"I just wanted to hear your voice."

"That's sweet, Angel. It's wonderful to hear your voice, too. We haven't talked for a couple of days."

"It's been *four* days, Dad."

"You're making me feel like a neglectful parent. By the way, I transferred some money to your checking account. Did it show up?"

"It was posted today. Thank you *so much*. If I were a car, I would have been running on fumes."

An uneasy feeling swept over him every time Julie mentioned cars. She'd dropped her request for a car going into her junior year at prep school, which had been a bone of contention between them, but he'd been concerned ever since that the issue wasn't dead. "You should have let me know if you were that short," he said.

"I managed to get by," she said. "I'm trying to emulate you and show some discipline. Say, what are our plans for Thanksgiving? It's only a month away you know."

"I hadn't really thought about it. I expect I'll be invited to Rona and Harry's house again."

"This is the year your daughter is supposed to have Thanksgiving with you, remember?"

"I do remember. I'm sure they'll be delighted to have you, too."

"Do they know I might have a guest this year?"

"Guest?"

"You know, in case Remy comes."

"Oh, right. As soon as you know for sure, let me know. It won't be a problem, I'm sure."

"Dad?"

"Yes?"

"I got some papers from the housing department that they'll want us to sign. Do you want to look at them?"

"As the only lawyer in the family—so far anyway—I think I should, don't you?"

"I'll send them to you."

"That's great. I'll look at them right away."

"And Dad?"

"Yes?"

"To give you a heads up, I'd say it's fifty-fifty as to whether Remy will be coming."

Pete's interest picked up, but he tried to show concern. "Oh, has something changed?"

"We had a fight on the phone the other night."

"I see."

"Remy told me he wants to start dating other women."

"Mmm," Pete murmured, wondering at what age a high school girl started to use "women" and "men" rather than "girl" and "boy." He detected a sniffle at the other end of the line.

"I mean, I've had a lot of opportunities to go on dates, too, but I always said no because I thought Remy and I were sort of committed to each other, you know?"

Pete wanted to parrot back to her what she'd said to him about long distance relationships, but he let his heart sing to him and said only, "These things have a way of working themselves out."

When they finished their conversation, Pete turned off his bedside light and was buoyed by the feeling that on the home front at least, maybe things were trending his way.

THIRTY-THREE

Pete dropped off his supplemental response to the ethics complaint at the post office and then called Andy Tate. It was too early in the day for Tennessee Whiskey so his speech sounded crisper.

"I have another question about Marlin Hines," Pete said. "Do you know if he was born in Toledo? I'm guessing he might have been because that's where he moved to after he left Ridge College."

"I don't know where he was from to be honest. It could have been Toledo. Why is that important?"

"If Thomas Edinger were blackmailing Hines as you suggested, it might have involved something Edinger knew about Hines from the past. I thought I'd dig a little deeper and see if anything turns up."

"I told you, blackmail was just a guess."

"But a good guess. The possibility never occurred to me until you mentioned it."

Tate was silent for a moment, then said, "Millie might be able to help us with Hines' background. I seem to remember that when I applied to Ridge College, I had to fill out a detailed questionnaire that included things like where I was born, schools I attended, stuff like that."

"Could you ask her? Or have we gone to the well with her too many times already?"

"I wouldn't worry about that," Tate said. "Millie liked Marlin Hines just as much as I did. I'm sure she'd be happy to check, assuming the college still has Hines' records." Tate promised to call Pete back after he'd spoken with her.

Harry had called while Pete was on the telephone with Tate. He returned the call.

"Time has gotten away from me," Harry said. "Rona's birthday is the day after tomorrow and I'm putting together a surprise party for her. I can't very well do that at the Bayview so I've arranged to take over The Fusion for three hours that night. I want to be sure you're available."

Pete said, "I guess I'm going to have to change my plans. I was planning to sneak away for a quiet dinner with Rona at The Manitou that night."

"You're a real card," Harry said. "Besides, I know you have a thing for Carla and she's going to be at the party, too."

"A thing?" Pete said. "That sounds so old-fashioned."

"That's a joke coming from you," Harry said. "Do you know who else is going to be at the party?"

"Darth Vader?"

"No, wise guy. Ira Manning. He's coming up to give a press conference on the Edinger case the next day."

"When did he decide that?" Pete said.

"I just found out. He sent an e-mail to all of the media early this morning to alert us."

"Why a press conference? Has there been some new development in the Edinger case?"

"Beats me. Maybe it's just Ira being Ira and fighting the battle on two fronts—in the courtroom and in the court of public opinion."

"I'll call him," Pete said.

"As soon as I got the notice about the press conference, I sent him an e-mail inviting him to Rona's birthday party. He accepted by return e-mail three minutes later."

Pete returned a couple of other calls and then dialed Ira Manning's number and waited while his secretary tracked him down. "Norske!" Manning bellowed. "You were on my list of people to call."

"I understand you intend to grace us with your presence in a few days."

"Decided this morning. There are some things I have to go over with your boy Spencer, but the main reason is that sheriff of yours. He keeps putting out this pap about how he has a sure-fire case against Mr. Dahl. I need to get up there and even the playing field a bit."

"Richter has some holes in his case."

"Holes," Manning huffed. "If I were Walter Payton—remember him, he was the ace running back for the Chicago Bears in the old days?—I'd be able to gallop right through one of those holes without anyone laying a paw on me."

"It sounds like you're now fully committed to the case," Pete said.

"I'm tending that way. The case is gaining more traction publicity-wise than I thought it might for a while. An article just appeared in the *Detroit Free Press* and before that there was one in the *Cleveland Plain Dealer*. The Cleveland story irritated the crap out of me, though. They misspelled my name in one place. Left out an 'n.' 'Manning' isn't that hard to spell, for crissakes. My PR guy is trying to get them to print a correction, but you know how that goes. The error is on page one and the correction is buried somewhere on page twenty-two. We're trying to generate some more stories in other papers with my name spelled right."

"We can talk about it when you're up here," Pete said. "Let me bring you up to date on what I've discovered so far about that poem." He summarized for Manning the relationship between Edinger and Marlin Hines and Hines' suicide after he resigned from Ridge College.

"Interesting. So you think blackmail might have been involved?"

"Not my idea," Pete said. "A retired professor at the college who knew both of them raised that possibility."

"It could be dynamite if it's true."

"We'll see. I have to do some more digging."

"Blackmail would show that someone had a real motive to kill Edinger. With the other chinks he has to deal with, that would blow your friend Richter's case against Dahl right out of the water. Does Dahl know any of this?"

"I haven't seen or talked to Spencer Dahl since that day I walked out of the courtroom. I don't think we should say anything to him, either, because he'd find a way to blab it around town even though he's in jail. Besides, it's possible I'll hit a dead end after I dig around some more."

"How about the press? Can we work any of this stuff into the stories my PR guy is trying to plant? Not as fact, of course. Sometimes working in innuendoes or hypotheticals can be almost as good as if the facts established it beyond question."

"I wish you wouldn't do that, either. We'll have time enough to use the information if I'm able to establish the tie-in I mentioned."

"Jesus, Norske, you really tie a man's hands. How am I supposed to get new clients if I can't get my name out there and throw ice-water on the prosecution's case?"

"Patience, my friend, patience. See you in two days."

Shortly after he got off the phone with Manning, Andy Tate called back and confirmed that Marlin Hines had indeed been born in Toledo. The address he gave when he applied to Ridge College was 19 Long Street. Tate also gave him Marlin Hines' work history "just in case he needed it."

Pete checked his atlas and found that Long Street was on the north side of Toledo. He sat back in his chair and began to wonder whether Hines and Edinger knew each other before they both landed associate professor jobs at Ridge College. Pete called up Thomas Edinger's website and confirmed his recollection that Edinger was also from Toledo. Pete then looked at the notes from his telephone conversation with Andy Tate; they showed that Hines got his undergraduate degree from what is now Wittenberg University, the same college that Edinger attended. They had to have known each other before Ridge College.

He grabbed the phone and dialed Andy Tate's number again. "I hope your relationship with Millie is solid because I need some more information, this time on Thomas Edinger. Do you suppose she'd be willing to check Edinger's application when he applied to Ridge College and see what address he gave in Toledo? I'm almost positive Edinger and Hines knew each other before they joined Ridge College, but I'm trying to confirm it."

An hour later, Tate called him back. Thomas Edinger's application showed his Toledo address as 3601 Evergreen Lane. Pete got out his atlas again and found that Evergreen Lane and Long Street intersected and that Edinger and Hines had once lived little more than a block apart.

Pete thought back to his previous inquiry to the Toledo Police Department. If they'd actually run a search as they said they did, and Hines' name didn't turn up, that suggested there might not have been an investigation. And, possibly, no body, only a story. The three-line obituary that appeared in one of the papers could have been a plant, and the fact that Hines' wife disappeared shortly after the incident would be consistent with a fake-suicide scenario.

He thought about that for a while and decided he was letting his imagination run wild. He had to take one step at a time and find out what it was that Edinger held over Hines' head. Assuming the blackmail theory had validity, that is. There were probably a myriad of reasons that would give one person cause to blackmail another, but in academia, two possibilities loomed large. First, plagiarism, the kiss of death in academic circles. Or second, a criminal past, which if it came out, would be equally damaging to a person professionally.

He didn't have the foggiest idea how to go about determining whether Hines had committed plagiarism, but he did know how to have the criminal records searched. Ohio and Tennessee were logical venues to begin the search. He logged on the website of the search service he'd been using and went through the hoops to order court searches in those two states for Marlin Hines. In a half-hour, the search results came back. There was nothing of public record on Hines in either state.

Pete thought some more about the plagiarism possibility. He ran a Google search on Hines and came up with a list of nine articles he'd published in various academic journals around the country. Seeing the references to the articles reinforced his initial conclusion that it would be sheer luck if he came up with any problems with any of them. A person would have to have an intimate knowledge of the work of others in his field to be able to spot something in Hines' work that smacked of plagiarism. Thomas Edinger might have that knowledge, but Pete knew he did not.

Pete's options were limited. He'd gotten lucky with his trip to Toledo when he'd stumbled onto a busybody who knew everything about everyone in the neighborhood, but ferreting out someone's criminal past was different. It had to be twenty-five or thirty years since Hines lived on Long Street. Pete's chances of getting lucky again and finding someone who knew Hines from his early years were virtually nil.

Still, it was worth a try. Either that or give up, and giving up wasn't something that was in Pete's DNA.

THIRTY-FOUR

Pete was on the road to Toledo again before seven the next morning armed with some of his favorite oldies and a jumbo bag of trail mix for sustenance. He tried to focus on things other than the odometer as he motored south and occasionally hummed along with an Eagles song or a Johnny Cash favorite.

Shortly after noon, he was on the city's northwest side searching for Long Street. The number Tate had given him, 19 Long, turned out to be the address for one of three low-rise yellow brick apartment buildings that looked like government subsidized housing. Modest bungalows lined the other side of the street. It was typical of many aging inner city neighborhoods.

Pete scanned the plastic name plates in the vestibule of the building at 19 Long Street and didn't see "Hines" listed. That didn't surprise him and he was prepared to knock on doors to see if he could find someone who remembered the Hines family. Chicken soup seemed to be the day's menu item of choice for the residents because the aroma seeped from the apartments and permeated the halls.

He began on the ground floor and worked his way up. As he proceeded from door to door, he got a variety of receptions that ranged from occupants who slammed the door in his face before he could get his question out to those who listened politely and then said they didn't know the Hines family. When he finished with the first floor, he moved on to the second and then the third. No luck with any of them.

On the outside chance that someone in one of the other buildings might know the Hines, he decided to try those apartments as well. He followed the same routine with the same result until he knocked on a door on the second floor of the adjacent apartment building.

"Are you looking for Mary Hines?" the elderly woman with a walker asked.

Thinking Mary was probably Marlin Hines' mother, he said, "Either Mary or someone else who might know Marlin Hines or where I might be able to reach him." He explained that he was the attorney for the estate of a man who'd named Marlin Hines in his will as one of his heirs and he was trying to locate him. The white lie had worked for him before, although if Jeffery Rodes knew what he what he was doing, he'd almost surely cite it in his ethics complaint as yet another example of how Pete went around deceiving people.

"Oh," the woman said.

"Does Mary live in this building?" he asked.

"Mary passed on years ago."

"I'm sorry to hear that," Pete said.

"Whose will are you talking about?"

"His uncle."

"That's funny," she said. "Mary never mentioned having a brother."

"The uncle is on his father's side," Pete fibbed, scrambling to be consistent.

The woman didn't look convinced. To get the conversation away from genealogy and flowing in the right direction, Pete asked, "Do you know Marlin?"

"I haven't seen the young man in years. Since before he graduated from college, I believe."

"But you did know him in his early years I gather."

"Out of respect for Mary's memory, I'd rather not say anything."

Pete sensed he might have stumbled onto something and he pressed the woman for more details. "If there's something about Marlin, as the attorney for his uncle's estate, I should know about it. I don't have a copy of the will with me, but I'm almost certain there's a clause in it pertaining to the ethical and moral behavior of each of his heirs."

"Mary and I had conversations about Marlin. I don't feel comfortable discussing them with a stranger."

Pete had a feeling that he'd pushed the woman about as far as he could and shifted gears. "I can understand why you feel the way you do. This would be a much better world if everyone had your integrity. Please understand, the only reason I'm asking about Marlin is that I'm trying to do my job as an attorney. There are some rumors floating around about things he might have done in his youth and I'm trying to determine whether or not they're true. It will have a bearing on how I give effect to his uncle's will."

"Thank you for your kind words. Would it help if I gave you the name of someone you could talk to about Marlin?"

"Thanks so much. That would help a lot."

The woman came back with a slip of paper that contained a name and telephone number. "You don't even have to drive. Mr. Werling lives in the building next door now. Not the building Mary used to live in, but the one on the opposite side."

Pete thanked the woman and did everything but skip down the hall and race over to Werling's building. He knocked on his door and tried to appear nonchalant. When Werling opened the door, Pete introduced himself as an attorney and said, "Mrs. Hatcher gave me your name, Mr. Werling. She said you might be willing to talk to me about a man named Marlin Hines."

Werling was a block of a man with a brush cut. He appeared to be in his middle or late sixties, but was still muscular and his biceps bulged beneath his gray tee shirt. He looked at Pete with steady gray eyes and said, "Marlin Hines. Boy, that was a long time ago. Why are you interested in Marlin?"

Pete repeated his story that he was attorney for the estate of Hines' uncle who had named Marlin as one of his heirs. Pete added that the uncle had included a morals clause in his will and Pete was trying to determine the facts to make sure Marlin was a qualified heir.

Werling invited him in and said, "You're lucky you came along on a day when a broken down old street cop doesn't have a lot on his plate."

They chatted briefly about superficial things, including Pete's pre-occupation with the Toledo Mud Hens when he was a boy. Then Pete said, "I sense that Marlin Hines might have had a run-in with the law when he was younger."

"Maybe that's putting it a little too simply. When Marlin and the other kids his age were growing up, Toledo adopted what's known as community policing. Things were getting a little rough in a lot of the neighborhoods and the theory was that community policing would bring the people and law enforcement closer together for the benefit of the city."

"A lot of cities do that."

"Right, but we did it back when it was still a new concept. Long Street and the surrounding blocks were my beat area and I spent a lot of time on foot getting to know the kids. Shoot, I wasn't much older than most of them. Marlin was always a quiet boy and not one of the real troublemakers. I think it was about his senior year in high school that he started hanging around with the foster daughter of one of the families in the area. She was younger than him. Fourteen or fifteen years old at the time as I recall. Anyway, Marlin went away to college, and when he was home for vacation one year, the foster parents claimed they stumbled upon Marlin having sex with the girl. The foster parents raised holy hell and insisted that Marlin be prosecuted for statutory rape. It's been so long ago now that I don't remember all of the details, but the girl refused to testify against Marlin and it eventually came out that the foster parents were abusing their foster children, including the girl in question. The prosecutor quietly deep-sixed the case and the family lost all of their foster children. Marlin Hines faded into the woodwork."

"Did the community know about all of this?" Pete asked.

"Oh hell yes. For some reason, they didn't blame the foster family, but poor Marlin's reputation took a real beating. He came out as the bad guy in what would be a very sordid incident. I think that's why he stopped coming home. Even his family shunned him."

"I assume there's no public record of any of this because Hines was never prosecuted."

"Right, and we didn't have sex offender registries and things like that in those days."

"Question, Joel. Do you remember a kid named Thomas Edinger?"

Werling snorted and said, "Remember him! Hell yes I remember him. I always thought he was one of the instigators of things that went down in the neighborhood, but we never caught him at anything."

"And I assume he knew about the incident between Marlin Hines and the foster girl, right?"

"How could he help but know? Like I said, everybody in the community knew the story."

Werling had been so straight with him that it made Pete want to confess his real reason for wanting to know about Hines' background, but he couldn't think of a graceful way to do so. There was one more thing he wanted from Werling, though. He wanted a contact at the Toledo Police Department he could talk to about Marlin Hines' suicide.

"This has been extremely useful in view of the morals clause in the will. But there's something I should have mentioned at the outset. There's a rumor floating around that Marlin Hines killed himself and that's the reason I've been unable to find him."

"Suicide? I hadn't heard about that."

"It might not be true. Do you have any contacts at the Toledo Police Department I could check with and find out if there's anything to the rumor?"

"Sure," Werling said. He wrote a name and phone number on a piece of paper and handed it to Pete. "Captain Yarborough isn't in today. He's at a conference in Columbus and isn't due back until late tomorrow morning. Knowing what a workaholic he is, he'll probably go straight to the office. I'd try him around noon or a little after."

"Thanks," Pete said. He calculated how long it would take him to drive back to Frankfort. He knew he couldn't miss Rona's birthday party.

"Now let me ask you a question, Pete. Assuming Hines committed suicide as you said, and assuming further the morals clause in the will comes into play, what happens then?"

"It depends. I'll have to research whether the *per stirpes* rule applies or whether the remaining named heirs take everything. *Per stirpes* means, essentially, that Marlin Hines' share would flow through to his children or other heirs."

Werling nodded.

Pete thanked him and headed out to his Range Rover feeling excited that another piece of the puzzle had fallen into place.

THIRTY-FIVE

The underwear and shaving gear Pete bought at K-Mart the night before made his unexpected overnight stay in Toledo less disruptive of his routine than it might have been. He loaded up on the complimentary breakfast in the lobby, scanned the newspaper, and then headed for Armand Lukitsch's house to ask him some follow-up questions about Marlin Hines.

"Pete," Lukitsch said, shaking his hand warmly, "I didn't expect to see you down here again."

"I didn't expect to be here, either, but some lawyer stuff came up that I had to deal with. I had some extra time and I wanted to ask you a couple more questions about Marlin Hines' suicide." He took a seat on the couch and glanced at his watch while Lukitsch rushed into the kitchen to do his usual tea-and-cookies routine. Freddy had been lurking out of sight and suddenly flew through the air and landed on the back of the couch inches from his shoulder. Pete recovered from his momentary surprise and soon Freddy was purring in his ear like the finely-tuned engine of a Lamborghini.

Pete accepted a cup of tea and a cookie and said, "I'm a bit pressed for time so I'll get right to the point. When we talked the other day, you said that Marlin Hines committed suicide. Did you actually see Hines' body?"

Lukitsch looked horrified. "Heavens no."

"So you didn't see the body either inside the Hines' house or when it was taken out to an ambulance or a hearse."

"No," Lukitsch said again, shaking his head, "it happened at night. If it had happened during the daylight hours, I might have seen it."

"Who told you Marlin Hines committed suicide, then?"

"A real estate lady. I try to keep on the good side of the real estate people because they can do so much to support the property values in a neighborhood."

"When did she tell you about the suicide?"

"The next day I think," Lukitsch said with a thoughtful look on his face. "Yes, I'm sure it was the next day in the afternoon. If you need an exact time, I might have made notes of my conversation with her and could look for them if you like."

"No, that's good enough. So as far as you know, no one saw the body except Hines' wife."

"And I suppose the police and the ambulance people who picked it up."

Assuming they were ever called, Pete thought. "Did the police come by and ask you or any of the other neighbors about Hines?"

"No, they never asked me anything. I'm sure they didn't ask any of the other neighbors, either. I'm sure I'd know if they did."

I'm sure you would, Pete thought. He thanked Lukitsch for his time, gave Freddy a scratch under the chin, and headed downtown to the police station.

A junior officer told Pete that Captain Yarborough, a district commander, wasn't in yet, but was expected shortly. Pete read a two-month-old copy of *Law Enforcement Today* and sipped coffee from a Styrofoam cup while he waited. Not exactly like Armand Lukitsch's china and cookies, he thought ruefully.

At exactly three minutes past twelve, a trim man with a pencil moustache and an immaculate police uniform burst in and suddenly the large room buzzed with activity. A sturdy policewoman asked the captain whether he wanted coffee and another officer showed him a clipboard with a stack of papers attached. The officer pointed toward Pete and said something Pete couldn't hear. Captain Yarborough looked Pete's way and a few moments later, walked over to where he was sitting.

"You've been waiting for me?" Yarborough said in a clipped tone.

"Yes, sir. Do you have ten minutes to talk to me?"

Yarborough fixed him with a steely gaze and said, "You're catching me at a bad time. I just got back in town. Helene," he called, waving a hand in the direction of the policewoman, "can you set up an appointment for this gentleman?" Yarborough turned and started towards his office.

Pete played the only card he had. "Joel Werling thought you might be able to fit me into your schedule today."

Yarborough stopped and turned to face Pete. "Do you know Officer Werling?"

"Yes," Pete said, stretching the truth. "He helped me with a matter and thought you might be able to fill in the gaps in our knowledge. I have to leave town this afternoon and—"

"How the hell is he? I haven't been very good about keeping in touch with my officers after they retire."

"He looks great," Pete said. He tried to inject a little humor into the conversation by adding, "I think he misses the action."

Yarborough laughed. "That's typical. We spend our entire careers bellyaching about everything, and then once we're retired, we miss not being in the loop anymore."

"Isn't that the truth," Pete said.

Yarborough looked at him through narrowed eyes and said, "Are you plainclothes with another force?"

"No, I'm a lawyer."

"I see. Well, I guess I can spare ten minutes since the request came from Officer Werling. He was one of the best damn officers the Toledo force ever had."

"Could we go back to your office? I'm not comfortable talking about this out here."

"Sure, why don't you go back and make yourself comfortable. I'll be along momentarily as soon as I take a whizz."

Another officer directed him to Captain Yarborough's office. It was good-sized, but outfitted with utilitarian hard-edged steel and laminated wood furniture. The walls were filled with framed certificates, family pictures, and other photographs. Captain Yarborough obviously was a fisherman because fully half of the photographs were shots of him or members of his family landing fish, holding fish up for the camera, posing next to a Gulfstream camper, or sitting on a dock that jutted into some evergreen-rimmed lake.

When Yarborough came back from the men's room, Pete said, "A lot of your pictures look like they were taken in an area like where I grew up."

"Where's that, Pete?"

"Northern Wisconsin."

Yarborough walked over to the wall and pointed to one of the photographs and said, "Eagle River." He pointed to another and said, "Hayward. That's big fish country as you undoubtedly know. Here's one at a small lake in Vilas County. That's God's country. Why did you move away?"

"Do you know what we called my area when I lived there? The Demilitarized Zone, after the no-man's land between North and South Korea. It wasn't good farming country and it wasn't good resort country. If I'd stayed up there, I'd be cutting poplar trees for the paper mills half the year and on welfare the other half."

Yarborough shook his head. "I know what you mean. Some places are better to visit than to live in. Sorry to rush you, but what's on your mind?"

Pete gave him his business cards both from Sears & Whitney in Chicago and the one he used in Michigan. "I'm semi-retired from the practice of law, but still take on things from time-to-time to keep my hand in." He then told Captain Yarborough his well-honed story about representing a decedent's estate and trying to track down one of the heirs named Marlin Hines. He'd traced Hines to Toledo, he said, and was told he'd committed suicide years ago, but hadn't been able to confirm that.

"When there's a suicide, you investigate, don't you?" Pete asked.

"Sure," Yarborough said, "if the incident is reported to us."

"Would you have time to run a computer search to see if Marlin Hines' name pops up?"

"Absolutely," Yarborough said, logging on his desktop computer. "When did this man Hines die?"

"I don't know the exact date. It was about ten years ago, give or take."

"We had everything computerized by that time and it should be here if it happened in Toledo. It did happen in the city, right?"

"Yes," Pete said.

Yarborough keyed in information and waited. Then he keyed in more information and waited again. He did it a third time.

He looked up at Pete and shook his head. "Nothing. Are you sure you got the name right?"

"Positive."

"Let me try one more thing," Yarborough said. He keyed in information again and told Pete he was doing another search under "suicides." After a couple of minutes, he looked up at Pete and shook his head again.

"One final thing, Captain. There's a morals clause in the will and I picked up rumors that Hines might have been involved in some sort of incident in Toledo years ago. Officer Werling remembers the case—a sex crime incident involving an underage girl—but said that charges were never brought against Hines. Could you search to see if the computer validates Joel's memory?"

"How long ago would that have happened?"

Pete thought for a moment and said, "Maybe forty years?"

"And you said it was a sex crime?"

"Yes, sex with an underage girl."

"Mmm," Yarborough murmured. "Everything was paper back then and no one had even conceived of a sex crime registry. At least not in our area. When we computerized, we put some of our files on the system, but it was a hit-and-miss process. I'm not optimistic a search will turn up anything." Ten minutes later, after keying in information several times, Yarborough shook his head and said, "Sorry. Tell you what I'll do, though. I have your business cards. I'll have someone look through our paper records and send you an e-mail if we find anything."

Driving north again, Pete summed up what he'd discovered during his second visit to Toledo. The first was that Marlin Hines had once been accused, rightly or wrongly, with a sex crime involving an underage girl. Charges had apparently never been brought against him, but everyone in the community knew about the incident and blamed him anyway. Second, Thomas Edinger and Marlin Hines unquestionably knew each other growing up and it seemed impossible that Edinger wouldn't have known about the accusations against Hines. And third, Hines reportedly committed suicide ten years ago, but Pete hadn't been able to find any record that the incident actually occurred.

The information he'd uncovered didn't solve the puzzle, but it was more than he had before his visit. He'd reassess the situation after he heard back from Yarborough following his staff's search of the paper records.

THIRTY-SIX

Rona's birthday party was in full-swing when Pete walked in The Fusion. Harry and Rona were holding court at the bar wearing silly cone-shaped birthday hats that looked like something Harry had purchased at the dime store down the street. The other seventy-five or so people in attendance were scattered around the room talking or dancing to the three-person band in the corner opposite the bar. The band's vocalist had long red hair and a skirt that was short enough to stop traffic had she been sashaying down Main Street.

Pete walked up to Rona and gave her a kiss on the cheek and said, "Happy birthday, Doll."

"Thanks, Pete. The party can begin now that you're here."

Harry, never enjoying a conversation where he wasn't the focal point, chimed in caustically with, "Nice of you to show up an hour late. You missed the surprise 'Happy birthday' greeting when Rona and I walked in. Course, since you can't sing, it was probably just as well."

"Harry," Rona said in a scolding tone. She patted Pete's arm and added, "We're just glad you're here."

Harry continued to bore in and said, "I'll bet you'd have been here on time if you knew what a hot band I'd lined up."

"Oh, is there a band? I hadn't noticed."

"Hadn't noticed." Harry spat out the words contemptuously. "I thought you were going to run into that post staring at Vicki Jean when you walked in."

"They do have a nice sound," Pete said.

"They play everything from that ancient stuff you like to more modern tunes some of us prefer."

"Right. Did Ira make it?"

"He not only made it, but he arrived ahead of time to be polite. I'll tell you, that man can sing. He led the group. He's over there regaling some of the guests with his stories." Harry gestured toward a table where Ira Manning was sprawled in a chair with a beer in his hand and surrounded by six or eight other people who were hanging on every syllable he uttered.

"I think I'll go over and say hello."

Harry moved closer to him and asked in a low voice, "Before you do, did you learn anything new in Toledo?"

"Several things."

"Well?" Harry said.

"Let's wait until Ira can join us so I don't have to tell it twice." Then to torment Harry, he added, "Or we can discuss it tomorrow before the press conference."

"If you tell us tonight," Harry said earnestly, "we'll have time to digest it."

"Okay. As soon as Ira's finished with his stories."

"I have a feeling he's never finished. I can go get him," Harry volunteered.

"No, let's wait until he begins to circulate again. Remember, I know the guy."

Harry lowered his voice again. "Be on your guard when you talk to Carla. She knows you were late because you were in Toledo digging up information to help Spencer."

Pete looked at him sharply. "How does she know that?"

"Rona and I were talking to Ira before you got here. You know what a quiet voice he has. I'm positive Carla overheard him ask if we'd gotten a report from you on your latest visit to Toledo. He asked some questions about your trip to Chattanooga, too. I was going to try to smooth things over with Carla, but she just walked away. She didn't look happy."

"Great," Pete said, shaking his head.

"When you talk to her," Harry suggested, "maybe you can explain that you were just in Toledo tying up some loose ends for Ira and you're completely out of the case now."

"Yeah, I'm sure that would be persuasive," Pete said sarcastically. "She's really likely to believe that when she knows I was in Chattanooga the day after I had dinner at her house and now in Toledo."

"Can't you think of some way to explain those trips?"

"I already gave her a cock-and-bull story about a business trip. What makes you think she'd believe any new story I cook up?"

"I could try to talk to her again," Harry offered.

"No, don't make it worse. Let me handle it."

"Sorry."

Pete circulated through the crowd and exchanged pleasantries with people he knew. He saw Carla across the room and had pretty much decided to confess what he'd been doing and throw himself on her mercy. She apparently saw him, too, and as he walked her way, she grabbed the hand of a paunchy man with a fringe of hair rimming his head and began to jitterbug with him. She moved fluidly to the music in her tight black pants and after about a minute, her dance partner looked like he was a candidate for cardiac arrest. Pete continued to circulate through the crowd and tried not to be obvious when he occasionally looked their way.

When the number ended, Pete began to edge toward where Carla was standing again. The band switched to a slow number and the man she'd been dancing with whisked her out on the floor for another number. As he watched out of the corner of his eye, he saw Carla throw her head back and laugh like her dance partner was the wittiest man in the room.

Pete sighed and drifted back toward the bar. He saw Ira Manning getting another beer and went over and tapped him on the shoulder. Manning looked his way and bellowed "Norske!" in a voice thunderous enough to drown out the band. "You folks up here really know how to get down and party. Shoot, the people I associate with in Chicago are a bunch of tight-asses compared to these folks."

"Are you all set for your press conference tomorrow?"

"When you've done this as long as I have, Norske, you don't need a lot of preparation. You learn what plays with the media and what doesn't."

"I saw you regaling the locals a while ago."

"You know, that's part of it," he said seriously. "You never know when a friend or relative of a person you talk to is going to need criminal representation and it's nice to have advocates spread around who'll mention your name."

"So it has nothing to do with the fact you love to tell stories, huh?" Pete asked mischievously.

"Oh, that too, but it's mostly marketing. Say, Harry tells me you learned some things in Toledo that might be helpful, but he didn't know the details."

Pete beckoned Harry over and summarized the results of his latest visit to Toledo for them, including that Hines and Edinger knew each other growing up and that Hines had sex offender charges against him as a first-year college student. He also told them he couldn't find any corroboration of Hines' suicide other than that it was reported in the Toledo newspaper.

"So what you're saying is that this Hines guy might still be alive and could have been the shooter."

"I don't have evidence of that, but think we can't completely discount the possibility. If Hines were alive, he clearly would have a motive to kill Edinger because Edinger not only ruined his career, but probably his life as well."

Manning looked thoughtful for a few moments, then said, "Do you think your sheriff would take a more balanced look at this case if we got this information to him?"

Pete scoffed at the comment and said, "Not likely." He told them what happened when he tipped off Joe Tessler about Calvin Seitz.

"Tessler's the plainclothes detective with the sheriff's department, right?" Manning asked.

"Right."

"Do you think you'd have better luck talking directly to the sheriff?"

"Ask Harry. The sheriff refers to me as Public Enemy Number One around his department. I'd have as much chance of reasoning with him and convincing him that he might have the wrong man as I would of getting the wind in Chicago to stop blowing."

"That hopeless, huh?"

"That hopeless," Pete said.

They stood quietly for a few moments, then Pete said, "You've been in this game a long time, Ira. What kind of defense are you thinking about for Dahl?"

Manning grinned and said, "Insanity might be a possibility. The guy's certifiably wacky. But more realistically, the prosecutor has to prove guilt beyond a reasonable doubt. That means all of the things I've been hammering at so far come into play. Now we have the blackmail possibility, too. Maybe Hines or someone close to him getting revenge for what happened years ago."

"We'll need more than I presently have to make that stick," Pete said.

Manning looked thoughtful, then said, "I'm not talking about hard evidence. I'm talking about planting seeds of doubt in the minds of jurors regarding others with a motive to kill Edinger. And just as important, planting the same seeds with the media. Kind of a two-front war."

"Listening to the two of you talk," Harry said, "gives me a great idea for a feature story. A high-priced criminal lawyer from Chicago—"

"High priced? Maybe I missed it, but I haven't noticed any half-million dollar checks come into my firm's account from up here."

"Well, you see," Pete said, feigning earnestness, "you have to monetize all of the pub you've been getting on the case."

"Yeah, all of the pub I've been getting with a misspelled name and everything," he said dryly.

"Hey, I'm a lawyer myself. I happen to know that the filing fee in Cook County for a name-change petition isn't more than fifty bucks. You can net that off from the monetized value of the publicity."

They agreed to caucus again in the morning before Ira's press conference and Pete went in search of Carla Neville. He spotted her standing alone with her back toward him. The band had slowed their pace again and he tapped her on the shoulder and said, "May I have this dance, young lady?"

Carla turned and saw him and her face clouded over. "Well," she said, her voice dripping with sarcasm, "if it isn't my travelling lawyer friend."

"How are you?"

"I'm the one who should be asking you that. You must be tired after all of your 'business' trips."

"Let's dance and I'll explain."

"What could you explain to me that I don't already know?" she said nonchalantly. "Besides, I'm all danced out. Maybe you should ask your co-counsel Mr. Manning or whatever his name is. He looks like a dancer."

"I know I should have—"

"Should have what?" Carla said, her voice rising. "Told me you were going to Chattanooga, Tennessee, on a secret mission for the Spencer Dahl defense team the day after I fed you dinner? Or maybe that you were making two trips to Toledo for the same purpose?"

Pete was beginning to feel uncomfortable. People around them heard her outburst and were staring at them. "Let's go somewhere where we can talk," he said quietly.

"Where would you like to go?" she screamed. "Chattanooga? Toledo? Spencer Dahl's jail cell? Maybe you can bring that scumbag a cake with a file in it at the same time!"

"Carla . . ."

"You're just as sleazy as that rapist you're trying to protect!"

Carla stormed toward the front of the restaurant where the coats were hanging. Rona had seen her confrontation with Pete and went over and took her by the elbow and said something. Carla shook her arm loose, grabbed her jacket, and left. By now, half of the people in the room were aware of the spat and they watched in embarrassed silence.

THIRTY-SEVEN

ra Manning's press conference started off as a non-event. He adopted an old-shoe approach, and judging from his remarks, seemed to be almost understanding of the sheriff's position in the Dahl case. He allowed that he might have seen things the same way in view of the evidence found at Dahl's house and the fact his alibi for the time Thomas Edinger was shot was in question.

Then Manning explained the standard that applied to criminal cases and point by point proceeded to dismantle the prosecution's case against Spencer Dahl. But he wasn't finished. He went on to imply coyly that the defense was on the cusp of unraveling the mystery behind the cryptic poem that Dahl allegedly sent to Edinger. There had been blackmail alright, Manning intoned in a melodious voice, but the blackmailer was Edinger himself, not Spencer Dahl, and the person being blackmailed, who Manning said he couldn't disclose yet, was the one responsible for Edinger's murder.

He then invited questions from the media. The reporters fell over themselves trying to pry information from Manning about his blackmail allegations. He deftly parried their efforts, but from time-to-time added some gloss to his earlier remarks.

When they were in Harry's office after the press conference, Pete said, "Thanks a lot for going public with the blackmail angle. I thought you weren't going to do that unless I came up with more information."

"I thought about it some more last night," Manning said. "Apart from whether Marlin Hines is still alive, or whether someone else that was close to him did the shooting, I feel we have enough on the blackmail thing to plant a few seeds."

"But no proof," Pete said dryly.

"I'm confident that by the time the case goes to trial, *if* it goes to trial, you'll have that, too. And remember what I said. Seeds, if well planted, can be almost as good as proof."

Pete rolled his eyes.

"How do you think it went, Harry?" Manning asked. "You were sitting with the other reporters."

"Judging from the way they were hanging on your every word and taking notes," Harry said, "I'd say it went great. You created a feeding frenzy with those blackmail comments."

"That was my goal. Level the playing field without attacking your sheriff and toss some red meat into the arena for the media to chew on." He looked at Pete and added, "Now all you have to do, Norske, is find that fellow Hines."

"Oh, that's easy," Pete said sarcastically, "he's probably having lunch right now at the Mayfair Tavern."

Manning laughed. "It would make a helluva story if he *were* still alive, wouldn't it? Man returns from the dead after ten years to exact revenge against another man with a nineteenth century musket at the same time as the victim's wife was balling a self-styled mystic. You show me one newspaper in the country that could resist that storyline."

Harry grinned at Manning's comment and nodded.

No one spoke for a while. Then Manning said, "It's a long way to Chicago so I'd best be on my way. I'm going to think about what kind of papers I can file with the court to put pressure on your boy Richter. We're entitled to see everything the state has against Mr. Dahl, but sometimes they hold things back until close to trial to gain a tactical advantage. If that's the case here, I'd like to know sooner rather than later." He nudged Pete with his elbow and said. "And you keep digging, Norske."

When Manning was gone, Rona put her hand on Pete's arm and said, "Thanks for arranging all of this. And for your help. Now I'm comfortable that Spencer's interests are being capably looked after regardless of how the case turns out."

"No thanks necessary," Pete said. "I seem to remember that you've done a few things for me over the years, too." He remembered in particular how Rona had coaxed him back into the world of the living after his late wife, Doris, had died suddenly of an aneurysm while he was away on a business trip.

"I'm sorry for Carla's outburst last night," she said.

Pete feigned nonchalance. "I tried to straddle the fence and it caught up with me. I can't say I wasn't warned about her feelings."

They sat quietly for a few minutes until Pete said, "Well, I think I'll walk up to my office and see what I can find to entertain myself for the rest of the day."

"If you boys want," Rona said, "you can stop by in a couple of hours and I'll have my chef make you something for lunch."

Pete and Harry looked at each other and it was clear they had a date.

When Pete got to his office, he had a voicemail message from an attorney named Alan Doar in Lansing. Doar's message said he'd been retained by the Attorney Grievance Commission to give them his independent recommendation concerning the ethics complaint and wanted to set up a conference call among all parties. Pete called him back.

"Thanks for getting back to me, Mr. Thorsen. As I said in the message I left, I've been retained as the investigator and hearing officer in the ethics complaint against you. Unless you insist on a face-to-face hearing, I propose we do it by conference call. Any objections?"

Pete thought about it for a moment, then said, "I don't think so. Let me check with my counsel in Chicago and I'll get back to you today."

They then talked about possible dates if the conference call went forward. Doar said he was available any day for the rest of the week and then would be gone on a cruise with his wife for three weeks so the call would either have to be on short notice or sometime in November after he returned. Pete checked with Angie DeMarco and called Doar back. They agreed on a conference call on Friday of that week.

Only a dozen or so of the Bayview Grille's tables were occupied when Pete walked in. Not like the summer months when people often waited in line if they hadn't had the foresight to make a reservation. Harry was already seated at their usual table perusing the menu.

"I've been seeing a lot of you recently," Pete said as he sat down.

"Lucky you. A lot of people would die for the opportunity to have lunch with the editor of the leading newspaper in the area."

"The *only* newspaper," Pete corrected him.

Pete had never told Harry about the ethics complaint against him for the very good reason that he didn't want to listen to his lecture. He got enough of that from Angie. He was tempted to tell him now, but changed his mind. His original reason for keeping it confidential still applied.

"The town is quieter with Ira gone, isn't it?" Harry said.

"He's like a storm. Quiet while it's building up, then pyrotechnics, finally calm again after the turbulence passes through."

"Isn't that the truth," Harry said. Then he added after a few moments, "Carla stayed with us last night. Her bedroom door was closed and her light was out when we got home. Then this morning she was up and gone before we were out of bed."

"I didn't say this in your office," Pete said, "but I think it's over. It's obvious she's convinced that I lied to her. I thought I could reason with her, but . . ."

"The irony is that you can't stand Spencer."

Pete shook his head and said, "That's an understatement."

They talked about other things while they ate, and on the way out, Harry said, "Joe Tessler was in the audience at the press conference. He's probably dying for more details. I wouldn't be surprised if he calls you."

Harry proved to be prescient because Pete hadn't been back in his office for more than a half-hour when Tessler called.

"Are you calling from your car?" Pete asked, knowing the answer.

"Of course. You know I can't talk to you on an office phone."

"Are you sure that the sheriff doesn't surreptitiously check your cell phone call records?"

Tessler sighed. "Not yet anyway. Say, I wanted to ask you about something your pal Manning said at his press conference."

"I can't imagine what," Pete said innocently. "Overall, I thought he was pretty complimentary about your position."

"He started out being complimentary, but then proceeded to blow holes in our case. I expected to hear most of the stuff he put out, but what I wanted to ask you about was the blackmail angle he harped on at the end. It's clear as the nose on your face that Dahl sent the poem to the deceased to extort money from him. But Manning implied that Edinger was blackmailing someone himself. That doesn't make sense."

"He's right," Pete said.

"Right," Tessler said, scoffing. "And when are we going to meet this bogeyman Edinger was supposedly blackmailing?"

"In due course. I've done some digging into Thomas Edinger's background and discovered some interesting things. Want to hear?"

"I believe that's why I called."

Pete laid out everything he'd learned on his trips to Chattanooga and Toledo, beginning with the fact that Thomas Edinger and Marlin Hines knew each other as boys and Edinger almost certainly knew of the sex charges against Hines. They both wound up as associate professors at Ridge College, Pete continued, and were collaborating on a book about Colonel Thaddeus Clayton that was to serve as the basis for their applications for tenure at the college. Then in the middle of the process, Hines abruptly resigned from the college and advised the tenure committee that all of the work product on the Clayton biography was really Edinger's. Hines moved back to his boyhood city of Toledo and shortly afterward was reported to have committed suicide although Pete said he couldn't find any evidence that this actually occurred.

"So what you're suggesting is that this Hines fellow is still alive and he's the one who actually killed Edinger."

"Either Hines or someone close to him who was seeking revenge for what Edinger did to Hines years before. What better symbolism than to kill Edinger at the festival that bore Colonel Clayton's name. The books about Clayton made Edinger's career, remember."

"Pete, I like you and I've grown to respect the instincts you've shown on these matters, but I think you're really gone off the edge on this one."

"I expected you to say that, but nothing else makes sense. Your case against Spencer Dahl is full of holes as Manning said. No motive, no eyewitnesses, no murder weapon, nothing."

"There's plenty of motive. Your boy Dahl was leeching money off Mrs. Edinger and the deceased found out. Plus we have all of the stuff we found at Dahl's place, the history of conflict between Dahl and Edinger, Mrs. Edinger's statement contradicting Dahl's claim of an alibi."

"She's lying, Joe. She's trying to cover up the fact she's been screwing Spencer Dahl for months. If you're relying on her, you're in trouble. Ira Manning will rip her to shreds if this case goes to trial. As far as the stuff you found, we believe it was planted."

"Okay," Tessler said, sighing, "but until you deliver this Marlin Hines to me on a platter, this mysterious man who somehow has returned from the dead, I'll continue to believe that we have enough to convict Spencer Dahl."

THIRTY-EIGHT

Pete planned to hunker down in his office to prepare for the telephone conference with Doar and Jeffery Rodes that afternoon, but decided to stop at the post office and pick up the latest registered letter from the Attorney Grievance Commission first. It was probably just written confirmation of the hearing, but he wanted to be sure it wasn't something he needed to take into account in mounting his defense.

He heard shouting inside the post office even before he opened the door. The three customers waiting at the counter for service looked embarrassed as Jake Rossum's mother, looking as disheveled as she had the other times Pete had seen her, harangued the postal worker who was standing nose-to-nose with her near the bank of mail boxes.

"Somebody's been stealing my mail!" Mrs. Rossum complained in a high-pitched shriek. "I haven't gotten a letter from my husband in months!"

"Mrs. Rossum, everything that comes to the post office for you or your son goes right into that box and you have the only key. I assure you, no one has been stealing your mail."

"How about letters for Carrie Hines?" she asked. "This box is supposed to be for mail that comes in for both the Hines and the Rossums."

Pete's eyes widened when he heard the name. Had he heard her right? Carrie Hines was Marlin Hines' widow.

"If I don't start getting all of my mail," Mrs. Rossum screamed, "I'm going to write to the president and demand that he fire you!"

The sturdy looking postal worker stared at Mrs. Rossum wearily for a moment, shook her head, and returned to her station behind the counter and began to serve other customers. Pete handed her the registered letter notice when he got to the head of the line. As he signed for the letter, he said in a low voice, "Things are a little rambunctious in here today."

The woman rolled her eyes and said, "This happens at least twice a week. One time that woman comes in and says her name is Carrie Hines. The next time it's Mrs. Rossum. I don't know what she's looking for, but it never seems to be in her box. She always accuses someone of stealing her mail."

"Is she right that mail for both names goes into the box?"

"Yes, but I can't remember the last time anything came in for Hines."

"How long has this been going on?"

"Forever, it seems. At least three or four years."

The Northern Sentinel's offices were on Main Street midway between Pete's office and the post office. Pete literally ran up the street and burst in while Harry was on the telephone. He stood impatiently in front of the editor's desk waiting for him to finish his call. When he did, Pete asked before he could say anything, "Did you ever meet Jake Rossum's mother?"

Harry appeared taken aback by Pete's question which seemed to come out of the blue and said, "I don't think so. Why do you ask?"

"Because I was just at the post office and Mrs. Rossum was making a fuss about not getting all of the mail addressed to her or to Carrie Hines."

"So? A lot of people complain about the mail these days."

"Harry, doesn't the name Carrie Hines mean anything to you?"

"Should it?"

Pete's frustration was evident. "Have you been listening to anything I've told you about my trips to Chattanooga and Toledo?" he asked. "Carrie Hines is Marlin Hines' widow."

Harry processed the information and then a look of disbelief crept over his face. "You're kidding. She's up here?"

"That's the way it appears."

"That doesn't make sense."

"Think about it," Pete said. "We believe Thomas Edinger was blackmailing Marlin Hines, and now we find that Hines' widow is up here with her son. The next thing we know, Edinger is dead. Is the picture coming through?"

"You don't think Carrie Hines shot Edinger . . ."

"I doubt that *she* shot him," he said, thinking about the night he'd given Jake Rossum a ride home and his mother had literally chased him off the property. "But I'm beginning to think that someone close to her did."

Pete could tell from the expression on Harry's face that everything he'd been saying was finally sinking in. "Jake Rossum," Harry murmured softly.

"Uh, huh."

"Because of what Thomas Edinger did to his father."

"Yes."

Harry had emerged from his shock and now was in his action mode. "This clinches it for me. You have to go directly to Richter and lay all of this out for him."

Pete sighed. "If only it were that simple. Joe Tessler called me after I got back from lunch, just as you predicted, and wanted to know what Ira was getting at by his blackmail comments. I told him everything I'd learned during my trips to Chattanooga and Toledo and thought I made a pretty good case. Tessler essentially blew me off. If I couldn't convince him, what chance do you think I'd have with Richter?"

"I see your point."

"They've made up their minds on this case and aren't prepared to move off their position."

"So that avenue is closed."

"I have something I have to do this afternoon," Pete said, "then I'm going to decide what to do next."

"Can't you put off whatever it is that you've got planned and focus on this instead? This could be a major breakthrough for Spencer's defense."

"Screw Spencer Dahl's defense. I'm not thinking about that. I'm thinking about getting the man who committed the crime."

"One follows the other, doesn't it?"

Pete shot him a look and stared out the window at the quiet street.

Harry said, "Getting back to what I was saying about your plans for the afternoon, sometimes it's best to attack matters like this while the juices are flowing."

"I can't change my plans."

"Okay," Harry said, shaking his head and clearly not understanding.

"One more thing. Don't breathe a word of this to anyone, including Rona."

"You mean about Carrie Rossum Hines?"

"Yes."

"I won't, but I don't see why you won't share what's going on with a friend."

"I will, but just not now."

Back in his office, Pete reread his response to the ethics complaint for about the tenth time and reviewed Lorraine Edinger's statement and his supplemental response. He wondered if Lorraine was going to participate in the telephonic hearing. Having met her and seeing her statement, he knew he could expect some interesting if not entirely rational pyrotechnics if she did participate.

He waited for the AT&T conference operator to call and tried to keep his mind on the ethics hearing, but what he'd learned at the post office kept intruding.

THIRTY-NINE

Angie DeMarco was already on the line when the conference operator called him. They limited their conversation to small talk because they didn't know who else might be on the line and listening. He smiled when he thought back to a conference call on one of his deals. The lawyer on the other side, thinking he couldn't be heard, said to his people that they should fight tooth and nail on a critical issue, but be prepared to give in if necessary. The end result in those negotiations wasn't hard to divine.

When the operator called the roll, Michael Stojac, Jeffery Rodes' law partner, answered "present." Rodes apparently was aware that Angie was participating in addition to Pete and wanted to even out the numbers. Lorraine Edinger was on the call as well.

Alan Doar then identified the complaint for the record, told the parties he was going to record the proceedings for his convenience, and summarized the ground rules for the hearing. The strict rules of evidence that would apply in a court proceeding didn't apply, Doar said, but he warned all parties against making statements they couldn't support factually.

"Mr. Rodes," Doar said, "you're the complaining party. Do you want to make an opening statement?"

"Yes sir, I do."

"Proceed, then, but please hold your remarks to no more than five minutes."

Pete listened as Rodes laid out his case. It was essentially as he'd outlined it in his complaint. He sounded pompous, like he was arguing a landmark case before the United States Supreme Court, and sprinkled his presentation with words like "allegedly" and "putative."

"Since I filed my complaint," Rodes said, "Mrs. Thomas Edinger has come forth with a statement in support that describes another incident involving Mr. Thorsen. It was an attempt by Mr. Thorsen to trick Mrs. Edinger and threaten her and bully her into admitting things that weren't true. All of this is part of a pattern of behavior that wouldn't even be acceptable in a place like Chicago which is known for its 'sharp elbow' ways, as they say, and certainly isn't acceptable for a member of the bar of the great State of Michigan."

Lorraine Edinger blurted over the speaker, "This man Mr. Thorsen came to my house and tried to trick me! Then he threatened me with one of those subpoenas and implied bad things about my husband and—"

"Please, Mrs. Edinger," Doar said, "you'll have an opportunity to tell your story at the proper time."

"But—"

"At the proper time, Mrs. Edinger. Are you finished with your opening statement, Mr. Rodes?"

"Yes, sir. I'd just like to close by saying that in all my years of practicing law, I've never seen anything so deceitful, so abusive of the public trust, as Mr. Thorsen's conduct in this case."

"Okay," Doar said. "Ms. DeMarco, I understand that you're going to make the opening statement in Mr. Thorsen's defense."

"I am," Angie said. "I've known Pete Thorsen for over fifteen years both as his law partner and as a colleague and friend. I can honestly say that I've never known a lawyer who has a greater sense of integrity and honesty than Pete, nor a man with a stronger thirst to see that justice is served. All of the testimonial letters from Pete's former law partners, former clients, and colleagues in other firms who know him say the same thing." Angie then gave a couple of examples to illustrate Pete's character and said they would explain why Pete did what he did as the hearing progressed.

"Now it's your turn, Mrs. Edinger. Is there anything you wish to add?"

"When I hear someone say what we just heard about Mr. Thorsen, it makes me want to puke. He's deceitful and conniving and a bully. He'll say anything to get his way no matter who it hurts. They say a person is known by who he hangs around with. Mr. Thorsen claims that he's the lawyer for Spencer Dahl. I happen to personally know that Mr. Dahl is the biggest piece of crap God ever put on this earth. That's all I have to say right now."

"Alright, Mr. Rodes," Doar said, "let's get to the heart of your complaint. You claim that on several occasions Mr. Thorsen wrongfully represented to your sister, Barbara Rodes, that he was the attorney for Lynn Hawke's estate and had the authority to set aside an executory contract between Barbara and Ms. Hawke. How do you know that? Were you present when Mr. Thorsen made those statements?"

"No, sir, I wasn't present, but I have Barbara's account of those meetings recorded in her own hand. She kept copious diaries of everything that happened in her life, including the meetings and telephone conversations with Mr. Thorsen."

Ah, Pete thought, that explains how Jeffery Rodes knew so much about what transpired in the meetings he'd had with Barbara Rodes.

At Doar's request, Jeffery Rodes read the passages from Barbara's diary that supposedly supported his claim. When he was finished, Doar asked him to send all conference participants photocopies of all pages of the diary that related to the meetings or conversations between Pete and Barbara Rodes.

"Mr. Thorsen, it sounds like you said something to Barbara Rodes that, at a minimum, was misleading," Doar said. "Do you have an explanation?"

Pete and Angie had agreed in advance that Pete would handle questions dealing specifically with his conduct. He said, "I do, and to understand this, you have to go back a couple of years. I dated Lynn Hawke until she moved to Seattle. I'm sure you'll find that somewhere in Barbara Rodes' diary as well. In March of this year, I received a call from the sheriff of a neighboring county asking me to come to the morgue to identify Lynn's body. He said Lynn had died in an accident in an ice storm and they'd found my business card in her purse. Besides me, Lynn's closest friends in the area were Rona Martin, a restaurateur here in Frankfort, and Harry McTigue, who publishes the local newspaper."

Doar interrupted him to get the spelling of their names.

"Both Rona and Harry thought, as did I, that Lynn had a daughter in Seattle and a son in Los Angeles. I was delegated to try to reach them, tell them of their mother's death and find out what they wanted to do about a memorial service. I was unable to locate them and even drove down to Grand Rapids to see Lynn's father who was in an Alzheimer's facility. I—"

Angie broke in to remind him that he'd gone to Seattle, too, to try to locate Lynn's daughter.

"Right, I also went to Seattle, and while I was there, I uncovered information that led me to believe that Lynn might have been mixed up in something illegal and her death might not have been accidental. That's when I went to see Barbara Rodes, and during one of our conversations, I told her I was the attorney for Lynn's estate. I didn't think that statement was out of line in view of my previous relationship with Lynn and the fact she had no competent relatives I knew of."

Jeffery Rodes broke in and said, "Except that what you did got her killed."

"That's false and you know it," Pete snapped.

"Settle down gentlemen," Doar admonished them.

"Sorry," Pete muttered. "Anyway, what I told Barbara had absolutely nothing to do with her death. She was killed because she happened to be the accountant for another client, Arne Breit, who was mixed up in the illegal activity I mentioned and the people who ran the ring thought she had something that belonged to them. She knew nothing about Breit's illegal activities, but they thought she did."

"Mr. Thorsen," Doar said, "what did Barbara Rodes have that the perpetrators, as the police would say, claimed belonged to them?"

"A package of forged documents. She had the package because Breit was having his mail forwarded to her out of fear that someone was going through it."

Jeffery Rodes interjected himself into the conversation again. "And Barbara couldn't give them the package because she'd already given it to Mr. Thorsen thinking he was Mr. Breit's representative. That led to her death."

"You know," Pete said, "I'm getting tired of listening to Mr. Rodes twist the facts and make baseless allegations. Mr. Breit was my client, too — you can check if you wish — and Barbara Rodes called *me* and asked *me* what she should do with his mail. I picked it up from her office and promised to look through it, which I did. I'd appreciate it if Mr. Rodes would get his facts straight before he makes these ridiculous charges."

Doar said, "For the last time, gentlemen, keep this civil. You say this Arne Breit was your client, Mr. Thorsen?"

"Yes. I represented him on assault charges several years ago. He didn't have me on a retainer agreement, but I know he still regarded me as his lawyer."

"And just so I'm clear, you maintain what you told Barbara Rodes about being the attorney for Lynn Hawke's estate and the Arne Breit situation are two separate matters," Doar said.

"Completely," Pete said.

"How convenient," a female voice that had to be Lorraine Edinger's muttered loud enough to be heard over the speaker.

"Was that you Mrs. Edinger?" Doar asked.

When there was no answer, Doar added, "I warned you before, Mrs. Edinger, not to make these kinds of gratuitous comments. I've tried to keep this hearing civil in the interest of all parties. Now, Mrs. Edinger, you've made clear your feelings about this matter, but is there anything you wish to add? Civilly, of course."

"Just this. When Mr. Thorsen came to my house, he implied he was with the sheriff's office so I would talk to him. Then when he saw I wasn't buying that, he switched and started bullying me with threats of subpoenas and things like that. It was a very unprofessional thing to do. I think lawyers should be above that sort of thing or they shouldn't be allowed to practice law."

"Mr. Thorsen," Doar said, "in what capacity did you go to Mrs. Edinger's house?"

"Strictly as co-counsel for a man named Spencer Dahl who's a defendant in a murder case in our area. I never once told Mrs. Edinger I was with the sheriff's office."

"To the best of your knowledge, was Mrs. Edinger represented by counsel at the time?"

"Not to my knowledge."

"So you didn't go out there knowing that Mrs. Edinger had a lawyer?"

"Absolutely not."

"How about the subpoena charges?"

"I did raise that possibility. A defendant in a criminal proceeding is entitled to subpoena witnesses who might have information relevant to his defense but won't come forward voluntarily."

"Okay," Doar said, "unless someone has something else, I'll give each side two or three minutes to sum up your positions."

Both Jeffery Rodes and Angie DeMarco availed themselves of the opportunity. Lorraine Edinger only muttered, "What's the use?"

Doar explained his schedule and promised to get his recommendation to the Attorney Grievance Commission as soon as possible. "I have one last question for Mr. Thorsen. Are you licensed as a private investigator in the State of Michigan?"

"No," Pete said.

"Don't you think you should be? Many of your activities sound investigative to me rather than legal."

"Everything I've done that's investigative in nature has been done incidental to my legal work for a client."

"That's your position?"

"It is."

FORTY

fter rehashing the ethics complaint hearing with Angie DeMarco for twenty minutes, Pete refocused his attention on the scene at the post office. He was now more convinced than ever that he was on the right track. Someone in the Hines family—Marlin if he were still alive or alternatively Jake Rossum, assuming he was Marlin's son as it now appeared—killed Thomas Edinger and planted incriminating evidence against Spencer Dahl.

Pete remembered Armand Lukitsch telling him that Marlin Hines had a son who was in the army at the time Hines and his wife lived on Long Street in Toledo, but wasn't listed in the brief obituary as one of his surviving relatives. He also remembered Andy Tate telling him that Carrie Hines' middle initial was "R," which presumably stood for Rossum based on everything he now knew. He had to confirm that Jake Rossum was in fact Marlin Hines' son before he went any further.

He remembered several years earlier when he'd used a former army acquaintance named Bill Sullivan to get information he wanted about a man who served in the military. Bill held a high position with the National Personnel Records Center in St. Louis and had access to records that weren't available to the general public. It was 5:00 p.m. and an hour earlier in the central time zone where St. Louis was located. He wondered if he could still catch Bill at the office.

Pete called Sullivan's private line. "Christ, Pete, I didn't expect to hear from you after the Cubs had another hundred-loss season."

"Ninety-six," Pete corrected him.

"I was rounding," Sullivan said. "If you're looking for World Series tickets, I just sold the last pair I had. As a matter of fact, I might have sold one pair twice." Sullivan laughed. "I might need a good lawyer. Do you know any?"

"I know a criminal lawyer in Chicago, but he'd charge you more than a dinner at Stan Musial's restaurant."

"Damn, that was a weekend, wasn't it?"

"Yeah, fun to catch up," Pete said. They were talking about a baseball weekend in St. Louis three years earlier.

"I got to watch the Red Birds kick the crap out of the Cubs—what was the score, fifteen to two?—and then chow down for free on the juiciest, priciest steak in Musial's. It doesn't get any better than that. Do you want to go for a repeat next spring?"

"The steaks and companionship, but not the score."

"Say, what's going on up there in your city? I thought that when you guys landed the Red Sox *Mafioso* management team, you'd start giving us some competition, but instead you've gone the other way."

"Don't ask me about it," Pete said glumly. "It's come to be known in Chicago as the 'PR' strategy—perpetual rebuilding. Bill, I know it's late in the day, but the reason I called, other than to be treated to some St. Louis Cardinal propaganda, was to ask a favor. I'm trying to pin down whether a certain guy was in the army and thought you might be able to help."

"Didn't I do something like that for you not long before our Cardinals–Cubs weekend?"

"For which I handsomely repaid you by sitting through two humiliating baseball games at your ballpark and springing for dinner both nights."

Sullivan laughed again. "I don't come cheap," he said. "Who are you trying to find this time?"

"A man named Jacob Hines," Pete said, using the first name Carrie Rossum had called him by at the Rossum place that night. "He served beginning maybe fifteen years ago and mustered out eight or ten years ago."

"Do you have any other information on him? Where he was from, middle initial, Social Security number, dog tag number, that sort of thing?"

"I know he was from Toledo, Ohio, but that's about it."

Sullivan sighed. "I'll see what the computer has to say. This will probably take ten or fifteen minutes. I'll call you back."

"Bill, one further thing. Could you also check under the name Jacob Rossum? Also from Toledo, same period."

While he was waiting for Sullivan to call back, Pete remembered Rossum telling him that he was in Grand Rapids attending a sporting goods show on the day that Thomas Edinger was shot. He went on line and called up the Grand Rapids Chamber of Commerce website. The website had been recently updated and showed only events that were scheduled in the future.

When Sullivan called back, he said, "I found eighteen Jacob Hines listed for the period you mentioned, but none were from Toledo."

"How about Chattanooga, Tennessee?" Pete asked, realizing the Hines family likely would have been down there by that time.

Silence at the other end for a minute, then Sullivan said, "One Jacob Hines from Chattanooga." At Pete's request, Sullivan read the man's 201 file.

"That sounds like him," Pete said. "What did the search under Rossum show?"

"Twenty-nine hits, but I was just scanning the list as we were talking and none were from Toledo or Chattanooga."

"Okay," that fits with the other information I have."

"What are you doing snooping around trying to find people who used to be in the service? I thought you were a corporate lawyer."

"I am, but since I semi-retired, I get involved in some other things from time-to-time."

"Some of that major you used to drive a Jeep for must have rubbed off. What was his name?"

"Major Baumann."

"That's right. Baumann. The army detective."

"He was with the CID."

"Right. You loved that job. Why didn't you go to Officer's Candidate School like I did? You could have been Major Baumann's successor."

"I was a poor boy and wanted to make money. You can't make money being a career army guy. That's why I'm mostly retired and you're not."

"Ain't that the truth," Sullivan said. "I can't complain about this job, though. It's pretty damn cushy, and I get to leach big steaks off guys like you who're looking for favors."

After he was off the phone with Sullivan, he got back on his computer and tried to find information concerning the sporting goods show in Grand Rapids. He couldn't find anything, so he walked down the street to Harry's office and caught him just as he was closing down for the night.

Harry eyed him as he walked in and said, "It looks like you survived whatever it was you were involved in this afternoon. I was just looking for someone to go to dinner with."

"I'm up for dinner, but first I need your help." He recapped for Harry what he'd told him earlier, and then said he was double-checking Jake Rossum's claim that he'd been at the outdoors show in Grand Rapids the day Thomas Edinger was shot.

"You say you can't find any evidence of the show?"

"No, I'm saying that the Grand Rapids Chamber of Commerce site, which I'm sure would make some mention of it, has been updated to show only prospective events."

Harry grinned at him. "You came to the right place if you want information. Are you buying dinner if I tell you whether there was or was not a sporting goods show in Grand Rapids that weekend?"

"I'll even buy two desserts."

"Okay, let me see what I find." Harry tapped on his keyboard for a few minutes and then looked up with a triumphant expression on his face. "Here it is. The Midwest Outdoors Exhibition was held at the DeVos Place Convention Center in Grand Rapids from noon Friday through Sunday evening of that weekend."

Crap, he thought. Everything he'd found out so far fit together until now. He didn't know whether to be happy or sad that Jake Rossum had told him the truth.

Harry must have noticed the look on his face because he said, "You look like somebody let the air out of your tires. Did you think Jake lied to you?"

"I considered that possibility."

"What does this do to your theory that Jake is Marlin Hines' son?"

Pete stared at the floor and after a moment said, "It has nothing to do with whether Jake is Marlin Hines' son. It might have something to do with whether Jake was the shooter."

Harry broke the silence and said, "Does this mean that Marlin Hines is still alive?"

"Possible."

"That was your theory at first, remember? Then you switched to thinking Jake was Marlin's kid and—"

"Sorry to interrupt, Harry. Just because the show was held that weekend doesn't mean Jake Rossum was there, does it?" Pete asked.

Harry looked thoughtful. "No," he said, "it doesn't."

"Do you know of any way we can check on whether Jake Rossum was really at the show on Sunday?"

After a few moments, Harry said, "I assume the show sponsor has registration records of some kind. We can check and see what they say."

"Who would we check with?"

"Like I said, the show sponsor."

"Which is?"

"Let's find out," Harry said. He called up something on his computer screen that Pete couldn't see, then dialed a number. "This is Harry McTigue of *The Northern Sentinel* in Frankfort," he intoned. "I'm putting together an article on outdoors shows in northern Michigan and wanted to include the show held in your city a couple of weeks ago. Who should I talk to about that?"

"Right," Harry said, "right." He made some notes on his pad as he talked. Then he hung up and said to Pete, "The show was put on by the convention center itself. I've got the name and telephone number of the man who was in charge as well as of his assistant. They're both gone for the day, but will be in again in the morning."

FORTY-ONE

Pete was standing outside *The Northern Sentinel's* office the next morning when Harry arrived. He eyed Pete grumpily and mumbled, "Am I late?"

"No, Sunshine," Pete replied, "I'm just a few minutes early."

Harry fumbled around with his keys and finally got the door open. Pete was right behind him as he turned on the lights and raised the shutters on the plate glass window that fronted on Main Street. Harry looked at him owlishly and said, "Is it okay with you if I make some coffee before you get me on the phone again to do your bidding?"

"Of course. Follow your usual routine. Pretend I'm not even here."

Harry shot him a look. Pete watched as he rinsed out his glass coffee pot, held it up to the light and examined it, then poured Columbian-blend coffee into the mechanism on top. Harry stared at the pot as though in a trance as the fresh brew percolated. When the coffee was ready, he filled a mug with "Journalists Do It Best" stenciled on the side and carried it back to his desk. He took a sip, smacked his lips, and waved a hand in Pete's direction that Pete interpreted as an invitation to help himself.

Harry cradled the mug and continued to sip his coffee. The mug was never more than a few inches from Harry's mouth as he peered over his half-glasses and said, "As I understand it, you want me to use my position as editor of this fine newspaper to find out from the show sponsor whether Jake Rossum was registered for the Sunday session."

"And whether he actually attended that session."

"How, pray tell, do you expect me to get that information. Calling to inquire about a particular individual isn't exactly what a newspaperman does."

"I thought we went through this. You need to paint Jake Rossum as an anti-fishing, anti-hunting zealot who's out to damage the sports by saying he saw this or that at outdoors shows. Tell whoever you talk to at the convention center that you want to challenge Rossum's credibility by pointing out, among other things, that he never even attended the Midwest Outdoors Exhibition."

"That's fine, genius, but how about if they tell me that Mr. Rossum registered for their show under the name Jake's Outdoors? That doesn't exactly sound like an anti-fishing, anti-hunting group. What do I say then?"

Pete shrugged. "I'm counting on them not picking up on any of that."

"This sounds like one of the Pete Thorsen fabrications that gets you in trouble."

"Well, if you're not willing to do it, I'm just going to have to tell your girlfriend Rona that there's nothing more I can do for Spencer Dahl because you won't cooperate."

"You can't do an about-face on us now, not when we've got everything trending our way."

"Everything except the critical links I'm trying to establish."

"How about if I use some other story to try to get the convention people to tell me what I want to know?"

"Use any story you want. I just have to know whether Jake Rossum actually attended the Midwest Outdoors Exhibition that Sunday as he claims."

"And if he did?"

"Then we're either going to have to find Marlin Hines, if he's alive, or reexamine our entire premise."

"Jesus, this is turning into a byzantine mess."

Pete just stared at him.

"I know, I know," Harry said. "Rona came to you."

Pete didn't comment on that, saying only, "Are you ready to make some calls?"

Harry lumbered over to the coffee maker and refilled his mug. Before he set the pot back on the burner he said, "Aren't you having any?"

"I had some decaf before I came over. If I have a cup of your stuff, I'll be jumping back and forth over the bay all morning."

Harry sat quietly for several minutes as though Pete weren't there. He stared at the piece of paper with his notes from the night before and several times reached for the phone only to draw his hand back again. He looked at Pete over his glasses again and said, "Which person do you think I ought to try first?"

Pete considered that and said, "I'd try the assistant. Sometimes it's easier to get an underling to talk. The worst that can happen is that she bucks you up to her boss."

Harry seized the telephone with a determined look on his face and punched in a number. After a few seconds, he caught Pete's eye and pointed to the receiver, at the same time saying, "Ms. Ladd? This is Harry McTigue, editor of *The Northern Sentinel* in Frankfort. I called last night and was given your name as someone I could talk to about the Midwest Outdoors Exhibition." Harry listened for a few moments and said, "It was a great show, huh?" He listened some more.

"Let me tell you why I'm calling," Harry said in a conspiratorial voice that must have sounded comforting at the other end. "*The Northern Sentinel* is a small newspaper and we depend upon contributing editors and correspondents for many of our stories. We've been trying to vet one gentleman who's been trying out for a position. He's in the outdoor business himself, but lately we've become suspicious that he may just be making up stories and not doing the field work he claims he's been doing."

Harry listened for a few moments and then said, "Yes, that's very serious and a breach of journalistic ethics." He listened again and said, "I'm glad you understand the seriousness of this sort of conduct. Anyway—and this is very confidential—the man who was supposed to cover the Midwest Outdoors Exhibition for us is Jake Rossum." He spelled the last name for her. "I'm interested in checking on two things—whether Mr. Rossum ever registered to attend your show, and if he did, whether he actually attended on the last day. I believe that was a Sunday."

Harry gave Pete the thumbs up sign and kept the receiver to his ear. He spelled Rossum's name again for her and listened some more. "So he did register for the show on Sunday? Yes, yes," he murmured. "Can you tell me if he in fact attended that day?" Harry asked. He listened some more, then "So he registered, but never showed up. That's what we were afraid of."

"No, no," Harry said. "We would never cite this information as coming from you." More listening, then, "No, you absolutely will *not* get in any trouble for talking to us. The position Mr. Rossum was angling for—that's a pretty good pun, huh?—was an unpaid position anyway. We'll just quietly phase him out."

Harry put the receiver back in its cradle and grinned at Pete. "You were right. Jake registered for the show, but he wasn't there on Sunday. They have a procedure whereby they manually check off the name of each attendee as he or she arrives and then give the person a show packet. Jake's packet is in a box along with the packets of a dozen other no-shows."

"You were masterful. The next time I need a white lie told, I'm going to check with you as to how I should frame it."

"The bit about considering Jake Rossum for a contributing editor position sounded convincing, huh?"

"Very. For a while there, I was worried that Rossum might take my job."

"Speaking of that, I've been meaning to—"

"Sorry to cut you off, but can we talk later? I have to run right now. Can I stop by about 1:00 p.m. and buy you a late lunch?"

"I was hoping you'd suggest that. We need to plan our next step in this case."

When Pete drove past Jake's Outdoors, he saw Jake's pickup parked in its usual spot at the side of the building. He continued on and picked up the highway to Benzonia, then turned on the county road that would take him to the old farm Rossum rented south of town. He needed to confirm what he thought he remembered from the night he gave Jake a ride home. He also wanted to have a look and be gone before noon just in case Rossum came home for lunch.

There was no traffic on the county road. He turned left at the hand-lettered wooden sign that marked the Rossum driveway and proceeded slowly up the unpaved road. He saw the buildings up ahead and stopped and scanned the farmstead for signs of Mrs. Rossum. He didn't see her or anyone else. He proceeded again, and when he got closer, he saw the outdoor fireplace he thought he remembered. He wanted to go over and examine it to see if it had been used recently, but recalled how Mrs. Rossum had popped out from behind the sheets hanging on the line and knew that would be foolish. He turned around and went back out the driveway, and when he reached the county road, took a roundabout way back to Benzonia just in case someone he knew was driving south and might recognize his Range Rover.

FORTY-TWO

Pete clicked on his upper beams so he could see better as he headed for the Rossum farm for the second time that day. The county road was shrouded in darkness except for occasional periods when the moon poked through the cloud cover and illuminated the landscape. He'd dressed to blend with the night — a navy blue windbreaker, a pair of blue jeans that hadn't yet been bleached out, a dark cap with "Save the Boat" embroidered across the front in letters the same color as the cap itself.

He came to the Rossum driveway and continued on for a quarter mile, then turned around and pulled his Range Rover off to the side next to the brush and dry reeds that bordered the shallow ditch. He instinctively pressed the "lock" button on his key, but almost immediately had second thoughts and unlocked the doors again. He didn't anticipate having to leave quickly, but if he did, he didn't want to have to deal with locked car doors.

Pete walked back along the road and took comfort in the darkness. He reached the driveway and peered down the long chute bordered by trees on both sides. In the distance, he could see lights on inside the house. He made his way slowly toward the farm buildings. When he got closer, he could make out both of Jake Rossum's trucks, including the Toyota Tundra he normally drove. They were parked between the house and barn and the light from a side window reflected dimly off their exteriors.

He left the driveway and headed to the right side of the yard where he knew the outdoor fireplace was located. He heard and saw nothing. When he got closer, he saw the fireplace outlined in the glow from the house lights. He didn't like that, but decided there was nothing he could do except wait for the Rossums to turn off their lights and go to bed. He didn't want to hang around that long, and in any event, he planned to have a look at the fireplace and be gone in less than ten minutes.

Just as he started to move again, he heard a door open and saw Jake Rossum come out a side door, look around the yard, and walk to his Tundra. He got in and sat there with the door open for several minutes. He appeared to be looking for something. Suddenly the clouds parted and the farmstead was bathed in moonlight. Pete stood behind a large tree, hardly breathing. After what seemed like an eternity, the clouds knit together again and the moon disappeared from view. Rossum got out of the pickup, closed its door, and walked back toward the house. Pete didn't see him go in, but figured he must have because he heard the screen door slam and saw a light next to the side door go off.

Pete waited behind the tree a while longer. As he stood there and considered what to do, the clouds parted a second time. Pete cursed his luck; no moon for the past hour, and now when he needed cover, it seemed insistent on breaking through the clouds every five minutes.

He was fairly confident Rossum was back inside, but that didn't give him the solace he needed and conflicting thoughts swirled around in his head. He knew he was crazy to prowl around the Rossum's farmstead while they were still up, but at the same time he was determined to get a look at the fireplace. After thinking about it some more, he decided to retreat until the Rossums went to bed and the house lights were off, an option he'd initially rejected. No use being foolish.

When the moon was behind the clouds again, he looked around and seeing nothing, moved as quietly as he could to another large tree twenty feet farther away from the house. He waited a minute to satisfy himself that everything continued to be clear, then repeated his retreat to another tree. Then to another. Finally, he felt comfortable enough to turn and walk hurriedly out the driveway to the county road. He crossed the road and sat in the brush on the other side where he could watch the entrance to the driveway.

As Pete waited, the moon poked through the cloud cover again. He checked his watch impatiently and waited for the Rossums to retire for the night. In the summer months, he would have been eaten alive by the mosquitoes, but now with the temperature in the fifties, he felt nothing but his jeans absorbing moisture from the damp earth.

He was sure he was close to finding Thomas Edinger's killer and felt a surge of adrenaline when he thought of the way he'd pieced together his case. He felt frustration, too, over the way he'd been unable to convince Joe Tessler to look into his theory that the killer probably was a member of the Hines family and not Spencer Dahl. He could understand Tessler's position in a way, but it left him no option but to plow forward in an effort to find more evidence against Jake Rossum. Spencer Dahl, however much he despised him, wasn't guilty of Thomas Edinger's murder and Jake Rossum, who he happened to like, very likely was. That was a cruel twist of fate, but it also was reality.

The clouds parted once more and he glanced at his watch. He'd been sitting in the brush for nearly two hours and it was almost midnight. The last of the lights inside the house were finally off. He brushed at his jeans, ran a hand through his hair, and clamped his cap back on his head. Time for another try. If something spooked him again, he'd decide whether to take a chance or abort for the night.

Everything around him was silent as he crossed the road to Rossum's driveway again. His visual purple, something he'd learned about in his army days, was finely tuned as a result of sitting in the dark so long. He navigated the driveway without trouble, and as he got close to the house, the moon appeared again. He waited behind a tree and scoped out the yard.

When it was dark again, he let his eyes readjust and fingered the Mini Maglite flashlight in his pocket. Then he moved to a closer tree and finally to one still closer. The fireplace was thirty feet away with no trees to shield him. He took a deep breath, glanced at the sky and moved forward. Seconds later, he was kneeling in front of the fireplace opening. He pulled out his Maglite and flashed its focused beam inside. The ashes were gone. Either Jake Rossum was a neat freak, which wasn't consistent with the rest of the yard, or the ashes had been cleaned out recently.

Pete examined the inside of the fireplace more closely. The ashes that remained on the brick hearth looked fresh, as did the sprinkle on the ground where they'd spilled during the cleaning process. He thought back to the weather in the area for the past couple of weeks. It had been cloudy on many days, but he couldn't remember any rain since that Sunday when Edinger was shot. The fireplace had been cleaned sometime since then and Pete suspected he knew why.

As he was rising to his feet, something heavy hit him in the back of his head and everything went black.

FORTY-THREE

When Pete regained consciousness, everything around him was a black haze and his head throbbed mercilessly. He wanted to put his fingers to his temples to ease the pain, but his hands were bound behind him and he could barely move. He had no idea what time it was or where he was, although he seemed to be in a basement judging from the cement floor and the dank musty odor.

He felt sick to his stomach and turned on his side in case he upchucked. With his feet also bound together, he could do no more than roll his body. His nausea got worse and he could feel the room spinning. He closed his eyes and willed it to stop. It didn't and he felt the bile rise in his throat. Finally he couldn't control it any longer and everything erupted from his mouth. When it was out, he spit several times and rolled over to get away from the vomit.

He rested his cheek on the cold floor and tried to figure out what had happened. Jake Rossum somehow knew he was there and had been waiting for him, how he didn't know. He hadn't told a soul where he was going that night, not even Harry, so someone couldn't have inadvertently let his plans slip. He felt more bile rising in his throat and rolled back so any additional vomit would be in the same area.

When his stomach quieted down, he rolled over several more times to get farther away from the vomit. The rolling aggravated his nausea again and he had to lie still for several minutes to calm his system. He dozed off—he had no idea for how long—only to wake with a start when he felt something crawling over his body and scratching at his jacket. A mouse or, worse, a rat! He flailed with his feet and arched his back and let his body fall to the floor to scare it away. He repeated the movement and kicked with his feet, then kicked again. The throbbing in his head got worse as a result of the jars.

He tried to doze off again, but could think only of the animal exploring his body. He lay there, unable to sleep. Finally a faint glow appeared at the other side of the room. He figured it had to be a window, and as it got brighter, it confirmed his earlier assessment that he was in the Rossum's basement. He stared at the opening and wondered if it was large enough for a man to fit through. Then he heard footsteps above him. They seemed to go from room-to-room. Finally he heard water running through the pipes. Someone was taking a shower. He wondered how long it would be before Jake Rossum came down to check on him.

Pete put his head back on the floor and tried to rest. The light coming through the small window was brighter. The time must be around 7:00 a.m. he estimated. The water stopped. Whoever had been in the shower was out. He heard more footsteps above him and again wondered what would happen when Jake was dressed for the day and ready to deal with him.

He heard voices, probably Jake and his mother talking. A door slammed, then everything was quiet again. He tested the restraints that bound his hands and feet and found them as tight and unyielding as before. With the light from the small window, he could faintly make out the features of the basement he was in. The floor was concrete, something he already knew, and overhead there seemed to be a maze of pipes. The house's plumbing system presumably. A water heater and small furnace occupied one corner. One of the walls had been plastered over and the others seemed to be made of fieldstones fit together the way a fireplace would be constructed. Shelves lined one wall and a few pieces of old furniture were scattered about the room.

Pete heard a car engine outside, then it stopped and a door slammed. He heard more footsteps above him, then nothing. Ten minutes later, Pete heard footsteps again and a key turned in the basement door lock. Pete tensed. He didn't have a direct view, but saw a cone of light appear in the stairwell as the door slowly opened. Then someone switched on the overhead light and the sudden brilliance blinded him. He was unable to shield his eyes with his hands so he squeezed them shut. After a moment, he opened one enough to see Jake Rossum coming down the stairs with a pistol in one hand. It was pointed directly at him.

"Did you sleep well, Pete?" Rossum asked. He looked at the pool of vomit a few feet away from where Pete was laying and grimaced.

Pete's eyes were open now and he stared at Rossum without saying anything.

"Are you feeling okay?"

Again, Pete didn't reply.

"You're probably wondering how I knew you were here last night."

Pete continued to stare at him.

"The guy we rented this place from wasn't much on maintenance, but he was long on security. He had sensors installed everywhere, including in the driveway. I knew someone was coming when you were a hundred yards away. Then it was a matter of waiting you out while you sat in the brush across the road."

Pete spoke for the first time and said, "You're not going to get away with this, Jake. I know everything."

"Really."

"Yes, really. I know you killed Thomas Edinger because he ruined your father's career and drove him to suicide."

"Jacob!" a shrill woman's voice called. "Is that man still down there?" She started down the stairs.

Jake Rossum looked that way and said sharply, "Stay up there, Mother!"

Carrie Rossum Hines was already halfway down the steps. She saw Pete bound hand and foot and propped up against the basement wall and her son standing near him with the gun in his hand. "That's the man I saw in the post office! He's the one who's been stealing our mail!" She retraced her steps and a couple of minutes later clumped back down with a pitchfork like the one Pete had seen leaning against the outdoor fireplace.

"Mother," Jake said sternly, "get back upstairs."

"We should take him to the post office. Mail theft is a crime."

"For the last time, *go upstairs!*"

"You're not going to let him go, are you?" Carrie Rossum Hines said as her son nudged her up the steps. She screamed at Pete over her shoulder, "You're a criminal!"

She stood at the head of the stairs with her pitchfork and stared down at Pete and her son below.

"I know how you did it, too."

Jake looked at him sadly. "Why couldn't you leave things alone, Pete? I like you."

"I like you, too, but it's over. You can't kill a man and expect to walk free."

"Thomas Edinger deserved to die."

"Maybe he did, but that's no defense."

Jake continued to stare at him and said softly, "You know I can't let you go."

Pete tried to keep his voice steady even though his head was throbbing again and he felt like his words were coming from outside his body. "Why compound your problems?" he said. "With Edinger, a jury may very well be sympathetic and possibly even let you off on a reduced charge. If you kill me, you'll never see daylight again."

"I'll take my chances. The sheriff is pretty fixed on Spencer Dahl, I'm told. With you, I'm sure there'll be an investigation into your fatal accident, but I don't see how they can find that I had anything to do with it. Old cars like yours are so unreliable and people who know you are aware that you have a drinking problem and occasionally go on binges."

"Jacob!" Carrie Rossum Hines screamed from above them. "Shoot that man before he steals any more of our mail!"

"For the last time, Mother, go back to your bedroom right now!" he shouted at her. "I'll talk to you before I leave!" Then he turned back to Pete. "I've got to get to the shop. Would you like some water before I leave?"

"That would be nice, but I don't see how I can drink it with my hands tied behind my back."

A thin smile appeared on Rossum's face. "Nice try." He went upstairs and returned with a bottle of spring water. He held the bottle for Pete while he sipped it. The water lubricated his mouth, which was like flannel, and also seemed to make his whole system feel better.

Rossum said to him as he climbed the stairs, "I'll be back after we close for the day. By that time, I'll know where you're going to have your unfortunate accident."

The overhead light went off and everything was black again. He heard the key turn in the lock, and ten minutes later, he heard Rossum's pickup pull out. He heard looney old Carrie Rossum Hines walking around one floor above him, periodically testing the basement door. He prayed that she didn't have a key to the lock.

He pulled at the plastic restraints binding his wrists together with all of the strength he could muster, but there was no give. He'd gotten a look at the restraints on his ankles when the overhead light was on and figured the one on his hands was the same. They didn't look like the plastic handcuffs that the police commonly used, but seemed equally effective.

He thought back to Jake Rossum and the lack of emotion he'd shown when he said Thomas Edinger deserved to die. Like John didn't deserve the promotion or Mary didn't deserve to get into Princeton. Rossum didn't seem like a cruel man, in fact far from it, but the matter-of-fact way he discussed Edinger's fate was unnerving. The same was true when he talked about the "accident" Pete was going to have that night. Thinking about it made Pete's blood run cold and he had no doubt Rossum planned to make it happen.

Pete had faced death once before, when he'd been bitten by a venomous snake while on bivouac in the piney woods of Louisiana during his army basic training days. The army was his first step out of a life he hated and he literally willed himself to live during the seemingly eternal ambulance ride to the hospital. He felt the same steely will coursing through his body now.

FORTY-FOUR

Pete figured he had eight hours at most to come up with and implement an escape plan that had a reasonable chance of success. He reduced that to seven hours to be on the safe side. Even that was uncertain because Jake Rossum might come home early or possibly might return during the day to check on him. Rossum's mother's footsteps above him were like a metronome, ticking off the precious seconds and minutes and hours.

He knew he had to find a way to free his arms and legs because without that, nothing else was possible. He got to his knees and laboriously inched his way around the room, looking for something he could use to cut the plastic restraints. He could barely see in the dim light from the small window and his knees ached from contact with the cement floor. It seemed like every ten feet, he'd lose his balance and topple over and had to exert a lot of energy to get back in position.

The only thing metal he could see was the shelving. As best he could tell, the shelves were empty except for a couple of cardboard boxes, a stack of bamboo poles, and a plastic bucket filled with musty old rags. He struggled to his feet and stood with his back to the corner of one shelf so he could feel the metal. The support uprights consisted of angle irons that were smooth on the outside where the steel wrapped around and a little rougher on the two inner edges. It wasn't ideal, but it was something.

He continued around the basement looking for an alternative, but found none. Overhead, Mrs. Hines continued to pace. *For crissakes, doesn't she ever sit down?* Pete thought irritably. Occasionally, he heard scratches or thumps on the basement door as she apparently tried to open it. He couldn't waste any more time; he had to give the rough edges of the metal shelves a try.

He inched along back toward the wall. It took him five minutes to cover a distance he'd normally cover in seconds. When he reached the shelves, he turned around so his back was to them just as when he first examined them and pulled his hands as far apart as the plastic restraint would allow. Because of the angle iron, he had to lean against the shelf and twist his arms around so that the restraint binding his wrists was against the rough inside edge. Then he moved his hands up and down in a sawing motion.

After a half hour, his arms felt like they would fall off, but he kept sawing, willing the pain away. Up and down, up and down, up and down. He couldn't tell whether the metal edge was cutting into the plastic restraint or not because he couldn't see his wrists. He wanted to quit, but forced himself to continue. How long had he been at it? An hour? Two hours? Longer?

He continued the sawing motion. Sweat ran down his face even though it was cool in the basement and his shoulders ached and his arms ached and his wrists hurt and his hands were covered by a sticky substance he assumed was blood. The nausea was back, too. He wondered if Mrs. Hines could hear the sawing sound in the basement and had enough of her senses about her to call her son. He didn't care, he had to continue. Up and down, up and down, up and down. He swiveled his neck around as far as it would go in an effort to see his hands, but it was useless and the light was too dim anyway.

He thought he felt a tear in the plastic where he'd been sawing, but couldn't be sure. He sawed some more. He desperately wanted to crumple to the floor and sleep, but kept on sawing. He stopped for a moment and stretched his hands apart as far as they would go. Was there some give in the plastic or was he imaging things? He stretched his hands apart again and felt give again. He resumed sawing with new energy and felt his heart pound! It was working! He alternately sawed and stretched his hands apart and sawed some more. Suddenly his hands were free and fell to his sides. Every part of his body ached, but he was free. He clenched his fists a few times and he could see that the sticky substance coating his hands and wrists was blood. He wiped his hands on his jeans.

He pushed up the left sleeve of his windbreaker and angled his wrist so he could see the face of his watch. It was almost 2:00 p.m. He'd been sawing at the restraint for over five hours if his initial time estimate was correct. He knew he didn't have that much time to free his legs.

He heard a door to the house open and close. That had to be Mrs. Rossum, he thought. Pete was able to hear Jake's pickup when he left for work and he hadn't heard anything outside since that time. The light through the small window suddenly got dimmer, like a shadow had passed across it, and as he stared at it he saw why. Mrs. Hines was trying to see in the basement. Her hatchet face was flattened against the dusty, cobweb-covered glass and her stringy gray hair made her look even more frightening than usual.

Pete froze. He didn't think it was possible to see through the window into the basement without an interior light on, but didn't want to take a chance. He wasn't feeling any sympathy for Jake Rossum, but wondered how he felt comfortable sleeping at night with a deranged old woman stalking around his house with a pitchfork. In a few minutes, the face peering through the window disappeared. He expelled air in relief and resumed his search for an alternative to the inside edge of the shelving to cut the restraint that bound his feet.

He moved along the shelves feeling for something, any kind of tool, that might be there but wasn't clearly visible. Before long, his hands were filthy with dust and grime from the surface of the shelves, made worse by the sticky blood. Finally he touched what felt like pliers. He held them up to the dim light that filtered through the window and saw he was right. They were rusted and covered with dust, but it was a serviceable pair of pliers! He wiped them on his jeans and banged them against the wall a couple of times to loosen the mechanism and worked the jaws. With the pliers, he knew he'd be able to cut the restraint binding his ankles in far less time than it took him to free his hands.

He put the pliers in his shirt pocket and hopped over to the window and used his hands to ease himself to the floor in a sitting position against the wall. Then he moved over a few feet just in case Mrs. Rossum looked in the window again. He adjusted the pliers to the maximum gripping size and examined the wire cutting feature. His back was still killing him, but he leaned forward and began to work on the restraint binding his ankles. Cutting through the plastic was a lot tougher than snipping a piece of copper wire, but in a fraction of the time it had taken him to saw through the restraint on his wrists, his ankles were free. He rose to his feet and walked back and forth across the basement a few times to regain the feel of his legs. He looked at his watch again; it was 3:00 p.m.

Pete stood quietly for a few moments and didn't hear Mrs. Hines. He felt his way up the steps, being as quiet as he could, and cringed whenever they creaked. A sliver of light showed at the bottom of the basement door. He tried the inside door knob, but as Mrs. Rossum apparently had found from the other side, it had been locked with a deadbolt and wouldn't budge. He ran his hand over the door. It didn't feel like an ordinary flimsy basement door. He guessed that it had been reinforced with steel, possibly by the man who'd installed the sensors on the property.

He made his way back down the steps and tilted his wrist again to pick up light from the small window. His watch showed it was 3:30 p.m. One or maybe two hours left to devise some kind of makeshift weapon to use when Rossum returned.

He went to the metal shelves again and poked around on the top where he knew the bamboo poles were. He grabbed one and tested it and found that it had good elasticity. He put the pole back and as he was feeling around, his hand touched something that felt like a fishing rod. He took it over to the light and saw that it was a spinning rod and reel. From the look of it, it hadn't been used for some time because it was coated with dust and grime. He tugged at the stub of line dangling from the reel and more line came out.

That gave him an idea. Maybe he could fashion a crude bow and arrow from the materials at hand. It didn't have to be powerful like his Viking longbow at home. Something that would stun Rossum long enough for him to make his move now that his arms and legs were free would be enough.

He took the bamboo poles down and tested each of them for tensile strength. He selected the one that felt best and pondered how he would cut it down to manageable length. He decided his best option was to use the steel shelving again. He selected a place on the bamboo just above a joint and began to saw off a six-foot length. It was far easier than cutting through a tough plastic restraint, and after ten minutes, he was able to break the pole where he wanted. He then sawed notches at each end of the pole.

He went back to the spinning outfit and tested the line. It didn't break when he yanked it several times, but he decided to use a double twist just to be safe. He tied the reinforced line at one end of the pole, striving for a secure tie rather than neatness, then bent the bamboo wood and tied the other end.

He could barely see his handiwork in the near darkness, but it felt right. He decided to test the bow before trying to fashion an arrow out of one of the back spokes of the old wooden chair he'd seen in the corner. He pulled the makeshift bowstring back six inches at first and then progressively farther. Now if he could just find a way to grind the point of the chair spoke to a sharp point, he'd have a serviceable weapon. When he pulled the bowstring all the way back on his final test, he heard the bamboo break and splinters of wood snapped out just above his hand.

He stood there with his handiwork in his hand and felt his rage build. *Damn it,* he swore under his breath. He flung the useless bow across the room where it slapped against the wall and clattered to the floor. The footsteps above him started again and he feared Mrs. Rossum had heard the disturbance in the basement. He stood silently while she tried to open the basement door for about the tenth time. A few minutes later, he heard the house door open and close and then saw her hatchet face press against the small window again. *Go inside!* Pete pleaded silently. *I don't have much time!*

The face disappeared. As Pete had been fashioning his bow, he'd been thinking about an alternative in case that didn't work. By now, he could get around the basement with his eyes closed. He headed for a corner, holding out his hand for protection in case he miscalculated, and returned with a long-handled push broom. He unscrewed the brush and moved the chair closer to the window so he could see what he was doing. It was now 4:15 p.m.

He adjusted the pliers and began to work on the screw-end of the broom handle. He removed bits of wood and gradually fashioned the end into a taper. Slowly it began to resemble a point. He worked on it some more and then walked across the basement to the metal shelves and ran his hand over the second shelf until he found the sandpaper he'd noticed earlier. He selected the coarsest sheet and began to work on the tip. It was almost 5:00 p.m.

Pete continued to grind away at the tip of the handle, banking on being able to hear Rossum when he got home. His hands were already raw and bleeding from his struggle to free himself from the plastic restraint and his work with the sandpaper aggravated them. He kept sanding, eventually going to a finer grade of paper. He worked on lengthening the taper and making the point sharper.

At 5:45 p.m., Pete saw lights flash through the small window. He heard a door slam and knew Rossum was home. Pete felt the point of his spear and prayed it would be sharp enough. He headed for the stairs, spear in hand, and climbed silently to the top of the landing. His heart thumped so hard he feared that someone on the other side of the door might be able to hear it.

The basement door opened to Pete's right and at first he thought he should position himself on that side to conceal his presence as long as possible. After further consideration, he opted for the left side. He'd only have one chance at Rossum and being on that side gave him the best angle with his spear.

Pete heard voices. Obviously, it was Jake talking with his mother. He waited, telling himself he had surprise on this side, and tried to stay calm. *Why didn't Rossum open the door for crissakes?* He heard footsteps, but then everything became quiet for an inordinately long time.

He kept wiping his grimy, sticky palms on his jeans as he nervously waited with his spear and stared at the locked door. How much time had passed since Rossum had gotten home? An hour? Two? The light from the window had long ago disappeared and the basement was completely black. Suddenly he heard footsteps again, getting closer, and a key scraped in the lock.

FORTY-FIVE

Pete kicked the heavy basement door as hard as he could just as Rossum was opening it. It flew all the way open and slammed into Rossum, sending him reeling backward. Pete lunged at him with the makeshift spear pointed at the middle of his chest and felt it make contact. Rossum sagged against the hallway wall, clutching at his breast. He started to raise his pistol and Pete aimed a vicious kick at his hand. The pistol skidded across the floor.

Pete bolted for the door only to find a startled Mrs. Rossum standing in his way with the pitchfork. She saw what had happened to her son and jabbed at Pete with the fork, screaming, "You hurt Jacob! You hurt Jacob!" He felt the tines prick his side and sent the old woman sprawling with a violent shove. He wrenched open the door and ran outside into the night. His only thought was to escape before Rossum recovered.

Earlier, when he looked through the basement window, he'd seen his Range Rover standing by the barn where Rossum had moved it. He ran in that direction. His key ring wasn't in his pocket and he assumed Rossum had taken it. When he opened the car door, he saw that there was no key in the ignition. His heart pounded wildly as he considered what to do. Then he remembered the emergency valet key he kept secured by a magnet under the car's frame. He dropped to his stomach and groped around desperately for the key. His fingers touched the magnetic sheath, but in his haste, it fell to the ground. He felt around hurriedly, but was unable to find the key. He looked back toward the house and saw Rossum coming out with a rifle in his hands.

Pete started to run. He sprinted around the barn to put an obstacle between himself and Rossum and then ran straight back toward the woods. About fifty feet into the tangle of trees and underbrush, and breathing hard from fear and the exertion, he paused to look back. He didn't see Rossum even though he was sure he'd seen him run behind the barn. Maybe the makeshift spear had hurt him worse than he thought. Pete went a hundred feet farther into the woods and saw nothing in front of him except the hulking shapes of trees.

He knew that if his sense of direction was correct, he was headed east. He had no idea how far the woods extended in that direction or if there were woods to the north of him as well. It was too dark to see, and for the moment, the moon was obscured by the clouds. He cursed his lack of foresight for not scoping out the terrain more carefully ahead of time.

He stood without moving, hearing and seeing nothing, and thought about what to do. He knew that if Rossum caught him again, he wouldn't wait to stage a "fatal accident" as he'd originally planned. He also didn't know what kind of equipment Rossum had. He remembered when Adam Rose was helping him try to find Les Brimley's killer and Rose showed up that night on the golf course with military-grade night vision goggles. If Rossum had similar equipment, Pete knew he'd be easy prey for Rossum.

The clouds parted and the moon brightened the landscape. For the first time, Pete could see the edge of a field some fifty yards east of him. He debated whether he should continue to move in that direction, but then realized he'd have little chance if Rossum were close behind and saw him out in the open.

Pete concluded that his only option was to stay in the woods and veer north. Maybe he could go west again after a while and figure out a way to get back to his Range Rover so he could retrieve his cell phone and call Joe Tessler for help. Better yet, he might be able to find the valet key he'd dropped and escape from the Rossum farm. That meant taking a chance, but it didn't seem any riskier than some of his other options. It also had the advantage of surprise because Rossum probably wouldn't expect him to double back and return to the farmstead.

He picked his way through the trees, trying to be as quiet as he could. He cringed every time a twig snapped underfoot and resisted the urge to swear when an unseen branch snapped against his face. The clouds parted again. He stopped and stood next to a tree and waited for the cloud cover to return. He saw nothing behind him, but maybe Rossum was doing the same thing that he was. Waiting, watching, the hunter and the hunted.

In the moonlight, he could see the woods ahead of him jut west where a narrow strip of trees and bramble separated an open field to the north from the Rossum farmstead on the south. When the clouds covered the moon again, he made his way farther north and then headed west. The bramble tore at his jeans and every step he took sounded excruciatingly loud in the still night. The moon broke through the clouds again and he stopped and surveyed the scene.

The farmstead where his Range Rover was parked looked to be about a hundred yards south of him. Half of that distance was across an open field. He considered continuing to walk west as an alternative, but he knew there were risks to that as well. The woods wouldn't go on forever and there would be other fields he'd have to cross where Rossum might be able to pick him off. Sticking with his plan of retrieving his cell phone and hoping he could get Tessler and some deputies out to the Rossum farm seemed like the best of bad choices.

He moved to the edge of the field, but even though it was dark again, he couldn't force himself to step into the open. He visualized Rossum waiting to put a bullet in him as he was halfway across the field. Second thoughts raced through his mind. Maybe he'd made a mistake by not trying to end it in the house when he had surprise on his side. He could have grabbed for Rossum's pistol when it fell to the floor. But it was too late for that now.

The moon shone through again, and when it was obscured by the clouds once more, Pete knew he had to go. He drew on his military training from decades earlier and dropped to his stomach and began to worm his way across the field. His back and arms still hurt from the basement ordeal, but he snaked along as fast as he could. The grass covering the meadow wasn't as lush and high as it would have been in the summer months, but it still concealed most of his body. Fears never go away completely, however, and as he crawled toward the barn he had visions of Rossum suddenly appearing in front of him with a cruel smile on his face and a high-powered hunting rifle pointed at his head.

The moon poked through the clouds once more and he flattened himself against the ground, relying on the grass to conceal his body. It seemed like an agonizingly long time before the moonlight faded and he felt he could move forward again.

He finally reached the edge of the farmstead. Nothing separated it from the field he'd just crossed, except the brown grass around the buildings was shorter, like it had been mowed. His Range Rover was only twenty-five feet away. He scanned the area and saw no sign of Rossum. He considered whether to make a dash for his vehicle or continue on his stomach, and opted to continue to crawl notwithstanding there no longer was anything to shield his body. When he reached the Range Rover, the first thing he did was to pat the ground under the driver's-side door in an effort to find the valet key. Nothing, and he knew he couldn't afford to waste time searching for it.

Rossum had closed the Range Rover's door and Pete hoisted himself to his knees and opened it as quietly as he could. The inside dome light went on! Suddenly he felt like a spotlight had been focused on him, and he hastily leaned across the seat and opened the middle console and grabbed his cell phone. As he was sliding out of the car, a loud

Crack! reverberated through the still night and he felt something hit the car window above him. Tiny shards of glass sprinkled his neck. *Christ, Rossum was shooting at him!*

He slid the rest of the way out of the vehicle and slammed the door to cut the light, then wriggled on the ground to the back of the car. Another *Crack!* broke the silence and he heard the shot strike metal close to him. He got to his feet and ran in a low crouch past the house in the opposite direction from where he thought the shots came from. A third *Crack!* shattered the night. Pete kept running away from the dim glow the house's lights cast over the area. He finally saw trees ahead of him.

Branches snapped him in the face as he plunged into the wooded area. It was too dark to see clearly and he banged into a tree, sending him sprawling to the ground. Pain shot through his shoulder. He got up and continued to run, using an arm to shield his face from the branches and tall underbrush. He paused to catch his breath. His chest heaved, and between gulps of air, he stared back at the farmhouse and listened for sounds of Rossum coming after him. He heard nothing, but was certain Rossum was headed his way.

Pete knew he had to call Tessler now! He did his best to calm his nerves and listened some more. Nothing. He pulled out the cell phone he'd retrieved from his Range Rover and pressed the button and waited for the "Welcome!" sound to tell him the phone was on. He held the phone against his windbreaker to shield the light he knew was coming. Then he cupped a hand and punched in Tessler's cell phone number. Damn, busy!

Pete didn't want to chance Tessler calling him back so he ended the call rather than leaving a message. He continued to walk west, pausing frequently to listen, and thought about what Rossum's strategy would be to find him. Contrary to what he'd assumed, Rossum must have had a hunch he'd double back to his Range Rover because he'd obviously seen the light as soon as Pete opened the car door. He had no idea how far away Rossum had been when he fired the shots or whether he'd been hurt badly enough by the spear to slow him down.

He punched in Tessler's cell number again. This time Tessler answered. Before the detective could say anything, Pete whispered in an urgent voice, "Joe, it's Pete. Listen carefully because I can't talk any louder. I'm in serious trouble and need your help right now. Jake Rossum killed Thomas Edinger and now he's after me. I'm at the Rossum farm south of Benzonia, in the woods west of the house. He's got a rifle and a handgun and he's already shot at me. Get here as fast as you can or you're going to have another body on your hands. I've got to go."

Tessler started to say something, but Pete cut him off. "Trust me, Joe. I wouldn't call if I wasn't in trouble." He was about to end the call, but added, "Leave your cell phone on in case I have to call you again. And don't call me. No sirens either. I don't want to give Rossum advance warning that you're coming." Pete ended the call.

He listened for sounds of Rossum moving through the woods, and hearing none, began to walk west again as quietly as he could. The woods brightened briefly as the swirling clouds parted again. He leaned against a tree to rest for a moment and prayed that Tessler would get there soon. As he peered into the darkness, his stomach knotted when he thought he saw a small light bobbing around among the trees maybe a hundred yards away. The light disappeared and he wondered if he were imaging things. It reappeared a few minutes later in a slightly different place and this time Pete knew it wasn't his imagination. It was Rossum.

Pete had planned to go west a safe distance and then gradually work his way south to the county road in order to flag down Tessler or some other sheriff's department personnel when they passed on their way to the Rossum farm. Now he decided that might not be a good idea because of where he saw the light. He decided to wait a few minutes and see if he could tell where Rossum was headed.

He saw the light again. Closer this time. He wondered how long it would be before Tessler arrived. It was difficult to imagine Joe *not* coming after Pete's call, but he couldn't be absolutely certain in view of the politics in the sheriff's office. He needed to think of an alternative plan in the event Tessler didn't arrive within a reasonable time period.

Besides the obvious one of picking a direction that made sense and continuing to walk until he found someone who could help him, he considered doubling back to the farm house a second time and taking a chance he could find the valet key to his Range Rover, or just as good, a key to Rossum's Toyota Tundra.

He saw the light bobbing among the trees again. Get out of there he told himself. He veered north and suddenly the moon illuminated the landscape again. As he waited behind a tree, he consoled himself with the thought that Rossum probably didn't have night-vision goggles. If he did, he'd have no need for a flashlight.

He heard a vehicle on the county road. It was easy to hear traffic in the still night air, but Pete was too deep in the woods to see who it was or the direction the vehicle was traveling. He thought it was going east, though. Then he heard a second vehicle and a third. From the flashes of headlights through the trees, it seemed like all of them had turned into the Rossum driveway. His spirits soared. Let this be Joe, he prayed. He dialed Tessler's cell phone number again.

"Pete, where are you?"

"I'm still in the woods west of the house. Rossum is searching for me. He's close, less than a hundred yards away I think."

"Why don't you come out to the farmstead area and join us? I don't want to send our people in and have them shoot the wrong man."

"I can't just walk out in the open. Rossum has a high-powered hunting rifle. He'd pick me off and then try to get out of here."

"What do you suggest?"

"I'm going to walk north and then back east through the woods," Pete said in a whispered voice. "I'll call you again when I get north of the house. If you have a loudspeaker or a bullhorn, you might announce yourselves now and demand that Rossum surrender."

Before Pete could end the call, a bullet tore into a sapling near him. He panicked and began to run north. Another shot clipped a tree not far from him. *Christ, Joe, send your people in now!* He continued to run and branches switched him in the face and he fought to stay on his feet as he stumbled over the rough terrain. A third shot rang through the night.

As he ran, he heard someone say over a loudspeaker, "Stop firing, Jake Rossum, and come out with your hands up! I repeat, come out with your hands up! We have seven men out here. You're surrounded and can't get away!"

Pete heard two more shots, followed by return gunfire from Tessler and his men. He reached the strip of woods north of the house and ran east. After he'd gone a hundred yards, he stopped, gasping for breath, and pulled out his cell phone and called Tessler again.

"Joe, I'm north of the house now. I can see you and your men."

"Stay put. I'll announce over the loudspeaker or call on your cell when it's safe to come out."

Pete huddled on his knees in the brush and watched the shootout unfold. After a few minutes, the guns went silent and a man came out of the woods into the bright headlights of the sheriff's department's vehicles that had been trained on the woods. His hands were behind his head and Pete couldn't see any weapons. Pete's cell phone burred. "It's over, Pete. We've got him."

When Pete got to where the cruisers were parked, he saw Rossum bent over the hood of one of them. He was handcuffed and being searched by two deputies. Another deputy read him his rights. Rossum didn't have a jacket on despite the fact it was a cool evening, and when he was allowed to stand erect, Pete saw that the front of his shirt was matted with blood. Rossum locked eyes with Pete as he walked up, then looked away.

"Hey, Joe," a deputy called, "I ordered an ambulance because there's an old woman in the house with a broken hip or something. Plus the perp has some kind of chest injury"

Tessler walked over to where Pete was standing by the cruiser and sized him up. "Jesus," he said, "you look terrible. "Do you want to ride back in the front seat of the ambulance? I can have someone drive your car to Frankfort."

"Thanks, Joe, I'll be fine." He needed to be alone and the last thing he wanted was to be reminded of what Thomas Edinger had done to the Hines family.

FORTY-SIX

Pete's day brightened when he got to his office the next morning and listened to a telephone message from Alan Doar. Doar reminded him that he was about to leave on vacation, but wanted to give him a heads-up about what his recommendation to the Attorney Grievance Commission was going to be.

Doar said that although he was troubled by some of the things Pete had represented to Barbara Rodes and others, he didn't find anything in his conduct to warrant disciplinary action. A mitigating factor in his decision was that he understood why Pete had said them. Doar was also critical of Jeffery Rodes for having brought the complaint, saying he seemed to be more concerned with assigning blame for his sister's death than for anything else. Doar concluded by mentioning the private investigator point again and said he was considering referring the matter to the appropriate state agency when he got back.

Pete was basking in the good news when Joe Tessler walked into his office, and after giving him the once over, said, "You look better this morning than you did last night. Did you have that side looked at like I suggested?"

"Just came from the hospital. They cleaned it up and gave me a tetanus shot."

Tessler nodded. "For your information," he said, "they took your assailant, Mrs. Rossum, to the Traverse City hospital with a broken hip. She's a little looney from what I hear and they have her in a special ward."

Pete didn't say anything, but images of the face plastered against the basement window flashed through his mind.

"But the real news is what we found when we searched the Rossum farm. You know that outdoor fireplace you were looking at when Jake Rossum conked you on the head? It's been mostly cleaned out as you know, but Rossum didn't do as thorough a job as he might have. We found one of the buttons from the Confederate uniform that was burned and our forensics people are examining the remaining ashes to see if they match those we believe he planted in Dahl's fireplace."

"You know," Pete said, "if you'd taken more seriously what I told you on the telephone that day, you would have had that evidence without me spending the night in Rossum's dungeon."

"Oh, so now we're to blame for what happened."

"No, I'm just pimping you," Pete said. "I'm not sure I would have believed the story I told you either. Plus, you bailed me out when my butt was on the line. Thanks for coming out last night, Joe."

Tessler looked at him for a long moment. "I would have felt terrible if we'd been late getting to the Rossum farm."

"We both would have," Pete said dryly.

"Getting back to the search, do you know what made Frank the happiest?"

"Besides what you found in the fireplace?"

Tessler nodded. "Besides that. We think we now have the murder weapon."

"Really?"

"One of the gun cases in Rossum's house had a false back. We found a smoothbore hidden behind the panel."

"Interesting," Pete said. "But that's not likely to be conclusive, is it? As we talked about before, they can't trace a round to a smoothbore."

"That's true, but the fact Rossum had a smoothbore together with everything we found in our searches plus the stuff you dug up, he won't have room to twitch. And because of what he did to you, we now have him on attempted murder charges as well."

Harry McTigue burst into Pete's office and said breathlessly, "They arrested Jake Rossum for Edinger's murder last night!" He looked at Tessler and then back at Pete and came down to earth. "But I can see you guys already know that."

"We were just talking about it," Pete said.

"You were on target with your analysis right down the line," Harry said to Pete. "Jake is Marlin Hines' son, just as you thought."

Pete nodded, but suddenly felt empty again when he thought about the human wreckage Thomas Edinger had caused.

They chatted for a few minutes longer, then Tessler said, "Well, I've got to run."

"Before you go," Pete said, "I assume you guys are going to release Spencer Dahl now, right?"

"Yes. I'm handling that announcement. Frank has to make an unexpected trip out of town."

Pete and Tessler exchanged knowing glances as the detective headed for the door.

When he was gone, Harry said, "I guess it doesn't make any difference now that Lorraine disputed Spencer's alibi, huh?"

"I guess not."

"You seemed to feel that she turned on Spencer for some reason. Any theories?"

"Probably money."

"I don't understand."

"I suspect it had something to do with her inheritance. Thomas Edinger had two children by his first marriage and I'd be surprised if he didn't leave them something. What do you think they'd do if they found out their father's new wife was sleeping with another man at the time he was shot?"

Harry seemed to think for a while and then said, "Contest the will? I mean as it pertains to Lorraine."

Pete nodded.

"Umm," Harry murmured. He studied Pete and then said, "I didn't want to say anything while Tessler was here, but what are those scratches on your face?"

"Just scratches."

Harry looked at him some more and said, "And your hands. Jesus. You were at the Rossum farm last night, too, weren't you?"

"For a while."

"Want to tell me about it?"

"Not now," he said wearily.

"But—"

"Please, Harry."

Harry knew better than to press Pete when he didn't want to be pressed and said, "Rona's on her way over. She wants to thank you personally."

"That's not necessary."

"She thinks it is. When Spencer is released, she intends to drag him over to say thanks, too."

"I'll tell Rona myself, but between you and me, I don't want to see Spencer Dahl again. Ever."

"I can understand that. Well, here's something I think will boast your spirits. Your daughter called yesterday to pick my brains about a few points for her composition class. During our conversation, she told me her French boyfriend, Remy, won't be spending Thanksgiving with us."

Pete's eyebrows shot up and he said, "No kidding."

"Yeah, no kidding. She went on a rant about what an unfaithful jerk this guy had turned out to be. She said she was looking forward to spending the holiday with family and friends who really loved her. She wants to tell you herself so don't let on that I tipped you off."

Pete tried to conceal the smile tugging at his face as he gazed out at the bay.

ABOUT THE AUTHOR

Robert Wangard is a crime-fiction writer who splits his time between Chicago, where he practiced law for many years, and northern Michigan. *Payback* is the fourth in the Pete Thorsen Mystery series. The first three, *Target, Malice* and *Deceit,* were widely-acclaimed by reviewers. Wangard is also the author of *Hard Water Blues*, an anthology of short stories. He is a member of Mystery Writers of America, the Short Mystery Fiction Society, and other writers' organizations.